"New Politics" . . . or Programmed Anarchy?

Tom Gavin's real education began when he kidnapped his favorite professor. He was suddenly a Kampus hero, sought after by every radical group. Each night a different commando squad went out with bombs, grenades and greaseguns . . . and Gavin was the guest of honor.

Gavin realized the nightly raids were organized to keep the students battling against an enemy that didn't exist. But he was helpless. He had to keep playing the charade . . . or be killed in the latest revolutionary craze . . .

KAMPUS

A Novel by

JAMES E. GUNN

BANTAM BOOKS · TORONTO · NEW YORK · LONDON

RLI: $\dfrac{\text{VLM 6 (VLR 5–8)}}{\text{IL 9+}}$

KAMPUS
A Bantam Book | July 1977

ISBN 0–553–02693–3

Published simultaneously in the United States and Canada

Bantam Books are published by Bantam Books, Inc. Its trade-mark, consisting of the words "Bantam Books" and the por-trayal of a bantam, is registered in the United States Patent Office and in other countries. Marca Registrada. Bantam Books, Inc., 666 Fifth Avenue, New York, New York 10019.

PRINTED IN THE UNITED STATES OF AMERICA

KAMPUS

1 ↔ Karnival

Karnival is a bit like a circus, a bit like a bacchanalia, a bit like a Beaux Arts ball, a bit like a mass orgy, a bit like a slave market, and nothing at all like a university. It was invented as an excuse for doing in public what everyone else does in private. The students call it honesty, and the faculty call it lewd, but what it really is is an affirmation of the students' devotion to sensuality and their uninterest in education. In other words, it is a completely appropriate beginning to a new academic year.

—THE PROFESSOR'S NOTEBOOK

Gavin dopedrifted through the sensemadness of Karnival like a molecule enslaved in one of the Savages' amplifiers, vibrating with the chords of the bass guitar, beaten from side to side by the hammering drum, darting with the stringplay of the lead, in unrelenting, irrelevant motion. . . . Throb, boom-boom, tinkle, twinkle, plink. . . .

Someone, somewhere, had slipped him a hallucinogen. In the hideyholes of his mind he tried to remember what he had eaten or drunk or smoked, tried to decide what friend had meant him well or what enemy had wanted him neutralized, and for what purpose, on this most important day of the school year. But, carereleased, he floated above that central core of concern, like a red balloon over a lava pit, and reveled in his liberation from the demon that sat on his shoulders, riding him this way and that, while its metalstudded whip lashed down through skin and muscle and heart and liver to his guts.

He gave himself to the slugbeat and the kaleidoscene with an emotion that resembled joy. The familiar arena of the fieldhouse was strange tonight, the roofreach fading into night, the balcony glittering with flickerlights and swirlpools, the air thick with burncense and leafsmoke and mansweat. Some of the effect, he was sure, was sensetwist, the strange swim and shimmer of passing students, their aura, their iridescence, but how to explain the grotesqueries of their faces and the way their proteanskins melted into motley?

And then Gavin remembered: tonight was Karnival, with masks and costumes, Truce, the suspensions of all conflicts, freedom from fear and license to do those things which position or timidity or reason ordinarily prevented.

"Hi, Gavin," said one mask as it loomed out of colored mists, and a firm hand to his shoulder staggered him before the mask disappeared.

"Hello, Gavin," said another mask, more lightly, more meaningfully, and lips like burning snakes writhed upon his lips before the crowd swept from him the figure that his hands yearned toward.

He held his hands in front of his face, looking at them as if they were strange and new, while the crowd buffeted him, and then blindlifted them to his cheeks. His cheeks felt stiff but not like a mask, more like skin rigid from shock or rigor mortis.

He did not feel in shock, only disoriented by the hallucinogenic, deafened by the screamsound, battered by the slugbeat that seemed to originate in his bowels and radiate outward to jar the mobscene and rattle the roofreach.

He looked up and saw the Savages, naked save for loincloths, surrounded by amplifiers, seemingly hooked into them umbilically, pounding madsweat at their instruments, swaying on their precarious platform suspended by a cable from invisible heights. He didn't know what they were playing, maybe nobody did except the Savages, but it was update and gutlow.

Dazzled and deafened, Gavin let himself be buffeted, moved Brownian around hugespace, surrendering his senses to the violence that raped them. And in that brightnoise crazysea, bits of flotjet bumped against him . . .

A tall lean man in hardhat and bluecollar in pursuit of . . .

A scaredeyed girl in nunhabit . . .

A Jesusfreak with crown of thorns and stigmata that left blood smears on Gavin's hand . . .

An acidhead with pupils black and vague . . .

A longhaired straight with mortarboard and gown . . .

A towering black with an incredible erection . . .

A nearly naked girl who lashed . . .

The bleeding back of the naked man who walked in front of her . . .

A weeping clown who tried to press joints into everybody's hands . . .

A girl with three bare breasts . . .

A Kampuskop with upraised club who pounded indiscriminately each head he passed . . .

A Roman emperor carried on a litter, who scattered candy bars among the mob . . .

A naked girl with strapped-on dildo who carried a sign Gavin couldn't read . . .

A tall lean man in hardhat and bluecollar . . .

A scaredeyed girl . . .

A revolutionary with bomb in either hand and greasegun bandoliered across his back . . .

A Jesusfreak with crown of thorns and stigmata . . .

A longhaired straight with mortarboard . . .

A janitor with pushbroom that had no bristles . . .

Two strolling gaylibs . . .

An acidhead with pupils . . .

A weeping clown who tried to press . . .

A girl with three . . .

A longhaired straight . . .

A towering black . . .

A Kampuskop . . .

A Jesusfreak . . .

A nearly naked girl . . .

The bleeding back . . .
A tall lean man . . .
A scaredeyed girl . . .
A revolutionary . . .
A janitor . . .
An acidhead . . .
Two gaylibs . . .
A naked girl . . .
Christ! thought Gavin. *What are patterns for?*

Gavin found himself mobtossed into one of the booths that lined the underside of the balcony. Here, somewhat sheltered from the screamsound, people could make themselves heard. Dazed, Gavin felt hands upon each arm, heard voices alternately in each ear like a stereo demonstration tape:

Left: "Find Jesus. Be saved."
Right: "I was a sinner. Like you."
Left: "I shot dope."
Right: "I screwed girls."
Left: "I cheated."
Right: "I fuckedover people."
Left: "I spit upon my fellow man."
Right: "Until I found Jesus."
Left: "Jesus."
Right: "Jesus."
Left: "You're a sinner."
Right: "Just like us."
Left: "If you ain't saved by the blood of Jesus, man, forget it!"
Right: "You're damned to the pits of hell!"
Gavin's head cleared for a moment and his eyes confirmed what his ears had learned; he was in the grasp of two Jesuspeople determined to save him.
Left: "Burning forever."
Right: "Forever."
Left: "And ever."
Right: "Amen."
"Amen," Gavin said, and broke away before he was dragged farther into the den of iquity. As he dopedrifted on, he saw that the Jesuspeople had soulgrabbed another student, a scaredeyed girl in nunhabit. . . .

Gavin's feet were not as light as his head. He stumbled through heavy curtains into another booth where men and women sat crosslegged in midair, his bedazzled eyes told him, their eyes focused on a distant, invisible reality, their faces and bodies forgotten and relaxed as though empty, and, Gavin thought, perhaps growing transparent.

A low, omnipresent voice said, "Ooom." And then again, "Ooom."

Between "oooms," which seemed to resonate like prolonged chords, a voice said, "Come in. Meditate. Discover the true nature of reality. Liberate yourself from temporal passions. Release the true power of the self. Become all that you can be. Unite yourself with the universal. Meditate. Control your body. Release the self. Unfetter the soul. Ooom."

But Gavin thought he had tried that path once, and as he remembered it, or recalled his dream of it, the self was fascinating and the powers that seemed to be released were strange and exhilarating, but the process and even the results were personally unsatisfying.

He staggered back through the heavy curtains into the equally hypnotic and compelling ambience of the Savages. Before he could recover control over his own destiny, he was swept into another booth where quietly efficient young men and women were persuading students to place their identity cards against one of three translucent readin plates under labels spelling out Radicals, Revolutionaries, and Nihilists. Under the first label was the simplified drawing of a student carrying a placard; under the second, a student mounting a barricade and waving for others to follow; and under the third, a bomb and a torch.

"Join the political party of your choice," one of the young women called to Gavin. "You aren't truly serious unless you're prepared to put your body on the line for what you believe. Join up and discover what politics is all about. Learn the truth about government. Get three credit hours for fieldwork in political science."

"But which one?" Gavin asked.

"This is a nonpartisan booth, brother. They're all equally good. The differences are matters of tactics.

The important thing is to get committed. Don't drift, brother. Get involved in the age-old struggle for justice. Free the slaves. Topple the establishment. Let's get things moving again. . . ."

But it was too much for Gavin. The whole scene seemed too fraught with religious intensity, and he had not yet discovered a cause for which he would put his life on the line.

The next booth had a ceiling full of stars. A masked astrologer in a peaked cap and a black cloak glittering with zodiac signs offered to cast his horoscope for a dollar and a blood sample. "Guess your weight?" he called after Gavin. "Read your fortune? Love charms? Amulets? . . ."

In the next booth, as Gavin was weakswept, a magnificently figured girl was tied with silken ropes, face-up and naked, on a black-draped altar. A high priest stood behind the altar, spectral hands outspread above the girl, and a double-handful of monkhooded students surrounded the tableau and pleaded for a thirteenth to complete the coven.

"Master the dark arts," one said.

"Get in touch with the real powers in the world," said another.

"Exorcise God. . . . Name the Nameless. . . . Evil without guilt. . . . Be yourself. . . . Enjoy ceremony without boredom. . . . Join the Brotherhood of Blood. . . ."

The next booth offered a prosaic computerlist of communal living opportunities, with pictures and psychological indices of all the present communists. Students were invited to register for rush week by punching out the proper holes in a computercard while a terminal asked a long series of personal questions. If student cards matched communal needs, a student would be invited to spend a couple of days in the commune, and if the eating, working, and sleeping arrangements suited him and if the commune members wanted him, he would be invited to move in permanently, as permanence went.

So many more booths followed that Gavin lost count and track as he was mobtossed around the perimeter of the lower floor over the burn-marred, spit-stained man-turf. It was Karnival, the semiannual festival held on the Friday before classes started on Monday. It was a time for joy and a time for commitments. All student groups offered their opportunities for service or for pleasure, for serious avocation or for extracurricular activity. New students could sample the attractions of student life; former students, who were not soliciting in the booths themselves, could swap interests, switch life-styles, pick up new mates, or enjoy a casual experience. The more predatory males seized their chance to annex a new student before he or she had an opportunity to canvass the field, and the womanlibs were almost as active. . . .

Even the faculty were on display, course-touting in the upper corridors . . . and Gavin knew then why he was lost, why he had dopedrifted around the scene, why he had mobfloated. He belonged on another floor.

Gathering together his volition, he edged his way toward an exit, let himself be eddied toward the stairs, and mobsurged up to the second floor. Released at last, he heard voices and found himself outside the doorway of a small auditorium. A short, fat student was making a politspeech to some fifty students packed into dilapidated theater seats. Gavin admired how the words came rolling off his tongue like marbles off an assembly line.

"The time is come," the speaker said, ". . . no, let us be honest with ourselves—if nothing else, let us be honest—the time is long past when we should have destroyed a system that has not abolished unemployment, exploitation, and war." At each keyword—"unemployment," "exploitation," and "war," carefully spaced to allow response time—the audience growled in sympathy.

"What war?" Gavin asked, but nobody heard him.

"The lackeys of the establishment ask what we will put in its place." Again the growls. "That ain't our responsibility. First we'll make the revolution—then we'll find out what for."

Cheers.

"This society is concerned only about higher prices and higher profits." Growl. "A rational new system will

stress production for use." Cheers. "Instead of a heartless
Amerikkka in which the poor get poorer and the rich get
richer"—growls—"in which the middle class exploits the
workers, we will build a nation with a heart." Cheers.
"Democracy has failed. This slow, inefficient system
which has been seduced into the embrace of big money
and corporate power must be junked in favor of participatory democracy, where what the people want and need
will be provided: security"—yeah!—"opportunity"—
yeah!—"freedom"—yeah!—"and power." Yeah, yeah!

Gavin backed away from the groupritual, hearing
fragments of speech and antiphonal response as he
went.

". . . leaders crazed with power . . ." Rannh!

". . . deceive the people . . ." Rannh!

". . . freedom . . ." Yeah!

". . . establishment . . ." Rannh!

". . . Marx . . ." Yeah!

". . . Marcuse . . ." Yeah!

". . . Mao . . ." Yeah!

". . . Ché . . ." Yeah!

". . . tyranny . . ." Rannh!

". . . liberty . . ." Yeah!

Until there were only growls and cheers like a response without a reading, like counterpoint without a
point or a scoreboard without a game, or . . . or, he
thought more wildly, like a grin without a cat. " 'I've
often seen a cat without a grin,' thought Alice; 'but a
grin without a cat!' "

Gavin backed into an object that moved and then
clutched his shoulders to keep him from falling.

"Ah," said a precise, monotonous voice, "here we
have someone in need of elementary mathematics. . . ."

"Sorry," Gavin said.

"You see? He is sorry that he cannot add, subtract,
multiply, and divide. Simple arithmetic is what we offer
here. What you need to get by in this world—or to progress to algebra, geometry, and eventually to the calcu-
lus itself and the entire range of disciplines dependent
upon them, such as engineering, chemistry, physics, yes,
and even economics."

Gavin struggled free from the hands that held him

and turned to look at the small thin man who stood in blue cap and gown outside a booth faced with blackboards. The teacher was covered with chalkdust and the blackboards were covered with simple additions and subtractions, by multiplicands, multipliers, and products, by dividends, divisors, and quotients. The professor, who was barking for his own course, had in his hand a mechanized collapsible pointer with which he tapped the blackboards for emphasis, as the pointer kept shooting out and returning to its pencil size.

"How many students know their times tables? How many have to waste time punching eight times seven on their pocket calculators? Eight times seven is fifty-six, ladies and gentlemen, a fact that would require twice as long to discover electronically—while the rest of the class has gone on and left you behind. I can teach you new methods of multiplication and division which do not require laborious memorization. I have pills which are guaranteed to encapsulate the entire development of mathematical thought since the Arabs invented numerals, pills which need only be triggered by lecture and brief exercise. Sleep learning, of course. Free tutoring if necessary. Absolute guarantee. Success or your money back. Step right up. . . ."

Gavin noticed that a student who had been nodding vigorously throughout the spiel and making approving noises strode forward to place his identification card against a readin, but he was clearly a shill, and only one or two doubtful students followed.

In front of the next booth stood two heroic lucite figures, male and female, of the naked human body, and between them a fat man in a white coat. The fat man looked like an obscene caricature of the kind of human ideal represented by the figures that flanked him. The sign over the booth, also in lucite, and like the figures infused with cold flame, announced: HUMAN ANATOMY AND DISSECTION.

"Learn the marvels and delights of the human body," the fat man shouted. "A requirement for students who wish to go on into medicine, nursing, pharmacy, physical therapy, and physical education, as well as altered states of consciousness, and a pleasant diversion for those who wish to astonish their friends with a scientist's knowledge of musculature, nerve stimulation, and amatory skill."

As he spoke, the statues seemed to shift on their pedestals like alien shapechangers; their original internal flame became daylight yellow, the lucite skin disappeared, and they became articulated skeletons; when that color faded into pink, the skeletons were overlaid with muscles, and when pink became green, the body was reticulated with nerves; blue, underlaid with veins; red, with arteries; and purple, with obscenely throbbing internal organs. As the colors shifted more rapidly, the statues seemed to pulse with their own lewd life like ultimate perverts.

"Visual aids such as you see before you now make memory work easy—of course, learning pills are keyed to every lesson. And we will not depend upon models alone. We will dissect real cadavers, authentic preserved dead people, men and women. For this reason laboratory fees must be charged; bodies—particularly youthful bodies—are hard to come by. But we will have fun. When we come to reproduction"—the statues seemed to move lasciviously, and Gavin thought he saw something twisting into shape in the female figure's lower abdomen —"we will have live demonstrations as well as the opportunity for personal experimentation by lab partners, who will be appropriately and congenially paired. For only seven hundred and fifty dollars, students, you can have a great time this semester and learn something that will always be useful. . . ."

Students rushed to the counter; anatomy was always popular.

Beyond the surgeon was an English teacher. His visual display was a large screen upon which scattered words were shaping themselves into phrases, clauses, and sentences. "Learn to read and write," he said wistfully. He was dressed shabbily, in a kind of tweedy suit that was old twenty years ago. His hair had grown thin on top, and his face, like his clothes, drooped with the expectation of defeat.

"You think now that you will never need these skills," he said. "Everything you will ever need to know will be available in visual form; everything you will ever need to communicate can be spoken or taped. . . . Not so, ladies and gentlemen. Many works of literature, many exciting—yes, even pornographic—passages have never been translated into visual form. Imagine the delight of reading *Fanny Hill* in the original or *Justine* or *The Story of O*! Even the best of translations leaves much to be desired; you cannot imagine, if you have never experienced it, the exquisite pleasure of summoning up your own images instead of having someone else's ideas thrust upon you."

A single word formed upon the screen and grew into a monstrous shape. "This is a word some of you can recognize. The word is 'you.' You! The person to whom you are talking. And this is 'I.' Easy, isn't it? Now, something more difficult—a four-letter word. 'Love.' Put them together"—the words reappeared and swam around until they formed a straight line—"and you have a simple sentence: 'I . . . love . . . you.' A statement of delightful meaning, of infinite application." The "I" began to caress the "you"; the "you" writhed with pleasure until the "I" concluded its performance by diving into the middle of the "o" and disappeared.

"Imagine being able to write that to your lover. Imagine the depth of the response. There are, of course, other uses. Astonish your friends by signing your name instead of presenting your identification card to an anonymous readin. Write down your thoughts where they cannot be heard; be immune to bugging and eavesdropping. Perform research into documents which few can read; read that which few can share. Secrets of a thousand sorts lie hidden in books which never have been coded into a computer. . . ."

But nobody rushed to the English teacher's counter.

The next booth was labeled: PSYCHOLOGY. In front of the booth was a clear crystal pillar which supported a glistening, spinning apparatus; it shattered light and scattered it in beams and glitters across the wide corridor and the faces of the students who stood watching. On one side of the pillar was a dapper, youngish man with a line of smooth patter and a sleek seal look; on the other side was a slender girl with large breasts crossed by bikinistrips. Her eyes, like those of the students standing in front of the booth, were fixed upon the spinning apparatus; Gavin noticed that they did not seem to blink.

"Psychology, my friends," said the huckster, "is the now science. Learn how to predict the behavior of others! Eminently useful in salesmanship, politics, group dynamics of all kinds, as well as personal relations." The professor dug a knowing elbow into Gavin's ribs. "And we all want personal relations, right?

"Learn not only to predict but to influence. Once you can predict how people will behave, influence is but a small step beyond. Without your apparent intervention, people will behave as you wish them to do. On a large scale the science of psychology is applied most obviously in advertising and motivational research; on the smaller scale of the community or the group, it provides a pleasant environment for the individual who knows his subject—things happen to satisfy his or her desires." Gavin's ribs received another blow from the psychologist's elbow. "And the satisfaction of our desires is what the game is all about, right?

"Learn not only to influence but to control. This young lady of such exquisite proportions is completely under my control. She will do whatever I command. For instance"—the elbow swung toward Gavin, but he evaded it—"I could tell Helen to go into the booth with you and make passionate love, and she would do it. Is that right, Helen?"

"Yes," the girl said.

"Are you under my control?"

"Yes," the girl said.

"Tell these students your name."

"My name is Janice."

"Helen, Janice." The psychologist shrugged. "Have we ever met before tonight?"

"No."

"Have you ever stripped for an audience before?"

"No."

"I want you to remove your clothes for these wonderful people," the psychologist said.

Automatically the girl's hands went behind her back and twisted twice. The bikinistrips fell away. Her body was more magnificent than before.

The psychologist turned toward the student audience with his hands thrown out, palms upward, in a gesture of simplicity. "These, of course, are parlor games that anyone can learn. Beyond control of the individual is the serious business of social control, of shaping an entire society into a rational, reasonable, desirable arrangement in which satisfactions are maximized and frustrations are minimized, in which such sicknesses as war, murder, and other crimes cannot exist. Skinnerism is not yet a science, ladies and gentlemen, but we are working on it.

"In addition, we will devote some of our time in this course to the study of altered states of consciousness, the proper use of drugs, and their effects. Now," he said to the students in the same tone he had used with the still-naked girl, "you will sign up for my course. Janice will help with your enrollments." The students lined up mechanically in front of the counter. "Cash, of course, will be accepted, as well as credit cards if they have been co-signed by your parents. Please have your identification cards ready. . . ."

Gavin moved on. He had been too fascinated by the girl and the psychologist to more than glance at the glittering mechanism on the pillar.

Beyond the psychology booth was a computer. A lighted panel at the top carried the printed words: COMPUTER SCIENCE. In a pleasant feminine voice the computer said, "Every student knows that the computer is the creator of our society. It has taken the drudgery out of man's life; automatically, without complaint, it performs the simplest repetitive tasks as well as the most complicated computations. It manages the economy while it economizes on management. Because of the computer, man is free to do not what he can but what he wishes."

The computer's voice dropped an octave, became more personal, more seductive. "But you must learn to handle your computer so that your computer will produce the results you want." The computer made it sound like a love affair. "You must know what the computer can do and what it cannot; what is simple and cheap, and what is difficult and expensive. Computer science is the essential course in the University curriculum. Learn how to talk to your computer. Learn how to obtain the exact answer by asking the exact question, not the approximate answer or even an incorrect answer by asking a careless question."

The computer's voice rose again to the efficient and the impersonal. "A knowledge of computer science is useful to everyone. It is, however, a prerequisite to careers in business, economics, engineering, and all the sciences including chemistry and physics. Sign up for this course by placing your student identification card against the blue readin plate in the counter and your credit card against the red plate. No cash or checks, please. You may sign up for your own computer terminal by pressing the button between the two plates.

"I need not remind you how much easier and more satisfying your university life will be with your own computer terminal, providing answers as well as services, tutoring and tapes for class exercises included—this service covers all classes offering within the University, of course—and even printed term papers for teachers barbaric enough to require such arcane skills. As a matter of fact, all courses offered within the University may be taken by computerized instruction, with the single exception of laboratory courses.

"Of course, fascinating games can be played with your own computer terminal—space war, chess, computer dating, terminalhop—as well as sending and receiving personal messages, and even prompt delivery of late-night snacks or drinks, pills or dope. No student ever again need be lonely, oppressed, or depressed. With your own computer terminal you need only describe your mood and be matched with some other student who at that very moment wants to give what you need. . . ."

Inside the glass housings, the broad tapes turned, and on the panels the colored lights flickered like genies anxious to be liberated into the service of man, but Gavin had the uneasy feeling that it was all a fake and that somewhere some unshaven man sat in his underwear punching buttons and answering questions out of a Book of Records, an unabridged dictionary, a a tattered 1994 almanac.

The next booth spelled PHARMACY in glass tubing filled with bubbling fluids that changed colors as Gavin watched. Beneath the lettering, on a frosted screen, full-color pictures appeared, split, merged, and disappeared, split screen and quadruple screen, film and stills, illustrating the wonderthings a pharmacist does. But in front of the screen, tradition reigned: colored water in fancy jars, a plump, smooth-skinned man with a waxed moustache wearing a white jacket, and on a counter in front of him, a mortar and pestle, bottles of pills, liniments, and lotions, and squeezetubes of toothpaste.

His patter went back an even older tradition, of snake oils, patent nostrums, and curealls. "Students," he said, his moustache twitching, "this is it. This is what you've been looking for. How many times have you told yourself, 'I don't know what is in this pill. I don't know whether this stuff has been cut or adulterated. I don't know whether I ought to take it or not.' So you take a chance and run the risk of blindness, madness, a bummer, or even death; or you don't—and miss that great experience, that mystic high. Ladies and gentlemen, you need take those chances or miss those highs no longer. A few simple tests—easily mastered in the course I teach—can confirm or refute the claims of your dealer. Don't pay horse prices for sugar or strychnine. Don't buy poison when you are paying for peace. Don't trade a headache for an upset stomach. Don't let life give you a bummer. Don't settle for a bad trip. For only five hundred dollars, ladies and gentlemen, you can guarantee yourself a pleasant saunter through life's happy groves.

"And that isn't all, ladies and gentlemen. For that same five hundred dollars—only half a grand, students, you can't even support a modest habit for half a grand anymore—you can learn the effects of drugs upon the human metabolism and the human brain through animal and human experimentation as well as self-dosing under carefully controlled conditions. Learn what pro-

vides a superior high. Learn what kind of comedown to
expect and how to ease down instead of crash. Learn
how to substitute simple cheap drugs for the expensive,
hard-to-get kinds. Learn your own tolerances. Each
single person is unique. Each one of you responds differently to the same substances.

"Moreover, ladies and gentlemen, for that same five
hundred dollars—why, you can't even bribe a local
judge for five hundred dollars anymore—you can learn
how to prepare your own drugs. Of course, it ain't easy
to obtain the raw opium or morphine base, but we will
learn how to handle the poppy from field to consumer.
Some of you may wish to enter the production business
yourself. We will learn how to prepare the psychedelics,
the hallucinogens, the amphetamines, and the tranquil-
izers from simple substances you might find in your own
kitchen. This course will return its initial cost many
times over just in the ability to prepare your own uppers
and downers."

The pitchman put his hands on the counter and
leaned forward confidentially. "You will, of course,
learn how to prepare simple pharmaceuticals—aspirin,
for instance, antacids, and many others—for fractions
of the cost of purchasing them at your local dispensary.
Need I point out the burgeoning opportunities awaiting
the young man or woman in the knowledge industries,
in the fields of chemical learning now just in its in-
fancy. Learn how to prepare your own learning pills.
Why, I venture to speculate, ladies and gentlemen, that
not many years from now we will not even have courses
like this anymore. You need only take a pill or a series
of pills and you will know everything a course can teach
you. Well, ladies and gentlemen, you can get in on the
ground floor of that industry now. Sign up! Put down
your five hundred dollars, and receive an education you
can always use."

While the students thronged to put their cards down
upon the readins, the pitchman's voice dropped until
Gavin could scarcely hear it. "And, for advanced students," the pharmacy professor said, "there is an opportunity still for research in the fields of human response,
ethical drugs, antibiotics, and delivery systems. . . ."

Next to pharmacy was a booth with no one in front of it. Over the booth, in simple, handpainted letters, a sign read: PHILOSOPHY. Beside the entrance to the booth was another sign that read: ENTER FOR PERSON-AL INTERVIEW.

Gavin, who had drifted past the other booths in a kind of mind-blasted euphoria, unimpressed and un-motivated, hesitated in front of this blatant disregard for the proprieties. Who was being interviewed? Who was hiring whom here? But the approach—or lack of approach—stopped Gavin long enough to think with what he had left for brains.

Eventually he realized that he was offended, but he was also intrigued—he was sufficiently intrigued that he stooped, pushed aside the bare canvas closure of the booth, and entered. He stopped just inside and blinked while his dope-dazed eyes adjusted to the dimmer inte-rior. Finally he saw that the small space contained two ragged upholstered chairs, a floor lamp behind one of them, and between them a scarred wood coffee table on which sat a cup and an ashtray overflowing with ashes and cigarette butts. As Gavin watched, another cigarette butt was stubbed out in the heap.

"Come in, come in," a voice said impatiently. It was a voice that had grown weary and testy trying to whip bored students alert, or at least awake, but still a bugle of a voice which could throw words at student heads like erasers. Now the voice was irritated and high-pitched, but even so it compelled attention. "You've done the Anthony-to-Cleopatra imitation. Sit down."

The chair beneath the lamp held a man who was dressed stylishly—though not in student style—and then was careless of his appearance. He was an ordinary good-looking man who, well into middle age, no longer cared what he looked like, with graying brown hair down almost to the collar of his long-lapeled, open-necked yellow shirt and cigarette ashes dribbled down the front of his gold jerkin.

"What are you looking for?" he said to Gavin.

"What do you mean? Here?" Gavin asked.

"What do you want?" the Professor insisted.

"Maybe a course?"

"What is your goal?" the Professor boomed. His hands rested like stone paws on the arms of his chair.

"You mean now? Here? On campus? In life?"

The Professor shrugged. "On campus, in life, what does it matter? The campus is life, young man. And the goals you adopt here will never really change; they will only fade into dreams of what was or might have been."

"I don't understand you," Gavin said, trying to pull his head together, wondering if the hallucinogenic was affecting his hearing as well as his eyes. The Professor did have a golden aura about him, and there seemed to be an aura of ambiguity about his words, something delphic and layered and significant. But it might be the drug. The evening had been strange already, and it promised to get stranger. "This is enrollment, you know. . . ."

"Sir," said the Professor.

"What?"

"This is enrollment, you know—'sir.' "

" 'Sir'? What do you think this is—the Army?"

"This is normal human intercourse between a teacher and a prospective student, who, if he shows promise, the ability to learn, and a proper attitude, may be accepted. It is a situation eased, rendered tolerable, and perhaps even pleasant, by a proper use of respect terms which clarify the relationships between the two. It is a modest effort which costs the student nothing if he is not insecure or neurotic, and places him in a proper social frame for learning."

Wordshit, Gavin thought, and felt his eyes beginning to focus. "Clearly I've come to the wrong place. You seem to have matters all turned around."

"Sir," said the Professor. " 'Curtsey while you're thinking what to say,' said the Red Queen. 'It saves time.' "

"Sir," Gavin said. Let this odd Professor cherish his ancient ways and his archaic forms of address, he thought; he soon would leave the Professor to his well-deserved solitude and never see him again. But he did wish to get one thing straight before he left. "You're selling your services and I'm buying. *Caveat emptor* may be the operating principle, but this is a buyer's market, and the buyer may purchase or not, as he chooses."

"A misleading comparison," the Professor said airily, and blew a smoke ring into the air above his head, "though not ill-argued. You see, I am in possession of that which few have and some want, even though it may do them no good to have it. Nevertheless, this makes me a monopoly; you must come to me. What do you want?"

"What is it you have?" Gavin asked cannily.

"I cannot teach you a skill with which you can amaze your friends and satisfy your baser needs. What I have will not give you power over others; it will not make you famous or well-liked or happy. What I have, if you want it and I decide to communicate it to you, may make you miserable, and certainly will make you discontented. As with the most habit-forming drug, you never will be able to get enough. It will ride your back from now until you die. If you do not get your daily fix, you will suffer from withdrawal. All this and more."

"Why would anybody want something like that?" Gavin scoffed, but he was intrigued in spite of himself.

"Why does a man seek beauty he knows he cannot possess? Why does a man keep probing his guilt, like an abscessed tooth? Why does a man torment himself with dreams of immortality when he knows that he must die? Man is perverse, and the sooner you learn this simple fact, the sooner you will stop asking foolish questions. Besides, there is a consolation that creeps like hope from Pandora's box." The Professor lit a cigarette with an old-fashioned kitchen match and broke into a fit of coughing as he inhaled the smoke from the cigarette and the sulfurous fumes from the match as well.

"Why does a man smoke when he knows it will kill him?" Gavin echoed. "Why don't you get to a medcenter anyway?"

" 'Get thee to a nunnery . . .' " the Professor said.

Gavin had a nearly subliminal glimpse of a scared-eyed girl in nunhabit.

". . . besides," the Professor was saying, "I am a dying breed, and no amount of medical rigor will save me. I am the last of the old-time professors, about whom Chaucer could have been thinking when he wrote 'gladly wolde he lerne, and gladly teche.' You will not see his like again." His voice assumed the scornful flamboyance of the snakeoil salesman in front of the pharmacy booth. "Get him while you can. Only a few days more at this special price. A vanishing species, ladies and gentlemen. A nearly extinct bird mostly found today in dusty libraries and deserted studies, abandoned by students and family, scarcely worth preserving were it not for the nostalgia involved in his occasional appearances before the unwary student, who, baffled by this apparition from the past, stares at his performance unaware that he may be viewing the last grand fling of the old-time professor."

"What is it you teach?" Gavin asked.

"What do I teach?" the Professor repeated, sucking hard on his cigarette and, as a consequence, coughing the smoke out again like billowing phlegm. "I teach man—and woman, too, when I can get close to one. I teach beginnings and endings, creations and cataclysms, holistics and holocausts. I teach proportion and people, life and death, love and hate. I teach all things and nothing."

"I think . . ." Gavin said, not knowing why he said it, "I think I'd like to take your course. Where do I sign up? But you aren't going to get a class filled like this, taking students one at a time, putting them off even more than you're putting them on. There aren't very many like me who are going to come in here out of curiosity and put up with your idiosyncrasies. Sir."

"You presume too much," the Professor said. "I haven't decided yet that I will accept you. As for the rest—we live in a fragmented world—more like Chicken Little than Humpty Dumpty, who was a fragmented person in a whole world—and the truest words to be spoken today surely are these: the sky is falling.

"Fragmented," he said somberly, "each person an atom unto himself, whole and impenetrable, each group clinging only to its own kind, reacting with others not at all or violently. No longer do we feel the social pressure of necessity to rub us together, to smooth our rough edges, to fit us into a smoothly operating system of civility and custom.

"Where are our rites of passage, our initiations by which the youth is admitted into the mysteries of the tribe, those sacrifices and sufferings by which he or she proves a fitness to join the adults, by which he or she accepts tribal values, by which he or she gains the right to procreate, to commingle their consecrated seed and ovum for the greater glory of what is right and good and true? What happens when there is no longer right or goodness or truth? What happens when children procreate without sanction? What happens when they pass, unproven, into postpuberty states without ever becoming adults? What happens when nobody wants to be an adult, when childhood is so much more attractive that it becomes a lifelong state? The old ways crumble . . ."

"None too soon," Gavin muttered.

"And with what savageries are they replaced?" the Profeessor mourned. "With what new traditions do the young console themselves? Youth!" The Professor dismissed the entire generation with a wave of the limp hand in which he held aloft his cigarette.

"What do you want?" he said again to Gavin.

"I don't know," Gavin said savagely, feeling the clawed hand which had cupped and protected his brain beginning to relax its grasp. "No, wait—I want to know . . . what you're talking about. I want to . . . know—"

The Professor hit the coffee table with the fleshy part of his fist, and the end of his cigarette, ash and glowing coal together, flew into the air. "That's it!" he exclaimed. "You have said the magic word and you have won a one-way trip for one to misery and despair. I will accept you as a student, you poor, unhappy fellow."

Gavin felt an uncharacteristic wave of delight. "May I get some others to sign up, too?"

"Why?"

Gavin rummaged for words. "This . . . this experience . . . I'd like them, a few of them, to try it, too."

The Professor shrugged. "It doesn't matter. One or a dozen. As long as there is one." He dropped the cigarette stub into the ashtray, lit up another, and coughing, picked up a book from the floor beside his chair. The interview was over.

But Gavin, dopefreed, feeling a kind of frustrated sexual excitement, wanted to go on. He had an intuition that he would never be this close to the Professor again. The truce of enrollment was over; the war between teacher and student would resume on Monday, and between them would descend all the barriers and precautions the teacher could devise. From this moment they would be like lovers separated by traditions or feuds or divided loyalties, or walls.

And yet, all the frustrated and voiceless longings that Gavin had experienced through his twenty years yearned toward the Professor, all the unanswered questions he had never asked rushed simultaneously to his lips, and he wanted more than he had ever wanted anything what he had not known existed until this moment, that for which he had never known a name.

"What?" he said to the Professor, extending both hands toward the seated teacher. The Professor did not look up from his book. "How?" Gavin asked, his need turning him inarticulate. The Professor flicked his ashes in the general direction of the tray. "Why?" Gavin asked, and let his hands fall.

Burning, aching, he turned and left the smoke-filled booth. The corridor with its endless array of booths circling the building seemed tawdry. The canvas was tattered and dirty, the bunting faded and cheap, the pitchmen sleazy, the milling students bestial. Dirt gritted under his feet, and he kicked trash out of his way as he headed for the nearest stairway leading to the arena.

What had happened to him? Then he realized that the hallucinogenic had worn off, burned out, perhaps, by the emotion with which he had responded to the Professor's provocation. His mind was clear, and he hated it. "You have won a one-way trip to misery and despair," he heard the Professor say, and he almost turned to find a joyseller and resume his pillstate of innocence and well-being, but something stopped him.

He looked down at his hand. It was shaking. "God help me," he said softly. "I want something more than joy or peace or even happiness. And I don't even know the name of it."

Distantly he heard the Savages. They were playing more softly now, either through fatigue or choice, and someone—a nasal girl, he thought, or a tenor—was singing. Gavin could not make out all the words, but occasionally one would come through, accompanied by an appropriate response from the audience.

". . . lonely . . ." sang the voice, with a throb of self-pity.

From the remote audience came the sound of a sympathetic moan.

". . . friend . . ." sang the voice, with a whine of despair.

Another antiphonal moan.

". . . only . . ."

Moan.

". . . end . . ."

Groan.

". . . you . . ."

"Ah-h-h," the audience responded.

". . . shove . . ."

"Ah-h-h." The sigh was like an exhalation.

". . . true . . ."

"Mmmmm," said the audience.

". . . love . . ."

"Ah-h-h-h," said the audience, as if it had received final satisfaction.

Gavin searched his memory for a similar experience. Then he remembered: the political rally in the little auditorium. He reached the foot of the stairs and went into the main area, expecting a more complete information flow, but it did not occur. There were no connectives. The abstraction was sufficient to arouse in the audience the suspense of foreplay and the release of orgasm. By the time he was in the midst of the swaying students—some were dancing by themselves or in vague relationship with someone else—the Savages themselves had begun to shout another song:

"Aggression/repression/regression/depression. . . ."

And then a roll of the drum, a wail of guitar strings, and a shout of "Digression!"

"Deflation/'flagration/cessation/elation!"

The students swayed or danced, responding to the revolutionary lyrics and the music. Gavin listened, too, caught up by the rhythms and the ambience in spite of himself and his newfound hunger. The moodspell of the manyheaded beast had the power to entrance and to reward.

And then someone said in his ear, "Whatcha takin', Gavin?"

Gavin looked to his right. The voice belonged to a suckass named Simpson, a body without a leader, a follower eager to attach itself to any directing force, but not a bad sort really. "Philosophy."

"Ah-h-h," Simpson said, his face brightening as if someone had turned on his light. The choice was offbeat enough to become a fad.

Well, Gavin thought, let the Professor make a few bucks. Maybe he would be able to afford to get that cough taken care of. Some of the teachers who were not very popular were really poor.

As Simpson moved away through the crowd like a conspirator with a message, Gavin saw him dip his head by a series of students and whisper a word in their ears. Gavin knew most of them: Marlin, Miro, Buck, Ridgley. . . . And Gavin knew the word.

As he turned from watching Simpson's progress, a girl bumped into him. He knew it was a girl before he saw her, from the firmyielding of her body against his, from the yearning of his body to hers. Then he recognized the face from his earlier fantasies—the scaredeyed girl in nunhabit—and dark, frightened eyes looked at him, searching for something.

"You've got to help me," the girl said. Her voice was husky and exciting, like the girlflesh that lurked hidden within the robes, that had pressed itself briefly against his body. Her hand caught his arm.

"What's the matter?"

"There's someone . . . following me."

His eyes followed where hers looked. Some yards away through the crowd was a tall lean man in a hard-hat. Gavin recognized him now. His name was Gregory, and he was a man of growing power in campus politics.

"That's what Karnival is all about," Gavin said.

"I know," the girl said. Her hand quivered on his arm. "But I don't like him. He's . . . ugly."

He was ugly, Gavin saw now. He had a big nose that still did not separate sufficiently a pair of mean eyes, and thick, wet lips, and yet he fancied himself a stud. Gavin had seen him with some of the choicest girlgirls on campus, had seen him moving in with the natural grace of a ferret, all his attention fixed upon his mesmerized prey.

"You can always say 'no,' " Gavin said.

"He won't let me."

"How do you know? Have you told him?"

The girl shook her head. "I know," she said simply. "I'm afraid."

"What can I do?"

"Take me home," she said.

"Your home?"

"Yours. I don't have a place to stay."

"No place?"

"I'm new," she said. "I just got in today from California. I thought I might find . . . a place to stay . . . here."

"Somebody to stay with?" he asked.

She nodded.

"Me?"

"Yes," she said.

He could not be certain what she looked like behind the white linen that clasped her face, what she was shaped like beneath the folds of that black robe, but her face was attractive, with vulnerable lips, a small, short nose, feathery dark eyebrows—her hair, too, he decided would be long and dark and silky when it was uncovered—and eyes now that were frightened and all pupil, fixed now upon him with all her attention and what seemed to Gavin like love. She seemed, he thought, not like a girlgirl but perhaps a womangirl.

"All right," he said. "I like your looks and your voice, and I don't want to see you hurt. I think maybe I could love you."

He took her hand. It was cold and small and tense in his. He turned and threaded his way through the crowd toward the nearest exit. When they emerged into the still dark and breathed the clean air, she said, "Is love important?"

"To me," he said. "You?"

"Maybe," she said.

While they were walking up the hill and over the campus toward his pad, she told him that her name was Jenny and she had been born and raised in California, in Oakland.

"That's near Berkeley, isn't it?" he asked.

"Right next."

"I never was any good at geography," he admitted. "But why didn't you . . . ?"

"Go to Berkeley? I spent three years in a college for Catholic girls until I couldn't stand it any longer. A few days ago, when my parents were sending me back, I just took off across the country—hitching—and I ended up here this morning."

"Weren't you afraid?"

"Not until I got here." She hesitated. "Actually, everybody was wonderful to me."

Gavin took her arm in a gesture that was meant to be comforting but sent shivers through his body. "You're safe now," he said. "As safe as you want to be."

She smiled at him in the moonlight, as they passed between the shadows of the long, low administration building on the north and the long, low humanities building on the south, and suddenly her face was transformed in a miracle of beauty. "I know," she said.

They descended the steep hill on the other side of the campus toward the large, decaying houses that clung to the slope. The houses were more than one hundred years old, and there were blocks of them, with an occasional gap like the place where a rotten tooth had crumbled away. Several hundred yards away was the wall, but Gavin didn't tell Jenny about that. Daylight was soon enough to warn her about snipers.

They climbed stony steps in the darkness, and went through a plywood-reinforced door, and up narrow, creaking stairs redolent with the old odors of onions and beans and potatoes and dirt. Directly opposite the head of the stairs was a door. Gavin fumbled in his pocket for a key to the padlock that held the door closed.

"Is this a commune?" Jenny asked, pressed against him in the dark.

"It's just a place to live," Gavin said. He opened the lock and swung the door back. "It's not much," he said as he switched on the overhead light, a naked bulb hanging from a cord that dropped through a black hole in the ceiling. "But it's better than the dormitories and favelas on the other side of the campus. It's not so clean." His mattress was on the floor under the bay windows at the other end of the room; the sheets, Gavin noted with relief, had been changed relatively recently, but beer cans and bottles littered the floor and were stacked in the corners, and cigarette butts and ashes mingled with the dust and cobwebs and balls of lint like miniature tumbleweeds.

"I don't mind a mess," she said as she closed the door behind her.

He looked around the room. "I wish I had a beer or something to offer you," he said, keeping his back to her, "but they're all gone."

"I don't mind," she said.

He turned toward her. She had removed her headdress. He had been right; her hair was long and black and silky, and her face was lovely. He looked at the mattress and then back at her. This was the difficult moment. He understood the proprieties, but did she?

He cleared his throat. "There's only the one mattress."

"I don't mind," she said.

With great courage he took her face between his trembling hands and bent to her lips. They were cool and mysterious under his, and then they warmed and parted and welcomed him into the erotic plains and valleys of her mouth.

The light went out, and he realized vaguely that she had reached out with her right hand to turn the switch, but he did not have time to think of that as he heard a rustling sound in the dark and his hands slipped from her face to the naked velvet surfaces of her shoulders and her sides and indrawn waist and rounded hips.

She pulled him down to the mattress, sinking beside him like a lily when the sun has set, and the firmyielding of her silksmooth flesh surged quicksilver through his veins and moltengold into his brain. Under his melting hands and charring lips he found her buttonhard and breathhastened. Into roughsmooth moistpink he surged, and in that spinblurred, joysmeared, throbcentered universe he was lovelost, and he thought, I love you, Jenny, stranger, bride. . . .

But later, sweateased and sane, he held her against him and listened to her even breathing. He thought again about the experiences of the past few hours, and the memory of his encounter with the Professor filled him with a new excitement that he carried with him into his dreams.

2 ← The Kidnapping

You students think you are dedicated to the ideals of
revolution or justice or freedom, but you haven't yet
understood the word. Dedication—that's the word you
use to describe the mother whose son has fallen in
love with a beautiful, greedy, vicious young girl who
asks him to prove his love for her by giving her what
he values most. And he gives her his own treasures
and then those of his mother—china, silverware, heir-
looms. And yet, unsatisfied, the girl asks for one more
gift which finally will prove his love, his mother's
heart. Sadly he returns home, and his mother asks
what the girl wants now. "Your heart," he says.
"Then take it, my son," she says, and hands him a
knife. And after he has ripped it from her bosom and
is running with it through the forest, he stumbles, and
the heart says, "Careful, my son, you will hurt yourself."

—THE PROFESSOR'S NOTEBOOK

The morning they kidnapped the Professor, Gavin
awoke with the clear certainty that everything was going to happen just as he had planned. His happy calm
survived the discovery that Jenny had awakened early
and was gone, as well as a foul cup of coffee in the
cockroach-infested communal kitchen and the distur-
bances that had hit the campus overnight.

He was almost never alone with Jenny during the
day. Their relationship was nocturnal and dark. She

would not make love when the sun struggled past the dust-smeared windows or when the naked bulb above their heads chased shadows around the room. But in the blinded night she was wanton and insatiable.

"You are my dark love," he told her when he was feeling gentle and relaxed. But other times he would scoff at her exposure neurosis—he had never seen her without her clothing, which she had rescued from a hostel just inside the walls—and he would say, "You're afraid that God will see you sinning in the light," but she just shook her head and would not change. Sometimes, in the night, as they listened to the cockroaches wrestling in the kitchen, she would ask him what that noise was, and he told her, "Those are angels rustling against each other in the dark because they cannot see."

To avoid the heart of the disturbance, Gavin took the long way to class. Ordinarily he went down the curving boulevard, past the museums, between the old law building and the behavioral-sciences building, past the library, between the journalism building and the education building, to the side door of humanities.

But the administration building had been occupied by the Revolutionaries. They had taken the Chancellor hostage, and they had liberated some machine guns from the military museum, and nobody was going to drive them out until they got what they wanted. Nobody was sure what they wanted, but the rumor was spreading that their leaders would present a list of seven nonnegotiable demands before noon. Their attitude, expressed in the words of Tom Hayden, an early hero, still was "First we'll make the revolution, and then we'll find out what for."

Gavin went the long way, past the political-science building, where the Radicals had thrown up a picket line. One professor had been accused of trying to proselytize in his classroom for parliamentary democracy. Now pickets were stopping students and shaking in their faces signs printed with fluorescent ink. They must have been told what the signs said, because they were shouting their messages, "Abolish propaganda," "Reactionaries Against the Wall," and "The Telos of Tolerance Is Truth."

Gavin stopped the last picket and asked him if he knew what his totesign meant. The student looked at him blankly and then turned to another picket. "Hey, Jack," he yelled, "what does my sign mean?" The other picket shrugged, and the student Gavin was questioning passed it along. "Like, man, you know," he said.

But Gavin knew what it meant. "Telos" was a Greek word meaning "end," and the quote was from Marcuse, comparing liberating tolerance with repressive tolerance. The Professor had discussed Marcuse one day, and his concept of personal freedom and democracy at the end of a long tunnel of repression in the name of truth and virtue. "Truth is the end of liberty, and liberty must be defined and confined by truth." For now, scholarship must serve the ends of a "liberating tolerance." When we encounter doctrines that are regressive and repressive, we know they are false, and cannot enjoy the same right of propagation as those that liberate. "This tolerance cannot be indiscriminate and equal with respect to the contents of expression, neither in word nor in deed; it cannot protect false words and wrong deeds which demonstrate that they contradict and counteract the possibilities of liberation."

The Professor was no Marcusian. As concerned as he was with truth and virtue, he was even more concerned about the conditions from which truth and virtue might emerge; and he was by no means sure that final truth and ultimate virtue had been discovered by anyone— with the possible exception of himself—and the hostility he encountered led him to suspect that *his* truth and virtue might be the first victims of a liberating tolerance.

The Professor quoted what Marcuse called his "apparently undemocratic means": "They would include the withdrawal of toleration of speech and assembly from groups and movements which promote aggressive policies, armaments, chauvinism, discrimination on grounds of race and religion, or which oppose the extension of public services, social security or medical care, etc." The final "etc." bothered the Professor almost as much as the means.

"Moreover," Marcuse went on, "the restoration of freedom of thought may necessitate new and rigid restrictions on teaching and practices in the educational institutions which, by their very methods and concepts, serve to enclose the mind within the established universe of disclosure and behavior—thereby precluding *a priori* a rational evaluation of the alternatives."

The Professor re-created for us there in the classroom the old, didactic, bigotsure Marxian—Herbert Marcuse —from his published words, and knocked him down again and again. And if the sainted Revolutionary were stuffed with straw, why, it only made up for the fact that Marcuse had already won, that we were living in his world, in which everybody already knew what was truth and what was virtue, and knew that whatever was necessary to be done to liberate it excused—no, sanctified—the deed. The only problem was that every individual or little group had its own version of truth and virtue.

Sometimes the Professor called our institution "Marcamp-use," when he was not calling it a "playground" or a "sandbox." And after the dwindling figure of Herbert Marcuse, losing straw as it fled, he called out, "How do you like your blueeyed boy Mister Death?" That last was a quote from an early-twentieth-century poet named E. E. Cummings.

Gavin walked behind the library and heard the ululations of the Kampuskops as they raced from their distant sallyport to remove the picket line. They would not touch the Revolutionaries—they had machine guns and a willingness to risk injury or even death in their cause —but the daily encounters with the Radicals was a ritual which both participants missed when for some reason they did not come off.

In the river valley below, the smog was thick this morning, but the hilltop campus was clean and bright like a green island in a gray sea. The white buildings gleamed in the sun. Gavin drew in a deep breath of air. He smelled the incense of grass and trees warming in the sun, and only a trace of sweetish tear gas from a feminist confrontation the night before.

He walked behind the journalism building where the little offset presses were grinding out the day's handouts and ultimatums, and down the driveway with the word

STRIKE stenciled in red on its blacktop, upon other fading messages like a palimpsest history of campus politics.

Dealers were hawking their pot and their pills at the entrances and on the open concrete levels around it and through it. But Gavin shook his head at all of them. He had not touched drugs since Karnival. He was hooked on harder stuff. If others wanted to shoot or sniff or swallow, that was their trip, but what he needed was learning. The Professor had been right about that.

Up close, the buildings did not look so much like white temples. They were pitted with the pox of random bullets, painted with calls to forgotten battles, punctured with stones and bricks, until few unbroken panes remained among the plywood surrenders.

One of the dealers angled eagerly toward him as Gavin approached the exterior steps that led concretely up to the classrooms of the second floor. Gavin knew him. He was a big-boned, broad-faced boy with no neck and medium-length blond hair. His name was Johnson. In earlier days he would have been a tackle on the football team, but now he drifted on the calm seas of campus life looking for a compass, or at least some bit of flotsam which seemed to be heading somewhere.

"Tom," Johnson said, "I got some ponies here for the course." He opened a large-knuckled hand to display some pink-and-blue capsules in his palm.

"What course?" Gavin asked, but he knew what course it was. They shared the Professor's course in philosophy. Johnson never attended. He said it was beneath his dignity as a human being, but Gavin thought he was either lazy or afraid. He kept trying the chemical route, kept trying to find that Northwest Passage to learning.

"You know," Johnson said.

"Who made them?"

"Some boys at the biochem lab. They swear they're the real stuff." Johnson's big face was sweating; his eyes wanted to believe.

"How would they get the real stuff?" Gavin asked, trying to get around him, but Johnson was too broad.

"Maybe they got some blood at the Medcenter?"

Johnson asked. "Anyway, the son-of-a-bitch doesn't put out a class issue. These got to be better than nothing. Right?"

"Maybe, maybe not," Gavin said. "What makes you think the biochem boys can put together synthetic peptides? How can you trust them?" He feinted right, then sidestepped left, and got around Johnson to the steps. "Besides, I happen to know the Professor hasn't been to the Medcenter."

Johnson hadn't heard him. He was wailing, "But, Tom, they're on our side."

The building smelled sweetly smoky like pot, and sour like sweat, and pungent like tear gas. It was Gavin's madeleine; every time he smelled that mixture, he was magically transported back to the classroom.

The wide corridor was only dimly illuminated by an occasional fluorescent light recessed into the ceiling. In other places fixtures gaped darkly like unhealed wounds or dangled from the ceiling like strangely shaped stalactites.

Gavin walked along the corridor nodding to students as he passed. They slouched toward their classes like rough beasts or sat along the walls smoking and sipping coffee or soft drinks. Like him they were dressed in grubbies carefully preserved from disintegration by colorful patches, or artfully aged to achieve the same appearance, but all were based on simple peasant trousers and workman's blue shirt. Steel toe and heel caps on their boots rang occasionally on concrete exposed where carpet had been worn or burned or ripped away.

A few students affected jeans and tanktops in response to a nostalgia craze for the late sixties and early seventies; a few more wore one-piece suits or skirts from the straight world to show their independence of student culture. Of course, that was useful if you wanted to sneak outside the walls occasionally. Not many tried it. Of those who did, some never came back. Sometimes in the late hours, when topics of sex and revolution dragged, students would talk about eloping and somebody would tell a horror story he had heard directly from the source, or almost. Gavin didn't believe any of it; not much, anyway.

Jenny was waiting for him outside the classroom.

"Today?" she said.

He nodded. Outside most of the doors along the corridor were dispensers labeled with the name of the course and the number of the lecture, but here the dispenser was empty.

"You're going to class?" she said.

Sometimes he wondered how serious his fellow students were about the revolution. None of them wanted to make any sacrifices that involved effort. "Aren't you?" he asked.

"I guess," she said, looking up at him with submissive brown eyes, willing to be led.

Gavin smiled. She wasn't exactly lazy, he thought, just a bit weak when it came to pushing herself. It was a small flaw—he thought of it as a womanly flaw, and then struck it from his mind as sexist—and he could forgive it. He was in love; he could forgive her anything, even that her relationship with him did not compare in intensity with his relationship with her. She was, he thought, a practical girl besieged by all sorts of fears and fancies. He didn't care.

They walked into the classroom together. They were the first, but not, Gavin hoped, the last. He did not want to be obvious. Even though the Professor did not take roll, some members of the class thought there were monitors or informers among them. In fact, a couple of his more impulsive classmates had beat up another, and the boy had almost died. It turned out to be only a misunderstanding.

Three more students drifted through the door a few moments later. One, George Simpson, was involved in the project. In his sleeve pocket he had the detonator disguised as a package of marijuana cigarettes. Two more students wandered in, then a group of five, half a dozen, and three more. Four more came in after the class had started. Eventually about half showed up out of an enrollment of fifty or so; there always were a few students who wanted to attend class and a few others who had awakened early and couldn't get back to sleep and hadn't anything better to do.

The Professor hadn't arrived. He liked to make his

entrance when the class, such as it was, had already assembled. Gavin didn't think he delayed out of any sense of the dramatic but that he didn't want late arrivals distracting the class. Gavin looked out the one window which hadn't been boarded up. The Professor's car wasn't in its customary parking place. Gavin felt a flash of panic: perhaps the Professor was going to skip class himself; he hadn't seemed well lately, and his cough was worse than ever. Gavin realized, for the Professor had taught him to be honest with himself, that his panic was tinged with relief.

And then the armored car was pulling up in front of the classroom. The machine gun in the administration building splattered bullets against its other side for a moment, and then stopped. It had jammed, perhaps, or someone had turned on the ad building's built-in teargas jets.

The guards stepped out of the car. They were big men, as big as Johnson, with black beards and mean eyes. They swung their riot guns from the hip, watching the passing students, daring them to move incautiously.

The rear door of the car opened. The Professor stepped out, looking small and tired and average. Then he raised his head, seeming to stare through the window where Gavin stood looking out. Gavin pulled back, his heartbeat accelerating, not wanting to be seen, not wanting to look into the Professor's eyes.

"What's the matter?" Jenny asked.

"He's coming," Gavin said.

He looked at her, saw her eyes looking at him, her mouth composed and a little prim, but still desirable even at this moment, her long hair framing her dramatically colored face, and he thought, "You're beautiful. How could I ever have had you in my bed, flesh to longing flesh? How could I have known you so intimately, and still not know you? Were you ever a child, sexless and cute? Will you ever grow wrinkled and old?"

And he saw the outlines of her breasts and the roses of her nipples through the thin shirt, and he wished they were home in bed and he could put his lips against them and hold on to her.

"Are you all right?" she asked.

"I'm all right," he said. He would have put his arm around her, but he knew she hated a public display of possession.

They took seats at the back of the room where they could see everything. The other students scattered around, none of them together, most of them toward the back of the room, in keeping with immemorial custom. In front were ranks of empty chairs looking like the incomplete skeletons of students waiting for flesh to gather and idea to shape.

Gavin wondered what they would think tomorrow—the students who showed up—when the Professor did not appear. He wondered if he should show up—he had not yet missed a class—and decided that it would depend on whether the grapevine reported the Professor missing.

And what would he think, he asked himself, when he knew what the Professor knew? Not just what was in the Professor's lectures, not what he had time and thought to formulate, but everything.

Gavin shook his head. He thought too much. That was, after all, the Professor's fault. He reached out for Jenny's hand. It was slender and firm and passive. Jenny let him hold her hand. That was all right.

Gavin looked at his watch. It was right at the half-hour, and he looked up. At that moment the Professor came through his doorway into the podium. The bullet-proof glass that surrounded him caught his reflections and made him seem four instead of one, a solid original and three pale shadows that all moved and gestured and opened their mouths together.

Many professors never ventured inside the classroom—or even inside the campus walls. They played it safe: electronics carried their three-dimensional images to the students, and electronics returned the student responses. The difference was subjective, but the Professor said the issue was morality. The Professor had a strong sense of morality, and he felt that the personal contact was irreplaceable. He would not shirk his responsibility to provide it.

"I want to see you," he had said the first day of class. "I want you to see me. You children of McLuhan don't

think that's important now. You think those aspects of
life that are immortalized on tape, with fade-ins and
fade-outs and jump cuts and nonlinear developments,
are the only things that are important—next to the
mysteries inside your own head and the fleshpressing of
your contemporaries—smooth, firm, young, tumescent
flesh. But one day, if you live long enough, you will
understand that there is another contact which is of
greater and more lasting importance—the contact between the past and the present, between wisdom and
ignorance, between maturity and youth. They can react
in many ways—as teacher and student, as master and
slave, as contemporaries, as colleagues before eternal
mysteries. But react they must, and react they will, and
the only way to make that reaction less than catastroph-
ic is face-to-face, mind-to-mind."

"Face-to-face," Gavin recalled. "Mind-to-mind."

As the Professor opened his mouth to speak, Gavin
impulsively pressed his thumb against the little window
in his desk under the engraved word "Record." The
desk buzzed briefly. Jenny looked at him. He shrugged.
Maybe it was sentimental, but he wanted the Professor's lecture on tape. He would pay for it somehow. His
parents would add the credit to his account if he threatened to come home.

"Today," the Professor said, "we shall hold a Socratic
dialogue about learning and life." His voice was husky
but strong. He moved restlessly around the enclosure of
his podium as if impatient with the barriers that separated him from those reluctant vessels into which he
poured his wisdom. Gavin was shocked, however, to
see how the bones of the face pushed through the skin
in some urgent effort to break free.

"In the past few weeks," the Professor continued,
"we have discussed the contradictions implicit in our
society. Marcuse's concept of 'liberating tolerance'
which practices tyranny in the name of freedom. The
state of education which glorifies the democratic ideal of
political equality into a debilitating doctrine of educational equality. The decay of the so-called Puritan ethic
into a general acceptance of pleasure-seeking hedo-
nism, of man's unique time-binding ability into a hatred

of history and a forgetfulness of the future, of language itself into degraded meanings, autonomic responses to abstractions, and ritual words scarcely distinguishable from the grunts and sighs of cavemen. The elevation of youth into a cult, and ignorance into a virtue. How did we get here?"

"Who cares?" someone muttered at the back of the room.

The Professor's eyes searched the room for the speaker. "Will the barbarian who spoke please identify himself? No? I could quote Whitehead to you: 'Those who ignore history are condemned to repeat it.' Instead I shall suggest that you cannot live rationally without knowing what your society values, and why."

"Rationality is a middle-class prejudice," said a student halfway toward the front. He was a bright, fat boy named Brucker, who was continually arguing with the Professor. Gavin thought maybe he was an agent provocateur for the Radicals, at the least an informer.

"So we are condemned to irrational behavior because we must not be bourgeois," the Professor said. "Or do we elevate something above rationality—an instantaneously perceived truth, intuitively recognized and not subject to rational analysis? Which is to say, we should turn off our minds and let the truth roll in—or roll out, as the case may be. Implicit in that concept is a definition of truth as an absolute, existing independently of man, his circumstances, his perceptions, and his understanding—like God. Now, I am as willing to postulate God as the next man, and if you wish to argue that since we are created in God's image we instinctively recognize God's truth without the intercession of our minds, I would not quarrel with you, although I might sympathize with the situation in which your convictions limit your potential. But that, I gather, is not what you mean."

"Certainly not," Brucker said.

"Nor do you, I believe, mean your remark to be interpreted in the Platonic sense of ideals existing somewhere of which we perceive in this world only shadows or imperfect imitations but which we can intuitively recognize if we allow ourselves not to be deceived by appearances or by the confusions implicit in our attempts to analyze and synthesize."

"Ridiculous," Brucker said. "Where has traditional thinking got us?"

"Which must mean," the Professor said, coughing a bit in his elation at reaching a critical point in the dialogue, "that we have alternate methods for acquiring knowledge and power, methods which are undescribed and perhaps undescribable, hence mystic, arcane, cabalistic, cryptic, occult, intangible, impalpable, and no doubt supernatural."

"Of course," Brucker said.

"And so we have elevated the unknowable over the knowable, the magician above the scholar, sensation above thought. And yet you are here, the end product of a series of definitions of education beginning with Bishop Wilson's 'Culture is the desire to make reason and the will of God prevail' to Montesquieu's 'The pursuit of knowledge is to render an intelligent being yet more intelligent,' Matthew Arnold's 'Culture is the acquainting ourselves with the best that has been known and said in the world, and thus with the history of the human spirit' and 'The great aim of culture is the aim of setting ourselves to ascertain what perfection is and to make it prevail,' and Bertrand Russell's 'Reason is, and ought only to be, the slave of the passions.' But . . . how did we get here?"

"Here is where it's at," George Simpson said. Gavin was surprised; Simpson never spoke in class. Perhaps possession of the detonator had given him delusions of competence.

"And wherever it's at is right," the Professor concluded.

"Aw," Brucker said. "It's right because it's right. It's right because it's good. It's good because everybody's equal. No phony degrees. No phony teacher-student shit. You do your own thing, and it's just as good as anybody else's thing."

"And so," the Professor said, "we are content, having arrived at a state of perfection, to allow our route here to fade into oblivion. Yet, suppose we lose our permissive paradise, suppose reaction or necessity forces us from our heaven and sets at the east of the garden of Eden cherubim and a flaming sword which turns every way? Having once tasted the fruit of the tree, shall we be content not to eat of it again? If we do not know how we got here, how shall we return?"

"In the beginning," Gavin said, his mouth dry but unable to resist any longer the urge to give the Professor what he wanted, "Mario Savio created the Free Speech Movement at Berkeley. The civil-disobedience techniques learned by students in the southern civil-rights campaigns of the late fifties and early sixties were applied for the first time to questions of campus power. University governance, based for a century or more on a master-apprentice relationship disguised as a community of scholars, was not equipped to handle disobedience, much less violence. Slowly but inevitably administrative authority crumbled. First went control over the private lives of students subsumed under the phrase *in loco parentis,* then control of the classroom and the curriculum. Power drifted inexorably toward the student constituency, which was bored and affluent and reckless. . . ."

The Professor held up his hand as if to place it against a dike. "Enough," he said. "Who gives the lectures here?" he asked, half-mocking Gavin, half himself, and coughed. When the seizure subsided, he continued in a half-strangled voice, "And so we find ourselves in this student culture, in this youth-centered environment—and not just us, but the world itself, the society outside the walls, which exists, at least in part, in response to what is here inside the walls. We paranoid schizophrenics have rejected thinking for feeling, and feel, therefore, that we are gods, and noble gods at that. And who is inside the walls and who is outside?"

Jenny looked at Gavin. Gavin frowned and shook his head. Jenny thought the Professor was raving, but Gavin knew better. Everything the Professor did was planned. Every response he elicited from the class was anticipated. In spite of the fact that the Professor issued no capsules containing his lectures encoded into chemicals, everything that happened in the class still had, for

Gavin, an overpowering sense of déjà vu, every lecture sounded like an echo, every thought seemed graven on the clay tablet of his mind.

The Professor was still talking. Gavin had missed part of the lecture. Well, that was all right. It was there in his mind. He had heard it, and all he had to do was think it through. And he would have the tape to remind him.

Gavin glanced at his watch. Ten minutes had passed. Forty minutes to go.

"But we make a mistake," the Professor was saying, "if we restrict our concern to the history of ideas, or even the history of politics. We shape ideas, and our ideas shape us, and it is difficult to tell who is shaper and who is shaped, who Pygmalion and who Galatea. 'Who is the potter, pray, and who the pot?' Other forces move us. Tradition, say. You, 7527679, what do you think of tradition?"

He was pointing at Simpson. A chill raised the fine hairs on Gavin's arms. Had he picked Simpson deliberately?

"As little as possible," Simpson said.

The machine gun began to rattle again across the street. A soft crump sounded outside, like a tear-gas canister exploding, and then another. Gavin nodded. They could use all the extra diversions they could get.

"Of course. And yet tradition exists, whether you think about it or not, and it affects you, whether you accept it or reject it. And yet tradition is but one force, like ideas, that make us what we are."

The Professor coughed again, and Gavin felt a quick surge of sympathy.

When the Professor had regained his breath, he said, "And what of our animal natures, our needs for food and rest and shelter from the heat and cold, and mother love, and after all of these, said Freud, came sex, and of them all, sex was not the strongest but only the most important, because only sex could be denied the individual without depriving him of what he must have to survive."

"But why should sex be denied?" Jenny asked.

Gavin was surprised to hear her speak in class for the first time. So was the Professor. "Why, indeed? Can any of you suggest a possible answer?"

A brisk fifteen-minute dialogue ensued, in which most of the class participated. At the end, some of them conceded that their permissive culture might inhibit creativity and social stability and delay emotional maturity.

Jenny was not willing to admit even a possibility. "It's just a game," she whispered scornfully. She didn't like games and wasn't good at them.

Gavin motioned for her to be quiet. He didn't want to miss anything today. The Professor turned Jenny off, but he turned Gavin on like speed, racing through his veins, accelerating his time sense.

Gavin looked at his watch. Five after. Only fifteen minutes left.

"And then there is technology," the Professor said, "an idea materialized which shapes our environment, and we are in turn shaped by our environment. At very nearly the same moment in time when Mario Savio was standing on a police car in front of Sproul Hall, experiments were being conducted at the University of Michigan and at the Baylor University College of Medicine, at UCLA, at the University of Göteborg in Sweden, in Denmark, and in Czechoslovakia, which would change our lives fully as much as the ideas Savio unleashed."

The students waited passively for the Professor to continue. He sighed. "James McConnell and his flatworms at Michigan, George Ungar and David Krech with their rats at Baylor and Berkeley, even earlier Holger Hyden and his RNA experiments at Gotëborg. From their beginnings we derive today's learning methods; we have perfected their primitive habituation studies so that we can transmit precise information in the form of synthesized peptides. Just as television created the age of McLuhan, so chemical learning has created the age of chemistry. And we have just begun. Who knows what may come next: not only information, but sensory experience one day may be coded into proteins, and not only aptitudes, but talents themselves. Beyond the transfer of learning may lie an improvement in the general level of intelligence equal to the improvement in the general level of health in the first half of this century."

Outside, something went whoomp-whoomp again. Into the room, through the air-conditioning system, drifted the faint, stinging odor of tear gas.

"But, Professor," Gavin asked, "how do we know that information is being coded correctly into the peptides? Or, alternatively, that correct information is being coded in?"

"Good," said the Professor, "good. But that is why classes in which encapsulated lectures are distributed still must be attended, if you are wise. To compare what you think is true with what someone else thinks is true or says he thinks is true. And that is why one reads —if one is able to read—or watches tapes, or looks around him at reality. 'The unexamined life is not worth living.' " He coughed.

"But who is master?" Gavin persisted. Jenny tugged at his sleeve, but he ignored her. "Our peptides or our will? How do we know we can cope with what the peptides tell us is true? Or do we accept these, as we accept our prejudices, and seek only to justify them, as Bertrand Russell said? And what if, through chemical means, a government should pass along to its citizens an inhibiting respect for laws rather than a revolutionary insistence on truth and justice?"

"You have one good test for all such concerns," the Professor said. He lit a cigarette and coughed. Soon the odor of marijuana joined that of tear gas in the room, and some of the students began to light up as well, all except Simpson, who looked uneasily at the disguised detonator in his sleeve.

"Reality," the Professor completed. "Look around you. Is this campus inhibited? But we live in an age of chemistry, when drugs are available to tire or invigorate us, to ease pain, to increase or suppress hunger, to put us to sleep and wake us up, to increase or diminish sexual drives, to induce or suppress fertility, to terminate pregnancy, to improve or impair our ability to think, to create temporary or permanent insanity, to induce the mystic state, to improve physical performance, to create or depress aggressive behavior, to produce pain or pleasure—to affect, that is, every aspect of man, including his memory. We can be whatever we choose to be."

"Or whatever someone else chooses us to be," Gavin said.

"Possibly," the Professor said. In spite of his seeming approval of the age of chemistry, Gavin thought the Professor reserved another opinion that he hoped, by natural opposition, the class would derive from discussion. "But what do we laymen know about chemicals, about peptides, chemical learning, technology, the state of the art? Surely we have some chemistry majors in the class."

There were two, and the discussion was off again and winging toward a destination that only the Professor knew.

He was the wisest and wittiest man Gavin had ever met—and he had met him only briefly except with a layer of bulletproof glass between them. Gavin ached with the desire to know everything the Professor knew. This was, he thought, the best class session the Professor had ever conducted. Premonition?

"Here I stand," the Professor said, "tearing my breast to bleeding shreds like the fabled pelican to feed you ungrateful chicks, in a place where learning has fled, where man has retreated from intellectual activity to ritual. I have lived through it all. I have seen the University retreat from educational standards and academic freedom through autonomous black-studies curricula, general studies, and student participation in University governance to total lack of concern for objective educational criteria and to the abandonment of the campus by serious scholars and scientists. Where has learning fled?

"How many of you know that when you matriculate in this University you are automatically awarded a degree? Of course, most of you stay around to play in the sandbox you call a university, and a few of you, to seek out an education. Where has learning fled?

"The practice of students hiring and paying their own teachers goes back to the first university, at Bologna, founded in the eleventh century, but it soon was recognized as the pure bologna it was. Students do not know what they need to know; if they knew, they would not need teachers. Well, the Dark Ages returned as public support for higher education gradually was withdrawn from campuses, enrollments began declining, and faculty became increasingly dependent upon student fees; the ancient pattern of student control and student hiring, firing, and payment of faculty reestablished itself. The result, you see around you—not teachers but charlatans, pimps pandering to student lusts in the name of relevance. Relevance—that's what we call it when our prejudices are reinforced. A basic principle of education is that you cannot learn anything from someone with whom you agree.

"Where," he said, "has learning fled?"

And it was over, reaching its conclusion at exactly the moment the class-break whistle blew, and the Professor nodded, turned, and vanished through the door that led, Gavin knew, to an interior stairway walled off from the rest of the student-controlled building. Eventually, joined by other stairways from other podiums in other rooms, it led to a single, guarded outside door where the armored cars waited.

Gavin looked at his watch and counted the seconds. The other students were getting up, introspective, withdrawn, collecting their belongings absently. Gavin waited, Jenny waited. Gavin looked up and nodded at Simpson. Simpson drew a cigarette out of the pack on his sleeve.

The single unbroken window brightened, turned blinding. A fraction of a second later came the sound of an explosion. The window shattered. Gavin had his eyes closed. He opened them again as the brightness faded, and was on his feet heading toward the door. Jenny was beside him; he was pleased by her effectiveness.

Behind them something whirred, then clicked. Gavin glanced back and then turned.

"Tom! No!" Jenny said.

But Gavin ran back and grabbed the cassette that had popped out of his desk.

At the door he grabbed Jenny's hand and pulled her

behind him from the room. Outside, the machine gun hammered. A riot gun roared. Gavin and Jenny looked at each other.

As they reached the door that looked out onto concrete stairways and broad expanses of open pavement facing the administration building, they saw masked students fading into the pedestrian traffic.

Many students were standing still, rubbing their eyes, or moving cautiously, stumbling, their hands held out in front of them as if they could not see.

The armored car pulled away, threading a path through masses of students; they fell back, seemingly startled by the noise. Several masked students passed by, supporting another. Above the administration building a helicopter swooped lower.

Blind eyes lifted toward the noise, and a cry of "Tear gas!" went up from several students. Many fumbled plastic masks from pouches at their hips and put them over their faces.

Gavin looked at the spot the armored car had stood and saw no sign that told him whether the abduction had been successful.

"Come on," he said to Jenny, "let's get back to the house."

When they left the humanities building, the students who had been facing the administration building when the light bomb exploded were beginning to regain their sight, and the machine gun in the administration building had started up again.

They walked the entire distance in silence, not touching, not looking at each other. For the moment their being together had no undertone of sex. They shared only the feelings of conspirators.

This day, successful or not, had changed his life, Gavin felt. He had never felt as alive, as much a thinking man, as he had felt in the classroom; he had been able to sense, almost, the Professor's thoughts as they had occurred, before they were phrased into those precise and witty words. He had even felt the emotions behind the thoughts, the moral force that drove the man to do what he should do rather than what was pleasant or easy or convenient. . . .

"Wasn't it terrible?" Jenny said. "God, I can't stand that man!"

In the daylight, as they descended the hill, the wall was not shadowed mystery, but ugly, utilitarian reality made up of ill-fitting concrete blocks and old stones salvaged from fallen walls and broken foundations, the remnants of someone's shattered dreams of home and permanence now transformed into a barrier between the old and the new. The wall was ten feet high on their side, perhaps eleven on the city side, but they kept well away from it; in spite of the cleared hundred feet beyond, some kid or redneck was always sneaking up to the wall when a guard's back was turned—sometimes on purpose—laying his gun between the barbed wire and the broken glass, and practicing his marksmanship at the expense of the students. The freakshoot, they called it.

Gavin's room was in one of the older buildings; it was more than one hundred and twenty years old, and it should have fallen down years ago. Wire and faith held it together. Every few years a movement would get started to repair the place, and everybody would play games with nails and hammers for a day or two. But the enthusiasm burned out before any permanent improvements were accomplished.

The house was a two-story frame structure perched on the hillside like a boulder deposited there by a retreating glacier. Its paint had long ago weathered away, and the boards were gray streaked with black. The porch had fallen off many years ago and been burned in a bonfire protesting or celebrating some long-forgotten issue. But they were lucky to have something so substantial. Many students were living in corrugated-metal favelas, and others had to endure the mass living in the crumbling dormitories on the other side of the campus.

They climbed concrete blocks to the front door and then up the worn, turning stairs, dusty and smeared in the gray light that fought its way through the cracked window partway up the stairs. Gavin unlocked their door and they went into the room, leaving the door open behind them. A closed door in the day meant you weren't home.

The room was neater now. The cans had been thrown away, the floor had been swept, and Gavin had built a framework to raise the mattress off the floor. Jenny laughed and called it Gavin's homebuilding instinct; she didn't care how the room looked. It made Gavin uneasy, as if she invested nothing in their relationship and preferred the impermanence of disarray and dirt, but he supposed his small improvements made her uneasy too.

He turned and looked at Jenny. She was looking at the doorway as if willing someone to appear in it, not thinking of him or of sex, and he felt suddenly lonely.

"What do you think?" she asked.

"We'll know soon enough."

And footsteps pounded up the stairs, and Bob Marlin filled their doorway, beard bouncing. "You're a genius," he shouted. "Better than Mario What's-his-name or Mark Rudd or Rubin or Hoffman or any of the old-timers."

"Everything came off?" Gavin asked.

"Just like you laid it out, every step."

"The guards?"

"Out cold in the armored car where we abandoned it on the other side of the campus. When the flash went off, we tapped them where the medic showed us, and they fell back into the car."

"A riot gun went off."

"Reflex. Nobody hurt."

"The Professor?"

"Grabbed him as he came out just after the flash, clapped the mask on his face with the chloroform in it, and took him away as if he had been injured. He never said a word."

"Where is he?"

Bob pointed a finger straight down.

Excitement filled Gavin's throat. The Professor was here. In this house.

"Where's the medic?"

"With him."

"Let's go," Gavin said.

The basement was dark and damp, filled with cobwebs and cockroaches, micedroppings and mildew, and
the old unidentifiable shapes of discarded furniture and
implements and rotting things in cardboard boxes lurking in the shadows like ghouls.

Behind the old converted furnace was a small room
that might once have been a coal room. It had been
scrubbed recently and was lit by a single high-intensity
lamp focused on the arm of the Professor. Everything
else had been amputated by darkness.

The medical student looked up. His syringe was purple with blood. He withdrew the needle from the swollen vein in the Professor's arm and emptied the contents
of the syringe into a test tube.

"You could have waited," Gavin said.

"The longer we wait, the more danger of being discovered," the medic said. He was a tall, thin boy with
pimples and a prominent Adam's apple that went up
and down when he talked, but his hands were thin and
strong and sure. The fingers twitched as if, independently, they wished to be about their job.

"Who'd discover us?" Gavin said. Now that the plan-
ning and the execution were over, he felt a strange reluctance to hurry this moment to its conclusion. He
took Jenny's hand and led her around the door set on
sawhorses which held the Professor's body. "Put the
lamp at his head," he said. He wanted to look into the
Professor's face. Jenny tried to hold back, but he pulled
her along.

"Well," the medic said, "there's the Kampuskops or
another student group. We could be hijacked, you know.
Or maybe even the townies might think it important
enough to . . ."

"They'll never find us in time," Gavin said absently.
He was looking at the Professor's face. The shadows
cast by the light at his head made the Professor's face
look like a skull. He thought he saw a flicker of movement in the shadows that fell like eclipses from his eyebrows. "Is he awake?"

"I gave him a hypo that will keep him out until we're
through with him," the medic said. "If you don't
waste too much time," he added. "I've got to get blood

out of the other arm if I'm going to have enough to analyze."

"Don't rush it," Gavin said. He looked the Professor over from his head to his shadowed feet. He seemed much smaller here, laid out. "Here we are, Professor," he said softly, "come together for a rite more primitive, more traditional, than the rite of teacher and student. If you were awake, you would be the most interested person here. Speak of the fabled pelican!"

Again Gavin thought he saw a flicker of movement in the eyesockets. He leaned closer, but he did not see it again. "I wish you were awake so that you could truly share this moment with us," he said. "We do like you. We like you better than any of our teachers. That is why we picked you to be part of our ceremony of learning."

"Let's hurry it up," the medic said nervously.

"It isn't enough just to have the words," Gavin said. "Not even the words and the peptides, if you had been willing to issue them. One is just a synthesis of ideas, and the other, a synthesis of molecules. We want the real thing. The real thing, Professor. The memory locked in the peptides of your own blood, Professor, not not just a representation or an imitation."

The Professor's arms flopped and fell outward on the improvised pallet. When they stopped moving, the Professor's body was different. Something had gone out of it. "What's happened?" Gavin asked.

The medic already was listening at the Professor's chest. He looked up, a face half-light, half-dark. "He's dead," said the dark-light mouth.

"Dead?" Gavin echoed. "Dead? Do something!"

"Me?" the medic said, straightening into complete shadows. "Here? In his condition? With what? Anyway, he shouldn't have died. There must have been something wrong with him. I want to do an autopsy."

"Let's dispose of the body," someone else said. "Fast." There was a grumble of agreement.

"No!" Gavin said. The whole thing was going wrong. It would be a disaster. He couldn't let it go wrong, be wrong. Not when it was so right. "You've got a drill," he said.

"Yes."

"And a blender?"

"Yes."

"Open his head," Gavin said. His voice didn't shake when he said it. "We respect you," he said to the body stretched out upon the horizontal door, "the way the ancient warrior respected his fallen enemy, and we want you to be part of us. We want you to be part of us as long as we live, and this is the only way we can do it now."

"He can't hear you," the medic said.

"Let's get it over with," Simpson said.

"Yes, let's get on with it," said several other voices.

Gavin looked up. While he had been talking to the Professor, the little room had filled with people. He had difficulty recognizing them in the many-shadowed room, but he knew who they were—all the members of the class who had been involved in the project. All of them had gathered to get from the Professor his store of knowledge, his innermost thoughts, his wisdom, his wit. . . .

"Fellow ghouls," Gavin began, "vampires . . ."

"Shut up, Tom!" someone said.

Gavin looked down again, urgency rising in him as if he stood upon a hill waiting for nails to be driven into outstretched palms, waiting to see if death could conquer love, and if spirit could conquer death. "They're eager, Professor," he thought. "Eager for their last supper at your table, impatient for the feast of ideas to begin. The class is ready to start. I wish you were here to share with us the mystery and the magic of this moment."

"Are you ready, Professor?" he asked aloud.

He imagined he saw the Professor's lips twist upward, as if smiling, but it was only a shadow moving as the medic jostled the lamp.

"Let us begin," he told the medic.

The scalpel descended, and a few moments later came the sound of a drill whining its way through bone.

Gavin continued to look at the Professor's face, refusing to think of him as dead, but he did not see or think he saw any other movement. He stared at the face as if he were trying to fix it in his memory forever. "I love you, Professor," he thought. "Even more than Jenny. I love you in a way I could never love Jenny. I want to possess you in a way I never wanted to possess Jenny. I will grieve for you, but more than that, I will celebrate you."

Then he heard the thin, high sound of the supersonic blender, and he knew the time had come.

"Who's got straws?" someone asked. "Didn't anybody think to bring straws?"

But straws suddenly were being passed around. As soon as they were inserted, the light was turned off so that no one had to look, although the medic had been skillful and there was remarkably little blood.

What Gavin drew through the straw was the consistency of malted milk, but not really like that, because it was lukewarm and salty. For a moment Gavin thought he would not be able to swallow, but he thought of the Professor and how wise he was, and wonderful, and he swallowed and swallowed again, and yet again.

And they were through, wiping their lips, not looking toward each other in the dark.

"I don't feel any smarter," somebody said.

"You think it works in seconds?" someone else said.

"I'm sick," Jenny said.

"You'll be all right," Gavin said, and he put his arm around her, but he felt a little sick too. He knew he couldn't be sick. That would ruin everything, make everything wrong, and it was wrong enough as it was.

"Come on, fellows," the medic said, "let's get this thing over to the anatomy lab. I can use the rest of the blood, and by the time we get it pickled and floating among the other cadavers, nobody will know the difference."

"No," Gavin heard himself say.

"What do you mean?" the medic said. "It's a good plan. Nobody ever looks at a cadaver."

"No," Gavin said again.

"Well, I guess I can cut it up here. A bit of a mess, but—"

"No," Gavin said.

"Then what's your idea?"

"You can take all the blood, but then we're going to bury him."

"You're crazy!"

"Where?"

"In front of the library," Gavin said, suddenly sure of himself again. This would make it right.

"We might as well dig up the middle of the boulevard," someone protested. "The library lawn is as wide open as a billiard table."

"We'll skin off the turf, dig the grave, cart off the extra dirt, and lay the grass back like it had never been touched," Gavin said.

"How'll we do that?"

They were still objecting for form's sake, but they had accepted it, the way they always did. Gavin felt a choking sense of power and a strange new sense of moral right.

"It's right," he said. "That's where he would want to be, where great thoughts are kept. It's the least we can do." He was silent.

He felt Jenny's arm slide around his waist. She leaned her head and body against him as his arm encircled her shoulder. It was her first open demonstration of affection, and the thought exhilarated him.

"We'll create a diversion on the other side of the campus, a demonstration, a real confrontation. That will draw off the Kampuskops, the students, everybody. By the time it's over, the Professor will be in the ground." He thought of it as sanctified ground, and if he arose on the third day, everyone would be there to see it.

"Bob," Gavin said, "you're in charge of the diversion. "George," he said, looking around in the shadows for Simpson, not finding him. "Sam, then, you're in charge of the burial detail. And, Fred, you'll have the Professor there at the proper moment. Any questions?"

"What time?"

"There's no moon tonight. Midnight, say. No, three-fifteen."

There were no more questions.

As he and Jenny went toward the basement stairs, they heard somebody vomiting in the corner. It was Simpson.

In their room Jenny slowly detached herself from him, slowly closed the door, and slowly, as if she were listening to some distant music, removed her clothing. First she removed her peasant trousers and then her thin shirt, letting them drop unnoticed to the floor, and there she stood, weaving slightly in front of him, as beautiful as he had imagined, as his hands had told him she was. As he looked at her and the dreaming smile upon her face, his hands trembled and his eyes burned, and he felt desire rise in him as he had never felt it before.

She moved toward him, for he seemed unable to move, and they made love in the light, seeing everything, the sights accentuating the touch and the smell and the taste, as they had never made love before, interminably, without satiety, like gods. . . .

Later he lay quietly in the dark listening to her even breathing beside him, and he felt a great joy—remembering all that they had been to each other and the promise that this was not everything but only the beginning—and at the same time a great sadness. He did not know why he was sad, but he knew he had to think about it. He had to think about it until he figured it out, even if it took a long time.

Looking into the darkness, he felt as if he were looking into a tunnel that was so long he could see no glimmering of light at the end, but he knew he was going to have to go down that tunnel to its end, no matter how far.

3 ⊷ The Raid

Wherever creatures have organized a society, the basic question is power. Among the social insects, instinct and diet determine who shall do what. In the hen yard and the rest of the animal world, a pecking order or its equivalent is soon established to minimize useless and disruptive battles over supremacy and mating rights. Among humanity, everyone seeks a situation where he or she can exercise power: the patriarch seeks the family; the matriarch, children; children, the schoolyard and eventually the campus. Some of them never want to leave.

—THE PROFESSOR'S NOTEBOOK

The Union was student country. No faculty, no Kampuskops, no civil authorities, no federal agents of any kind ever came there. That principle had been finally established in the riots of eighty-five which followed the law-and-order tyranny of eighty-four, when a choice had been made between the destruction of certain campus strongholds, and possibly the campuses themselves, and surrendering those buildings, and possibly the campuses as well, to the rioters.

"We are your children," the students echoed, and the adults surrendered.

Once proudly called by its professional manager "the University's living room," the Union now was sanctuary, flophouse, hash house, burger bar, co-op, and play pen. Students ran it for students, and if the food was greasy and the floors were dirty, the students didn't mind. Perhaps they didn't notice; it was theirs, and what was theirs was good.

Gavin saw the building as if he had never seen it before. When he had awakened, the day was well into afternoon. After the Professor had been safely, secretly, and reverently planted in front of the library, Gavin had returned to Jenny's side and slept like a baby—restlessly, turning, whimpering. . . . When he awakened, he still was tired. The medic awoke him with a hypodermic filled with a faintly yellow fluid. Jenny was gone, and Gavin felt sad and old, and the medic said it was an extract of what he had been able to get from the Professor, and did Gavin want the shot. "Yes!" Gavin said, wanting everything of the Professor that he could get.

Afterward he didn't want to stay at the house. The kitchen was filthy. The dirty dishes stacked in the sink and on the table, and the pans on the stove, all smelled like decay, and the cockroaches hopped around tamely. He didn't want to see anybody who had been connected with the project.

The Union was brick and limestone; it had been weathered by midwestern summer heat and winter cold, by thunderstorms and wind and snow and freezing rain. The building had been constructed in stages, over the years, like a Gothic cathedral, as enrollment increased, and cupolas sprouted unexpectedly from green copper roofs, and stone balconies, from red-brick walls.

It was, Gavin thought, a wonderful, surprising mélange of a building. Gavin wondered what the Professor had thought of it, but as the thought occurred to him, he knew with an odd certainty that the Professor had liked it.

Gavin wished the Professor were here with him now, that he could walk with him into the Union and talk to him about life and philosophy and the way things are, and then his mood lightened. The Professor was with him and always would be, he thought.

The Union had been set afire twice during the past twenty years. The first time, the arsonist was never identified; the second time, the students knew who the culprit was, and they had punished the poor screaming wretch for a month, keeping him from all drugs and at the end of the period expelling him from the campus, as a warning to others.

After the second fire, but before the riots, the students assumed complete jurisdiction over the building. Student fees had built it. The students seized it first, and no one wanted to make an issue of it, least of all the administration. The alumni had protested, saying that their fees had built it when they were students and they didn't approve of what was being done with their building, but this argument was brushed aside by student leaders as invalidated by the nonstudent status of the alumni, who had joined the establishment. And they pointed out that the students had possession of the building and were going to keep it, and that was that, there was no need to argue about it, and subsequent uses were sanctioned by time, strike, and struggle.

Gavin opened one of the plywood doors—they replaced the glass that had once served—and walked into the north lobby. The marble had been worn down by shoes and sandals and bare feet over the years, and plastic tiles that had been placed over the marble were worn through as well, until only ragged fragments remained around the edges. A few blankets and bedrolls were scattered along the walls, a few of them still with occupants, some of them sleeping.

Several students were walking aimlessly through the lobby or leaned against the painted pillars, talking aimlessly. One of them looked up and saw Gavin. He rushed over.

"Gavin!" he said, grabbing Gavin's arm at the shoulder, squeezing it. "You're a hero, you know that? Everybody's talking about it."

The boy was blond and thin and short. His name was Phil, and he reminded Gavin of a spider monkey. His hands on Gavin's arm didn't hurt, but Gavin didn't like the feel of it, and he moved away. He walked on toward the stairs at the far end of the lobby, stepping around a sleeping bag with two heads that was beginning to thrash around.

"What did you do with the Professor?" Phil asked. "Where've you got him stashed? Gonna hold him for ransom, get some bread, get a grade?" Phil trotted along beside Gavin, his monkey face bright and eager.

Gavin walked on. "I don't know what you're talking about," he said. He kicked some loose papers out of the way and started down the stairs.

" 'At's a way, boy," the other said. "Keep it to yourself. Who's listening, right?" Phil made a show of looking up and down and around as they reached the basement landing and started down the next flight of stairs to the sub-basement. The walls were plastered with old signs and notices advertising films and strike meetings and protest demonstrations and goods and services of all kinds, from the most ordinary to the most intimate, including many that once were found only on the inside of men's toilets; some were printed on squares of colored cardboard, but they ranged down through notes scribbled on scraps of ruled paper or on the walls themselves.

"You can tell old Phil, though. Just between us, right?"

Gavin didn't answer. Phil scuttling at his heels, he went through swinging wooden doors into the rathskeller. Plastic-covered booths lined the walls and filled the center of the room. The place was gloomy. Gavin couldn't see much after the glare of the afternoon, but he could smell the familiar odors of stale beer, old grease, and thrice-breathed smoke.

"Everybody knows you swiped the Professor," Phil said. "That's no secret. Nobody else would've had the guts to try it, much less carry it off in daylight. You got spirit, man! You're a real dude. Everybody's saying it."

Gavin looked at Phil and shrugged. He didn't care what everybody said, and Phil sucked.

Gavin found an empty booth and slid into it, catching his pants for a moment on a split in the imitation leather upholstery. Phil waited for him to move over, but Gavin sat on the edge. After a moment Phil sat down on the seat opposite, undeterred.

Phil winked at him. "Now you can tell me, right? What did you do with the Professor? Gonna release him? Hold him hostage?"

"I don't know what you're talking about," Gavin repeated wearily.

Phil nodded conspiratorially. "That's right. Don't tell nobody. Who may be listening, eh? Or what?" He rolled his eyes toward the ceiling and leaned down to peer under the cluttered table. When his head came up, he tried to look into Gavin's eyes. "What I wanted to tell you, dude, is that next time you get something on, I'm in. Anything you say, no matter how heavy." Phil lowered his voice and reached over to tap Gavin on the hand with his forefinger to indicate that "anything" included "everything." "Can I get you something?" Phil went on. He swept the dishes and glasses toward the wall with his arm. "Let me get you a beer."

He half-rose from his seat, but Gavin shook his head. Yesterday anybody could have bought him anything, but today was different. In particular he didn't want Phil buying for him. Phil always seemed to have money, and he always wanted to spend it on other people.

A student waiter slouched down the cluttered aisle toward them and stopped by the table. His apron was decorated with food stains, old and new. "What'll it be?" he asked.

Gavin fingered the few coins in his pocket and estimated their purchasing power. "Burger," he said.

"Beer?"

Gavin shook his head. "Has Jenny been in?"

"Ain't seen her."

"I saw her," Phil said. "She was at the Health Service. In line at the dispensary. Getting her pills, I suppose. Some lay, right?" He looked at Gavin slyly.

"She's a person," Gavin said. Suddenly he was no longer hungry; Phil and the rathskeller made him sick; between Phil's suffocating admiration and the odors, he couldn't remember what he was doing here.

"You?" the waiter said to Phil.

"Naw," Phil said, and when the waiter was gone, he leaned across the table again. "Look, Gavin," he said softly, "there's gonna be an election soon. I'm gonna nominate you for raid chief. You'll get votes, too, a dude like you. Damn, you could be president, you know, or a member of StudEx."

Gavin did not want to feel impressed, but he did. He could not deny it—the abduction, the operation, the interment, the whole project had gone as smoothly as the most classic revolutionary venture, and in spite of unforeseen and unlikely events that threatened to sour it all. *Ah, there, Professor!* "Who wants to be president?" he said.

"Somebody's got to be," Phil said. "Why not you? Then maybe we'd get something done, not screw around like we seem to do alla time."

Why not, indeed? Except he had meant what he said. He didn't want to be president. The president was a figurehead with lots of responsibility and no authority, a hostage to the good behavior of his fellows; none of them lasted long. What Gavin wanted was not power but knowledge, which maybe was ultimate power; he had the conviction that if he knew everything there was to know, the questions that disturbed him would fade away and he would have all the time that queer feeling of certainty he felt now only on rare and beautiful occasions.

His friends kept urging him to take alpha-wave training.

A hand clapped him on the shoulder. A deep voice said, passing, "Good show, man!"

Gavin looked up. The man who had spoken was a big broad-shouldered black named John something. He passed on, bandoleers shifting on his back as he moved. Two other blacks followed him, shotguns in their hands. "Thanks," Gavin said.

The waiter was back with the hamburger. Gavin fumbled in his pocket. "Forget it," the waiter said. He sounded as if he had learned something while he had been away. "The manager said it's on the house."

Gavin took his hand out of his pocket. "If I'd known that, I'd have had some fries and a glass of beer."

"I'll get 'em," the waiter said. "You really pulled one, didn't you?"

Gavin shrugged.

The waiter turned to Phil. His voice changed. "You sure you don't want anything?"

"Got a joint?" Phil asked.

"There's a cigarette machine right outside the door," the waiter said.

"How about Big H?"

"We're all out, but there's a guy in number three says he's got some good stuff."

Phil pulled a roll of bills out of his shirt pocket and turned off a couple with his thumb. "Get me an envelope," he said. He not only liked to buy things for people, he liked to send waiters on errands for him.

"You know where it is," the waiter said. "Any food? Drink?"

Phil crumpled the bills in his hand. "I wouldn't eat here if it was the only place on campus."

The waiter shrugged. "So starve."

Gavin bit into the hamburger. Phil was right about that, at least. It was pretty bad. Old meat with lots of fat and gristle that had been cooked too long on a dirty grill. It reminded him of the old joke about professor-burgers, and he put it back on the plate. He tried to remember why he ever ate here.

Phil glanced both ways and leaned forward. "There's gonna be a raid tonight," he whispered.

Gavin looked bored.

"In town."

Gavin looked surprised. Phil smiled.

"They're gonna ask you to go along," Phil whispered. "They liked the Professor bit. Gonna check you out. Get it on, and you're in all the way to the jackpot."

Gavin swallowed. His throat felt dry, and he wished the beer were in front of him. "Who are 'they'?"

"Names are bad news," Phil said, crumpling and straightening the bills in his hand. It was his turn to be noncommunicative, but Gavin knew Phil couldn't sustain it.

"What are they going to hit?"

Phil leaned even closer. "They'll tell you the police barracks, but it's really the power plant."

Gavin sat back. "The big generators north of town?" His hand felt for the split in the upholstery and rubbed it like an old sore. "The coal-steam or the reactor?"

Phil shrugged. "I don't know. Both, maybe. Or make a feint at one and hit the other. Don't make much difference. It'll cut off power to this whole end of the state."

"Including the campus," Gavin said.

"So?"

"Students would suffer, food spoil, maybe some sick students might die. . . ."

"So?"

"And if they hit the reactor, we could get some contamination here. Even if it's only the coal-steam plant, the fire and explosions could spread to the reactor."

"That's their lookout."

"Yeah," Gavin said. "Yeah." He could imagine some ambitious raid leader turning projects over in his mind, starting up in the middle of the night, sweating, thinking "the generating plant," knowing that this was it, this was the big one, the raid that would make his reputation for life, the project that would affect everybody and write his name in the stars. . . .

"Get me a beer, Phil," someone said.

Gavin looked up. Standing beside the table was a student named Gregory, the fellow Jenny had run from into Gavin's arms. Behind him was Jenny. She was looking at the floor. Neither of them had seen Gregory since Karnival; at least, Gavin hadn't.

"Sure, Greg," Phil said, and slid out of the booth.

"Nice operation, Gav," Gregory said.

Gavin didn't like people who called him "Gav." He didn't like Gregory much anyway. He was tall and dark and wiry thin. Gavin thought he was probably very strong in spite of his apparent lack of muscle. He moved with the grace of a natural athlete who did well everything physical. Gavin had seen him win first place in both bottle-throwing and tear-gas-canister return.

Rumors of his sexual prowess hung about him like a miasma. That he was ugly, that his nose was too large and his eyes set too close together, that his lips were thick and wet and his complexion was bad, didn't seem to matter. His air of aggressive sexuality challenged everything female to prove itself against his masculinity. Phil skulked around like a neurotic mink; Gregory asserted his male dominance over his territory.

Gavin had heard stories about Gregory taking by

force what was not freely offered, and that bothered him, but not as much as the afterword that nobody complained. Gavin didn't know why it bothered him— as if he and Gregory were in competition for all the girls on campus and what Gregory touched he ruined. It was not a sensible feeling, but there it was—a kind of sexual tournament in which Gavin felt himself destined to come in second.

At least he recognized the source of his attitude, Gavin thought, and that was the beginning of wisdom. He slid over in the booth so that Jenny could sit down beside him, but she slid into the other side.

"Hello, Jenny," he said, wanting to touch her, trying to give his ordinary words special meaning.

She didn't speak. She didn't look at him. Gregory sat down opposite him.

"Careful, neat, precise," he said. "I like that."

"Why?" Gavin asked. He felt belligerent, and he knew it was not only because he resented Gregory, but he didn't like the way Jenny was behaving.

"Well, it's not my style," Gregory said, "but I admire it in others."

The waiter was back with Gavin's french fries and beer. He looked at Gregory and Jenny. "Anything?"

Gregory shook his head. "I'll eat some of these." He reached toward the fries. "Bring the ketchup." The waiter reached into the next booth and put a greasy bottle on the table. Gregory doused the potatoes with ketchup.

Gavin didn't like ketchup on his french fries, but he just looked at Gregory coldly. He wasn't hungry anyway. He tried the beer. It was cold and astringent. They couldn't do much to beer, he thought, except to let it get warm or go flat.

He looked at Jenny. "I missed you," he said. He hadn't said that to Jenny before—it implied a sense of unfair obligation on both sides—but he wanted her to know. Last night had been something special. "I wondered where you went."

"I . . . had to go out," she said, still not looking up. "I had to go to the dispensary."

"Yeah," Gavin said. He was going to say that Phil

had seen her, but he didn't want to link them together.
And he was thinking, too, that Jenny's voice sounded a
bit weak. Gregory's right hand was underneath the
table, and Gavin wondered if Gregory was fooling with
Jenny. It was the sort of thing that Gregory would enjoy
—enjoy it more because Jenny hated it. Well, if it was
going on and Jenny didn't like it, she could object. Nobody owned her. Not Gavin, anyway.

"We've got a raid on tonight," Gregory said, his
mouth full of french fries. He ate with lip-smacking enjoyment.

Phil trotted back to the table with Gregory's beer. He
put it down and looked as if he were going to sit down
beside Gavin.

"Go screw," Gregory said, not looking at him. When
Phil was gone, Gregory said, "We want you to join us.
We need somebody like you."

"For what?"

"To go along," Gregory said. "Someone you can
count on to pull a trigger, to throw a grenade, to set a
timer under fire."

"That's not my style," Gavin said quietly, "and I
don't admire it in others."

"Ever tried it?" Gregory's eyes were brightly feral.

"No."

"Next best thing to getting laid," Gregory said.

"What are you going to raid?"

"I tell you, and you got to go along."

"Why?"

"Protection."

Gavin frowned. That wasn't the way most students
operated. If you were into it, you went along; if you
weren't, you went your way. Who was going to fink?
They might take different routes, but they all were heading for the same goal.

"Is it the police barracks?" Gavin asked.

Gregory smiled. "We tell you, and you got to go
along."

Gavin shook his head. "Even if I were into that sort
of stuff, I'd only go with something I had planned myself."

"What d'ya mean, 'that sort of stuff'?" Gregory

asked. He had finished the potatoes, and he sat back, wiping his mouth on the back of his hand and then rubbing that on his pants.

"I'm not an anarchist," Gavin said.

"Who is?" Gregory said. "So we use a little leverage, let 'em know we're here."

"Hurt them enough, and they'll hurt you," Gavin said. "No aimless violence for me. I've got to have a reason."

"We got a reason," Gregory said. "Tell him, Jen!"

"It's for the revolution," Jenny said.

"Right," Gregory said. "We're gonna hurt 'em so bad they can't hurt back."

"They're stronger than you think," Gavin said. "And we're not as strong as we think. Read the history of revolution. We need a bigger base; we've got to win people, not alienate them."

"Shit!" Gregory said. "Jen's going along with us, ain't you, Jen?"

Jenny nodded slowly.

"You better come, too," Gregory said to Gavin. The ordinary words seemed heavy with implication.

"No."

"I gotta take a crap," Gregory said. He turned to Jenny. "Come along. You can hold my hand—or whatever else you want to hold."

"Let her stay!" Gavin said. He looked squarely at Gregory, putting it up to him.

Gregory frowned, as if making up his mind whether to take up the challenge.

"I want to talk to her," Gavin said, giving Gregory an out.

Gregory laughed and stood up. "Sure," he said. "Talk to her." He leaned over the table, and Gavin got the full impact of his unwashed masculinity. "But I gotta tell you—I asked her to come live with me for a while."

Gavin looked at Jenny. His stomach lurched into his throat. "What did she say?"

Gregory laughed confidently. "She didn't say no."

He walked toward the door, swinging his buttocks as if they were weapons in the sex wars.

"Well?" Gavin asked. "What happened?"

"He caught me," Jenny said. Her voice was almost too faint to be heard. Gavin leaned forward. "After I left the dispensary. He said he'd been watching me for some time, and he'd decided I'd do. I was afraid, but I didn't think he'd do anything there, not at first, and then he backed me against the wall of the behavioral-sciences building. He pressed himself up against me. I was afraid he was going to rape me, standing there with the sunshine pouring down around us and the birds singing and people walking by."

"He touched you?" Gavin asked. His mouth was dry, and he had difficulty forming the words.

"Right out in the open there. People walked by, looked at us, but they didn't do anything. I was afraid to ask for help. He had his hands on me as if he owned whatever he touched." Terror was in Jenny's voice, but something else, too—a kind of horrified fascination with what she was saying or what had happened.

Gavin started to stand up. "I'll get him," he said.

Jenny put her hand on his arm to stop him. "He'll kill you."

"I can handle him," Gavin said, but he stopped and sat down, relieved. "Or if I can't, I can get some friends." He took a deep breath. "What else?" He really didn't want to hear any more. He couldn't keep himself from thinking about Gregory's hands on Jenny. But he knew he had to hear the rest.

"He said he was going to do me a favor," Jenny said. "He would let me move in right after the raid. And then he hurt me and let me go."

"I will kill him," Gavin said flatly.

"I'm afraid."

"Don't be afraid," Gavin said roughly. For the first time he felt as if he had a right to Jenny, a right to tell her what to do.

"Not for you," Jenny said, and added quickly, "yes, for you. But most of all for me."

"What of?"

"I'm afraid," she said, looking down at the table and tracing circles in the moisture on the tabletop. "I'm afraid I'll go to him," she whispered.

Gavin couldn't control his response. "Well, if you want to go . . ."

"I don't want to," she said miserably. "But I'm afraid I'll go anyway. I'm afraid I'll get to like what he does. I'm afraid I'll get hooked on it." She shuddered.

"Brutality?" She nodded. "Pain?" She nodded again. "Sadism? Male dominance?"

"I don't know," Jenny said, her eyes downcast. "I feel guilty somehow, as if I ought to be punished."

Gavin looked startled. "For what? The Professor?"

"I don't think so. For the other. What we did. I'm not sure people were meant to be happy."

Gavin felt the cold go away and his manliness return. "That's just your childhood religious training," he said lightly. "Your overpunitive superego. You can't shake that all at once."

"Maybe," she said, and then the expression of impending doom returned to her face. "Oh, Gavin, don't let me go!"

"I'll tie you to the mast," he said.

"What?"

"You may hear the sirens' song, but you can't respond. And me—as far as Gregory's attractions are concerned, my ears are already stuffed with wax."

"What's stuffed with wax?" Gregory said behind him.

"Your head," Gavin said.

Gregory smiled down at him. "Come on, Jen," he said. "Let's go."

"Leave her here," Gavin said.

"But, Gav," Gregory said reasonably, "we got to go get ready for the raid."

Gavin looked at Jenny. She wouldn't meet his eyes, and he knew she would be unable to stand up to Gregory. She would go, and she would return to Gregory's pad with him, if all went well, and she would be lost to him forever. He made up his mind.

"I'm going with you," he said. "I'll bring Jenny if I have to, although it's stupid to take her along."

Gregory thought about it. "Okay," he said. "We'll have a runthrough at midnight. My place. And about Jen—you have to. Else we'll send for her. You see, I value Jen more than you do." He smiled at Gavin, looked knowingly at Jenny, and walked away, giving them the full benefit of his confident pelvic thrust.

The tunnel was long and dark, but Gregory pushed them through it without pause. At first Jenny and Gavin were able to walk upright, brushing with their hands its crumbling concrete walls and asbestos-covered pipes.

"An old steam tunnel," Gavin whispered once.

Flashlights lit their way fitfully. Dust rose from their shuffling feet and made them sneeze. Jenny kept a hand on Gavin's arm. Every now and then Gavin felt it quiver.

Finally the large tunnel stopped. Two smaller brick-lined tunnels branched at its end. Gregory took the one on the right. From that point they crawled without lights, Jenny and Gavin in the middle of the column, Gavin's hand on her rounded bottom for contact and reassurance.

The bricks hurt his knees, and the tunnel smelled of damp earth and mildew. It grew steadily more moist, until they were sliding as much as crawling. Sometimes something mashed under a hand or scuttled away in the darkness.

Gavin thought about the tons of earth above him. The tunnel was student-dug and -lined, and he had no illusions about student thoroughness or responsibility. Perhaps they got the engineers to do it, he thought, and then he realized, with slumping shoulders, that the engineers would have done a better job, and it was probably the ceramicists.

"What am I doing here?" he thought. It would have been better to have had it out with Gregory and done with, one way or another, but there never had been a good time. And they couldn't just ignore him; Gregory's kind of violence could happen anywhere, anytime; Jenny was weak, and one decision point after another had slid past them, and here they were on a mad raid into the unoffending night.

Gavin thought the tunnel would never end, that they would keep burrowing deeper into the earth, that this was their punishment for allowing Gregory to lead them, to go on crawling forever through this midnight tunnel, but finally the column stopped. One by one they emerged into the basement of a burned-out house. Stars were overhead, but no moon. Gavin looked around, his night vision sharpened by the long darkness. A floor had fallen into the basement. Part of it, covered with charred and fire-stained debris, leaned precariously against the wall. From under that they had come, through an opening at the side which had been concealed by a pile of bricks carefully and artistically mortared together and hinged on one side.

It had been the ceramicists, after all, Gavin thought.

The place smelled of old fire. Gavin brushed the dirt from his hands and knees and took hold of Jenny's hand. It was as cold and limp as a dead frog. The others gathered around them, shadowy in blackened faces and black raid uniforms, pistols at their hips, or carbines, shotguns, or machine guns over their shoulders, grenades dangling on their chests like hard, knobbly breasts. Two had packs of explosives on their backs.

They were a dozen in all, counting Jenny and Gavin, who were without weapons. All but Jenny and a large, hard-bodied phys-ed major named Edna were male. Gavin knew the names of a couple of them. But all of them were a lot like Gregory. Physical types. He wondered if any of them ever went to class, if they were even enrolled.

Silently, imperiously, Gregory motioned for them to follow, and they climbed out one edge of the cellar, Gavin and Jenny still in the middle. Gavin wanted to break away, but he couldn't figure out how to get Jenny away with him.

When they were at ground level, Gavin looked back toward the campus. Between some still-standing houses, a few perhaps still occupied, he could see the wall in the distance, and behind it, shining faintly in the starlight, the hill and the campanile and the white buildings. From here it looked like a kind of fairy world, unreal and uninhabited. Gavin stood there, trying to memorize the location.

Someone pushed him forward, and Gavin stumbled, caught himself against Jenny, and straightened up.

Gregory's arm was raised again, and the line of raiders began to trot silently through the night, heading almost directly north. They avoided streets except where they had to cross. Luckily the street lights were out in this sector of town—or perhaps there was no luck to it; Gavin could imagine the straights crouched in the darkness behind their shotguns waiting for who-knows-what to toss a stick of dynamite on their front porch or throw a cocktail through their windows if they were not shuttered and barred, as most of them were.

Occasionally a spotlight blasted a street with brilliance, blinding them if they were too close, and then swiveling away as the armored car moved on.

Once, a spotlight came on and did not move away. Finally Gregory slipped off into the darkness. A few minutes later the light went off. Before their vision fully returned to them, crouching in some bushes near an intersection, Gregory was back, wiping a knife ostentatiously on the leg of his trousers before he slipped it back into his boot scabbard.

"We could have circled the light," Gavin whispered.

"This is my party," Gregory said. Gavin could see his teeth glinting in his blackened face. "We'll do it my way."

Gavin felt Jenny's hand twist in his. He thought he knew why Gregory wanted them both there. He was going to show Jenny how ruthless and reckless he could be, how much more of a man he was than Gavin, and he wondered again what he was doing here in the night on a mission he could not approve under a plan he had heard with unconcealed incredulity.

When Gregory had asked for questions, Gavin had exclaimed, "But that isn't any plan at all! Are you sure it's the barracks you're going to hit?"

"That's what I said," Gregory had replied.

"But you haven't got responsibilities assigned! You don't know who's going to do what!"

"We'll work it out as we go along," Gregory had said, grinning.

"The barracks will be well-guarded. How are you going to draw them off long enough to plant the explosives?"

Gregory had shrugged. "We'll think of something." He had nodded toward the other members of the raiding party lounging casually around the cluttered room. A couple of them were smoking grass, and one of them, Gavin suspected, had mainlined some speed. "These ain't your ordinary students. They're hand-picked for strength, quickness, guts, thinking on their feet. They're all veterans. You give dudes like this too many directions, and things is gonna go wrong, because things may not happen just like that, see? We been out before. We know what to do."

"It's the most haphazard, ill-conceived plan I've ever heard," Gavin had said desperately, "and anybody who goes out there with you is insane." He had looked around the room hopefully, but the others were unmoved.

"Maybe there's parts you ain't heard about," Gregory had said.

"I'll bet there are," Gavin had said grimly.

Gavin ran the conversation through his mind again as he trotted in line behind Jenny. Her stride was faltering now, and Gavin himself was feeling the strain on his lungs, but each time they tried to slow down, a shotgun muzzle was shoved into his back.

They were heading almost due north, or maybe angling a little bit west—not toward the police barracks, but north toward the river. Gavin had tried to complain to Gregory, but Gregory was too far away and Gavin was too out-of-breath.

They paused for a moment at an eight-lane street, part of the circumferential network around the small city, and Gavin had a momentary upsurge of hope that they had been stopped. Traffic streamed silently along the street, lighting the night with headlights, even though the overhead street lights were extinguished. But Gregory didn't break stride. He led them through an underpass redolent with the ammonia of old urine, over an old brick schoolyard, and through a small wilderness with a stream running through it that must have been a park.

Gavin thought he could smell the river.

What are you doing here, Gavin?

"What?"

"Quiet!" someone ordered.

What was he doing here? Gavin asked himself. He had tried to back out. "We're not going, Jenny and I," he had told Gregory.

Gregory had only smiled confidently. "Solidarity," he had said.

"Good luck," Gavin had said, and felt that his voice betrayed his insincerity. He had not thought himself capable of wishing something bad for a fellow student, but he had hoped Gregory wouldn't come back.

"We can't leave you behind now," Gregory had said in a tone of reasonableness. "You know too much."

"That's all right," Gavin had said, trying to maintain the discussion on the same plane. "We'll stay here until you get back. You can place a guard here if you don't trust us."

"We can't afford to do that," Gregory had said. "Besides, Jenny wants to go. Don't you, Jen?"

Jenny hadn't said anything, nor with any gesture or motion of her head communicated agreement or disagreement. She was not going to help. Or could not. She had said nothing since they had left the Union. In their room he had held her for a while, not trying to make love to her, and she had lain passive in his arms, as if she had surrendered herself to the whirlwind. It had seemed to Gavin that some vital element had gone out of her, and he had loved her and wanted to protect her more than ever.

But all those events, all those alternatives, were past now. They trotted through back yards and side yards and alleys, and finally they broke into fields and open country.

The river was close. Gavin could smell it, wet and muddy and decaying, and he realized he had been smelling it for some time.

Gregory led them down a wooded embankment, as confident as a cat in the darkness—"No lights from here," he had warned a block back—and they crossed old railroad tracks and went down another wooded slope that gave way slowly to sand and mud.

Gregory led them west along the bank. Jenny and

Gavin stumbled along, sinking into soft spots, pulling their feet out of the mud with nasty, sucking noises.

"Here they are," Gregory said.

Gavin's groping hands felt the rough wooden side or back of a boat. A hand grasped his shoulder. "You," Gregory said, "Gav, into the first boat with me. You too, Jen. Also Marvin, Erik, Gerard. The rest of you into the other boat. Straight across. No noise."

Gavin stumbled into the boat, shoved from behind. He fell forward over a seat and found himself up to his wrists in water standing in the bottom of the boat. Others were with him in the dark. The boat moved, grating on the bank. As it bobbed, other bodies clambered in, and the water in the boat sloshed.

For a moment Gavin was afraid the boat might sink, and then he wished it would. He felt around in the bottom of the boat, but he couldn't find anything like a plug. As they got away from the bank, the current began to pull at the boat. The bow swung east. Then oars were unshipped. After a few splashes, sounding loud in a night owned by bullfrogs, the oars caught, the boat straightened, and they headed north across the river, the oarlocks creaking.

Gavin looked up and picked out the North Star, but he couldn't see the other bank. Gregory pulled him down into the foul water.

"We aren't heading for the barracks!" Gavin protested. "The only thing out this way is the generating plant."

"Yeah," Gregory said. "Ain't that something?"

"You're crazy!" Gavin whispered violently. "If you don't succeed, we'll all be killed, and if you do, you could spill radioactivity all over this area."

"That's their problem. Teach 'em they shouldn't pollute the environment."

"But—"

"You listen!" Gregory said harshly, grinding his fingers into Gavin's shoulder. "This ain't no time to argue nothing. Something else you didn't know." He pressed his face close to Gavin's. His breath smelled of garlic and beer. "You're gonna be on point. I'll be right behind you." His arm slipped familiarly around Gavin's shoulder.

Gavin shrugged the unpleasant arm away. Gregory's hand fell more familiarly on Gavin's hip, squeezing it. "There'll probably be barbed wire," Gavin said, "and very likely electrified."

Gregory squeezed harder. "I'll be right behind you with the wire clippers," he said. His voice was happy and friendly. "Marvin will be right behind me with the plastic explosive, and Erik right behind him with the fuses and timer."

"You're putting a lot on an untested man," Gavin said.

Gregory squeezed him again and then patted him on the butt. "I've got faith in you, Gav. Besides, I'll be right behind you, and Jen'll be waiting for us to come back."

The hateful hand went away, and Gavin felt Gregory's body shift. A moment later he heard cloth rustle, and a gasp told him that Gregory had turned his hands loose on Jenny. Gavin wished he had a knife or some kind of weapon, but there was nothing in the bow of the boat but water. His hands clenched and unclenched helplessly.

He felt the current tugging at the boat and smelled the river close to his nose, fishy and muddy; then slowly the river began to relax its grasp. A few moments later the bow ground into something firm. The boat rocked as bodies left it at one side and then the other. Then he felt the boat being pulled higher on the bank. A hand reached in, clutched Gavin's arm, and pulled him out.

"You're gonna stay here, Jen," he heard Gregory whisper. "You and Gerard. Gonna give us cover, Gerard, if we're pursued, and be ready to shove off if we have to get away in a hurry. Jen, you'll keep Gerard company. No funny business with Jen, now," he said, and chuckled. "Want you alert, Ger."

He pulled Gavin's arm. "Come on, we'll find the others." But they didn't find the other boat, and after a few minutes of searching up and down the bank in the dark, Gregory swore and turned inland. "Who needs 'em?" he said.

They stumbled through scrub trees and brush, branches stinging their faces, before they came out onto a meadow. Or maybe it was a lawn. It was as smooth and closely cropped as a lawn. Gregory made them get down and crawl. They crawled endlessly, Gavin in front, feeling cautiously ahead with one hand, trying to peer through impenetrable darkness, Gregory pushing him from behind.

It was like all the nightmares Gavin had ever had rolled into one. Gavin couldn't believe it was happening.

What are you doing here, Gavin?

It sounded like the Professor's voice asking him a question in class. He had to answer. But he didn't know the answer.

I don't know, Professor.

Then get out of here, Gavin.

As he felt Gregory's grasp on his leg loosen as Gregory leaned his weight on that arm, Gavin jerked his leg forward and rolled quickly to his left, rose on all fours and then to his feet, and began to run back the way they had come.

"Come back here, you son-of-a-bitch!" Gregory shouted.

As if Gregory's voice was the cock's crow that split the night, the darkness turned to daylight behind Gavin. He saw the trees in front of him outlined like stick figures against the darkness beyond, and he threw himself forward and rolled over and over until he was in the midst of the scrub.

"Ahhhhh!" Gregory shouted behind him. It seemed almost like a scream of joy. A moment later came the whump of a grenade and the chatter of gunfire.

An amplified voice came from everywhere, like the voice of God. "Surrender! You are surrounded. You can't get away. Surrender or be shot!"

But Gavin was up and dodging among the small trees and tall bushes. Another grenade went off behind him, and more gunfire.

The best bottle-thrower in the University was doing his thing with grenades.

Someone was thrashing through the woods toward the generating plant. Gavin stopped moving until the noise had passed. Even then he couldn't bring himself to move.

But the guns began to bark singly behind him, and projectiles whistled through the leaves above his head, and Gavin moved. Shouts and explosions mingled in confused counterpoint behind as he ran. He thought he could hear Gregory's voice like a Norse berserker glorying in the combat.

He ran, crouched low to avoid stray bullets and flailing branches. In a few steps he reached the riverbank. The lights from the generating plant went overhead, leaving the bank itself in deeper darkness. Gavin ran along the bank looking for the boat.

"Jenny," he called softly. "Jenny!" He didn't care if Gerard heard him. He wouldn't be so insane as to want to hang around when so clearly the raiding party had run into a trap. "Jenny!"

He stepped into a soft spot and went in up to one knee. He dragged himself out and began to run again. "Jenny!"

Behind him and above him the battle intensified. Now the bullets were continuous rather than single, a solid sheet of noise rocking the world. Suddenly Gavin decided he was searching in the wrong direction, and he turned around and began running back the other way.

As he passed close to the gunfire, an explosion shattered the night, splitting it apart, throwing Gavin flat on the bank, his hands buried. The gunfire stopped. Gavin's ears rang with silence. "My God! The plastic!" Gavin thought, and got up and ran again, covered with mud. When he reached the bridge, long minutes later, he realized that there were no rowboats on the bank.

Trucks and tracked vehicles rattled the old bridge. Lights came on above. Sirens blasted. Gavin took a deep breath and edged along the top of the low dam.

Jenny was gone.

He took another few cautious steps. He heard the

water rushing over the spillway; it could not be far
ahead. He tried to remember what it was like. The water rushed, a dirty brown, over the edge, and fell
about ten feet, to splash white and foamy into the river below. He had not thought it a big drop when he
had looked at it from above as he arrived at the University, but then he had not thought about trying to
walk across the top of the spillway. He could be thrown
against concrete or drowned in the turbulence below
the dam.

A giant's voice echoed down the river. "Your com-
rades have been killed or captured! Surrender or take
the risk of being shot on sight! Curfew violators are
warned! Come walking out with your hands in the air
or suffer the consequences!"

Gavin edged along the dam. His groping hands met
the rough concrete of a pillar. He rested against it,
listening to the hiss, splash, roar of the water. It was on
the other side of the pillar. Gavin could smell the water
misting up.

Floodlights on the bridge began to swoop up and
down the river. Somewhere upriver a motorboat was
whipping the water into froth. The sound broke Gavin's
paralysis of will and body. He edged around the pillar and put one foot on the other side. Cold water
pulled at it, chilling his foot, sending shivers up his
back. He edged it out a little farther and swung around
the pillar. Both feet now were in the sluicing water; his
back was against the pillar, his arms thrown back to
clutch it.

Jenny was gone.

He forced himself away from the pillar and stood in
the raging water wavering for balance. Then he was all
right, and he pushed one foot forward and pulled the
other behind. The top of the spillway was slick with the
polish from a hundred years of river water. Fishy spray
rose around him, soaking his clothes, invading his
lungs. The thunder of the water hitting the river below
deafened him. How long was the spillway, he wondered,
fifteen, twenty feet? He had to be across it before the
boat arrived. If it had a spotlight, they couldn't miss
him. They could shoot him off the spillway like a duck

in a shooting gallery. If that happened, he knew, he would have to drive off the spillway and take his chances with the river below.

For a mad moment he wished he had gone along with Gregory, and then he realized that what he did or didn't do wouldn't have mattered. It was a trap. It had been a trap all along. Hadn't it?

He was in the middle of the spillway, and the rushing water was strong. It kept trying to pry his feet loose from the solid rock or concrete underneath, trying to pull his feet over the dam. One foot slipped as he edged it forward, and he swayed to his left, trying to balance himself on his back foot, his arms outspread, waving in the air as if to find a handhold. And then his forward foot found its place, and he inched on, moving a little faster now, getting the feel of it. The water seemed to get shallower over his feet. And then he was sure—it was shallower and the pull was almost gone. The water was gone, and he clutched another pillar.

He clung to it desperately. Jenny! Jenny!

A flash of light hit the bridge behind him. The boat had a spotlight! He moved around the pillar and was on the rough top of the dam again. Now he could hear the motorboat propeller chewing up the water. Gavin moved swiftly. The spot of light flicked on the side of the bridge and began to slide south along it.

Gavin reached another pillar. As he touched it he felt a metal cable, old with rust, dangling beside the pillar. Gavin put his hand around it and edged over the side of the dam, slipping into the water. He felt the cold water slither up his body, over his chest, over his shoulders and up his neck and face, until it closed greasily over the top of his head.

He looked up. The top of the water where his hand broke through turned bright and slowly darkened again to brown and then to black. His eyes stung. He shut them and slowly edged up for a breath, took a quick glimpse around through water-blurred eyes, and went under again.

Hours later, cold and wet and shivering, he waited in a clump of bushes not far from the ruins of the burned-out basement. The lights and sounds had slow-

ly ebbed. Now the sky was graying in the east and the
morning smog was swirling around corners and
creeping up slopes. Gavin rose shakily from the bushes
and trotted toward the basement, bent over simianlike
until his knuckles almost touched the ground, slithered
into the basement, swung back the bricks, and slipped
into the dark opening behind the fallen floor.

It seemed to him as if he were retreating to the
womb, with his terrible memories of confusion and
fear and pain that waited for people like him outside
the walls, and everything blurred for him, until, an eternity later, he found himself in front of the decayed old
building that was home.

Jenny! he thought. Where are you?

And he looked up and wondered if he would find her
in his bed, waiting to warm him with her body and her
love, and he leaped eagerly up the stairs to their room.

But it was empty, and the bed was empty, and he fell
into it, not removing his wet, filthy clothing, and he lay
there, shivering, curled up, his hands between his legs,
until his body warmed and he slept and dreamed and
woke screaming and finally slept again.

4 ⊷ Power Play

The young always are opposed to what is. They suck
in revolution with their mother's milk. "Change the
order!" they say. "Down with the establishment!"
"First we'll make a revolution—then we'll find out
what for." "Abolish injustice, destroy discrimination,
share the wealth, shoot the bastards!" To shatter the
old is easy; to make it work is hard. A civilized society
makes itself sufficiently difficult to overthrow that
the eternal young rebels must learn the system in
order to achieve their ends—and then, of course, they
have an investment in the system.

—THE PROFESSOR'S NOTEBOOK

Gavin was awakened by repeated pokes to his belly.
He struggled upward out of a dark puddle of nightmares. "What?" he asked, opening his eyes to dusty
sunshine. "Who?"

He found himself sitting upright in his bed, still
damp, still muddy from the river, still confused about
what had happened, about what was real and what was
dream. The room was buzzing. He wondered if someone had slipped him a hallucinogenic again; what he
was experiencing was more aftereffect than aftermath.

"Jenny?" he said, and looked around. An older
man, with a broom in his hand, was standing at the foot
of the bed. He was dressed like a student, but he wore
his clothing like a costume. He was not to the status
born.

81

He was no Gregory, violent, threatening, and reck-less. He was an average sort of man, neither very blond nor very dark, very large nor very small; he would have been unnoticeable except that his eyes were very steady and his voice was very quiet, and, Gavin thought, he probably was very efficient. At whatever he did.

At the moment he was poking Gavin in the belly with his own broom. When Gavin's eyes stayed open, the stranger tossed the broom clattering into a corner packed with dust kitties.

"All right, Gavin," the stranger said, "get up. It's noon, and StudEx wants to see you."

The room buzzed, and Gavin could scarcely hear him. "Stu Decks?" Gavin repeated. "Who's he?"

"The Student Executive Committee, dummy. They want to see you."

Gavin put his hand to his forehead and rubbed it. "Of course." He swung his legs over the edge of the bed and then froze his head in position as he was hit by a wave of dizziness. "Why does StudEx want to see me?"

"You know the answer to that better than me," the stranger said. "I'm just the sergeant-at-arms."

Gavin sat on the edge of the bed holding his head, smelling the river on his body, trying to summon the will to move, to comprehend. Except for the buzzing, the house was silent.

"Damn, you're a mess." the sergeant-at-arms said. "Do you go to bed like that all the time? I don't see how you freaks can live like this—all this filth and vermin and decay."

"You freaks?" Gavin echoed. "Aren't you a stu-dent?"

"You don't have to be a freak to be a student."

Gavin had never seen this man before, but he knew the man was no student, except in the general sense that anyone who lives on a campus is a student. Gavin doubted if he had ever been a student, although he might have enrolled briefly before dropping out. No, this man had drifted here and found the campus life easy and the pickings good—plenty of willing girls, money to be extorted or earned by extorting for others, power to be served. He was a scavenger, a parasite on the student body, a mercenary of the revolution.

"I ain't got all day," the sergeant-at-arms said quietly. It was a steely quiet, like the quiet of a knife slipping into an unsuspecting back. "I'd think you'd want to get out of a place like this."

"Yeah," Gavin said, standing up. The room did sickening things, and Gavin grabbed the wall until it settled down. "A guy downstairs sews leather into belts and bags and vests, and he starts up his machine about this time. A guy upstairs is on speed. He's been watching a stone idol for two weeks now. The other day we had to tie him down to his bed and gag him because the statue told him to put out his eyes, and he wouldn't stop screaming. . . ."

"You don't need to worry about the guy downstairs," the sergeant-at-arms said. "He didn't want to tell me where you lived, and he won't be using his hands for a while. If you want, I can take care of the guy upstairs, too."

Gavin shivered. His attempt to be casual had turned into reality. "No need, no need," he said. Poor Ned. Faithful and broken. "I've got to change."

"You mean you got another pair of those? Why bother? No, you come now, as you are."

Gavin wondered if those were the man's instructions, but he didn't want to ask. A brief tension had run through the room. Nothing obvious had changed, but it was like the difference between a cat stopped to observe and one that has gathered itself for a spring.

"Okay," Gavin said. He walked toward the door, his clothing clinging clammily to his body, his mind beginning to shake free the paralysis of sleep, remembering. . . . Jenny and Gregory. . . . The night and the river. . . . The lightning of battle. . . . "Jenny!" he thought, and anguish made him stagger as he led the stranger out the door and down the creaking stairs to the outside.

The sun hit him with shiny clubs. The day was bright and warm, as if it had never seen death or known sorrow. Gavin looked at the buildings around him with a stranger's eyes. He saw all their sad age and imperfections, the sagging walls, the weathered sides, the loose boards, the gaps in the patched roofs, the weeds that surrounded the houses like green savages, the trash and junk that lay scattered among the weeds like the weeds of an industrialized society, the grass sprouting in walks and streets as if they were some strange mulch.

This is how the Professor would have seen it if he had been conscious when they brought him into the house from the alley, Gavin thought.

The outdoors buzzed too, and Gavin realized that his ears were buzzing. Everything around him seemed brilliant and unreal.

The sergeant-at-arms pushed Gavin from behind, and Gavin stumbled down the concrete-block step onto what remained of a concrete walk, and the mood was broken. But Gavin had a strange feeling of parting as they walked to Fourteenth Street and then slowly climbed the Hill.

"What are you studying?" Gavin asked the quiet man who walked just a little behind him, a little to his left. Somehow, he felt, he had to force the situation into a more normal social occasion.

The man thought for a moment and then said, "People."

"Psychology?"

"Yeah, that's right. Psychology. And a bit of anatomy."

The sunshine was warm, but Gavin shivered again. "You seem older."

"I'm from New York. There you get old quick or you don't get old at all."

"Yeah," Gavin said. This man with him, a little behind, a little to the left, was a survivor of a tougher school than Gavin's. Gavin's chances with Gregory would not have been good, he knew, but he believed that his chances with this deadly nonperson of a man were nonexistent.

They had reached the top of the Hill, and Gavin was breathing hard. He didn't know whether it was emotional strain or the swift pace. He had the feeling of being pushed, as if a phantom hand was always in the middle of his back.

The air was clear on top of the Hill and the sun shone down upon them and students walked past on their way to class or lunch or rendezvous, as if everything were normal, and Gavin wanted to call out to them and say, "I am being abducted by this person who is walking a little behind me and a little to my left. Fellow students, *au secour!*" Only it would have seemed ridiculous, his being abducted by one average sort of man, and he knew it wouldn't do any good anyway. Either he would receive a switchblade or an ice pick in the side, or the sergeant-at-arms would fade away, average as he was, and later they would do it all over again, only this time without pretense of civility.

Better to go when he was summoned, as if willingly, than be dragged, twisting and hurt, into the presence of StudEx.

Even as he was thinking these thoughts, he received a guiding shove on the shoulder that sent him toward the front door of a small chapel set in grass and climbing roses. Both the grass and the roses were artificial. He stood inside the door for a moment, blinking in the darkness after the brilliance of the day, seeing nothing, and a hand pushed him forward and then to the right down a dim aisle between wooden benches that slowly swam into view.

"All right, Willie," said a high-pitched voice from the darkness in front. "You can wait in the back. You, Gavin, stand where you are."

Gavin stopped. To his right he could see now the red, blue, and yellow stained-glass windows that miraculously had escaped the riots of eighty-five. Then, slowly, three figures emerged from the darkness like corpses floating to the top of a lake. They were seated on a little platform in front of him, so that, even seated, they were taller than he was. The one on the left was fat and youthful; his round face, framed with golden curls and hanging with chins, was rosy and innocent. He wore a voluminous white robe, as if to conceal his bulk, but it overflowed the chair in which he sat, and the flesh of his arms overflowed the padded wooden arms of the chair. He was like a Roman boy emperor who had put aside for the moment his golden laurels.

The one on the right was big and black and strong. His hair was short and curly. He wore shorts and a ragged shirt through which his muscles bulged like fertility images carved from ebony.

Between the two was a girl. She seemed little more than a child. As she sat in her big chair her feet dangled six inches from the floor. Brown hair was cut short and ragged around a childish face. Shirt and slacks fit like doll clothes on a boyish body.

They were unreal, and Gavin did not believe in them.

"You've been busy, Gavin," the fat boy said. His was the high-pitched voice that had spoken to Willie.

"Yeah," the black said. "Busy."

The girl said nothing. Her dark eyes looked roundly at Gavin like shoe buttons in a doll's head.

Gavin nodded. His knees trembled, and he hated them for displaying weakness.

"We wish to compliment you on the skill and professionalism with which you handled the abduction of the Professor."

"Good job," said the black.

"Thanks," Gavin said. He felt as if he was answering talking statues.

"But . . ." The fat boy broke off. "Did you have to come here in such deplorable condition? Really, Gavin, you stink." He waved one fat hand in front of his nose like an aristocrat offended by the slums his actions have created.

"I wanted to change," Gavin said, and instantly wished he had not spoken. The words sounded defensive, and he felt weaker because of it.

"You freaks are all alike," the black said.

The fat boy shook his head at the back of the room until his curls wobbled. "Willie, you're so impatient."

But Gavin knew that they liked him muddy and damp in front of them, just as they liked looking down at him, and he tried to even things up by imagining them in other circumstances—in a sauna, for instance, or a shower room. Then he decided he would think of them as the three monkeys who saw no evil, heard no evil, and spoke no evil. Only, the last two monkeys were out of order. The girl had not yet spoken.

"But," the fat boy went on, "the operation last night was deplorable." He rocked back and forth in his huge chair metronomically.

"It wasn't my operation," Gavin said.

"How can you say that? You were there."

"Against my will."

"A leader like you?" the fat boy scoffed. "How could anyone make you go on a raid if you didn't wish to go?" He had an oily voice that seemed to go on and on, insinuating and subtle.

"Gregory intimidated Jenny. I went along to protect her." Gavin had a feeling that they knew all this, that all these questions were a net being slowly tightened around him. His legs shook again, and he locked his knees to avoid seeming in terror of these chimerical creatures.

"Jenny's your girl?" the black asked.

Gavin nodded, suddenly swept by grief.

"She *was*, Muhammad," the fat boy said.

What did they know about Jenny? Gavin thought in his misery.

"We know everything that happened," the fat boy said, as if in answer. "But we want to hear it from you. Whose operation was it?"

An odor like incense began to force itself upon Gavin's senses. He would have smelled it before, he thought incredulously, but his nose had been stuffed with his own effluvium. "I thought it was Gregory's," he said, "but now I'm beginning to think otherwise."

"You think it was ours," the black said.

"Of course he thinks it was ours," the fat boy said, rocking, "and of course it was. Gregory wasn't smart enough to plan a raid as ambitious as that."

"It was dumb enough to be Gregory's," Gavin said.

"You think it was dumb?" asked the fat boy. "What did you think was dumb?"

Gavin ignored the subtle menace in the fat boy's

voice and plunged ahead. "Everything. The lack of preparation, realistic objectives, briefings, methods. . . ."

"And yet," the fat boy mused, "it might have worked."

"And covered the campus with radiation."

"If the townies had not been tipped off."

"How do you know they were tipped off?" Gavin asked. He did not want to take them seriously, but sometimes a statement broke through his feeling of fantasy. Incense! Like gods!

"It was a trap."

"How do you know that? Perhaps it was only poorly done. As far as I know, I was the only one present who escaped alive."

"That is suspicious, isn't it?" the fat boy said smoothly.

"Shit!"

"But someone had to, didn't they?" the fat boy asked. "I mean, Gregory was dumb, but he wasn't clumsy. It would hardly be Gregory, now, would it? Or one of those in the squad with him. Why not the one who got away?"

"Maybe you were mad enough to tip off the townies," the black said. His muscles moved like ripples in a stream of tar.

The girl sat as motionless as a portrait by Gainsborough.

They were trying to make themselves real by irritating him, Gavin thought, but they couldn't succeed. They were too improbable. "I'm going to sit down," Gavin said defiantly, his jaw tight to keep his voice from shaking. He felt the raised left edge of the bench next to him and edged himself over until he could sink into the seat.

"Of course," the fat boy said. "We want you to be comfortable." That was a lie. They didn't want him to be comfortable at all.

"Even if I knew how to inform the townies," Gavin said, "which I don't, I didn't know the raid was for the power plant until we got there. Gregory kept saying it was the police barracks."

"We can't prove that now," the fat boy said, shifting from one grotesque ham to the other. "Nobody's left but you."

"Anyway," Gavin said, taking up another position, "anyone could have squealed. Someone told me about it that afternoon."

"Who?" the black said, leaning forward, rippling.

"Why should I get him in trouble?"

"He means the Monkey," the fat boy said. He looked at Gavin with clear, innocent eyes. "But that means that you knew all along."

"Who's going to believe an asskisser like Phil?" Gavin said. "And if he knew, who didn't know? But I suppose all this means that you sent Phil to tell me what was going to happen."

"Of course," the fat boy said. "There's no use trying to deceive you, Gavin. You're too bright for that. We won't admit it outside this little sanctuary, but nothing happens on this campus that we don't know about, and nothing important happens that we don't authorize."

He rocked. The black rippled. The girl watched.

"Like the Professor?" Gavin asked.

"Well," the fat boy said, "we didn't learn about that until afterward. As we told you, it was a nice, tight operation. What I want you to understand, however, is that we needed a fall guy for the raid if it didn't come off, and, Gavin, you're it."

"You think I'd risk not only my life but Jenny's?"

"You were angry," the fat boy said.

"You were out of your head," the black said.

"You weren't thinking straight, and you thought you could rid yourself of Gregory and get away. As you did," the fat boy said.

"Without Jenny?" Gavin's desperation broke through. "Where is Jenny?"

"We thought you'd tell us," the fat boy said.

For the first time Gavin thought he was telling the truth. "After the townies started shooting, I couldn't find her. She was gone."

"She isn't on campus," the fat boy said.

He rocked. The black rippled. The girl stared.

Revelation came to Gavin. "You tipped off the townies!"

"Of course," the fat boy said. "Rather, the Monkey —the boy you call Phil—tipped them off at our instructions."

"But why did you give them your own man, your own raid party?"

The fat boy shrugged. "Well, we couldn't have the campus showered with radioactivity, could we? You pointed that out yourself. Even cutting off the electricity would have been a bore."

"Then why order the raid at all?" Gavin complained. The words were going around in front of him like a spiral galaxy.

"We needed it right now," the fat boy said. "Revolutionary activity had been pretty light recently, and the masses have been restive. We needed something highly visible, but we needed martyrs more than we needed victories. Revolution feeds on martyrs and soon grows surfeited with success."

Gavin could feel the world fragmenting around him like a Steuben glass vase tapped with a ballpeen hammer. "How did you get Gregory to go along with it?"

"We told him only what he wanted to hear—that it was dangerous, even foolhardy." The fat boy rocked complacently. "That sort of thing never bothered Gregory. He had a touching faith in his own invulnerability. And then we promised him any girl he wanted. He had a foolish lust for this one girl. It doesn't make sense, really. . . ."

"My Jenny?"

"Your Jenny then, Gregory's Jenny later. The difference is infinitesimal. What does it matter?"

The pieces of the world began to fall, in slow motion, like glass snowflakes, leaving only black nonexistence where they had been. "People matter!"

"Of course people matter!" The fat boy was exasperated. "Individuals don't matter. People matter. And we must do what is good for people, for people and the revolution. We can't let ourselves get enmeshed in personalities."

Some Radiclibs, said the Professor, *are able only to love people abstractly because they hate people individually, and they are perfectly willing, therefore, to sacrifice what they hate for what they love.*

"But why would you want to get rid of Gregory?" He had to force himself back to reality, even though reality kept receding before him, buzzing in his ears, unfocusing his eyes. These three incredible creatures sitting in front of him had set them up like pieces on the chessboard of their world, each with its own move. "You move!" they told Gregory, and he plunged into danger. "You move!" they told Jenny, and she meekly followed. "You move!" they told Gavin, and he threw himself between the other two. Now they justified their cruel game with the name of revolution. They were the menace. They were the Moirae—Clotho, Lachesis, and Atropos. He had to destroy them. He had to deliver mankind from their fatal grasp. But he could not move. He was too weak. He felt himself becoming unreal.

"He was getting to be a bit of a problem," the fat boy said, serene again. "Always going off on his own, reckless, arrogant, hard to control. . . ."

"He didn't give a shit about revolution," the black said.

"That too," the fat boy said. "He even made Willie nervous, and not much makes Willie nervous. Gregory was dispensable. The others were dispensable. Actually, Gregory makes a better martyr than a raid leader. And, of course, we wanted you out of the way, too."

"Why me?"

"Elections are coming up soon. Ordinarily this would be no problem, but times are a bit unsettled. Students were talking about you for president."

"That didn't interest me."

"You say that now," the fat boy said, "but StudEx has its appeal, particularly for a sincere revolutionary who sees how the revolution can be operated more effectively: StudEx wields great power."

Power, the Professor said. *The basic question is power.*

"We could have avoided that unpleasantness," the fat

boy continued. "There was no question of that. But sincere rivals, we have found, are better removed than left to gather support and nurture dissent."

"You would have cheated in the election?"

The fat boy was shocked. "Nothing as crude as that. We would simply have got out the vote—our vote—and there isn't enough student interest in campus politics to overcome our well-organized minority."

The world continued to fall in tinkling splinters. "Why not let the will of the students prevail?" Gavin's voice sounded distant to him, as if it belonged to someone else.

"Students got no will," the black said.

"Right, Muhammad," the fat boy said. "Students don't know what they think until we tell them. We are the revolution. No one else is qualified to replace us. No one is capable of wielding power as effectively or as dispassionately."

"And my unfortunate survival upset your plans," someone said. "Sorry."

The fat boy raised a fat hand; his whole arm wobbled. "No need. We had considered that possibility. Clearly you are a resourceful person. If you escaped, then we had a clear choice: to dispose of you permanently or to persuade you to join us on our terms. Now it's your choice."

"Between what?"

"We're offering you the position of raid leader."

"Gregory's position?"

The fat boy spread his hands, palms up, and rocked in his chair. The muscles on the black moved. The girl sat quite still.

"Why would you offer me something like that?" someone asked.

"We have lost a raid leader," the fat boy said. "We need a new one. You are clearly qualified. You will have won a position of honor and privilege; we will have exchanged a hothead for a cool one, a confused mind for a clear one, a bad leader for a good one. The perquisites of the office are these: any girl you want, an automatic A in any course you wish to take, a virtually unlimited expense account, and free access to whatever drug supplies you need, so long as it doesn't interfere with your duties."

The light from the westering sun colored the rough stone wall behind the fantastic trio with motley like an effulgence of their power.

"And what must I do?" someone asked.

The fat boy shrugged. His shoulders rippled under the white robe. "Anything we say."

"It sounds," someone said, "like a sentence which you can execute anytime you wish. Is this what you do with all your rivals?"

"The alternative is more certain and less pleasant," the fat boy said.

"No." The word echoed.

"You're crazy, man," the black said.

"I'm not interested in power."

The fat boy frowned. "What else is there?"

"What else, man?" the black said.

The fat boy rocked. The black rippled. The girl watched, round-eyed and still.

"Knowledge. Truth." Someone else was in the room, answering for Gavin.

"Knowledge of what?" the fat boy asked. "The truth about what?"

The other person shrugged. "Everything."

"What about the revolution?"

"First you must know," the other person said. "Then you make the revolution."

"No, no," the fat boy said. "First you make the revolution. Then you find out what for."

"I never did think that made sense," the other person said. Where was he?

"Besides," the fat boy said, "what is there to know? Five percent of the people own ninety-five percent of the wealth in this country. We know that. 'The history of all existing society is the history of class struggle.' We know that. The revolution creates a classless society; in the process, the proletariat become the ruling class, until the state withers away. We know that; Marx told us."

"What he means," the black said, "is power to the people. The poor is gonna get rich, and the rich is gonna get shot. That's the revolution."

"Kill the oppressors," the fat boy said, "and liberate the oppressed. We will bring freedom and justice to the world if we have to destroy the world in the process."

The sunlight streaming, filtered and changed, through the stained-glass windows fell like clown's paint upon the terrible three. The fat boy was still. The black was tense. The girl's round eyes narrowed.

Someone giggled. "Eenie, meenie, and miney," someone said. "Words. Words." Gavin knew now who was talking: it was the Professor. A wave of dizziness rocked his head, and the scene wavered in front of him.

"It's all a game," he heard the Professor saying. "You're playing a deadly little game with people's lives, and you're making it seem real by dressing it up in ancient words and creeds. It's no different from the games you played as children, except this time it's for keeps. It's no different from the chickens establishing a pecking order, except that chickens don't kill. And the funny part about all this is that you believe it; you think it matters, and the only ones it matters to are those who get used. The funny part is that you don't know it's a game."

Gavin laughed. He was happy with the laugh. The sound was not too hysterical. It would have been a completely satisfying laugh if the room had not been shimmering and buzzing and the three student leaders had not loomed up and receded like a zoom lens gone mad. In the midst of his laughter, Gavin realized that they saw themselves not as see-no-evil, hear-no-evil, speak-no-evil, not as the Fates, not as eenie, meenie, and miney, but as a Roman triumvirate or a Soviet troika, and he laughed harder, laughed until the room blurred with tears and the world ached, and he laughed even harder when he thought he heard the fat boy call, "Willie," but all buzzy and distorted and strung out, like "Will-ell-eray!" and the little girl in the middle, whose feet did not touch the floor, who had not made a sound, seemed to say, "There are better ways than making martyrs. As we should know. Leave him."

When the laughter died, shivers shook him. He wrapped his arms around his chest to hold himself still, and half-rose to find his way back out into sunshine and sanity, but his thigh muscles jellied and his traitorous knees surrendered to the weakness of his body, and he sank back, the room spinning until he had to close his eyes. He could still feel it spinning, but he didn't have to watch it.

He fell over on the hard bench, on his side, his knees drawn up toward his chest for warmth, and shook. A few moments later lava poured through his veins, and his body uncurled gratefully like a flower in the sun. But sweat sprang from his pores and trickled icily down his sides, and he shivered uncontrollably when his clothing touched his nervestudded skin.

The roomwomb closed around him, and he relaxed, grateful for protection, grateful for warmth, grateful for darkness, beset as it was with ice and fire, alternating like a glass figurine being tested to destruction.

Later he had a vague memory, like the vagrant snatches of a dream, of people around him, looming over him, their faces large and distorted, of voices rising and falling, booming and whispering, coming and going, buzzing and buzzing, and of movement, like dope-floating, only better, through bright and dark, stopping and starting, of a finger of ice that burned his arm and a finger of fire that cooled his body, and of sleep that came, not like the blackjack of unconsciousness, but softly, gently healing, like cool fingers across his eyelids.

He came awake slowly. At first he thought everything had been a dream, that he was still lying in his bed, and he reached out for Jenny, for the reassurance of her magnificent flesh, but his hopeful hand met nothing but empty air. And then he knew that the experience with Gregory and the power plant had not been a dream, that Jenny was gone and he was alone, and he thought he still was lying on the old wooden churchgoers' bench in the onetime chapel where he had been interrogated and then taken on top of a mountain by StudEx, but he knew that was wrong, too. What he reclined on was too soft, too tacky, for wood; it felt like leather or vinyl, and he opened his eyes.

Looking down at him, close, concerned, was a face he liked instantly. It was a face that was older, kinder, and less competitive than those he had known for the past four years. The face was male, and it had gray at the temples and wrinkles in the forehead and around the mouth and nose, and Gavin realized what he had missed in the faces he had seen around him almost constantly for four years, all unlined, unformed, uncertain, unlivedin. Variety.

"You're better," the face said as it drew back.

Gavin could see now that the face had a well-shaped body, perhaps a bit shorter than average height, clad in a two-piece dark suit with a white turtleneck beneath. What Gavin had taken to be a high forehead was a tanned bald area surrounded on three sides by a neat fringe, like a tonsure with territorial ambitions. "What was wrong with me?" Gavin asked.

"A serious case of pneumonia," the old man said. He had a wide mouth with lips that moved with fascinating flexibility when he talked, and a nose that twitched when he sniffed. Gavin liked him even more. "But we shot you full of antibiotics. You'll be all right now."

"Yes," Gavin said, looking around him, "I think I will." The ceiling was clean and white. Gavin swung himself upright. A wave of dizziness swiftly passed. He was in a medium-sized office with white walls and red-leather chairs and a large dark wooden desk in front of him. The desktop was rough and splintered, as if people in hobnailed boots had danced on it, and the white walls were scrawled with slogans: "Kill the Motherfuckers!" . . . "Screw the Establishment!" . . . "Hang the Chancellor!" . . . "Workers of the World, Unite!" . . . "Victory or death!" . . . "No Treaty with Traitors" . . . "Keep the Faith!" . . . "For a great lay, call Maude —4-5130" . . . "Butcher the Butchers!" . . . "Sartre was a Fartre" . . . "Camus, too" . . . "Solidarity" . . . "Pigs against the wall!"

"You're the Chancellor," Gavin said, "and this is the Chancellor's office." He said it as if he had suddenly found himself in a place hallowed by history, like Jerusalem or the White House or Sproul Hall.

The older man nodded. He didn't seem formidable or evil, Gavin thought, but he knew he was in the presence of the Enemy, and his senses sharpened and looked for ways to escape. "How did I get here?" he asked.

"My officers picked you up at the old chapel," the Chancellor said. He leaned against the front edge of the desk, half-sitting.

"Kampuskops?" Gavin said.

"That's your name for them," the Chancellor said wistfully. "We prefer others."

Gavin shrugged. "Kampuskops are Kampuskops."

"Yes," the Chancellor said, "and students are students. That's one of our problems. Anyway, they took you to the outpatient clinic, got you diagnosed, treated, and brought you here."

Gavin looked at the windows on his left. They were set deep into terra-cotta walls. They framed black night. The only exit from the room was a door beside the leather-covered sofa on which he sat. "Why?" he asked.

"What did you do with the Professor?" the Chancellor asked.

"I don't know what you're talking about," Gavin said automatically.

A note of weariness crept into the Chancellor's voice. "You don't have to play games. We know you abducted him. We know who was involved besides yourself."

"If you knew all that and if what you knew were true, you wouldn't be asking me these questions," Gavin said. "And you couldn't prove anything." That was true, Gavin knew. No one would talk to the kops except under extreme duress, and anything like Ned's broken hands would invalidate any evidence he might be forced to give.

"Of course," the Chancellor said. "There's this unreasoning hatred and distrust of authority. But we're not concerned with proving anything. We're not going to punish you for that. Not that we wouldn't like to, you understand. Many of us liked the Professor. But he waived his legal rights when he came on campus; he didn't have to, but that's what he wanted. 'Don't punish anyone in my name,' he told me once. 'If something happens to me, it's one of two things: my own fault or my own doing.' We just want to know what happened to him."

Gavin heard the note of sorrow in the Chancellor's voice and what he would have considered in other circumstances an element of sincerity, but he hardened his heart. "If you think I'm going to tell you anything, you don't know students very well. We aren't going to cooperate with the authority that has been falsely placed over us."

They sat there looking at each other, Gavin defiant, the Chancellor sad, until Gavin said, "If there's nothing else, I'll thank you for the medical care and be on . . ." He tried to get up, but his knees wouldn't hold him. He sat forward on the sofa, breathing hard, massaging his thighs.

"I'm afraid," the Chancellor said, "it isn't that easy."

"It wasn't easy at all," Gavin said.

The Chancellor spread his hands helplessly. "You speak of authority. It isn't that way." He nodded as if he had reached a decision. "I want you to understand how it is."

"The Professor used to say," Gavin said, "when somebody tells you, 'I want you to understand how it is,' he means he wants you to hear his excuses for why he has to behave abominably."

The Chancellor nodded. "Quite right. Only, in this case I want you to know the situation not because I want your forgiveness, nor to absolve myself, but because you were the Professor's student and I think you respected him."

"And you want me to tell you what happened to him," Gavin added cynically. He shrugged. "If you won't let me go and I'm too weak to make a fight of it, I guess I'll have to listen." But he thought he could feel the strength flowing back into his thighs. Perhaps soon he could make a fight of it, or a flight of it.

"In the first place," the Chancellor said, "I have no authority. I have no power."

Gavin laughed. "The Professor used to say, 'Beware

of the power of people who say they have no power.' "

"And yet, in some cases it must be true. I am a figurehead, no better than a janitor—worse, really, because I serve no useful function. I neither govern nor direct. I do not admit, I do not grade, I do not dismiss or graduate."

"The Kampuskops," Gavin reminded him.

"My officers are actors in a play they do not understand. They do nothing important. They arrest nobody important. They play parts in this campus farce, and the fact that they do not know themselves as actors makes the farce even funnier."

"They arrested me."

"I was told where to find you by a student informer, who also told me who was responsible for the Professor's abduction."

"Phil?" Gavin asked. Was the little sycophant playing a dangerous double game?

"That is his name."

Why was the Chancellor telling him this? Was it a ploy to gain his confidence? "He works for StudEx."

"I know," the Chancellor said. "The orders to pick you up came from StudEx."

Gavin didn't believe it. StudEx might exert its petty tyrannies over individual students, but it would never connive with authority. "Did they also tell you to treat my illness?" he asked.

"That was my idea, I'm afraid. I wasn't told that you were sick, so I was free to use my own initiative."

It was all so ridiculous, and the most ridiculous part was that the Chancellor expected him to be taken in by it. "If you have no power, why are you here?"

"Call me a scapegoat," the Chancellor said, choosing his words with apparent care. "Call me a hostage."

"Not a Chancellor?"

"A hostage."

"For what?"

"For the good behavior of society."

Gavin laughed. "Why would society hesitate to act because of you?"

The Chancellor laughed too. Only, there was something hollow about it. "It wouldn't. That's funny,

right? Not for me as me. But for the position, that's
another matter. I have a title. Chancellor. And for
someone uniquely on a spot, extraordinary efforts often
will be exerted. Like an explorer in a cave or an astro-
naut headed for Mars. If they get into difficulties, hundreds of untitled men and women will risk their lives to
save him. He's there alone, and I'm here alone. I'm
a hostage for society, a scapegoat for the students."

"Why you?"

The Chancellor looked thoughtful. "I was . . . important, once. A physician. A scientist. An author. A
teacher. A man with a name. And now I'm none of
those things. The time I have spent here has eroded
them completely away. I'm a title, a scapegoat, a hostage, and I'm here because while I'm here conditions
may not get worse. Society still can exert some small
restraints upon youthful excesses. I remind students
of another world."

"You're a target for every student with a grievance,"
Gavin said.

"That, too. That goes with the office," the Chancellor said. "But if they didn't have me, what other targets
would they find?"

"You're being used," Gavin said scornfully. "By the
establishment you call society."

"And just as much by the students, which you call
the revolution."

"You're just playing games."

"That's what growing up is, right? Playing games,
trying on different roles, practicing for life?"

Gavin thought about that for a moment. The Chancellor was beginning to remind him of a gentler Professor, and unconsciously he was beginning to accept
what the Chancellor said as truth. "Maybe so, but if
this"—he swept his hand to encompass the campus and
all it implied—"is a game, all life is a game."

"Many wise men have used that metaphor," the
Chancellor said. "But there's a difference between metaphor and reality. In a sense, the games of the child
evolve into the reality of the adult along a continuum,
so that at no point between the two is a participant able
to say that this is all game and that is all reality. But

there is a point when, in spite of role-playing in adult life, a mature individual knows that he is seriously engaged with life, that this is real, no game-playing involved."

"That's just another ploy of the establishment," Gavin said, "to keep young people from pressing their demands for justice and revolution—the promise of jam tomorrow."

"Jam tomorrow?" the Chancellor asked.

"That's what the White Queen said to Alice: the pay is jam every other day—jam yesterday or jam tomorrow, but never jam today, because today isn't any other day."

"You humanities types always have the better of me," the Chancellor said, and sighed. "Never jam today. That's what it seems like when you're young and impatient, and the games seem real. So we have to isolate you. . . ."

"What are you talking about?"

"The walls," the Chancellor said. "I'm talking about the walls. That's what they're for. To keep you in."

Who is inside the walls and who is outside? the Professor asked.

"After the uneasy quiet of the Apprehensive Decade," the Chancellor said, "burned out by the riots of the sixties, alarmed by shortages and inflation and unemployment, the overall trend established in the late sixties resumed its progress toward anarchy—the energy problems were solved in a variety of ways; inflation was checked by cheap power and the increase in efficiency brought about by automation; unemployment subsided with the shortened workweek, student salaries, and early retirement; the guaranteed annual income took care of the poor; and the delayed adolescence of the middle-class young was further delayed." The Chancellor grinned apologetically. "That, at least, is the way our best historians have summarized it for me."

Increasingly Gavin began thinking of him as the Professor.

"On the other hand, the sociologists tell me," the Chancellor said, "that the behavior of young people was predictable. They are the products of two generations of permissive childrearing, egalitarian homes, praise for childish creativity no matter how poverty-stricken the imagination or inadequate the execution, primary and secondary education from which the concepts of discipline and content have disappeared, and personal freedom of movement and sexual activity. We gave you liberty and deprived you of society's voice, the superego. No wonder you began to believe that life was all freedom and leisure.

"Those haven't been the only influences: sociologists have identified the growing glorification of youth and the diminishing respect for age, the overpowering numbers of young people, the creation of a youth identity by advertising in pursuit of a market, and a tradition of youthful rebellion reinforced by peer approval and pressures."

"You've forgotten the law-and-order movement," Gavin pointed out.

"No," the Chancellor said, "this was as much a part of the youth movement as anything else, only it was an inevitable reaction to the pressures by youth to revolutionize society, and inevitably it only served to intensify the pressures. Inevitably, it led to the riots of eighty-five, and we realized—"

"Who realized?"

"Adults in general, but specifically Congress and the President and the electorate, which had consented in the law-and-order strategy, even if with misgivings—we all realized that we had been wrong. We had created a new breed of humanity—not just in the United States, but everywhere around the world as international travel and communication wiped out purely national cultures —a breed which like all newly created groups was sure that it had a monopoly upon virtue, that whatever it was was right, that whenever it wanted to know what was right it had only to consult its instincts. We had a choice of destroying it before it destroyed us, or of walling it off, encysting it. We couldn't destroy you. After all, you were our children—I myself lost two children to your Crusade—and we had created you, and there were new generations coming up behind, like you or worse. We had gone too far to change our theories and methods of childrearing. It is easy to loosen the reins of authority but difficult to tighten them again. That would have involved the kinds of effort we no longer were capable of making and would have revolutionized our society almost as much as you threatened. So we gave you the campuses. We walled you in. The serious scholars departed, and we left you here to play your games and survive, if you could, and maybe some of you would graduate."

"What do you mean, graduate?"

"Into adulthood and responsibility."

"You mean into surrender to the establishment," Gavin said. But he was becoming confused. This could not be the Professor who was lecturing him; the Professor was dead.

"No, that's what you mean," the Chancellor said. He sniffed, and his nose twitched to one side. "Well, I came here as Chancellor in eighty-six. I've been here nearly ten years, and I've lost hope. I've seen few graduate. I've seen conditions deteriorate. I have seen campus life become so personally satisfying that no one wants to leave in spite of the petty tyrannies that make existence perilous—I'm afraid they only add spice to a life of license that might otherwise pall. . . ."

"If there were an abduction on this campus such as you described earlier," Gavin broke in, "and if, by accident, the Professor died, I think the students would have buried him under the library lawn." Had that been only night before last? he thought.

"Under the library lawn?" The Chancellor considered it and then shook his head in admiration. "We would never have thought to look there. How did you manage . . . ? Oh, well, never mind. I can't approve what you did, but your choice of a resting place shows more understanding than any of us would have expected. We thought he would end up among the cadavers. But you don't seem like the kind of young man to indulge in casual pranks. Why did you do it?"

"A person such as you describe," Gavin said, "could have only one valid reason: admiration."

"Admiration?"

"Well, love."

"Love," the Chancellor mused. "Imagine that." He sighed. "Thank you for that. Now you may leave."

"I may leave," Gavin echoed.

"Let me put it a bit differently. You must leave."

"Where am I going?" Gavin asked warily, his muscles tensing.

"You're being expelled."

"You said you didn't expel students."

"I don't. This is the action of StudEx."

Gavin sprang at the Chancellor. The Chancellor tried to retreat, but the desk was behind him. Gavin hit him in the chest with his shoulder, and the Chancellor went back over the desk like an acrobat. Hope flickered that the middle-aged man wasn't hurt, even if he was a liar and a cheat, as Gavin turned toward the door. He tugged at the handle, and when the door didn't move, he searched for locks and hidden buttons. Nothing. He fumbled around the handle. As his fingers moved, the door clicked and then slid into the wall under his hands.

Standing in the doorway, shoulder-to-shoulder, were Willie and a Kampuskop. Each caught an arm and swung Gavin around to face the desk. The Chancellor was rising from behind it. Not an article of clothing was disturbed, not a hair was out of place, but something was wrong with his jaw.

"Take him to the southeast gate," he said in a strained mechanical voice. "Take him to the southeast gate. Take him to the southeast gate. . . ."

Too many realizations were pouring in upon Gavin simultaneously for him to adjust. The Chancellor was not a person. Gavin had been talking all this while with a robot.

The Chancellor-thing pulled itself upright and pushed its jaw back into shape with a click audible across the room. "By now," it said, "you will have recognized that I am a mechanical creation, not a creature of flesh and blood like yourself. But I wish to dispose of two misapprehensions." Human or not, this Chancellor could not let something alone. He had to keep chewing at it like a disputatious dog. "I was a real person, but, unfortunately, I was assassinated in the second year of my tenure here. Fortunately, my brain already had been cloned and this body created. It had been intended as my alterego, my stand-in for difficult moments, but it became the Chancellor. Since then I have been shot five times, hanged twice, stabbed more times than I can remember, and beaten almost daily. Resurrection is my fate. Only a machine could have endured it." It hesitated. "And even a machine finds it difficult."

Against his will, Gavin felt sympathy rising in him for this machine with feelings.

"I have not been replaced because I serve my function of hostage as meaningfully in this form as in any other. You may think it ridiculous to have a mechanical Chancellor. But it is no more ridiculous than having mechanical students. And that is what you are, responding mechanically to stimuli like so many robots." The Chancellor-thing slumped at its desk, its head cupped in hands like a statue of misery.

Willie and the Kampuskop wheeled once more and virtually carried Gavin between them out of the office and down the hall, through the bulletproof-glass doorway, and down the marble steps, his feet occasionally touching the floor. Gavin thought he could hear gears whirring in the Kampuskop, and he was not too sure about Willie. They threw him into the back of a two-man squad car and slid down the rear door. Gavin tugged at it, but the door was locked. A moment later an engine started, and the car rumbled along the avenue, its tires almost flattened by the weight of the armor. Gavin's cubicle had no windows; he could only guess at their direction.

The implications of Gavin's discoveries were beginning to piece themselves together. What was this Iron Chancellor? Were its words only clever mechanical responses to obvious verbal stimuli, or were they infinitely variable like the human mind? Was the mechanical man controlled only by programs in a distant computer? It had spoken of a cloned brain. Was that living brain hooked up inside the robot? Or was it protected somewhere else, nourished in some larger and more convenient receptacle, linked to the Iron Chancellor by radio receptors and transmitters grafted to appropriate nerve endings?

But apparently the Chancellor had been correct about his expulsion. Willie surely had been present to make certain the orders of StudEx were carried out. Which meant, no doubt, that he had been wrong all along about StudEx, and if that was true, wrong about the Chancellor as well.

Gavin's mind was whirling in his head, trying to grab the ring of reality, but all his images had been shattered, all the familiar signposts in his world pointed in the wrong direction, and he did not know where the truth could be found.

While he was thus confused, the car turned right, stopped, reversed, and backed, turning toward the left. Outside, something clanged and rattled metallically. The back door of the squad car rolled up, and in the faint starlight Gavin saw the stone gateposts of the southeast gate on either side of him. Between the posts a heavy metal gate had been raised high. He faced the featureless night, but he knew what waited for him in the darkness—one hundred feet of cleared land and then the beginning of town, with all its unknown dangers for the student.

He tried to squeeze himself farther into the car, but the wall behind him moved inexorably toward the back, pushing him into the night and uncertainty, pushing him out of the protected place he had come to know and to love, expelling him from paradise into the cold indifference of the outer world.

And then, on the edge of the car, clinging to it, he gave up and leaped into the night, yelling his defiance and outrage. As he leaped, the gate rattled down behind him and lights came on above him, blinding him, exposing him to his enemies.

And he stood alone upon a cold and light-blasted plain.

5 ⊷ No Place Like Home

Paleolithic man needed many children to replace the
men and women lost to hunting accidents, hardship,
and disease; neolithic man needed a large family so
that a few children would survive to care for him
in his old age; industrial man needed no children but
couldn't control his paleolithic instincts; modern men
and women can control their paleolithic fertility but
not their neolithic cultural heritage. Parenthood sur-
vives as a cultural fossil and is no sooner committed
than regretted. And so the university campus becomes
a place where students are sent by their parents so
that they will not have to be continually reminded of
their folly. Within the campus, students learn how
to extend delinquency into a career. The convent and
the military school were its historic counterparts, with
one significant difference; here the asylum is run by
the inmates.

—THE PROFESSOR'S NOTEBOOK

His arms thrown wide against the gate that barred
him from the campus, Gavin faced the night and the
enemies who hid behind it, and shouted, "All right,
come and get me! One at a time or all together! I'm
ready for you!"

He felt better for his outburst though a bit sheepish
about the heroic pose and the ancient formula in
which he had expressed his defiance. The words had
come to his lips unbidden, perhaps out of the long

107

hours of childhood he had spent with books or in front
of the flickering images on the wall screen.

The only answer was silence. It poured back upon
him like the cold waves of the sea upon the shore.

"Come on!" he shouted. "Don't be afraid! I'm all
alone! Surely there are enough of you to overcome
one student."

Again, silence. Gavin frowned, then shrugged and
marched forward across the rubble that separated the
campus wall from the town. It was performed bravely
enough, but when he reached the edge of the darkness
beyond the lights of the wall, he sidled into it, crouching, as if he was trying to slide between the heavy
black-velvet panels of a curtain.

He stopped and waited for his eyes to adjust to the
darkness, his body tensed for a blow that might hit at
any moment. Nothing touched him except a moth
blundering past him toward the distant lights. Gradually his fighting tension eased as the adrenaline was
washed from his bloodstream. When at last he could
see, he discovered that he was alone. In front of him
was a row of dark houses; a few steps to his left was a
paved street that led down the hill.

He felt like a fool. No one had been waiting for
him. No one had cared. And yet—the thought came
to him—perhaps they were lurking behind the houses,
waiting to see if he were point man for an ambush,
luring him farther into their territory before they
pounced.

That was more like it. He would play their game
because he had no choice. Here he was—defenseless,
alone, still weak from his illness, an exile from his
chosen country. He walked down the middle of the
street as the Israelites might have walked between the
parted waters of the Red Sea. His footsteps, light as
they were upon the pavement, sounded loud in the
night.

Streetlights began at the end of the first block. Bugs
buzzed around them and knocked against the protec-
tive glass with a staccato beat as if they were trans-
mitting some coded message to the world. Gavin
avoided the lighted areas. This was not like the

blasted part of town through which Gregory had led them. People lived here. Grass was cut neatly near the sidewalk, Gavin could see at the edge of the cones of light, and the sidewalks and the streets were in good repair.

Gavin took a deep breath. The air smelled good. For years he had not thought he could breathe the air outside the campus walls, but now, strangely, he felt freer than he had felt for a long time. He did not know why, but he decided not to think about that now.

He could, he realized, return to the campus through the secret passageway he had used last night. He was maybe a mile east of it, but he felt sure he could find it again if he were not attacked before he got there. But returning was pointless. Jenny was gone, and the Professor was gone, and the campus had nothing more for him, not even learning. And if he returned, he probably would be killed in some particularly nasty way by Willie or some other agent of StudEx, or perhaps even by the Kampuskops.

He could try to organize a countermovement to outvote or overthrow StudEx, and there was some merit in that; but he knew the notion was quixotic. Before he was more than started, StudEx or the Chancellor would act, and he could not operate completely underground in so small and organized a society. In any case, it was a corrupt society in which he no longer felt any interest.

"People get the government they deserve," the Professor said once.

Something moved in the darkness. Light came from windows in some of the houses here, as if they scorned the concealment of raidshades, and in their small glow Gavin glimpsed a head turning and a hand reaching, and he grabbed a bony shoulder and a thin arm.

"Hey, fella," a soprano voice said, "keep your hands to yourself!" And then, in a tone of delighted discovery, "Hey, Ma, here's a student! A real student!"

"Shut up!" Gavin said. "What are you trying to do?" As he spoke, he realized that the shoulder and arm he held in his hands belonged to a boy perhaps ten years old.

"Me?" said the boy. "Look around you, man!"

Gavin looked and saw no one. He shook the boy. "What do you mean?"

The boy opened his hand. In it was a small crawling insect. As Gavin watched, a part of its anatomy glowed and was dark, glowed and was dark.

"A lightning bug," Gavin said, and understood that what he had not seen around him were the flickering spots of light that appeared in the night, disappeared, and reappeared a few feet away. For a moment he was returned to the long, brown summer evenings when he was a boy.

"Young man," said a calm voice from the nearby darkness, "I got me a shotgun aimed at your head. I intend to shoot high with the first one so as not to hit Johnny, but I can't guarantee you won't get a few pellets. The second shot, Johnny'll just have to take his chances."

"Hell, Ma, don't shoot," the boy said with equal calmness. "This fella ain't much." As if to demonstrate the truth of what he said, the boy twisted in Gavin's hands and was gone.

"All right, young man," the first voice said from the darkness, "walk over here slow where I can see you."

Gavin estimated his chances of leaping into the darkness and decided they weren't good enough. Slowly he walked toward the voice. Within a few feet he was walking on the resilience of grass and could smell its sharp green odor. A few more feet and he made out the dim outline of a porch and a dark figure seated on it.

"That's far enough," the voice said. Gavin stopped.

The figure on the porch was small, and from the darkness came the creaking of wood against wood, as if a rocker were slowly moving back and forth.

"Why," the voice said, "you sure ain't much, are you? All ragged and bedraggled. Why you out here this time of night?"

Gavin was silent.

"Speak up, boy! I got all the patience in the world, but this shotgun—it ain't got patience one."

"I was expelled."

"Expelled, is it? Well, that's different. That means you ain't rightly a student anymore, doesn't it?"

"That's true," Gavin said, though all it meant was that he no longer was a student within the campus wall that he had known. Being a student, he realized now, was unrelated to surroundings or circumstances; it was a state of mind, as the Professor had said. He would never stop being a student.

The voice of the little woman on the porch softened. "Well, I wouldn't want a student in my house—not even one who's been expelled—but I don't like to see no one, not even a student, in a shape like you. Johnny, go get a shirt and a pair of pants out of Billy's closet."

"But, Ma," the boy protested from behind the woman, "someday maybe I can wear 'em."

"You ain't never gonna be as big as Billy," the woman said. "You take more after my side of the family; Billy took after his pa's side. And Billy ain't never coming home. While you're about it, Johnny, you might get this young fella an apple off the kitchen table."

The door opened and freed a shaft of light that briefly silhouetted the figure of the small woman sitting in a rocking chair, the long, straight barrel of a shotgun extending the right arm of the chair like a deadly iron tongue.

"You are in bad shape, son," the woman said, and Gavin realized that the spray of light had splashed him as well, and that the woman was calling him by another name. Gavin shifted to avoid the light when the door reopened.

"Not too close," the woman said. "I may be sentimental, but I ain't foolish. Where you heading?"

"Home," Gavin said, and knew suddenly that it was true. That was where he was going, and he didn't know why, except that there was nowhere else to go.

"That's good, son." The woman's voice had turned husky.

Gavin thought that her eyes probably were filled with tears, and he could spring now and get the gun, but he hesitated. And then the door opened again, and it was too late.

"Here, Ma," the boy said.

Clothing came flying out of the air toward him like giant winged monsters. Gavin caught them.

"Put 'em on, son," the woman said.

Gavin stripped off his mudcaked workman's shirt and peasant trousers and slipped into a cotton pullover and a pair of old soft jeans. He couldn't tell what color anything was, but they felt good. They took him back to his childhood—they were the kind of clothes he had worn before he went off to college and learned the proper dress for sincere revolutionaries—and smelling the soap-clean clothes brought back memories, and he wished he were home now, taking a long hot bath in the old marble bathtub, smelling the suds, and then sliding fresh, clean clothes over a towel-dried body, tingling with cleanliness. They were sensations he had not known for nearly four years, and they all came flooding back.

As he stood there, smelling an old world back into reality, a round object came toward him out of the darkness. He stuck up his hand, and the object hit it, and his fingers tightened around it. It was an apple. He bit into it gratefully, and with the first taste of juice he realized how hungry he was.

"There, now," the woman said with a note of finality. "Keep some citizen from taking a swing at you out of spite. Somebody stop you, why, just tell 'em you're on your way home. Like you told me."

"I want to thank you," Gavin said. The rusty words stuck in his throat, and he had difficulty getting them out, but when he did, he was glad they were said. "I don't know why you've done this, but—"

"Wasn't for you," the woman said. "Maybe someday, somewhere, my Billy will need help, and maybe somebody'll give him what he needs. Go on. Get."

Gavin turned and headed back down the street, biting off hunks of sweet apple as he went, and licking the juice from his lips, and thinking there was something to be said for the simple pleasures of life, uncomplicated by questions of revolutionary justice.

By midmorning he was nearing Kansas City on the rebuilt Kansas Turnpike, the wind of his passage blowing fresh and cool in his face out of a blue sky. He had slept well but not long in a shed north of town, been awakened by the sunrise, and risen, stretching, smelling the odor of dew evaporating from green growing things, hearing the sounds of large animals moving into nearby pastures. He was up earlier than he had been for years, and he felt remarkably good for all his recent experiences.

He had been picked up by the third car that passed, an old steam-turbine car driven by a middle-aged man with thinning brown hair which he combed carefully over a bald spot without concealing it. He was a large-boned man with a ruddy complexion that spoke of years spent exposed to sun and winter wind. He was a rancher, he said, and he had just sold fifty steers for good money, and he was going to Kansas City to buy him a new electric car.

"Operates from power broadcast from the nuclear-fission plant in the sky," the rancher had said. "Imagine that!"

"What do you know," Gavin said.

"Cost of the car includes the cost of the power," the rancher had said. He was looking forward to the silky quiet of a new electric.

"How about you?" the rancher had asked. "Why you going to the city?"

"Going home," Gavin said happily. "Going home."

And the middle-aged man beside him had glowed in Gavin's warmth. "By golly," he said. "That's good." And after a pause in which his mood seemed to change from reflexive to reflective, he said, "I had a daughter once."

"Oh," Gavin said politely.

"When she was fifteen, she run away to college," the rancher said. "Ain't heard from her since. She was mature for her age, you know. Guess she could have passed for eighteen all right. Cutest little girl. Loved her daddy. Yes, indeed. Loved her daddy. Pigtails. Ice-cream cones. Guess kids gotta grow up, lead their own lives."

"Yeah," Gavin said.

"But sometimes," the rancher said, looking straight ahead at the road, his knuckles white on the steering wheel, "when I think of my little girl, what mighta happened to her, what she mighta done, why, it makes you wonder if it's worth it, if anybody ever oughta have kids, if anybody ever oughta care that much about something that's gonna break your heart."

"Yeah," Gavin said.

"Young fella I picked up once, he told me he heard of her. Said he heard she was living out west somewhere in a commune. Said she had five kids and didn't know for sure the father of any of 'em. Imagine me a grandpa and never even seen a one of 'em. But he wouldn't tell me where that commune was. Thought I might go looking for her and make trouble, I guess. But I don't know—maybe he was just making it all up. They do that sometimes, you know. Kids make up stories they think you want to hear, just to pass the time. Or sometimes stories that'll hurt, just to see if you'll bleed."

"Yeah," Gavin said.

The rancher still didn't look at him. "You ever hear of her, Bonnee Belle Franzen?"

Now the rancher looked at him. Gavin shook his head. "Sorry," he said.

The rancher nodded. "Well, sure. Chances are you wouldn't."

And now the city itself loomed ahead, its concrete fingers etched cleanly against the morning sky.

"What happened to the smog?" Gavin asked.

"Been away quite a while, eh?" the rancher said. "They cleaned that up. No problem, once they set their minds to it. Cheap power means nothing's too costly, excepting food, maybe, and that's loosening up a bit. Me, raising cattle, I'm in a luxury business, you might say, but they're finding ways of making steers more efficient at turning grass and grain into meat, and one of these days they won't even be steers, so to speak, just meat factories with no waste. 'Course, they ain't got the smog and pollution cleaned up everywhere—in the little towns, say, where industry come late, but it's coming, and the rivers gonna run clean again and the air gonna be as pure as the Indians breathed. Maybe purer, considering there was smog then, with the pine forests and prairie fires and all."

"What do you know," Gavin said.

"Truth," the rancher said. He nodded, and Gavin nodded, and they agreed it was truly amazing.

The rancher parked in a large lot on the edge of the city. Even steam-driven cars weren't allowed inside the city limits, he told Gavin, but mass transportation was free and fast. They walked across the vast expanse of asphalt, softening in the sun, took the same monorail into the heart of the city, shook hands, and boarded electric buses to their separate destinations.

The buses ran swiftly, because no other surface transportation got in the way—a few electrics passed them in both directions, but they seemed to be official cars, mail or government, or delivery trucks—and Gavin stared out the window at clean streets and pedestrian traffic. None of it was what the revolution had led him to expect; he had to believe that conflicts were buried beneath the outwardly placid surface, ready to erupt.

Then he noticed that there were children and older people among the pedestrians, and among the other passengers with him on the bus, but there were no young adults—no one between the ages of eighteen and thirty—and he knew what had happened. The old people had isolated their rebellious youth on the campuses. This city was an old folks' home.

Gavin breathed easier.

But it was strange that the slums were gone and the signboards and the garish storefronts and the dirt. Before he was quite ready, the bus had stopped silently at the corner near his home. He got off and walked down the wide, tree-shaded boulevard; he remembered when the elm disease had turned all the elms to bare dead limbs, and the city had cut them down, one by one, and replanted new trees, and now they had grown tall again and everything was the way it had been. He walked between the quiet painted middle-class houses and their green lawns, which had never known trouble or misery or hardship, and he felt good. He felt better than he should have felt in this plastic environment, so far removed from reality, but he had grown up on this street, played games in these yards—run sheep run, and red light, and may I—caught lightning bugs like the boy last night, and rested on the screened front porch in the long, slow, wonderful evenings, thinking about life and people and nature and stars and books. . . .

He found himself standing in front of the screened porch. He was opening the screen door, and he was knocking at the front door, wondering what he would say to his mother and his father, now that he was home. "Hello, Mom. Hello, Dad. I've been expelled. I'm home to stay." "What are you going to do, Tom?" they would ask. "Oh, I don't know," he would say. "Sleep a lot and read and think. . . ." He had not thought about that part. He hadn't thought about what he would do after he got home. Home had been the end of it.

The door was opening. Gavin started to say something, started to enter, and he stopped, realizing that he didn't know the person standing in the doorway. It was a young woman, a girl really, attractive, though slimmer than he preferred, rather boyish even, with blond hair cut short, and a kind of turned-up nose and a generous mouth. . . .

"Yes?" the girl said. She had a pleasant voice, but it wasn't sexy. "Can I help you?"

"Well," he began, "I . . . I . . . I'm Tom Gavin. And I . . ."

The girl smiled and stuck out her hand boyishly to greet him. "Well, Tom, I never expected to meet you. Welcome home."

"Who are you?" he asked.

"I'm Elaine," the girl said, and then called over her shoulder, "Mrs. Gavin. There's someone at the door who'd like to see you."

Gavin heard a familiar pattern of footsteps approaching, quick, staccato, impatient, footsteps he had heard for eighteen years of his life coming toward him when he wanted something, and now he wanted something again, something he could not yet name.

He saw the familiar face, leaning forward, slightly turned, blue eyes looking upward, the way she did when she was ill-at-ease, meeting strangers or confronted by something distasteful. "Who is it?" she asked, and her voice was a cold hand wrapped around Gavin's spine.

"Mom," he said, "it's me. Tom."

"Oh, Tom," she said fretfully. "Tom? What are you doing here?"

"I came home," he said.

"Well," she said. "Well. I must say." She stood at arm's length, peering up at him, her arms at her sides.

"Don't you know me?" he asked. Somehow the edge of his excitement had been dulled.

"Of course I know you," his mother said. "Think I wouldn't know my own son? It's just that . . . It's just . . ."

Gavin took a half-step forward. "I know it's a surprise." He raised his arms and took her by the shoulders. He felt a shiver go through her body. She was a relatively small woman, five-feet-three, he thought. "But I'm home."

"Of course you are," she snapped, and then, as if apologizing, "but it is a surprise."

Gavin pulled his mother to him. She came stiffly, like some girls he had known who did not like him very well or were afraid of him, or themselves. He held her against him for a moment, trying to recapture the old warmth and comfort he had once felt when he was near her, even the joy with which he had held the thought of returning home, but they were both elusive, like trying to remember what it felt like to be in love.

For a moment her dark head bent forward to touch his chest, as if in response to some ancient hormonal instruction, and then her head snapped back and she pushed herself away. "Come in and sit down," she said. It was an invitation she might have issued to a door-to-door salesman or the local pollution inspector. "I'll call your father."

She turned and led the way toward the living room. She walked differently now, shuffling and slow. She was acting like an old woman, Gavin thought, and she wasn't old. She couldn't be more than forty-seven or forty-eight, and that wasn't old. She still looked good, he thought, still the most beautiful woman he had ever known—or, at least, the most beautiful older woman.

He didn't follow her. He stood in the little hall with the living room to his right and the dining room to the left and the breakfast room straight ahead, and he sniffed the odors of home, the old, delicate odors of favorite foods that had permeated the walls and the rugs, the musky perfume his mother wore, the deodorants sprayed in the air. He closed his eyes for a moment, and it all came back to him, all the feelings of childhood rushing upon him simultaneously, impossible to separate: a mingled emotional mixture of eating and of waiting to eat while the smell of cooking food drifted from the kitchen and set his stomach to working, of reading and the slightly mildewed, powdery smell of the old books, and of rushing to his mother and holding her by the knees, the thighs, the waist, as he grew taller, smelling the comfortable smell of her; of lying on the rug, feeling it springy under him, and watching television in the evening, looming tall and wonderful on the wall above, and of the strange electric smell of his father when he came home, and of friends who came to play while his mother tried to get them to go outside, and of bodies, sticky and warm, in the secret explorations in the garage or the attic with little boys and little girls. . . .

"I'm going up to my room," Gavin said, and he turned and ran up the stairs two and three at a stride.

"Tom," his mother called from below. "There's . . . there's been some . . . some changes."

But Gavin already was at the door, and he swung it open, and stopped. The old brass bed was covered with a frilly orange-and-white spread; swiss curtains matched the spread; and the walls had been painted white like the walls of a monastery. Where his old desk had been stood a white dressing table with a mirror attached, and the top of the dressing table was neatly arranged with bottles and brushes and combs and round boxes and canisters, and a picture of some young man.

Gavin walked slowly to the closet and opened the door. It was filled with dresses and blouses and other kinds of feminine clothing.

He turned toward the door, still not understanding, and the girl was there—what was her name?—Elaine. "What your mother was trying to say," the girl said— she was good-looking, all right, but not in a way that excited him—"was that your parents have taken in a boarder. Me."

He looked at her again. This time he saw her as something else, not a stranger, not a girl, not a possible bed partner, but as an interloper, a rival. "Why would they do that?" he asked, but not of her.

"It wasn't the money," she said. She had a pleasant, soft voice and a clear, precise way of speaking that he might have liked in any other girl. "I think they got lonely."

"For you?"

"Oh, not for me." She laughed. "But I think your mother always wanted a girl. They treat me just like one of the family. And it isn't all one-sided. I help around the house when I'm not working."

"Working?"

"When I met your parents I was still in school. Oh, not like you. Computer school. Very practical. That's how I happened to be here. Your father came to lecture, and they told him—the people at the school— how I needed a room . . ."

Gavin brushed past her on his way to the door. "I'm not interested," he said. He called from the head of the stairs, "Mom, where are my old clothes?"

After a moment his mother said something that he didn't understand. "I said," Gavin repeated, " 'where are my old clothes?' "

"We gave most of them away," his mother said more clearly. "We . . . we didn't think you'd be needing them again. There may be a few things left in a box in the attic, but they wouldn't fit. They're from when you were much younger."

He turned, angry now, and went toward the linen closet in the hall, pulled out a towel and a washcloth, and headed for the bathroom. It was coming back to him, how it had been, the arguments and the niggling little disagreements. All he had wanted was justice; all they had wanted was conformity. "I'm going to take a bath," he shouted.

"That's good," his mother called. "Maybe your father will be home when you get done."

He glanced at the girl standing in the doorway to his old room. She smiled a bit ruefully. "Well, do you want to help me?" he snapped.

"Thanks a lot," she said, shaking her head, 'but I think I'll pass."

He ran the old tub full of hot water. The room filled with steam and misted the bathroom mirror until beads ran down, leaving crooked clear tracks behind, and he steeped himself for an hour, letting his aggressions drain from him, letting the old memories return —water therapy, his parents used to call it, the hours he had spent in this tub, soaking, reading, keeping the water hot with a trickle from the tap while his parents pounded on the locked door and demanded to know if he was going to be in there all day, that other people had to use the bathroom once in a while too, and that it was sick to just sit in there and turn pruney day after day.

Maybe he had expected too much, he thought. Maybe he had exaggerated the reserve he thought he felt in his mother when she came to the door. Anyway, why shouldn't they let someone else use his room, even if it happened to be a snippy straight of a girl? He had been gone for almost four years, and they had no reason to think he would return, and if it hadn't been for an unusual combination of circumstances, he wouldn't have been here now.

He resolved to give his homecoming another chance.

When he got out of the tub and toweled himself

glowing dry, he was in a better mood. It was good to be home in spite of everything, and after he got rid of the girl it would be the way it used to be.

He found a pair of slacks and a shirt, topped by a pair of undershorts and a pair of dark socks, folded and stacked neatly in the hall by the bathroom door. Beside them were his shoes, now cleaned of mud and polished. The clothes weren't his, but when he put them on they fit pretty well. Perhaps they belonged to his father.

Dressed, he walked down the hall to the stairs and down the stairs to the living room. His mother and father were waiting for him. They were sitting on the brown plush sofa side-by-side. He had thought of his father as a big man, but he didn't look big beside Gavin's mother. He still wore his hair long and his face bearded, although the beard was a bit neater now than Gavin remembered it, and, like his hair, beginning to streak with gray.

Hair had been the big thing when his father was in college, a symbol of dissent, an expression of solidarity, a hint of virility; Gavin tried to imagine it, but it was difficult. Long hair had been popular with girls when his mother was a student, but since then her hair had been short and long and short again over and over. His father still was handsome, still looked like women would be interested in him, but different now, on the defensive, a little uncertain. Gavin remembered his father taking him to political meetings, standing up, denouncing injustice, arguing persuasively for mass action in his rich agitator's voice. And even earlier, or perhaps he only remembered being told about it, Gavin remembered riding everywhere, strapped like a papoose to his father's back.

"Thanks for the clothes, Mom," Gavin said.

"What clothes?" his mother said vaguely.

"Hello, Dad," Gavin said.

His father didn't get up, didn't move to embrace him or shake hands. "What are you doing home?" he asked.

Gavin sighed. "I got expelled," he said. He looked around the room. It was the same as it had always been: the easy chairs in the corners, a little shabbier now. The television on the wall opposite the fireplace. The tall color photograph of his great-grandfather as a child, dressed in a long gown, above the mantel. The little table covered with glass and porcelain knick-knacks and flanked by straight chairs with padded seats. He pulled the nearest one around so that he could sit facing his parents. He didn't feel like sitting in something soft. It was going to be a confrontation. He could feel it.

"Expelled?" his father echoed. "Nobody gets expelled anymore. What can you do to get yourself expelled? You'd have to kill somebody, and even then it would have to be the right person. If he were an enemy of the people, it wouldn't matter."

His father's voice had a querulous tone. Gavin remembered that, too, from the endless arguments before he left for college. "It was partly that," Gavin said. He hadn't meant to talk about that—he wanted to keep that part of him separate—but his father annoyed him.

"You really did kill somebody?" his father exclaimed. Gavin had succeeded in shocking him.

"It was an accident, and that really wasn't the cause of it."

"It wasn't the cause of it," his father repeated. "Damn!" he said, shaking his head. "What was the cause of it?" he demanded, as if by disbelieving in its validity he could reverse the whole turn of events.

"You don't want to know the bloody details," Gavin said. "It isn't important."

"I want to know," his father insisted, as if knowing would cauterize the wound. His half-closed eyes watched Gavin as if he were a rival.

Gavin remembered his father pitching a ball to him, over and over, while he tried to hit it with a bat. The sun was always hot in the sky, always shining in his eyes, and he always gave up, finally, defeated, unable to please his father, unable to keep up the pretense that he was personally involved. "Some campus politicians thought I was a threat," he said. "They had me expelled."

"Politics!" his father said.

Gavin shifted in his hard chair. "You and Mom were into political activity when you were in college," he said. "How many times have you told me about the sit-ins and the marches and the rallies and the arson and the bombs, about holding the Chancellor for ransom, presenting your ultimatums and your nonnegotiable demands, and about your refusals to negotiate without a promise of total amnesty?"

"That was when politics was important," his father said, brushing away the comparison. "That was when things were getting started, when we had to fight for student power. Why, if it hadn't been for us, your mother and me and our friends, the Vietnam war might still be going on, girls would still have closing hours, the fuzz still would be hauling students off to jail for smoking grass, and hitting them over the head with nightsticks for marching in the street."

"The fuzz?" Gavin said, momentarily lost.

"The heat," his father said impatiently. "The pigs. The cops."

"Oh," Gavin said. "Well, they aren't very important now."

"It's because of us they aren't," his father said. "We did it. We were the generation of Mario Savio, Mark Rudd, Bernadine Dorn, and Abbie Hoffman—the saints of the revolution. And we kept our political commitments. We worked for McCarthy and McGovern and all the rest. We've kept the faith, haven't we, Peg?" He nudged his wife.

"What? Oh, yes, dear."

Gavin remembered the strange men and women his father had brought home unexpectedly, the casual conversation about bombs and subversion and old friends, about political theory and weather. One of them kept saying, like an incantation, "You don't need a weatherman to know which way the wind blows."

"What you do now," his father said, "is play games. All the battles are over, and you don't know it. You're playing games and call them politics. You might at least have graduated."

"You don't understand," Gavin said. "I have my

diploma. I got that when I enrolled. What I wanted was an education."

His father shook his head. "What's the world coming to? At least your mother and I earned our degrees. You didn't get your—what is it?—your certificate? Your union card? You haven't got anything to help you get a job, have you?"

Gavin eyed his father without hope for understanding. "Not everybody can work, Dad. There aren't that many jobs."

"Not for those who don't want to work," his father complained.

"The good old Protestant work ethic, eh, Dad?" Gavin said bitterly. "I thought you were against all that."

"Oh, sure," his father said, "that's easy enough to say when you're young. You can be satisfied with the guaranteed annual income when you're young and single, when you have no responsibilities and can live on bread and peanut butter. But what happens when you get older? You can't spend all your time reading or playing the guitar or in the sack."

"In the sack?" Gavin repeated.

"In bed," his father said irritably. "In bed with some chick. A different girl every night. Making out. . . ."

Maybe that was what bothered his father the most, Gavin thought. His great balling days were past, and he envied his son the virility and the opportunity.

"When you've got a wife and a family," his father was saying, "you want something better for them than the minimum. You want walls around you that you own, a home that's yours, and you want a job to go to, something important to do. Call it the work ethic if you want to, but it's work by people like me that lets people like you collect your guaranteed annual income."

"Oh, Dad," Gavin exclaimed, "it's the surplus that does it, our economy of cybernated abundance. There's plenty for all, those who want to work, and those who don't—or can't. Maybe the lucky ones are the ones who want to work and can find jobs. It's all there in economics. You ought to remember."

"Don't tell me what I ought to remember," his father said. "I was remembering a lot of things before you were born. You can call it the surplus if you want, but somehow the economy of cybernated abundance doesn't come up with a check when you write home for money. It's your parents who send you the money. It's our pocket it comes out of, and it's us who have to do without something."

"What did you ever do without?" Gavin asked impatiently.

"Plenty of things," his father said. "Trips to Europe, new cars, a better house, clothes, a vacation home, a boat, lots of things we thought about and knew we couldn't afford, eh, Peg?"

"That's right, dear," his mother said.

They sat there facing him, next to each other on the sofa, his mother holding his father's hand, as if protecting each other from the threat that he represented.

"Oh, Mom," Gavin said, "you know that's not true. You've been collecting my educational allowance from the government all these years, and you've sent me only a few dollars from time to time, only what you had to send to keep me from coming home."

"Why do you keep calling me 'Mom'?" his mother said suddenly. "You always used to call me 'Margaret.' "

Gavin stopped and remembered. "That's right. I did, didn't I. All right . . . Margaret."

"I always used to hate it, too," his mother said, as if he hadn't spoken. "And you called your father 'Jerry,' as if everybody were equal. Your father used to say he didn't want to be called 'Jerry'—things would go better if you called him 'sir'—but you wouldn't. Now why do you call us 'Mom' and 'Dad'?"

Gavin didn't know the answer. He had returned home with a lot of false hopes and false memories. He remembered now: it had always been Margaret and Jerry, and he had to yell at them to make them listen.

"I've got a whole box somewhere of your grade-school drawings and your report cards with all the stupid comments on them by those stupid teachers. Why have I kept them? I'm going to throw them away. You drew terribly, Tom, and I was never able to tell you that, any more than I was able to tell you that I didn't want to be called 'Margaret.' I had to pin them up as if they were art. And we had to listen to your opinions at the dinner table as if they mattered, as if they were as good as anybody's. There really were a lot of things I hated about being a mother, and I never was able to tell anybody."

"Maybe you didn't do me any favors," Gavin said. He tried to remember the good things, how his mother had sat beside him and read to him endlessly. Had she hated that, too?

"How can you say that?" his mother said. "When we sacrificed for you all the time? We never left you with baby-sitters. We took you with us everywhere, even when you were a baby and an obnoxious little brat."

"I didn't ask you to do that."

"Oh, you did!" his mother protested. "Everywhere we turned, you were asking: get me this, get me that, take me with you, don't leave me alone, treat me like a person, treat me like an adult, love me, pamper me, spoil me, coddle me, tell me I'm wonderful. And when you weren't asking, the demands were in the air: society was asking for you, telling us that you were unspoiled and good and only if we didn't thwart you or kill your spirit would you grow up and be wonderful, be the sort of human being that we weren't. You were a terrible child. We didn't draw a peaceful breath until you went away to college."

"Besides," his father said, as if picking up an old cause, "it wasn't your educational allowance. It came made out to us. To help compensate us for the money we spent on you, for the trouble you caused, for the problems of raising a child. Anyway, all that's past and dead. What we want to know is why you came home."

" 'Home,' " Gavin quoted bitterly, " 'is the place where, when you have to go there, they have to take you in.' "

"Don't flaunt your newfound college learning at us," his father said. "We know Frost better than you do."

He could quote the Professor to them, Gavin thought. "Children should not expect love from their parents, any more than parents should expect obedience from their children," he remembered. "It is an unnatural relationship which is best terminated as soon as possible. The birds and the animals have the right idea. They don't keep their offspring around any longer than it takes them to fend for themselves. They push them out of the nest before the instincts wear thin."

His father stood up dramatically, looming over Gavin the way he used to do. "You can't stay here, you know."

Gavin rose to meet the challenge, and his father no longer seemed so big. He had shrunk. He could have looked Gavin in the eye, but he didn't.

"Now, you shouldn't say that, dear," his mother said helplessly. She turned to Gavin. "But you don't get on with your father, Tom. You're always at each other, arguing, like today. I don't think I can stand it if you're like that."

"It's your mother I'm thinking about," his father said. "You have a different way of life. You stay up drinking beer with your friends until all hours, and you come home early in the morning, waking your mother up, flushing the toilet, all that; then you sleep until midafternoon, lay around in the bathtub half the day, foul up the kitchen cooking ungodly messes for your mother to clean up. And you equate all this with greater sensitivity and moral superiority. Besides, there's no room for you. We've got a boarder."

"I know," Gavin said. He wondered if that was why they had rented his room, so that he could not move back in. He wondered, too, if there was something between the girl and his father. His father always had been a wanderer, a determined philanderer. That also would explain a great deal. Everything except his mother.

"Perhaps we could fix up a place for him," his

mother said. "There's that little room in the basement."

His father shook his handsome head, making his long hair toss from side to side. "It won't do, Peg. It just won't do. He's declared his alienation often enough; let him put it to practice. He's alienated! Hell, I'm alienated!"

His mother turned helplessly back to Gavin. "You mustn't blame your father, you know. It's me, and he knows it. I simply can't stand having you around. I know it sounds awful, like I'm an unnatural mother. But I didn't take kindly to motherhood. It was a shock and a trial. Not everybody is cut out to be a mother. You don't find that out until too late. And then there's the pain—seeing your child making the wrong choices and not listening to you. I can't stand that anymore."

Her voice faded as Gavin heard the Professor saying, "Children won't take advice—that's the basic problem. They refuse to profit from the experience of their elders. They think it's all new, that life started with them, that no one ever felt what they feel—but we've got an advantage, we older people: we may no longer be young, but we've been young, and you've never been old."

"Somebody called it the tyranny of the eternal now," his mother was saying. "If you won't let us help you avoid its consequences, or of your lack of understanding of yourself and the world, and the prices you must pay eventually for what you do now—why, we won't subject ourselves to the agony of seeing you heading for the nearest cliff, deaf to all our warnings."

Gavin looked at his father and then at his mother. "Thanks for the welcome home," he said, and started for the door.

"Where are you going?" his mother asked, anxious about him now that the decision apparently had been reached.

"I'll think of something," he said, recognizing the pathos in his voice, realizing the pain it would cause his mother, not caring.

"You can't just walk out of here like this," his

mother said, turning to his father. "You've been too hard on him, Jerry. Do something!"

"*I've* been too hard on him!" his father said. "Who called me at work all in a panic? Who insisted I come right home?"

The moment was familiar, a moment that at another time Gavin would have greeted with joy, knowing he had won, knowing that they had turned upon each other, knowing their united front was broken. . . . But it was too late.

His father turned to Gavin. "Look, Tom, I didn't mean you had to leave right this minute—only that you shouldn't plan on anything permanent, or allow the temporary to extend day after day into the same thing."

"Never mind," Gavin said. "You've won. I'm leaving."

"Not without lunch," his mother protested.

"I'm not hungry," Gavin said. It was a lie, but he knew he couldn't sit around a table with his parents and the boarder, exchanging little lies about what he had been doing and what had happened to people his parents knew that he had forgotten, if he ever knew them.

His father was rummaging through his billfold. "Look," he said, "I don't carry much money anymore, what with the new universal credit card, but you'll need something to get started. Here, take this twenty, and I think maybe I've got some more stuck away upstairs."

Gavin looked at the three bills in his father's hand, shaking just a bit now that Gavin had seized his position of moral superiority. "You can't buy peace of mind through me. And I'm not for sale either. 'Naked came I into the world, and naked must I go out.' "

"Yes," his father said, "and, you damned fool, you'll go through life tilting at windmills, too. Oh, I give up!" He turned and sank into an easy chair, his back to Gavin in renunciation. He tossed the money on the floor beside the chair.

"Oh, Tom," his mother said. "If you knew what I went through. If you knew what I'm going through now. Oh, Tom!"

But Gavin was beyond being blackmailed by his mother's trauma. He recognized the appropriateness of the moment, turned, opened the front door, and went onto the porch, closing the door firmly behind him. It closed like the door of a tomb.

"Hello, again," a girl's voice said. It was the boarder, sitting on a swing to his left.

Gavin looked at the half-open window to the living room. She had heard everything.

"I'm sorry things turned out this way," she said, swinging gently. She wore a white blouse covered with little blue flowers, and a matching blue skirt. She had good legs, and the skirt did something to Gavin's imagination that he tried to suppress. It was only that he hadn't seen a skirt for a long time, he told himself. "In a way," she said, "I feel responsible."

"Why should you feel responsible?" Gavin asked. He resented her pretending to an importance in his life that she could never have.

"You know," she said, frowning delicately, "if I hadn't taken over your room, your parents wouldn't have been able to use that as an excuse."

"Don't flatter yourself," Gavin said curtly, and reached for the screen door.

"Where are you going?" Elaine asked. She swung to and fro.

"What business is it of yours?"

"I do feel responsible," she said, and smiled. "I can't help it. I have an overpunitive superego."

Gavin stared at her. "If you must know," he said, the screen door open in his hand, "I've decided to head for the West Coast." The moment he said it, he knew it was true. Sometime in the period between his decision to leave home and her question, he had decided to go to Berkeley, where it had all started, where surely the revolution would be run properly.

Besides, Berkeley was adjacent to Oakland, and Jenny—dear, lovely, confused, frightened, lost Jenny—had come from Oakland. Perhaps, if she had survived that terrible night beside the river, she might have returned to her home.

He had hope, at least, which is more than he had felt for days. "What?" he asked.

"I said," Elaine repeated, " 'without money?' "

"I'll hitch my way," Gavin said. "There's always people who'll give a fellow a ride, always a freak who'll share his meal."

"But you don't know who might pick you up," Elaine said. "All sorts of strange people are around these days."

She looked childish and innocent. Gavin could scarcely keep from laughing. Instead he walked through the doorway and let the stiff spring slam the door shut behind him.

He walked slowly along the sidewalk under the arching oaks and Chinese elms and locusts and walnut trees. He had the feeling that the Professor was walking along beside him, nodding, saying, "Every adolescent must pass through two crucial periods: one when he identifies with a model—a father, an older brother, a teacher; the second when he dissociates himself from his model, rebels against him, reasserts his own selfhood." All right, Professor, he thought, I should have known I couldn't go home.

The houses didn't look the same as they had a few hours before. They were false fronts, hiding shame and misery and degradation and despair. He nodded at them as he passed, and spoke to them: "Good-bye, Mr. Cacciopo, and how are all the Cacciopos, and do the neighbors still send anonymous letters about Mrs. Cacciopo's indecent fertility? Good-bye, Mrs. Green, and does that strange car still park twice a week until early in the morning in front of the widow's house? Good-bye, Mr. Williams, and is your church still strangely empty on Sunday mornings while all the holy houses of the odd religious cults bulge six nights a week? Good-bye, Mrs. Stucker, and is your defective child all grown up now and still living with you to protect him from the institutions that might teach him how to go to the john and dress himself? Good-bye, Mr. Washington, and have the neighbors finally accepted their black family and do they invite you to their homes and their block parties? Good-bye, Mr. Froelich and Mrs. Mazanec and Mr. McCaslin and Mrs. Solsky, and how are all your little problems? Do your children grow up and become unmanageable? Do they discover that they know more of the truth than you, that they are born into this environment and you are only immigrants, that they are a new breed upon this earth who love each other, who don't want to compete with each other, who hate only war and injustice and repression, who have a vision of a better way and know that somehow, someway, they must reach it? Does it break your heart? Do you drive them out? Do you ship them off to college? Do you bribe them to stay away? Do you hate them?"

That was all very well, but Gavin couldn't forget that he was hungry. Pride was a wonderful companion, but he couldn't eat it. Pride made him feel as tall as Goliath, but hunger was the little David that brought him low. He thought about his mother's cooking, and wished, at least, he had stayed for lunch. What would it have cost him? And then he thought about the dialogue that would have followed his surrender to his belly's tyranny, the loss of face that his yielding would have involved, and he swallowed hard and moved on toward the bus stop.

The trip back to the heart of town and the monorail ride to the Interstate at the outskirts were remarkably different from his experience earlier that day. Then hope and expectation had brightened the streets and glorified the people. Now he saw quite clearly that the streets were only superficially clean; dust swirled behind the bus as they passed, and a paper wrapper danced in a gutter. The people weren't so much cheerful as they walked along the streets as sullen and unsmiling, the prey of secret doubts and conflicts. Gavin read their characters as he passed, and was content. This city wasn't so much an old folks' home as a concentration camp, cleverly disguised by facelifting and apparently free entrance and egress.

As if to confirm his diagnosis, the monorail out of the city was almost empty.

Gavin took his place along the north lane of the superhighway. The sun was warm, but he didn't mind: he was heading for Berkeley and the Coast. For a while he just stood there, waiting for someone to notice his need and stop to pick him up. No one stopped. He began to use his thumb and finally waved his whole hand at the advancing cars to indicate the urgency of his desire to get out of this unpleasant place. Still no one stopped, and the cars began to pass him less frequently, as if the very traffic patterns were beginning to conspire against him.

Finally he sat down on a boulder near the road and considered the desperation of his hunger. He couldn't go home. That would make him look like a little boy who returned from running away from home because he was forbidden to cross the street. Perhaps the best choice, he thought, would be to walk along the highway and leave at the next exit, if he didn't get picked up before then, find the first likely freak who might part with a little food and give him a place to flop. Then he could get an early start in the morning.

The more he considered the matter, the better he thought the idea was, even though it suggested a certain lack of faith in his fellow travelers. He began walking west.

He had walked about a quarter of a mile and was adding thirst and fatigue to his hunger when he heard a car's horn beside him. He looked up hopefully. It was a yellow electric, a small convertible with a narrow second seat behind the two bucket seats in front. The girl named Elaine was sitting in the front seat, her blond hair lifting in the light breeze, her blue eyes turned to him, her lips smiling.

"Well," she asked, "do you want a ride or not?"

"What are you doing here?" Gavin asked irritably.

"I'm offering you a ride."

"If you think I'm going to return to my parents' house with you . . ." he began.

She raised her left hand from the steering wheel. "Of course not."

Gavin walked along the road, his head turned to the left. The girl kept the car beside him, glancing at the rear-vision mirror occasionally to make certain that no car was coming from behind.

"Then what are you doing here?" Gavin asked.

"Do I have to say it again?"

"Where are you going?"

"Wherever you're going. The West Coast, I guess."

"You must be crazy!" Gavin exclaimed. This girl irritated him with everything she did. "You live in a room in my home. You eat at my table. You work back there."

"Not any more," Elaine said.

"You left?" Gavin asked. "Just like that?"

"Just like that. Get in."

"Not on your life," Gavin said firmly. "I really think you're crazy. Why would you do something like that?"

"I told you," Elaine said. "I feel responsible. Anyway, I've never done anything crazy before, and a person ought to do something crazy once in their life. Isn't that right? I'd get in, if I were you. Most of these cars are going short distances. Long-distance travelers take airplanes or trains or buses. You'd be weeks on the road, even if you got picked up. And nobody picks up hitchers anymore, not unless they've got a reason. Besides . . . I've got some sandwiches."

Gavin stopped. The car jerked to a stop beside him. "All right," he said. "It's your problem."

He got into the car. As he was settling back into the seat, the car began accelerating down the highway. The wind poured around the windshield, fresh and cool, blowing his hair, blowing Elaine's blond hair back from her head as she looked down the road. She had a good profile.

He wasn't sure he believed any of it—the succession of strange events that had evicted him from the campus, which had driven him from his home, which now had him traveling down a highway toward the West Coast with a girl he hadn't met until this morning, a girl he disliked, a girl who had tossed over her plans, her life, and impulsively, for no reason, was driving him toward the Coast and Jenny. . . .

Jenny, he thought, and looked at the highway unrolling in front of him. At the end of that long, unbroken ribbon was Jenny, and if things went smoothly, he might be seeing her again in as little as four days.

He bit into one of the sandwiches he found at his feet. It was peanut butter. He never had liked peanut butter, which was a great handicap to a revolutionary.

6 ↔ The Start of a Journey

To what more glorious or more natural existence do
we look back? Did the neolithic farmers envy the
more natural lives of their paleolithic forefathers,
and did those savage hunters, in turn, recall nostalgi-
cally the carefree careers of their arboreal ancestors?
Or did such romantic nonsense begin only with the
postindustrial-revolution factory worker? Among all
the varieties of lives that man has tried, which is the
most natural? To which shall we return? Or can we
say that man, as the adaptable animal, finds natural
that which conditions make most rewarding? The
countryside is no more natural than the city, though
a long tradition of pastoral writing has given us certain unnatural yearnings for sheep and meadows and
shepherds. Actually, the most natural condition for
man, if we define "natural" as that which has been
most prevalent, is hunger, privation, poverty, sickness, and an early death. Perhaps it is the scarcity of
these natural conditions which forces our reformers
to protest.

—THE PROFESSOR'S NOTEBOOK

The evening sun hung in a notch between the Flint
Hills as they advanced toward it at a sedate sixty miles
per hour, looping gently over the hills and into the
valleys. Fluffy clouds hung in the western sky, and
already their lower edges were kindled with the bright
promise of sunset.

The car swooped like a hawk along the black ribbon
of highway, the only sounds the friction of the tires
against the asphalt and the wind of their passing; it
came in the side windows or over the windshield to
run suggestive fingers through Gavin's hair and whisper strange thoughts in his ears. Gavin sat relaxed beside the girl who had picked him off this highway some
eighty miles behind, and he felt as if he were floating
through space, far from the ugly city and the busy
town filled with people and noise and the stink of
machines.

The land was hilly here; only a thin layer of soil
covered its stony shape. On either side the layered
white-and-gray limestone deposited when the area had
been an inland sea had been replaced by reddish
quartz. It emerged from the soil like the earth's bones:
in boulders or rounded outcroppings in the green hills;
or, occasionally, when the highway cut through a hill,
painted in strips along either side of the exposed rock.

In spite of the scanty soil, the grass grew thick and
tall. Red cattle with white faces stood knee-deep, or
grazed mournfully on the sides of hills as if they had
been bred for these pastures with downhill legs longer
than the other pair, or cooled themselves, broad chests
deep, in still ponds, or lay ruminatingly in their green
beds, jaws grinding their day's meal into more easily
digested form.

On a distant hilltop, silhouetted against the evening
sky, a lonely figure slouched in the saddle of a horse
like a statue raised to a vanishing way of life. Nowhere could Gavin see signs of man's habitation,
and for the first time he felt as if he had plenty of
room, as if he could never run out of green. He recalled how he had once flown over Illinois and Iowa
and Missouri, and how cities had appeared here and
there like amoebas growing wherever two roads met,
but mostly what he had seen from the air was green
geometry, squares of living things, with here and
there the brown rectangle of a plowed field and the
irregular blue oval of ponds, thousands of ponds, reflecting the limitless sky.

Gavin wanted to run through the pastures among

the cattle until his heart pounded and his lungs gasped, and then throw himself into the grass to look up into the sky and smell the air thick with growing things and listen to the sounds of the living earth.

Gavin did not know how long he remained in his pastoral reverie, but his peace was broken by the clamor of an old Greyhound steam-turbine bus which swung past them. The bus was painted from front to back and from top to bottom with fanciful designs in psychedelic colors like Day-Glo orange and purple and red and yellow and green, and in the midst of the designs, hidden like color-blindness tests, cabalistic messages like "The Kesey Express" and "You're on the bus or you're off the bus."

Inside the bus, bodies moved in rhythm to a hard-rock tape that assaulted Gavin's eardrums. It was like a gigantic coffin floating on waves of sound, with windows in the side through which could be seen surging masses of flesh and colored cloth like decorated protoplasm. As the vehicle passed, someone tossed a handful of pills in their direction, and over the noise of the tape a voice shouted, "Live! Grow! Experience the infinite!" Most of the pills missed, but a few landed in Gavin's lap—sugar-coated red pills, yellow capsules, blue capsules, yellow-and-green capsules, red-and-white capsules. . . .

In the middle of the bus, a girl waved her bare bottom at them through a window, peering over her shoulder to see their reaction, and a couple standing up in the rear seat were locked in the ecstasies of orgasm.

And then the bus was gone in a wail of Dopplered sound and a spurt of steam from the exhaust.

"Flaming youth," Elaine said disgustedly. "Precollege pranksters." She picked a capsule from her skirt and tossed it out of the car.

"We used to save that sort of thing for college," Gavin said. "What do they have left?"

"Remorse and reform," Elaine said.

The pastoral mood was broken, and Gavin looked once more to the road pulling the sun toward them. On the side of the road ahead he saw a stick figure against the horizon; it turned into a person trudging along the highway.

"There," he said to Elaine, pointing. "Let's pick him up."

The person turned a pale, unhappy face toward the car as it passed. He was a young fellow dressed in a ragged workman's shirt and peasant trousers; on his back he carried a pack complete with bedroll and guitar.

Gavin slapped the padded dashboard in disgust. "I don't know why you don't pick up people like that."

Elaine shrugged. "I feel no obligation," she said. "They've made their choice, and they might turn out to be murderers, thieves, rapists, carriers of a hundred contagious diseases . . ."

Gavin sat up a bit straighter. "That could be true of anybody anywhere."

"I don't pick them up, either."

"But these are brothers," Gavin went on.

"Not my brothers."

"They're like monks," Gavin said. "Like they've taken a vow of poverty. If they were thieves, they wouldn't be walking along the road in rags. They'd be driving, like you."

"I didn't steal this car," Elaine said. "I worked to buy it. If they want to ride, let them work, too."

Gavin shook his head sorrowfully. "You're just like my father. Don't you see? They don't want to surrender to the Protestant work ethic like their fathers did, and find themselves trapped day by day in a routine of hypocrisy and pollution and the kind of life that is built upon lack of concern for real values."

"Then I wouldn't think of seducing them into a collaboration with that society by picking them up," Elaine said. "That would be a surrender to the Protestant ride ethic, and it seems to me that their virtue depends on their walking."

"But your virtue depends on picking them up."

"I suspect that it's the other way around," Elaine murmured.

"You can redeem some of your own hypocrisy by sharing what you have with people who are less fortunate, like giving alms to beggars," Gavin went on, unheeding. "You might almost say that they are put on this earth to test you."

"Then I've just flunked the test," Elaine said cheerfully, "because they don't seem less fortunate to me. They chose their situation. They chose to be on the road without transportation. Fortune had nothing to do with it. If they are satisfied with their educational allowance or their guaranteed annual income, why should they be allowed to enjoy the material goods that other people have been willing to work for? And why should I encourage them in their folly by ameliorating the consequences of their decisions? How are they ever going to learn?"

"Everybody is exploited by society," Gavin said, "the rich man as well as the poor man. Those who work and those who don't. Over the years man—man, not individuals—has built up, with hard work and ingenuity, a substantial amount of capital, a production system that runs virtually without human intervention, that provides the affluence that some enjoy and others must do without but is sufficient for all, irrespective of work. It is our built-up capital which produces wealth today, not labor, which today is a sort of hobby with a peculiar social reward system.

"So we can't claim the rights of personal property and withhold its benefits from others. In the only meaningful sense, nobody owns anything, and we all own everything. The real nobility in our society are those who don't claim their birthright, who refuse to join the society of overconsumption, who save resources for others, including the poor, deprived masses in the underdeveloped nations of the world whose resources we are consuming at an ever-increasing rate. . . ."

Gavin could hear the Professor's ironic voice saying, "Who's giving the lectures here?"

"As a matter of fact," Elaine said, "the power output of our fusion and solar satellites has been made available to anyone who wishes to put up a receiving station."

"That's only elementary justice," Gavin said.

"There still are irreplaceable natural resources and food and—"

"Nobody uses oil and gas and coal for fuel anymore," Elaine said, "and with recycling and seawater extraction and mining the ocean beds, the usable amounts of metals and other valuable minerals are increasing rather than diminishing. We do ship agricultural products overseas, of course, in compensation for those minerals we don't have on this continent, but we can't feed the whole world and its constantly increasing population. That's a matter for birth-control policies in those countries."

"You mean," Gavin said, "it's all right for us to have all the babies we want, but not black and brown and yellow peoples."

"Look," Elaine said, frowning, "I'd like to have lots of babies, but I won't; at most, I'll have two because I feel a sense of responsibility. The rest of our people do, too. Our national birth rate has been below the replacement level for more than thirty years. We've taken care of our problem, and we can't take care of theirs. In fact, everything we do to help them avoid the necessity of facing their problems now— gifts of food and money—only builds greater problems for them later, when the food runs out and they have many more people to feed. Or to see starve."

"That's an easy way to avoid self-sacrifice," Gavin said.

"No," Elaine said firmly, "giving is an easy way to buy absolution. You wouldn't let your father do it to you, so why should you want us to do it to the underprivileged?"

Gavin sank back in his seat, remembering the Professor saying one day, "The Radiclib wants to do for others what he would find unforgivable if it were done to him." What was challenging coming from the Professor, however, was pure reactionism coming from a pretty girl driving along the highway in a yellow convertible. It was too bad—he had begun to think favorably of the girl; she was quiet, pleasant, not bad to look at, and she was taking him in the direction he wanted to go.

"Did you have something going with my father?" he asked. He studied her face. It was turned straight to the road again. He thought he saw color rise in her cheeks, but it might have been only the setting sun.

"That's none of your business," she said.

He shrugged. "Of course not."

"But," she continued, "there was nothing between us except the affection a daughter and a father might share."

"I see," Gavin said, "incest."

"Don't be ridiculous!" she said. "You seem to think the only thing a man and a woman can share is a bed." Her face really was red now.

"It's always there," Gavin said. "Not 'will she or won't she?' but 'with me or not with me?' " He had her on the defensive now. He suspected that she was a prude, perhaps even a virgin, and it all made him more pleasantly disposed toward her than reality justified.

"Your father was—is—an attractive man," Elaine said, fumbling for words, "but . . . he didn't appeal to me in that way. Besides, I was interested in someone else."

"Who?"

"That *is* none of your business," she said firmly.

"Look!" Gavin said suddenly, sitting up. "There's some more hitchers. Now's your chance to redeem yourself."

Two bedraggled caricatures sat on the concrete railing of a bridge ahead like scarecrows who had wandered in from a nearby cornfield. Worn packs and rolled sleeping bags rested on the railing beside them. They waved frantically at the car as it approached. Close-up, Gavin could tell that they were male and female. "For God's sake," he said, "aren't you going to stop?"

He held out his hand, widespread, in a gesture of helplessness and apology as the car sailed over the bridge and past the two disconsolate hitchers.

"Why are they always so miserable?" Elaine said.

"They have a chance to see human nature at its most inhumane," Gavin said. "You don't know what it does to me to reject my brothers and sisters like that."

"You can go to work and buy a car and devote the rest of your life to missionary work on the highways, picking up strays, transporting them from one spot to another," Elaine said.

"They'd give you anything they had," Gavin said.

"I suspect that all she'd have to give you is the clap," Elaine said. "Isn't it strange that people who have nothing are always willing to share it, and other people's plenty, too."

"I don't think it's strange at all," Gavin said. "It's just another example of the corruption of affluence." But he remembered the Professor saying, "A poor man's generosity comes to the same end as a rich man's parsimony. The poor man believes in equality; the well-to-do man in freedom. Beware of the man who wants to trade his penury for your freedom."

But he said to Elaine, "Where did you get your weary load of cynicism?"

"Easy," she said. "I was orphaned at the age of two. You learn a lot about human nature when you aren't protected from it. I grew up in a creche with a lot of other underprivileged children—black, red, brown, yellow, white—all there to give them an equal start in life, free from the inequalities of birth and environment."

"I'm sorry," Gavin said.

"Don't be," she said. "All I missed was parents to rebel against. Maybe that's why I enjoyed your parents so much. They gave their affection without demanding anything back. Oh, we had official surrogate parents in the creche, selected for warmth and empathy and emotional stability, but it wasn't the same. It was their job."

"The child-parent relationship is unnatural," Gavin said, quoting the Professor.

"Maybe it would have been different if I had been their child," Elaine said. "Maybe they'd have demanded something from me. But I was my own person, and that was all I wanted to be—beholden to nobody, independent of everybody, free from the constraints of poverty and of job alike."

"I can see," Gavin said considerately, in the attitude of "to know all is to forgive all," "how you might have grown up selfish—"

"Selfish! That's not the point. Free! Free to be myself! Free to be as much a me as I can! Free from the tyranny of equality and political justice and intellectual fads. That's why I never went to college—too much conformity in speech and dress and thought."

"Conformity!" Gavin exclaimed. "That was liberty."

"Then why did you all dress alike? Those ridiculous peasant clothes. None of you were peasants."

"That," Gavin said, "was an expression of solidarity. With workmen and peasants everywhere in all times. And with students who, like us, were protesting the conformity of forced consumption by advertising and styles and the uptight generation."

"You all talk alike, too," Elaine said. "Anyway, I wanted to be able to do what I wanted, as long as I didn't hurt anybody."

"That's a passive approach to morality," Gavin said. "And it will never help create a better world."

"On the other hand," Elaine said, "I won't do evil under the illusion that I am doing good."

Gavin found her attitude incredible. "I thought all young people were revolutionists!"

"I don't believe in philosophies," Elaine said. "They only serve to rationalize your prejudices or institutionalize your practices. But I have a rule of thumb: do good slowly, if at all. That gives people a chance to protest the damage you are doing to them. Or, if you like more elegance in your rules of thumb, don't do to other people as you would have them do to you, because they're all different."

"Then you consent to the oppression of the people," Gavin said.

"I don't know who 'the people' are or the nature of their oppression," Elaine said. "All I really know is that nobody authorized me to act in their behalf. And if 'the people' are 'oppressed' in sufficient numbers, they will know it and will do something about it."

"But they have no power."

Elaine shook her head. "What you revolutionists

object to is that they don't know they're oppressed, so you invent terms like 'brainwashing,' 'social behavior conditioning,' 'cooptation,' 'media massage,' 'unconscious rebels,' 'mute protest,' and all the rest—when what you mean is that you want revolution for your own purposes, to satisfy your own emotional needs, and you find that rationale distressingly insufficient to justify all the damage you are willing to inflict on others."

Gavin shrugged. "I'm afraid your political naïveté is showing. Perhaps you should have gone to college. In any case, all this has no relation to the simple kindness of picking up fellow travelers."

"Just as I would not do harm to others," Elaine said, "I choose not to put others in the position to do harm to me."

"Yet you picked me up," Gavin pointed out.

Elaine hesitated. "I didn't say that I took no risks; I choose them carefully. And I feel I know you—at least well enough to believe that you will do me no harm."

"I guess that's a compliment," Gavin said. "If it is, thanks." But he wondered if they had a common definition of "harm."

They followed the setting sun and a trail of pills and bottles and discarded clothing into the outskirts of Junction City. By then the sky was dark, and Elaine turned the car into the driveway of a motel whose illuminated sign had lost some letters and read "L———s Arms." As they passed beneath the sign, Gavin could read the missing letters. They were "over," and above the sign, unilluminated, was a reproduction of the *Venus de Milo*.

Gavin smiled and said, "It would be cheaper and more virtuous to sleep beside the car."

"I prefer a few comforts," Elaine said.

"I don't have any money," Gavin said.

"I have something better," Elaine said, opening the door on her side of the car and getting out, "a universal credit card and money in the bank. Of course, you're welcome to sleep in the car or in the nearest field."

Gavin got out of the car and followed her into a shabby lobby. Broken venetian blinds only partially covered the front windows, and the old green theater-type carpeting on the floor was worn down to the rubber backing in a pathway leading from the doorway to the desk. It looked like an animal runway through a meadow. To the left a flickering red neon sign spelled out "Restaurant." To the right, twin doorways were identified as "Fillies" and "Colts," and patches, about shoulder height, next to the edge of the door, had been worn through the varnish and stained by human oils. Between the doors were two vending machines, one for cigarettes, tobacco or marijuana, and the other for pills and capsules.

At first Gavin thought no one else was in the room, and then an old woman struggled upright from an easy chair behind the desk. A straw-colored wig was slightly askew on her head, exposing dirty gray hair beneath, and makeup made a clown's mask of her face. Once, perhaps, she had been a woman with a figure, but the figure had drooped and inflated until it was virtually impossible to carry. Gavin suspected that even stand-ing was torment. But the woman had not given up. She pushed out her pillowy chest and gave Gavin a challenging smirk that cracked her makeup.

"You two together, lovies?" she asked.

"Yes," Gavin said.

"Yes and no," Elaine said.

"Well, which is it, dearies? You want one room or two?"

"One," Gavin said.

"Two," Elaine said simultaneously.

Gavin shrugged. "Two," he repeated. "Just trying to save you money," he whispered loudly to Elaine.

"You paying, love?" the landperson said suggestive-ly. "No need to be coy with me. I know what it's like to be young. God knows, I'm not so old yet I couldn't give some fella a good time in a motel room, but it's different when you're young and your skin is smooth and tight, and you're all warm and excited inside so you can hardly—"

"Two rooms," Elaine said, removing her credit card from a small case at her waist.

"Well," the landperson said, winking broadly at Elaine, "you do it the way you think you should. You know best, love. Trust your instincts. Play hard to get. Sometimes it works out. They respect you more, and it gets them even hotter."

"Just give us the keys," Elaine said.

"Sure, dearie," the landperson said, and dropped the card into a slot in her computer. She pushed a button, and two keys fell out the bottom, a receipt came out the middle, and the card came out the top. She handed them all to Elaine. "Staying more than an hour or so?" she asked.

"All night," Elaine said.

"That's good," the landperson said. "That's the best." She turned to Gavin. "She don't treat you right, you come see me," she said, winking with both eyes. Her face seemed contorted with message. "Was the time," she began, "when all the young men came in from Fort Riley to see Maude Frumkin. . . ."

They turned and left her remembering. They got back into the car, and Elaine drove them around to the appropriate doors. They were side-by-side on the first floor of a two-story wing. The balcony of the second floor sagged a bit, but it looked as if it would remain standing for another night.

Elaine handed Gavin a key. She looked at the number of the one she retained. "I'm going to clean up," she said. "Then we'll get some dinner, if you're hungry." She got out of the car, took a small red suitcase from the luggage compartment, opened the door of the motel room, entered, and closed the door firmly behind her.

Gavin stared after her for a moment, recalling the brisk way her hips had swayed under the skirt, and wished she wasn't so reactionary and such a cold fish. He carried the thought with him through the doorway of his room and into the shower, where he stood soaping himself in the lukewarm spray from the shower head, thinking of Elaine standing not two feet away from him doing the same thing. What a waste it was, he thought, and wondered when the playfulness which began under the motel sign had changed to reality.

Dinner was available in the small dark restaurant just off the lobby. The landperson was the waitperson, the barperson, and the cook as well. She waddled to the table they selected, put down two glasses of lukewarm water, lit a candle inside a vase of red glass, handed them two menus bound in imitation leather now old and cracked and smeared with the dirt of a thousand fingers.

Elaine ordered a bloody mary and made a face at the first swallow. Gavin got bourbon and water. It was fair bourbon, not very good water. He told Elaine that travelers should never order mixed drinks.

"They also should carry money," Elaine said.

Gavin stiffened and stood up. "If you're going to keep reminding me of your charity . . ." he began.

Elaine put a hand on his arm. "Don't be so touchy," she said, "and I'll try to be less bitchy."

Gavin thought of the meal to come and sank back into his chair. "Well," he said, and thought of her room next to his, and tried to be as charming as he could.

Elaine lifted her drink. "I hope," she said, smiling, "that she doesn't salt the drinks with aphrodisiacs."

Gavin laughed. "Then you noticed the name of the motel."

"Only when it was too late," she said, and laughed. "I was afraid you'd think I suspected you of amorous intentions. You should see my room—red plush on the furniture, pink-nylon sheets on the bed, and a mirror on the ceiling."

Something magical happened to Elaine's face when she smiled. Only ordinary in repose, it became beautiful when she smiled, illuminated from within like a painting by Michelangelo. And with her eyes turned on him, pupils large, Gavin felt a compulsion to make her smile again.

The food turned out to be frozen meals thawed in a supersonic oven and hardly worth the pride he'd swallowed. But Elaine smiled several times as he told her about life on the campus, about Karnival and classes and the Professor, about how he had been expelled from the campus, making it all seem unimportant and amusing.

She ended up laughing with him at his bravado at the campus gate and at his illusions about coming home, although he thought he detected a bit of moist sympathy in the corners of her eyes as he described the way his expectations had turned out.

So when they left the little restaurant and walked back to their rooms across asphalt still radiating the sun's heat, Gavin felt faint stirrings of anticipation as they stood at Elaine's door. She turned toward him, and he bent his face toward hers, and she said, "Good night, Gavin," and turned, slipped through her door, and was gone.

Gavin stood for a moment, poised over nothing, and then straightened and impulsively knocked at her door. The door opened, and Elaine stood in front of him, her head turned to one side, looking up at him. "Yes," she said.

Gavin looked at her, silhouetted against the light of the room, and whatever ideas he'd had fled from his mind. "Good night," he said, and turned and went into his own room.

His sheets were dark red, though patched and faded in places, and he lay awake for a long time staring up at the dark mirror in the ceiling where his shadowed face looked back down upon him. He imagined he saw other faces and other events behind his own, and he thought, "Ah, love, let us be true to one another. . . ." And when he slept, he dreamed of Jenny and Gregory and the whine of bullets above his head. He woke up when they began to hit his body, and he rose and urinated, washed his face, and put on his clothes and went out into the morning sunshine.

Elaine was already up. She had changed into a lightweight white dress. She was putting her red suitcase in the luggage compartment when he came out his door. They breakfasted on soggy toast and weak coffee while the landperson simpered at them.

"Didn't get much last night, did you, young fella?"

she said. "Went in separate doors and never crossed over once, did you, now?" She chuckled. "How would I know something like that, you want to know. Got me a surplus nightscope when the boys were still at Fort Riley. Good-hearted lads, they were. When they didn't have money, they brought what they could. Anyway, I keep an eye on my customers, you see. A little extra service for which there is no extra charge. You'd be surprised what I seen in my time. Should've come to me, though, young fella. Wouldn't have gone to bed with your guts aching. . . ."

But Elaine walked out before the landperson had finished her description of what Gavin had missed, and Gavin followed her, arriving at the car just before Elaine pulled it away.

They drove in silence. Gavin didn't know what Elaine was thinking about, but he was beginning the long, difficult process of sorting out what had happened to him in the past month. *Professor,* he thought, *what happened? What price learning? What cost wisdom?* And he thought he heard the Professor say, "The price is a man's peace of mind, and the cost is his life."

Shortly before they reached the turnoff to Abilene, they began to notice objects scattered on the highway: first colored pills and capsules, then a broken bottle, articles of clothing, strips of rubber from a tire, black skid marks on the pavement, and finally, as they rounded a gentle curve, the bus itself lying on its side beside the road, pieces of it strewn behind, and a jagged, doorlike piece of the rear-left side ripped up. The bus was like an animal they had seen bounding along, brimming with vitality, apparently indestructible and perhaps immortal, now lifeless and still.

Marks on the road and the grassy median between the divided highways, along with broken glass, twisted metal, oil spills, and dried brown stains on the edge of the pavement, suggested that the bus had skidded into the median and then into the opposite lane of traffic, hit a vehicle, rebounded into its own lane, over-balanced, and skidded on its side for more than a hundred yards.

Elaine stopped behind the torn bus and scrambled out of the car. She ran to the bus, across the scuffed and scarred shoulder, to the doorlike opening at the rear, Gavin just behind. As Gavin got closer, he could see that the opening had been cut and then the metal wrenched outward. A vision flashed through his mind of a giant hand reaching down with a can opener while the screams of the frightened and injured and dying sounded from within.

Elaine turned from the opening and vomited in the grass beside the road. Gavin climbed a collapsed tire and then walked along the side of the bus to the hole. He peered into the dark interior and then climbed down into the bus carefully so as to avoid the sharp edges of the metal, and then the blood, splashed and puddled everywhere, most of it dried and brown, but some still sticky.

The bus was empty. All of the down windows and some of the upper windows had been broken, and glass was splintered into scythes and daggers. Clothing was scattered throughout the interior, hanging from seats and racks as if tossed there by careless children. Luggage and packs had broken open and lay with their contents exposed like entrails. Gavin had once visited a packing house on a primary-school educational tour, and the bus smelled like the slaughter room.

Gavin climbed out over the seats before he, too, was sick. He went to Elaine. She was still bent over, but she straightened as he came close. He put his arm around her. She was shivering.

"They must have taken everybody to a hospital last night," he said.

Her shivers grew less violent. "Or to a morgue," she said. "Poor buggers. Like mayflies."

" 'Don't pity the dead,' the Professor used to say. 'All their questions have been answered.' "

"Life isn't all questions," Elaine said. She took a deep breath and moved back to the car.

"The Professor would say, 'No, it isn't all answers,' " Gavin said, and followed her.

When he reached the car she was looking down at

her right arm. A brown handprint marred the white skin. She rubbed it away. Gavin looked down at his bloody right hand and turned to scrub it clean with a handful of grass. When he turned, she was seated on the passenger side of the car.

"Why don't you drive?" she said.

He nodded and got into the driver's seat. He had never before driven an electric, but it wasn't difficult to adjust. The car accelerated smoothly, and they swung out around the corpse of the bus. "So long, rite of passage," he said.

The silence of the electric motors was distracting, as well as the lack of power in a sudden surge. Gavin soon found, as the landscape began to slip behind, that he had to plan his maneuvers early, making his turns in slightly wider arcs, swinging out to pass a car several yards sooner than usual, but the quiet, even movement was exhilarating, like riding a silky roller coaster, gliding, swooping, turning, climbing, without end, without effort, or like flying itself. He felt pleased with himself and pleased with the girl who sat brooding beside him.

He turned toward Elaine and smiled. After a moment she smiled back, and the warm autumn breeze poured over the windshield of the car, and he felt good. For a moment or two he forgot the bus, forgot the campus, forgot the Professor, forgot even Jenny, and he enjoyed the day for what it offered him.

He felt so good he did not even think when he saw ahead of them a solitary figure walking beside the road. Automatically he pulled up beside the figure and stopped. The hitcher was a young man, blond and curly-haired, irresistibly attractive, with a curly blond beard, blue eyes, and neat clothing.

"Gavin . . ." Elaine began when the car started to slow, and then it was too late.

"Get in, brother," Gavin said cheerfully, feeling his pleasure multiplied by the prospect of sharing it with the less fortunate.

"Thanks, brother," the young man said, and when Elaine didn't move, he tossed his pack into the back

seat and vaulted over the back of the car to land beside it.

"Glad to do it," Gavin said, smoothly gliding onto
the highway and toward the horizon, which had leveled
off as they got farther into central Kansas.

Elaine said nothing. Gavin could feel the weight of
her disapproval in the seat beside him, but the comforting presence of the freak in back more than made
up for it.

"Where from, brother?" he asked.

"All over, brother," the other said. "I've been seeing the country for the past year, and now I'm going
home."

"Home?" Gavin repeated. He remembered his own
recent euphoria, and he felt a wave of sympathy for the
young man.

"Home to Dallas," the hitcher said.

"You're going in the wrong direction, brother,"
Gavin said. "We're going to the West Coast. Texas is off
south."

"I know," the hitcher said, "but you got to take
what you can get. Rides are scarce these days. Seems
like people are scared of hitchers."

"I wonder why," Elaine said.

"Well, sister," the young man said, "people are
afraid of a lot of things."

"Like thieves, rapists, murderers," she suggested.

"Well, of course, sister," the hitcher said. "But you
can't go through life looking for thieves, rapists, and
murderers. You might find them. And you'll miss all
the wonderful things, all the beautiful people."

His enthusiasm was like laughter. Gavin found himself smiling. "Just what I told her," he said. "My
name's Gavin. She's Elaine."

"Chester," the hitcher said, touching his chest with
his index finger, "but some folks call me 'Chet' and
others call me 'Jet.' "

"Is that because you're fast?" Gavin asked.

"That, and I move around a lot," the hitcher said.
"So much to see, you got to keep moving. And I
never met a stranger. Right, brother?"

"Right," Gavin said. "Is that all you do, Jet? You're not a student?"

"Used to be a student," Chester said, "but I wanted to get into something more active. So I became an activist—an organizer."

"What do you organize?" Elaine asked skeptically.

"People," Chester said breezily. "Movements, demonstrations, riots . . ."

"Bombings?" Elaine asked. She seemed immune to his charm.

Chester leaned forward to tousle her hair. She pulled away from him. "No need to be unfriendly," he said. "Those, too, but that's all in the cause of a better world." He tapped Gavin on the shoulder. "Right, brother?"

"Right," Gavin said. He hadn't felt such solidarity since he left the campus, and he hadn't met such a likable, attractive young fellow for years.

"I can't tell you how grateful I am that you picked me up," Chester said.

"That's what brothers are for," Gavin said. Joy rose in his throat, to make talking difficult.

"You don't often find brothers driving new convertibles," Chester said. He sat on the edge of the narrow back seat, looking from one of them to the other with delight, the breeze coming over the windshield tumbling his blond curls, twisting its fingers in his blond beard.

"It's not my car," Gavin said.

"Gavin . . ." Elaine began.

But Gavin continued, unheeding. "It's the girl's here. I'm just a hitcher, like you." He wanted to increase the solidarity, build upon it. "Got a ride yesterday."

"Yesterday, brother?" Chester said. He looked at Elaine with even greater pleasure. "A rider yesterday, a driver today. That's progress."

"That's right," Gavin said. He had a feeling he was babbling, but he couldn't help it. "Spent the night at a motel just this side of Junction City."

"At a motel, eh?" Chester said, grinning at Elaine.

"In separate rooms," Elaine said, and then looked as if she wished she had remained silent.

"Of course, sister," Chester said. "But where did a little girl like you get a new convertible and the money to stay in a motel—in separate rooms? I know Gavin here wouldn't have any money."

"That's right, brother," Gavin said. "The possession of money is the first surrender to materialism."

"I worked for it," Elaine snapped. "That's something you wouldn't understand, because you expect everything to be handed to you."

"Oh, I work, too," Chester said cheerfully, "but not for *it*. Not for money or for what money can buy, but for liberty and justice and equality. Right, brother?"

"Right," Gavin said.

"I didn't pick Gavin up because he was a hitcher," Elaine said, "but in spite of it. I knew him, so it wasn't what you think."

"What do I think?" Chester asked, spreading his arms wide to indicate his insignificance, grinning to indicate his harmlessness. "What do I matter? I'm just a knight of the road, a pilgrim of the revolution. I've taken a vow of poverty, and my opinions are just as worthless."

"Personal property is an illusion, brother," Gavin said happily. "Those who need and those who have are rightful partners in a process of equalization."

"That's right, brother," Chester said.

"God!" Elaine said.

"All men have created the wealth that man has accumulated," Gavin continued, "and so its use and benefits belongs to all men—not to the few who have expropriated it and wrongfully withhold its use from others."

"Right, brother," Chester said.

"Nobody owns anything, and everybody owns everything," Gavin said triumphantly.

"Right, brother."

"Then why do I work and others loaf?" Elaine asked.

"That's your hangup," Gavin said. "If everybody refused to perform the meaningless tasks this twisted society demands, it would soon order things better—distribute goods equitably, give people what they need, and let them use their time in the only meaningful way we have."

"And what's that?" Elaine asked.

"Self-discovery," Gavin said. "The exploration of one's humanity. The perfection of one's personality."

"Right, brother," Chester said, his white teeth sparkling in the sun.

"And what of this personality," Elaine said skeptically, "where did it come from?"

"Why," Gavin said in surprise, "we're born human."

"And the baby in the crib," Elaine said, "he's supposed to lie there exploring his humanity, growing up, alone, perfecting his personality which was given him at birth through a casual meeting of chance genes?"

"Well, there's an interaction with other people," Gavin said. "Exploring one's humanity is done in relation to other people who are exploring their humanity. One reacts, involves oneself, builds a sane society . . ."

"It isn't all studying one's own navel?" Elaine asked. "Sometimes you study other people's navels? It seems to me what you have is a program of equating man's genetic traits with man himself, ignoring his environment, ignoring the social evolution of ideas, ignoring the dynamic tensions which have made man first intelligent and then conscious of himself as a developing species. What about the mysteries of life, the birth and death of suns and worlds and universes? Where does your exploration of humanity make room for quest, for the sense of being human by pitting oneself against great odds, great questions, great challenges?"

"They're nothing beside the human mystery," Gavin said. "Right, brother?"

"Right," Chester said, and in the same cheerful voice added, "Now pull over to that rest stop."

"You mean you need a rest stop already, brother?" Gavin asked.

"I think we all do, brother," Chester said.

"Gavin . . ." Elaine said in a frightened, warning voice.

"Don't turn your head, brother," Chester said calmly. "There's the point of a knife at the hinge of your jaw."

Gavin could not control his head. It jerked to the right, and he felt a sharp pain in his jaw at the same time as he saw, out of the corner of his eye, a switchblade in the steady hand of the angelic Chester.

"There, now," Chester chided him, "didn't I tell you not to turn your head? Now you've cut yourself."

Gavin turned his face back toward the road, holding his head rigid. Something touched his jaw, and he drew back.

"Now, don't get nervous, brother," Chester said solicitously. "I'm just wiping away the blood. There! It's only a small cut, really, and you'll hardly know it's there by tomorrow. It'll be nothing beside the big cut in your throat if you don't slow down right now. Be careful, girl, or this blade will get knocked right into the neck of your boyfriend, here. That's it, brother. Slow. Slow. Now, turn off here."

"He's no friend of mine," Elaine said sullenly.

"I'd judge differently, sister," Chester said, "but that don't matter."

Gavin had swung the car off the road onto the gravel drive that led up to a little park area and a stone hut with a red roof. The gravel gritted under the car's tires.

"Now, swing the car onto the grass behind the shelter house," Chester said. "That's great, brother. Now, stop the car. Turn it off. Put on the hand brake. Move slowly! I wouldn't want this knife to slip. That's it. Now, open the door and get out of the car. Easy. Slow. I'm right behind you with the knife at your back, getting out. There, now, brother. You're a good student. You learn good."

Gavin stood beside the yellow car, his muscles tight,

his back conscious of Chester behind him. "Jet," he
said, "you wouldn't do anything to a brother, would
you? Somebody who took you off the road?"

"I wouldn't have a chance to do it to anybody else,
would I?" Chester asked reasonably. "Anyhow, you
know how it is with private property, brother. You
just convinced me. Nobody owns anything. Everybody
owns everything. Well, brother, I'm claiming a little
bit of mine and relieving you of something you don't
own."

"I told you," Gavin said, "it's the girl's." Back behind the rest rooms, he had no view of the highway.
Which meant that nobody could see them.

"As I understand you," Chester said, "it doesn't
belong to her, either. Right, brother?"

Gavin suppressed the automatic response.

"Don't move hastily there, sister, or this knife . . .
you know? I'll tell you when to move. Until then, just
sit there. Now, brother, lie down, here in the grass on
your belly, and don't move. You, sister, will find a
piece of rope sticking out of the top of my pack. Pull it
out. That's right—keep on pulling, and it will all come
free. Very good."

Gavin felt a foot in the middle of his back, shoving
him deeper into the grass. He struggled to keep his
head up out of the grass. Maybe he could roll out from
under the foot, he thought, but he didn't believe that
Chester intended to harm them, talking so calmly, and
as long as he talked about rope, there was hope for a
fate less than final. "Someone's going to hear you,"
he said. "Better get out while you have time."

"Now, that would be too bad, wouldn't it?" Chester
said. "They'd get hurt, and you'd get hurt, and the girl
would get hurt, and all for nothing. Right, brother?
Now, sister, I want you to tie up your boyfriend here.
Hands behind you, brother. That's fine. You learn real
good, brother. Now, tie 'em tight, sister. Real tight."

Gavin felt the touch of Elaine's fingers for the first
time, and he thought, inappropriately, that we go
through life not touching other people, not being
touched. There was something electric and meaningful
about her fingers as they twisted the smooth rope, and

then the rope bit into his wrists and he grunted with surprise.

"Now, run the cord down and tie his ankles the same way, sister," Chester said cheerfully. "That's good. That's great! Now, flop him over."

Gavin felt himself turned like a sack of potatoes. He faced into a blinding sun and then twisted himself until he could look at Chester for the first time since the organizer, if that was what he was, had pressed a knife against his face. "You lousy son-of-a-bitch!" he said.

"Don't be bitter, brother," Chester said. He was standing behind Elaine, his arm around her waist familiarly, his right hand behind her. "I'm just engaged in a process of equalization between those who have and those who need. Me? I need to go to Texas, so I'm taking the car." He plucked the credit card from the case at Elaine's waist and dropped it into his pocket. "With a little help, I'll make it by noon tomorrow. Now, I want you to understand that it's in my best interest to leave you two here dead, but I don't want to do that. Too messy, for one thing. I hate a mess, and I do like you, brother, and I wouldn't want to do that to you. So don't make any noise. As you said, it might bring somebody, and I might be forced to act against my will and my basic altruism. Right, brother? Now, there's something else I need, and I don't want either of you to make a sound. I could gag you, but let's consider this a lesson in self-control. Something else to learn, brother."

The birds sang and the locusts buzzed, and Chester put his hand on Elaine's shoulder and then pulled his hand back and down. The dress peeled away from her body like flower petals opening to the sun. Elaine jumped and then stood quietly, her head up. She was slender and pale in the sunlight. Gavin struggled against the ropes that held him. "You son-of-a-bitch!" he said. "You bastard!"

"Easy, now," Chester said, displaying the knife in his right palm. The sunlight rippled along its edge. "I'm trying to control myself. You must do the same thing." His left hand was on Elaine's bare shoulder

as his right hand moved behind her back. Her brassiere pulled tight and then loosened. Chester brushed
the strap from her left shoulder, and the brassiere fell
forward onto the ground at Gavin's feet.

Gavin clenched his teeth and struggled, as he noticed, inconsequentially, that Elaine was not as flat-
chested as he had supposed. Her breasts were small
but well-formed and firm, and the nipples were virgin
pink. And then he noticed that her face was tight, as
if she were trying not to cry.

And then her underpants fell away, the elastic sev-
ered, like the brassiere strap, by Chester's knife.

"You shit!" Gavin shouted. "You lump of filth!"

But Chester was no longer listening. With one hand
he closed the switchblade and slipped it into his pocket;
with the other hand he swung Elaine around to face
him, his face beatific.

As if the clicking of the blade were a signal, Elaine
moved with the turning hand and drove her right knee
toward Chester's crotch. He partially blocked the blow
with his right thigh, but he winced when the knee hit
him. Then he grinned, straightening, and hit Elaine
in the face with his fist.

She exclaimed, and turned as if to run. But Chester
had her arm and was hitting her methodically with
his left hand.

"I'm glad," he said, grunting with each blow, "you
. . . did . . . that! I like . . . a girl . . . who . . . strug-
gles."

After the first blow, Elaine was silent, but she
fought with him, raking at him with her fingernails.
Once she broke free and ran a few steps before he
caught up with her.

Gavin watched helplessly, trying to free himself, until someone's foot caught him in the head and turned
the world black.

Gavin didn't know how long he was unconscious,
but the sun was still high in the sky when he felt wet
hands tugging at the rope around his wrists, and he
opened his eyes. With one tug the ropes fell away. His
hands were free.

"What was the matter with you?" a voice asked

faintly behind him. "I tied the rope so that you could get free just by pulling the loose end. He . . . he was so busy talking, he didn't notice."

Gavin sat up, his stomach sinking with the thought of his stupidity, of what he might have prevented. Elaine was on her hands and knees. She was still naked, but her white body now was covered with red welts and darkening bruises. Her head hung down, and he couldn't see her face. It was obscured by limp, sweat-wet hair. The car was gone. They were alone.

"Is he gone?" Gavin asked.

"All hitchers," Elaine said, her voice breaking, "should be taken out and shot."

"We can't let one pervert destroy our faith in all the wonderful people," Gavin said.

"Damn you, Gavin!" Elaine said. Her hand swung toward his head. Too late he saw there was a rock in it. "Damn you!" And the day returned to darkness.

7 ⇥ The Organization Man

Radicals always complain about the resistance of the establishment to change. They might reflect that the conservative renders as great a service to revolution as the rebel. If every damn-fool idea were accepted and implemented immediately, we would all be engulfed in chaos. The conservative weeds out the casual impulse, the inept proposition, the ridiculous proposal, and the half-baked concept; only the fittest survive—those changes which have the force of truth and the irresistibility of historical necessity, and even then many ill-conceived and ill-fated innovations fight their way through social inertia, like Prohibition, and law and order.

—THE PROFESSOR'S NOTEBOOK

Gavin was forced to slip into the hospital by stealth. He was late for visiting hours, and the visitor's gate kept rejecting him. The hospital, always authoritarian, was the last remaining citadel of tyranny and the frustration of the individual.

"Visiting hours are over," the gate said in a flat, mechanical voice. "You may return at ten tomorrow morning."

Gavin's patience accepted euthanasia. Beyond the gate was a waiting room with plastic chairs and tattered old videotapes. A dimly lit corridor on the other side of the waiting room extended into the remote bowels of the hospital itself. Gavin vaulted the gate. As his feet hit the floor, a metal door slid from the ceiling to close off the hospital corridor, and the gate said, more urgently, "You have violated a regulation of this hospital. Regulations within this building have the force of law. Within thirty seconds the front entrance will be closed, and anesthetic gas will be released. Anyone found here . . ."

But Gavin already had retreated over the gate and did not hear the remainder of the fate that awaited him if he lingered. He moved around the dark building checking windows and delivery chutes, but they were all locked. He wondered what the patients were doing, why they were lying there in the dark.

Eventually he came to the emergency door where he had brought Elaine the previous evening. The mechanized litter stood just outside the door on tracks that extended to the curb. Gavin looked around. He could see no one. He could hear nothing except the distant stridulation of a cricket.

He slid himself onto the litter. Immediately it moved with him through a door that opened automatically. As Gavin entered the emergency room itself, the overhead lights came on.

A brusque, competent voice said, "What is the nature of your condition?"

Gavin looked around. On the wall toward which the litter was moving was a pair of flat binocular eyes, and below that a mass of black, waving tentacles like a deranged octopus. A plaque above the eyes read: DIAGNOSTICOM.

Before he came within view of the eyes, before the eager sensors could wrap themselves around and insert themselves into his body, he had rolled off the litter and crouched under the diagnosticom.

"Malfunction," the diagnosticom said.

The litter moved on its tracks through a hinged door marked: SERVICE. Another litter came through the doorway to wait patiently for an emergency. The lights went out in the emergency room.

Gavin waited, too. Seated underneath the unblinking gaze of the diagnosticom, he listened to the chuckle-gurgle-click of the emergency room, and as his night vision returned, saw the shadowy, mysterious shapes of machinery waiting to serve torn flesh and adulterated blood with cold devotion. Gavin began to feel like part of the room, mechanical, senseless, waiting. He wondered what he was doing here, what drove him to seek out Elaine now in spite of difficulties.

Half an hour later, as his legs reminded him that they were not machines, an ambulance pulled up outside, and a moment later the litter presented an unconscious body to the diagnosticom. The body was wearing a helmet and a black leatherlike suit that now was torn and bloody. Gavin watched the diagnosticom send its exploring tentacles over the body, measuring, testing, analyzing, and then, with an air of decision, stitching here, setting a broken bone there, and spraying with a quick-setting cast, injecting anesthetics and antibiotics. When the tentacles withdrew, Gavin started. For a moment he had thought of himself as part of the medical team.

As soon as the sensors pulled away, the stretcher trundled off through a doorway marked: HOSPITAL. Gavin went with it, crouched low.

Once into the corridors, Gavin moved with less care. The occasional stretcher or wheelchair had no eyes, though they moved with calm certainty on their twin tracks, swiveling without hesitation through a confusion of switches at the intersection of corridors; and he could avoid the infrequent monitors.

As he moved along the white, antiseptic corridors, dimly lit by an occasional panel glowing in the ceiling, he looked for a signpost or a directory. He felt out-of-place at first, like a visitor to an alien world, and then gradually he was reassured. His hospital memories were more than a decade old. As a child he had languished for a week in an old-fashioned, unautomated facility with rheumatic fever. But gradually he became aware that the hospital incense was the same: the corridors smelled like antiseptic and anesthetic, like alcohol and ether and Novocain.

He had to climb a flight of stairs before he discovered rooms with beds in them, and beds with patients in them, and signs painted on white walls:

GERIATRICS, PEDIATRICS, HEMATOLOGY, UROLOGY, MATERNITY, GYNECOLOGY . . . At gynecology he hesitated and then trotted down the corridor, sneaking glimpses through open doorways at people lying in beds. Most of them were asleep, and all of them looked as if they had sprouted.

One elderly woman looked up as he looked in. She registered surprise and then alarm. A tube from her arm to the wall above her head jerked as she opened her mouth. Her alarm faded. Her eyes closed over enlarging pupils.

At the eleventh room along the corridor, as Gavin was about to give up and try another specialty, he saw Elaine's blond head among the black spaghetti of sensors and delivery tubes, and he moved quickly to her bedside and pinched the tube that delivered medicine to her arm. He draped a towel over the watchful eye on the wall and stuffed a handful of tissues into the microphone below the eye. When he looked down, Elaine was looking up at him.

"Wait a minute," she said, and slipped a hairpin over the tube to her arm. Gavin released his hold gradually. The makeshift clamp worked. The tube jerked as it tried to deliver a dose of sedative.

Elaine reached down beneath the sheet that covered her slender body and removed a sensor. It writhed like a black snake to regain its intimate location, but Elaine tied a knot in it, and after that it flopped aimlessly. "That feels better," she said. "What are you doing here?"

Her visible bruises were beginning to fade under the cybernated care, but she still looked battered. Her left eye was black, and her right cheek was swollen. A wave of sympathy washed Gavin's stomach. She looked very small and helpless in the hospital bed.

"I . . . I wanted to see how you were," he said. He moved a chair over beside the bed and sat down. Until then he hadn't realized how tired he was. It had been a busy day.

"Why didn't you come during visiting hours?" Elaine asked. "They don't let anybody in here after dark."

"It wasn't so bad," Gavin said. "I would have come earlier, but I was busy."

"You could have waited until tomorrow."

"I wanted to see you tonight."

"Why?"

Gavin shrugged. He didn't know why. "How are you?"

"I'm all right," she said. "I'm sorry I hit you. Did I do any damage?"

He touched the left side of his head. "Just a lump."

She smiled suddenly and then stopped at the reminder of her bruises. "I should have said, 'One lump or two?'"

He rejoiced at her smile. "It was my fault. I shouldn't have been so philosophical about your trouble."

"No," she said, "I shouldn't have been so upset. After all, what did it really matter? If I hadn't struggled, maybe he wouldn't have beat me up."

"You had every right . . ." Gavin began.

"But it was really unimp . . ." she said.

They both stopped and looked at each other.

"He really was a son-of-a-bitch," Elaine said, "wasn't he?"

"He was no brother," Gavin agreed.

"How did I get here? I don't remember anything until I woke up here this morning."

"I brought you in to the emergency room," Gavin said.

"You carried me? All that way?"

"It was only a few miles."

"That's a long way to carry somebody."

"You don't weigh much," Gavin said. He recalled the endless night staggering along the dark highway. By the time he reached Salina, he thought she weighed several hundred pounds.

She gave him a look of appreciation. "What did you do today?"

"There's a park down the street a bit, across from the City-County Building," he said. "I slept there in the park under some old newspapers I found in a trash barrel, until the sun woke me. I cleaned up in the basement washroom of the City-County Building, and then I tried to report what had happened."

"You tried!" she exclaimed.

"You don't understand how things are," he said defensively.

The City-County Building had been new and modern some twenty or thirty years before, but now the painted walls were blackened from the touch of hands and careless mops, the corridor tiles were worn and warped, the dust of neglect had accumulated in the corners.

Gavin walked along the corridors with an odd reluctance, as if he had no reason to be there, but he attributed his unease to the natural feelings of a revolutionary for the environs of government.

He found what was left of an abandoned jail—the rusty bars on the window testified that it had been a jail—but the offices that led to the cells were vacant and dusty. He wandered the corridors, reading the names on signs jutting out above the doors: REGISTER OF DEEDS, CLERK, EXTENSION SERVICES, COMMISSIONERS, HEALTH, TREASURER, DATA PROCESSING, MENTAL HEALTH, COUNTY JUDGE, MAINTENANCE SUPERINTENDENT, COUNTY ZONING ADMINISTRATOR, PROBATE JUDGE, PUBLIC WORKS, FIRE DEPARTMENT, WATER DEPARTMENT, SANITATION, RECLAMATION, CITY ENGINEER, PARK AND RECREATION, BUILDING INSPECTOR . . .

He found a public telephone and checked the directory, but it listed no police or sheriff offices, and the front of the directory, which listed numbers to call in emergencies, offered fire and ambulance and ombudsman. The offices of the county judge were locked and empty. Finally Gavin entered the office of the fire department.

In the outer office a middle-aged woman in a stylish brown wig looked up from some kind of console with little lights that shone steadily in blue or flickered in yellow or red. "Police?" she said. "You don't have a fire to report?" She glanced back at the telltales in front of her.

"No," Gavin said. "I want to report a . . . a theft and . . . personal attack."

The woman looked at Gavin as if he had spoken Hindustani.

"I wish to report the commission of a crime," Gavin tried again.

The woman glanced back at her console. "I'm sorry," she said, "but we only handle fires."

"Isn't there anybody in this building who cares if someone commits a crime?" Gavin asked plaintively.

"Oh, we all *care*," the woman said sympathetically. "It's just that it's none of our *business*."

"What would you do if someone raped you?" Gavin asked in desperation.

"Are you threatening me, young man?" the woman asked sharply. "If you are, I must warn you that I am an adept in the latest form of personal defense, and you will be very sorry if you lay a hand on me."

"No," Gavin said humbly, "all I'm asking is, who would you report it to."

She thought a moment. "To my husband, perhaps," she said, "although he would only send me back to my personal-defense classes. I must say, young man, you do pose some difficult questions. Perhaps what you need is some personal assistance. If you've met with some misfortune and you need some help—food or clothing or funds to tide you over—there's a charity just down the street. They don't have much to do; it's really more a release for the charitable impulses of our citizens rather than an essential service. You go in there, young man, with your story of theft and rape, and they'll fall over you with excitement. They won't be able to do enough for you—new clothing, a shaver or depilatory, perhaps a little spending money. Of course, if you've been attacked—I didn't know men could be raped—did you meet up with a pervert who sodomized you? I mean, you shouldn't be reluctant to say so. The hospital is right down the street past the park if you need treatment. It's all free, of course."

"All I want," Gavin complained, "is an office to report . . ."

The woman looked back at her console. "Now, look

what you've made me do," she said, and pushed a button.

Gavin turned toward the door. As he reached it, the woman at the console called after him, "There's always the ombudsman." ·

The ombudsman. The last recourse. Of course. Gavin realized that he should have thought of that himself.

The door of the ombudsman's office was open. The ombudsman himself was seated with his back to the door, leaning back against his dark wooden desk, gazing out the window toward the little park where Gavin had spent the night. The walls of the small room had been painted a light tan. There was an old Persian rug on the floor, some Currier and Ives prints on the wall, and a large coffee urn on a table under one of the prints.

Gavin hesitated outside the door, and then, shaking off his reluctance, stepped forward into the room. At the sound, the man at the desk turned slowly. His gray hair clung tightly to his head; his features were prominent and the skin tight over them, as if his hair had pulled it back.

"How may I help you?" he asked. His voice was rich and resonant, and he sounded as if he really wanted to help.

Gavin found it difficult to speak, and then the words all came out in a bunch. "Yesterday, just a few miles east of town, a young woman and I were attacked by a young hitcher we had picked up. I was bound at the point· of a knife, and the girl was beaten and raped, and her car and credit card were stolen."

"I see," the ombudsman said. "And what do you wish me to do with this information?"

Gavin stopped and realized, inconsequentially, that he could smell the pleasant odor of hot coffee. "The hitcher should be apprehended and arrested," he said.

"You want him punished?"

"No," Gavin said. "I mean, yes, of course."

"You expect that this will deter him from committing similar crimes."

"Not exactly . . ." Gavin began.

"You're thinking that this will repair the damage done to you and the girl."

"Well, no . . . I mean, he won't do it to anybody else."

"The good of society is what you have in mind."

"Of course," Gavin said gratefully. "As well as the recovery of the girl's car and credit card."

"By now," the ombudsman said calmly, "the hitcher could be anywhere."

"That's true, but—"

"The first thing he would have done, if he managed to circumvent the identification, is clean out the girl's credit."

"At least there'd be a record of where and when . . ." Gavin pointed out.

"And perhaps he has arrived at wherever he was going and has abandoned the car."

"He said he was going to Dallas."

"Of course he would have told you where he was really going."

"Maybe not, but surely you can at least take the man's description, and the description of the car, and try to track him down so that he won't continue to steal and rape."

"For the good of society."

"Yes, of course." Gavin was becoming irritated at all the pointless questions.

The aquiline face of the ombudsman registered only an inner tranquillity. He put his hands carefully together, fingertip against fingertip. "I am concerned not with the good of society but with the good of the individual. My function is to protect the individual against social injustice."

"Well?" Gavin asked.

"But not against individual injustice. By the nature of my responsibility, you see, I must place myself on the side of the hitcher, who is in the most danger from society."

"But who is to protect the individual against him?" Gavin complained.

"No one. Except perhaps the individual. You see, even if I took the information you wish to give me,

I would have no one to accept it from me. We have no police, no one to track down the individual criminal, no one to try the accused, no one to incarcerate the guilty, no one to rehabilitate the prisoner, no one to commute the sentence or parole the convict. We have done away with all that."

"Then anyone can commit an act of violence or of theft against someone else and get away with it!" Gavin protested.

"Why should anyone want to?"

"Profit. Need."

"There are easier ways to get money. No one is in need."

Gavin thought about Chester's clear enjoyment of what he was doing. "Well, passion, then."

"Crimes of passion are impossible to prevent and seldom repeated."

"A criminal personality," Gavin ventured.

"Criminal personalities are infrequent, difficult to identify, and even more difficult to convict."

"This particular criminal personality was pretty easy to identify," Gavin said grimly.

"Perhaps," the ombudsman conceded. "Would you like a cup of coffee?"

"No!" Gavin said, and then, recalling the state of his stomach, said, "All right. Thank you."

The ombudsman rose athletically, gracefully, and poured two cups. As he handed one to Gavin, he said, "The problem that we faced a few years ago was the nature of society. We had solved most of the problems that led to criminal activity—"

"Come, now," Gavin protested.

The ombudsman raised one hand. "Hear me out. No one was hungry. All social services were free, financed out of the growing abundance of plentiful energy and cybernation. Anybody who wanted more than a minimum annual income could get a job."

"There aren't that many jobs," Gavin said.

"As an employment service of last resort," the ombudsman said, "I never have been unable to find some kind of suitable employment for anyone who wanted it: there always is need of labor to restore the land

and the waters to the condition of cleanliness and vitality in which we found them. We have, of course, our voluntary poor—our freaks and our indolent—but we cannot force them to labor, even if we wished to."

"What does all this have to do with criminal activity?"

"I'm getting to that," the ombudsman said. "We also have made education universally available, as well as liberating the underprivileged child from his poverty-stricken environment through creches and environmental enrichment. No longer is there any excuse for people to grow up deprived, maladjusted, perverted."

"Except," Gavin said, "for the fundamental injustice of a society which is based on unnecessary labor, which discriminates between the able and the unable, between the talented and the untalented, the motivated and the unmotivated, the deserving and the undeserving . . ."

"We have tackled," the ombudsman said, "what Gerard Piel called in 1961 'the nation's principal economic problem—that of certifying its citizens as consumers of the abundance available to sustain them in tasks worthy of their time.' I could point out that this is the most 'just' society man has ever known. But that isn't the point; nothing ever will seem just to the young. They have forgotten history and feel no gratitude to the past. What I am trying to demonstrate, however, is that the cybernated abundance which made possible our economic and social equality might have demanded payment from us. We might have had to pay for it with our personal freedom."

"I don't understand you," Gavin said.

"Our computerized world, the method of production and distribution, the individual records essential to the system, had implicit in them the possibility of government control of the individual," the ombudsman said calmly. "More than twenty years ago the big topic of concern was the threat to personal freedom, credit checks, government dossiers, wiretaps, police snooping, anonymous complaints. . . . We've done away with all that. It happened after the law-and-order riots of

1985. Purposefully, consciously, we have restrained the intrusion of computerized society into the affairs of the private citizen. The result: today everyone is free to be just as idiosyncratic, just as cantankerous, just as crazy, just as out-of-step as he wishes. But there's a price."

"What's that?"

"He also is free to be just as criminal as he wishes. You see, we could only get personal freedom by eliminating the investigatory arms of government, and I'm here to see that they do not get reestablished, that nobody starts using the information stored in the computers and their capabilities for intrusion and manipulation against the people. We phased out the police and the courts and the prisons. In this interim period, we haven't spread the information around, but as a matter of fact anybody can get away with anything that his neighbors or his victims will allow. Oh, there still are civil trials, and we don't allow conspiracies to go unchecked. You aren't suggesting, I take it, that this hitcher was part of some conspiracy?"

Gavin shook his head. There seemed nothing else to say.

"Well, then, we are helpless to apprehend him or to punish him. In the larger sense, of course, the hitcher was enjoying his basic liberty—although, to be sure, at the expense of someone else's liberty of action and enjoyment." The ombudsman put the tips of his fingers back together. "It is a difficult question. The act of rape might well be called an expression of existential freedom."

The Professor had once referred, with contempt, to Guillaume Apollinaire's opinion that the Marquis de Sade was the freest man who ever lived.

The ombudsman was silent for a moment, contemplating his tented fingers. "We can, of course, try to correct the wrong done to the girl. Medical care . . ."

"That she's already getting."

"We will place a hold on her credit account if it has not already been cleaned out, and we can provide some compensation for the unfortunate act committed against her and the loss she has suffered, as well as advice not to pick up hitchers. If you will have her get in touch with me . . ."

The account, from the appearance of Elaine's face, was no more satisfying for her than it had been for Gavin. The pinched tube jerked once more in an effort to calm her down. "That's why the monitor wanted my credit-card number, though I don't think there's any hope. Chester has done this before, and he'll do it again until he's stopped."

"You can try yourself, when you're able," Gavin said defensively.

"I'm not blaming you," Elaine said. "It just hurts to have him go free like this, enjoying himself. Talk about injustice . . ."

"The ombudsman said, 'Injustice endured by the individual is preferable to justice imposed by the state.' Well," Gavin said, getting up, "I've got to be getting back. I tried to call my parents, but they refused to answer. If you called them, I'm sure they'd come and get you." He hesitated. "I'm sorry you had to go through this. I feel responsible for that."

Elaine studied his face. "Don't. It was my own damn-foolishness."

"I hope you can forget it, anyway," Gavin said. "I hope your young man will make it up to you."

"What young man?"

"Well, maybe he isn't young. I assumed—you know—the one you said you were interested in when I . . . suggested you might be involved with my father."

"Oh," Elaine said, "that young man! Well, we'll have to see. What are you going to do now?"

"My plans haven't changed," Gavin said. "I'm still heading for the West Coast. But I'm going to have to delay a week or two while I accumulate a little money. I accepted a free meal from the charity the fireperson told me about, and some clean clothes, some toilet items, and a little cash to get me through the day. Then I enrolled in the local technical institute."

"Isn't that a comedown?" Elaine asked.

"It's just for the educational allowance," Gavin said. "Of course, it won't hurt me to learn something about computer programming or fusion generators."

"Fusion generators?" Elaine asked.

Into her question Gavin read a picture of stupid students tending miniature hydrogen bombs. "Only mockups," he said.

"How's it going?" she asked.

It was an idle question, and Gavin knew it was time to leave. "They're a different breed. Very practical. Desires, but no curiosity. However, I think they can be organized . . ." He leaned over and removed the hairpin from the tube in Elaine's arm. It thumped triumphantly.

"Organized!" she said distantly.

"I feel an obligation to lead them toward a moral commitment," Gavin said. "Up to the point beyond which there is no turning back." It was true, he realized. He had never been an activist before, but now he felt a strange compulsion to convert the heathen.

"Obligation," she muttered, trying to struggle up out of the sedation that overwhelmed her.

He bent over the bed and gently kissed her bruised lips. She would never know, but he would know, and that was enough. Her lips were pleasant, but there was no excitement. "Good-bye, Elaine," he said, and felt a twinge of regret for what might have been.

The technical institute was situated at the edge of what had once been a military air base, and the runways still extended through tall grass and weeds and sunflowers into the remote distance like mysterious markings on a Peruvian plateau. They served no purpose any more, although occasionally a small electric helicopter landed on a pad located across the field or a large passenger ship drifted in from the east or the west.

The buildings on this side of the old field were new. The old frame structures and barracks had been pulled down over the years, and woven and prefabricated plastic buildings and domes had been erected on concrete foundations. The institute was a thoroughly mod-

ern and up-to-date facility, in keeping with the
modern and up-to-date subjects taught within its walls:
electricity and electronics, mechanics, plumbing, recycling and reclamation, construction, carpentry, ac-
counting and bookkeeping, secretarial skills, data
recording, computer programming and repair, cybernation maintenance, aeronautics, solar-cell construction,
electrical generating, motion-picture projection, camera
operation, audio recording, hydrogen-fusion operation,
power broadcasting, electrical space propulsion, satellite construction and repair, telemetry, and many more.
There were so many subjects because the institute
taught practical application and no theory; each subject
had to be approached as an isolated series of actions
to be memorized.

The students were just as practical. They wore
jeans and knit shirts and tennis shoes, women as well
as men, and Gavin was one of them. Apparently this
uniform from a few decades ago had been adopted
not only by the institute but by the charity that had
given Gavin his clothing. But Gavin was not one of
them as they walked along the asphalt path, almost
marching, toward their classes in one of the domes.
He walked to one side and out of step, and listened to
them talk about the kinds of jobs they would get when
they were graduated and what they would do with
their earnings.

"I'm going to Kansas City," a young man said,
"and get me a job in recycling. They say it's better
than mining. Trash is the nation's third-largest re-
source."

"I got me a job already," a young woman said.
"Foreman in a solar-cell factory in Phoenix. Gonna
make five hundred a week and buy me a cottage on
the Gulf of California and get me a boat."

"Plumbing's got tradition as well as a future," said
another young man. "I got a job as an apprentice
in Coffeyville, and when the old man retires, he's gonna leave me the business. He promised. Gonna be
rich."

"Five percent of the people control ninety-five per-

cent of the nation's wealth," Gavin said conversation-
ally.

The students near enough to hear looked at Gavin
curiously. "Yeah," a young woman said, "and I'm
gonna be one of them."

"She may, too, you know," said a quiet voice beside
Gavin's ear.

Gavin controlled a start. Trotting beside him was an
older man. He was shaped a bit like a bird, with thin
legs leading to a body bowed out in front from chin
to waist; a red vest and a blue jacket were buttoned
tightly across the bulge, as if to contain it. His face
was like a rounded football, broadening from thinning
brown hair toward bushy eyebrows and red cheeks
and then tapering again to a narrow chin.

"New boy?" he said to Gavin. His blue eyes were
shrewd and observant. Gavin nodded. "Old boy," he
said, gesturing toward himself. "Superintendent. Keep
in touch, right?"

Gavin nodded again.

"Where'd you get idea about wealth?" the superintendent asked, elevating his eyebrows.

"Common knowledge," Gavin said airily, unconsciously falling into the superintendent's fragmentary
speech pattern. But he wondered: where had he heard
it? "Common knowledge," the Professor said once, "is
another name for common ignorance." And another
time, "There are some kinds of folk knowledge which
have been so often repeated that we can never now
know the truth: whether coffee grounds are good or
bad for kitchen drains, whether adults should or
should not drink milk, whether wet feet cause colds.
Along with this we can include most economic information."

"Not true," the superintendent was saying. "Real
per-capita income doubled between thirties and seventies; doubled again since then. Portion of national
income going to laboring man climbed from fifty-three
percent to eighty-three percent since 1900. Since 1929
share of national income of top fifth has dropped from
fifty-five percent to thirty percent, while three middle

fifths improved twenty percent, and bottom fifth by five percent."

"I don't believe it," Gavin said.

"Facts," the superintendent said.

"Whose facts?"

The superintendent looked at Gavin more closely. "Organizer?" he asked cheerfully. Gavin shook his head. "Revolutionary?"

"Isn't everybody?" Gavin asked.

"Not here," the superintendent said. "Practical men and women. Know what they want. Motivated. Ambitious. Black, white, red, brown. All colors. Not sophisticated, but backbone of society. Impatient with words. Good with hands. Word of caution: don't stir up."

Gavin gestured impatiently. "What's the use of a place like this?"

"Biggest social problem—maintenance," the superintendent said. "Machines break down. Can't fix themselves. Yet. Biggest economic problem—opportunity. Upward mobility. Opportunity here. Right?"

Gavin shook his head. "The biggest economic problem is distribution. Nobody needs to work."

"Not true," the superintendent said. "For many, work is psychological necessity. Maybe for all, though not proven. All people not alike. Some prefer leisure. Others, work. Some wish to improve economic situation. Others, develop selves. Give both chance."

"If that were so," Gavin said, "you wouldn't have to brainwash these kids into a psychological need for material possessions. And you wouldn't have to buy their services by paying them wages while those who prefer leisure subsist on the minimum annual income."

"People must learn what to do with leisure . . . and income. In spite of improvements in income and leisure between thirties and seventies, no social harmony: racial riots, juvenile gangs, city-life decay, national morals deterioration. Socialism also effective in producing goods, but no better in creating satisfaction. So—provide opportunity for those who want it, leisure for those who don't. Let people choose between work and affluence, and freedom and necessities. Nobody starves."

"The poor have you always with you," Gavin said, and he remembered the Professor saying, "Of course you do. You forget the past and re-create the poor by definition."

"Anyway," the superintendent said, "warning: if not here as serious student, may be trouble. Students here not idle, trouble-seeking bourgeois children. Hungry, rising lower class. May not appreciate revolutionary rhetoric."

"The biggest social problem is justice," Gavin said with simple dignity, "and the truth is recognized by everybody."

"Every man has own version of truth but can't force it on reality without occasionally reality biting back," the superintendent said, and trotted away on his spindly legs, puffing like a toy steam engine.

By the time Gavin got to the classroom building, the students already were scattered to their stations. As he entered through glass doors that swung open as he approached, he saw students in open cubicles partitioned from their neighbors and facing a large cylinder that rose from floor to ceiling. At the open end of the cubicles a corridor circled the exterior wall. Each cubicle was devoted to a different subject, and each had its own special equipment and demonstration facilities, but each had a television screen set into the slight curve of the cylinder surface that formed the front wall.

In the first booth a girl was hefting a pipe wrench, and the television screen showed a real wrench turning a real nut, and then a line drawing of wrench and nut progressively unloosening and tightening. A practical voice said, "The first thing a plumber must do is be sure the water is turned off. Once this is done, he is ready to undo the affected pipes. The wrench is fitted to the nut, or to the pipe or joint, as the case may be. This is accomplished by turning the screw at the base of the jaws. Now the wrench is applied and

turned by applying the appropriate amount of force
to the end of the wrench—clockwise for tightening,
counterclockwise for loosening. The demonstration pipe
is on your right. Now adjust the wrench to the size of
the joint. That's good. Turn the wrench counterclockwise. Stop! You have forgotten the first thing a plumber
must do; you forgot to turn off the water. . . ."

The young woman turned a damp face toward Gavin and grimaced. She wasn't pretty, but she had an
expressive face and a lively look. Gavin smiled at her
and thought that he would like to get acquainted.

The next booth seemed filled with trash, but Gavin
realized almost immediately that it was only simulated
trash. A voice was talking about the separation of
metals by magnets, while the television set showed
illustrations. The student in the cubicle watched crit-
ically as trash in the receptacles around him was emptied automatically into a large bin. From the bin it was
augured into rotating drums, where cans and other
metallic objects stuck to the sides while paper and food
wastes continued on out the other end.

The next cubicle contained a student and a motion-
picture projector and a stack of film cans. A voice was
telling him to check the name of the film on the can
and compare it with a list on the side of the projector, check the date and the time against his own
calendar watch, open the can and check the name on
the end of the film against the name on the outside
of the can, and if all these checked out, insert the film
into the projector with the white side of the film
reel facing out.

"The projector will do the rest," the voice said.
"Sometimes there will be something that will not check
out. In that case, you must know what to do. First . . ."

The student looked puzzled and reached toward the
pill dispenser beside the television set on the forward
wall. The sign above it said "Motion Picture Projection, Lesson Number Five."

The cubicles became more complicated as Gavin
moved farther around the corridor: computer maintenance had a real IBM 7000, secretarial training fea-
tured a voicewriter which printed the words spoken into

it on the television screen and corrected the student's pronunciation, solar-cell construction and molecular circuits, household wiring diagrams, stud hammers and laser saws, nuclear-fusion control. . . .

When Gavin passed the nuclear-fusion cubicle, he heard a voice saying, "The satellite is now an expanding ball of flame composed of hydrogen and helium and a lot of metallic atoms slightly contaminated with carbon compounds." The television screen was a mass of fire and hurtling objects.

The console in front of the student rippled with blinking lights and then turned dark. "Now," the voice said, "let us begin again. Ordinarily the fusion generator will function perfectly without human supervision. Perhaps once in ten years . . ."

The next cubicle was labeled "Computer Programming." It contained a keyboard, a voicewriter, a chair, and the ubiquitous television screen. The chair was empty. Gavin sat down in it, and the screen lit up with kaleidoscopic patterns.

"I am a Mark Seven computer instructor," a speaker said, "and this is computer programming. Please place your identity card on the readin plate, and take one of the pills marked 'Computer Programming, Lesson Number One.' "

Gavin took one of the pills and stuck it in a pocket. "My identity card is lost and has not yet been replaced. My name is Tom Gavin. I just enrolled."

"Very well, Tom," the voice said. "You must take the pill, you know. It won't do you any good in your pocket."

Damn! Gavin thought. Big Brother, for sure. He took the pill out of his pocket and swallowed it. It probably wouldn't do him any good, but it shouldn't do him any harm.

"Now," the voice said, "this is a picture of a modern electronic computer." The kaleidoscope patterns settled into the picture of a rectangular machine about four feet tall, judging from the height of the woman beside it. "As a programmer, you will not ordinarily be relating to the computer directly. Most of your work will be at a remote station much like the one you

have before you now. In order to become a skillful
programmer, you must become familiar with your
Mark Two keyboard and your Mark Three voicewriter.
In the process . . ."

"Get on with it," Gavin muttered.

"You must learn to pronounce your words more
accurately and say them clearly," the instructor said.
"The voicewriter is remarkably flexible, but it cannot
be expected to cope with sloppy diction or regional dia-
lects or slang usages. Now, repeat clearly after me,
'Clear. End. Readout. . . .' "

Lunch was a communal meal in the commons, another of the large domes. In this one the big central
column contained a computer and prepared meals on
metal trays. Students studied the menu in the computer readout windows, pressed a series of buttons, and
received their selections as the tray slid out of a slot
beneath the buttons. Students tried to be early; late-
comers had to take potluck. And once the half-hour
period for serving was over, the column sank into the
floor until it was only a platform about three feet off
the ground.

Gavin sat hunched over his meal, digging at pork
chops and mashed potatoes and green beans and thinking about the fate that had placed him here among
mechanics and mindless consumers. "What to them,"
he thought, "are Plato and the swing of Pleiades?"

He had never believed in any of the superstitions
that had sprouted on campus—not astrology or scien-
tology or satanism or spiritualism or theosophy. He
had not become a Jesus freak or a member of the
Aetherius Society or the Feedback Church or a Hare
Krishnan. But he had a strange feeling of certainty
that he had been brought to this place for a purpose,
and that purpose was to lead these poor benighted
mechanics into a realization of the true state of the
world. He felt words welling up in his throat unbidden,
a compulsion to spring up and shout them like challenges to the universe.

Revolutionary consciousness—that's what they
needed. The first thing, he decided, was to discover

causes of dissatisfaction in their personal situations and then lead them against the administration. Nonnegotiable demands, he thought. Unconditional amnesty.

"Where do they get this lousy food?" he said to his neighbors. "Out of the reclamation project?" Actually, it was pretty good food, but Gavin didn't reflect on the irony of the criticism from a person who had subsisted for almost four years on greasy hamburgers. He had to repeat his comment more loudly before his right-hand neighbor turned.

"I see you finished it."

Gavin shrugged and turned his attention to the center platform. A film had just finished about employment opportunities and fringe benefits at IBM, and a dark-haired woman stood up in the center of the circular platform. She was dressed in IBM tans, and she was apparently accustomed to speaking in the round. Her voice was confident and rich. It rang with power.

"As the personnel director for IBM," she said, "I want you to know that all the statements made in the film were false."

That quieted the audience. They turned their attention to the platform.

"They are false," the recruiter said, "because they no longer reflect the current conditions at IBM. Since that film was completed, the working week has been reduced from twenty hours to eighteen; these can be scheduled in three days or five. Stock options have been improved—a schedule will be available following my brief talk. Country-club dues *and* marina rentals have been authorized. Free group tours overseas are available as an alternate for those who aren't sportspersons. The rent allowance has been raised. Retirement now is at the age of forty-five—with full pay and a crash course on leisure activities and avocations.

"We know that you're here because you aren't satisfied with a handout from society. You want to do honest work. You want to become a producer, not just a consumer. You want to be an owner, not a renter. Some of you will go on to become part of management itself.

"I could continue, but those of you who have

personal questions can see me privately this afternoon. Oh, yes—the bonuses. We are prepared to offer substantial cash bonuses for those of you who sign up today. We want all you computer-maintenance students and programmers to know that we're eager for you to join IBM and become a member of our happy family."

Gavin was enraged. Rage was an emotion that started in his stomach and radiated out to his skin in hot waves. He could not remember when he had been so moved, and he found himself at the base of the round platform. The recruiter had walked off the platform. Gavin leaped up where she had been.

"Fellow students," he shouted.

A clattering of silverware and metal trays stilled as students turned toward the platform.

"You are too smart to be taken in by a patter of slick talk by the business conspiracy," Gavin said. "That's no happy family they're talking about. That's a savage, cannibalistic world out there, and they want you to come and be the food. They don't want to give you anything. They want to take from you your lives, your free time, your free will, and your basic humanity.

"They don't have anything to give you, because IBM belongs to you, General Electric belongs to you, Xerox belongs to you, the electric company and the nuclear-fusion company—all of them belong to you, because you are the people, and the people created them and built them. You own them, and you are entitled to all the wealth that pours from them, not just a pittance, what they spill from the horn of plenty."

He was moving them. He could sense their response, and the feedback made his voice stronger and his words more eloquent.

"This isn't a technical institute," he said. "This is a school for slaves. They're teaching you to be slaves to a society which doesn't even need slaves; they're forging your chains with promises, and binding them together with lies. They want you to trade your precious humanity for the role of a robot in this machine world. You're being brainwashed with pretty pictures of a wonderful world of consumption. Consume! Consume! Consume! That's all you mean to IBM. Someone has to devour the surpluses of the industrial machine."

They were on their feet now.

"Well, don't fall for their sucker game. Revolution is the only answer. Reform society! Take over the factories! Set them to turn out what people need, not what the factories want to sell. Don't let them parcel out your patrimony, give away in niggardly charity what the masses possess by right. The world was made for people, not for machines, and it should be run for people, by people, not for something called profits or production. Rise up and demand your rights!"

Some of them were shaking their fists at the ceiling. Soon they all would be ready to march with him. But —march where? And then, as he knew it would, inspiration came to him.

"Now, many of you are thinking: 'What can I do?' " Gavin said more quietly. "You're saying to yourself: 'I'm only one person. How can I fight a system, a whole society?' Well, I'm here to tell you that you're not alone. There's a whole world of brothers and sisters out there who want to join you, who are waiting to rise with you in the final revolution of humanity."

They were roaring now. He had them. He had them.

"But the time for that is not yet. We have to start where we are, and we are here at the technical institute. First we must reform this reactionary place. We will go to the administration. We will demand a revolutionary organization, a council of students to make whatever rules need to be made. We will run our lives through participatory democracy.

"We will demand better food. We will demand freedom—freedom to dress as we please, to come and go as we please, to go to class when we please and if we please. We will demand human instructors to be hired and fired by the students. We will demand the banning of recruiters from the campus. Our demands

will be nonnegotiable, and the first demand will be amnesty. Let's go! Let's take over the superintendent's
office!"

He leaped from the platform and ran toward the
nearby door. The students roared behind him.
"Come on!" he shouted, waving an arm in the classic
pose of the leader of troops, and they followed. Exulta-
tion rose in his throat like the sweetness of forbidden
fruit; and power was like an aura around him, lifting
his feet from the ground, propelling him forward.

He heard footsteps running beside him. He turned
his head, a word of brotherhood on his lips, until he
saw that it was the superintendent. He was running
well for a man who carried so much weight above the
waist, but he had difficulty speaking, particularly with
the crowd noise behind.

"Think . . . better . . . turn . . . . left," he gasped.
"Evade . . . mob!"

"You don't like it so well now," Gavin said triumphantly. "You're not so sure of your students as
you were."

"Don't . . . be . . . silly!" the superintendent got out.
"You! Get . . . away . . . while . . . you . . . still . . . can!"

And then he drifted back and away. Gavin was almost to the administration building, where he had enrolled the day before and received an advance on his
student allowance. He slowed as he neared the door,
and turned to guide the crowd, and the crowd ran over
him.

He got up, thinking "that's a stupid way to start a
takeover," and a large dark-haired student knocked
him down, shouting that he was a lousy rabble-rouser.

"You do that again," Gavin said, "and I just may
not lead this revolution."

Someone else kicked him and called him a chicken-
shit saboteur. And then they were all beating and kick-
ing him, each blow accompanied by an appropriate
epithet: liar, spy, seditionist, traitor, renegade, degen-
erate, pervert, scum. . . .

Finally, battered and hurting, he found himself lost
in a surging forest of legs, and he crawled between
them on hands and knees to the edge of the turbulence,

and then he was out of their shadow, on grass, with the sun shining down upon him. He would have collapsed, but he drew upon some secret reservoir of will and pulled himself up and staggered away from the crazy mob. When he had gone about ten paces, a man shouted behind, "There he is," and the pursuit began.

"Many a man," the Professor said once, "who thinks he is leading a charge actually is being pursued by a mob."

Gavin had limped only a few feet when an old steam-turbine panel truck pulled up beside him, the right door swinging open like a wall in front of him.

"Get out of the way!" he shouted.

"Get in!" someone yelled back. "Get in, you damned fool!"

He peered into the truck. A girl was sitting in the driver's seat. She was gesturing for him to get in. The girl was Elaine. Elaine! Elaine was in the truck telling him to get in. What was she doing here on the campus of the technical institute, driving where there was no street?

"Get in, Gavin! Get in!"

The footsteps were close behind him. He caught the handle of the moving door, staggering, put his right foot onto the doorjamb, and threw himself into the seat. The car took off along one of the old deserted runways, the door flapping painfully against Gavin's leg, the noise of the pursuit fading.

Gavin felt a hand on his shirt, pulling him into the cab, helping him sit up.

"Elaine," he said dazedly to the girl behind the steering wheel. "You should be in the hospital."

"No," the girl said, looking at him grimly, "that's where you should be. You're beaten up worse than I was."

"But what are you doing here?" Gavin asked. The events of the past day and a half were confused in his mind.

"After I woke up this morning, it took me several hours to talk myself out of the hospital. Finally I raised enough hell that they had to let me go."

"Why did you do that?"

The panel truck had reached the end of the runway. It plunged down a hillside, the tall weeds parting in front of the truck and thrashing against the sides. The door slammed shut.

"I heard your talk about organizing and moral commitments and obligations," Elaine said, her eyes on the hillside ahead, her hands white on the bucking steering wheel. "I know these students. I was one of them. I knew what they would do if you started spouting revolutionary nonsense. I'd have been here sooner, but it took me a while to steal this truck."

"You stole the truck?" Gavin exclaimed. He put his hand to his head. It came away bloody.

"We had to have transportation," Elaine said. "And I had to get you away from there before you were killed."

"But my parents!" Gavin said. "Your money!"

"I wasn't going back anyway," Elaine said. "Even if you hadn't kissed me. Oh, I know it didn't mean anything, so don't get uptight. Besides, you're such a simpleton, I felt responsible. What I can't understand is why you had to do it. Why can't you be satisfied just to get along for a while?"

The truck had reached the bottom of the hill. Now it slithered onto a graveled road.

"Why?" Gavin asked vaguely. He wanted the answer to that question himself.

"Yes. Why?"

The graveled road led to an asphalt side road and then to an access road for an interstate highway. It wasn't their highway. It went north, but it crossed the highway going west, and they were soon back on the road again, this time in a stolen car. But no matter! They were back on the road again toward the West Coast.

Gavin still was thinking about Elaine's question. He hadn't been such a radical on campus. Why had he turned into an activist when he left it? Was it only his natural reaction to the smugness, the hypocrisy, the sellout mentality of the world he had not seen upclose for nearly four years?

"Chester," the Professor said.

"It was Chester," Gavin said.

"Chester?"

"You know," Gavin said, trying to figure it out as he went, "I tried to turn him in, and I felt guilty. No matter what he did, it was like finking. He was a revolutionary, and I felt guilt about informing on him. I think, subconsciously, I was trying to make it up— to myself—by acting at the institute the way I thought he might have acted."

"That's strange!" Elaine said, shaking her head.

But she didn't know half the strangeness, Gavin thought glumly. Because that hadn't been what the Professor meant. He hadn't felt guilty for turning Chester in. He felt guilty because he wanted to do what Chester did. He wished that he had been the one who had beaten and raped the fair Elaine.

8 ⤙ The Cybernated Psyche

The ultimate cause or causes of our splintered society may never be known, but we can identify various contributing factors: the widespread use of cybernation to perform the necessary labor of the world; the development of chemotherapies, chemical mood changers, and chemical learning; the liberation of the individual to do his thing; a supportive intellectual climate; and the release of the innate cussedness of the human species. But the most dangerous human discovery may have been leisure. Hardship and necessity make cooperation essential; they rub people together and wear off the abrasive edges; they create a polite and gregarious society. Given half a chance, people will go off on their own tangents, cherishing their idiosyncrasies, glorifying their likes and dislikes into universal truths.

—THE PROFESSOR'S NOTEBOOK

As the sun rose like a mashed orange behind them, the Rocky Mountains rose ahead, jagged, dark, fading from the purple-black of nearer peaks to the pearl gray of those receding toward the horizon. Elaine woke Gavin to see it, but he only grumbled about his bruises and complained about his hunger.

"It's the first time I've really seen the mountains," Elaine said, sounding awed for the first time. "Don't you have any appreciation for beauty?"

"Not when I'm hungry," Gavin said, but he was

awake now, and he rubbed his eyes, wincing at the pain, and contemplated the mountains briefly before he began to survey the countryside through which they were passing.

They had driven all night after stopping at a clear stream outside town to bathe Gavin's face and inspect his injuries. Elaine's hands had been gentle and efficient.

Denver, Gavin decided, must not be far away. Isolated houses and then small communities appeared along the highway. He was contemplating a big breakfast in Denver when the old panel truck began to sputter.

"What's wrong?" Gavin asked.

"I think," Elaine said, "we're out of fuel."

"Why didn't you stop and get some?" Gavin asked.

"Where? Nobody drives a steam turbine on the highway any more. Not for any distance. So there aren't any service stations on the highway. The only place to get fuel is in town."

"You could have stopped in a town."

"What would I have used for money?"

Gavin shrugged. There was that. The little cash he had accumulated was still in his room at the institute, and Elaine had been robbed of everything. "I shouldn't take it out on you," he said. "I haven't been much help."

The engine sputtered again and cut off. The turbine rapidly slowed as Elaine guided the truck onto the shoulder of the road and stopped. "Here we are," she said, "on foot again. At least until we reach Denver." She opened her door and got out onto the highway.

Groaning, Gavin straightened himself and joined her. He stood stretching and shivering a little in the morning cold, but the air seemed as if it had been newly created in some chilly cavern of the world, and his depression lifted. "Let's go," he said.

They had walked only half a mile along the shoulder of the highway, and Gavin's muscles had just begun to loosen and slide smoothly over one another, when he saw a long, low, dun-colored structure off to the right. Almost simultaneously a delightful odor drifted to his bruised nose, which, nevertheless, had no difficulty recognizing the smell of baking bread.

There was something basic and primitive about the smell and his reaction to it. The Professor once had attributed the development of civilization to the discovery that grains could be ground and eaten. Paleolithic man had discovered the game he depended upon disappearing before the changing climate, and even in those long-ago days, hunted into extinction. He was forced to turn to the wild grains his women had discovered, but he had to be there when the seeds ripened and before the heads shattered and were lost. So he built his villages—many hands were necessary to harvest the grain—alongside the fields, and later, when irrigation was discovered and grains were cultivated, along the big rivers and flood plains. And he would roast the heads of wild wheat to make the seed easier to separate from the chaff, sometimes grinding the roasted grains and mixing with water to eat as a kind of paste, but then gradually learning to cook the paste on a flat rock near the fire into flatbread and later mixing with yeast and other ingredients to create a more enduring product which was still edible when cold. "Imagine," said the Professor, "this primitive hunter coming back to his fireside after an unsuccessful hunt, and squatting beside his mate, picking up a flatcake steaming from the fire's heat, and tearing at it with his teeth—it wasn't raw meat, but it was good. This was the start of civilization: the fire and the baking grain. . . ."

Gavin saw by Elaine's dilated nostrils that she, too, had smelled the bread. "Come on," he said, and scrambled down the ditch beside the highway and through the barbed-wire fence on the other side.

They walked through dryland grasses that rustled against their legs like whispers of the land. Meadowlarks were singing. Once a fieldmouse started up and ran in front of them. A few moments later a skunk walked imperiously across their path, tail high. It was as if this portion of the earth had never heard of man.

Finally, however, they came to a fence. Behind it

was a railroad track, and another fence on the other side. They walked along, following the protected tracks, until they came within sight of the building Gavin had seen from the highway. Here the smell of baking bread was almost irresistible. Gavin's mouth was watering, and his stomach was growling as they came to a point where the fence turned at right angles, admitting the train tracks but keeping out Gavin and Elaine.

The building within the fence was made of sheet metal enameled brown, probably prefabricated and brought to this lonely spot in sections. Gavin and Elaine stood outside the tall, chainlink fence that enclosed the four sides of the building, and looked at it longingly. On the front of the building were letters that had not been visible from a distance and not readable until they were at the fence. The sign said: FRONTIER AUTOMATED BAKERY. Underneath that, in even smaller letters, was: TRESPASSING FORBIDDEN. And underneath that: PROTECTED BY WatchComp, Inc.

The same legend was printed on metal plaques attached to the fence at regular intervals. The fence was unbroken, except where the railway tracks entered, and there the fence trailed off into the distance like the tail of a spermatozoon. Some fifty yards away a railway car stood against the side of the building. The end of the car was humped, as if to contain a motor and perhaps a small computer director.

But all that, and the bread, too, was on the inside, and they were on the outside. Gavin swallowed hard and said, "I'm going to get in somehow."

"Is that wise?" Elaine asked. "Couldn't we get fed easier somewhere else?"

"It wouldn't be the same," Gavin said. The disappointed hunter within him growled for bread. "Are you coming?"

"Lead on," she said.

Gavin started around the periphery of the fence again and stopped a few hundred yards around the corner. "Look!" he said. The sandy soil had been dug out around the base of the fence by some animal, perhaps a gopher or a prairie dog. Gavin attacked the hollow with his hands and soon had a space scooped out big enough for him to wiggle through on his back. Elaine followed him.

"Now," he said, and trotted back toward the railway track.

The railway car still was standing at the bakery wall, one entire wall of the car raised high against the building. The fit between the car and the building was so tight that not even the gopher or the prairie dog could have squeezed through. When they pressed their ears to the side of the railway car, they could hear rumblings and scrapings, as if something were being loaded.

As they walked past the car, they noticed other openings in the wall above the railway track marked: BUTTER, EGGS, MILK, FLOUR, SALT, SUGAR, YEAST, and so forth. All the openings were too small for human entry, even if they had not been sealed. The tracks disappeared into a wing of the building closed by a large railway-car-sized door. The door was immovable.

As they inspected it, the railway car behind them moved. Gavin whirled and ran toward it. Even as he turned, the big door they had been inspecting rattled. He glanced back as he ran. The door was going up. Another railway car was emerging. He almost stopped, but then he noticed that the car ahead had exposed a tall opening in the side of the building, about five feet up the wall.

The gap was still widening as he approached. Inside the dark opening he could glimpse what seemed like a clear space, and behind that the looming presence of something bulky and shadowed. He leaped at the opening and hauled himself up.

The railway car which had come out of the building was rolling down the track toward the opening in which Gavin stood. He reached down a hand to Elaine and hauled her up beside him just before the new car slid across the part of the opening in front of him. The inside of the building was lighted only by the sunlight coming through the narrowing loading

door. Before it closed completely, Gavin saw in front
of him a rack not two feet away, and beyond that
belts and machinery. To his left, under a network of
wires, under slotted strips of metal, Gavin saw an
open space, and he ducked into it, pulling Elaine after
him.

And then the railway car closed the doorway; only
daggers of light entered where the fit with the building
was not perfect. After the brilliance of the Colorado
morning, Gavin couldn't see enough to locate himself
in the omnipresent gloom. He felt, however, that the
room was big and filled with incomprehensible machinery performing mysterious functions. He could hear
it rustling and whispering and ratcheting, and he stood
there in the dark, holding Elaine's cool hand, smelling
the hot crusty odor of baking bread.

"Well, Mr. Mastermind," Elaine said, "what now?"

Indeed, what now? He hadn't thought about it, but
an automated factory needed no light. It could work as
well in the dark, perhaps better without the unnecessary and unregulated waste heat from light bulbs.
Somewhere there might be lights for human inspection and maintenance, but he had no chance of lo-
cating the switches even if they were not locked.

And even as he thought about them, the lights
went on. A giant voice shouted at them from above,
like the voice of God, "This is WatchComp, and you
are trespassing on the premises of Frontier Automated
Bakery. Stay where you are until you are given per-
mission to move."

Silence fell over them like fear. Elaine looked at
Gavin. "They're going to send someone out from Den-
ver," he said, putting on a confidence he did not feel.
"If they think we're going to wait for them . . ."

By the lights in the ceiling he could see the process
of automated baking. Apparently the openings in the
outside walls led to storage bins. Pipes led from the
bins to large closed kettles made of gleaming copper;
a larger pipe led from each kettle to nozzles above a
moving belt entirely composed of loaf-shaped tins. As
he watched, three globs of dough oozed from as many
nozzles, filled three tins, and the line moved forward.

Three metal disks sliced open the top of the dough. Butter sprayed from jets, and then the moving belt vanished into an opening in a wall.

Out of another rectangular opening came other tins, but these bulged with bread, their tops mounded with steaming brown crust. The moving belt reversed itself over a horizontal roller, and loaves of bread dropped like manna upon another belt, which moved the loaves toward them. The loaves were caught by slotted plates, sliced by a series of knives, and shoved into plastic bags held open by plastic fingers and a jet of air. Metal arms twisted plastic around the neck of the bag, and the wrapped loaves slid into racks that inched upward from the floor to accept them. As soon as the rack was full, it shoved its contents into the waiting racks of the railway car and slid down out of the way of the next rack.

The process had come a long way from the banks of the Euphrates. But hunger had not. Gavin grabbed a loaf of bread from the rack nearest him. The railway car was nearly full, and its racks left no room for Gavin and Elaine.

The car began to move. Light entered past its near end like a bright curtain.

"Be ready," Gavin said.

As the loading door widened to the width of a person, Gavin stepped into the space between the racks and the door, and then, still holding Elaine's hand, onto the humped housing on the rear of the car. Elaine had to jump, but the housing was big enough for both of them. They clung to air vents on the rear of the car as it picked up speed, passed beyond the line of the fence around the factory, and entered the long tunnel of fencing that led, Gavin believed, toward Denver.

Gavin tore the top off the load of bread with his teeth and offered the open loaf to Elaine. She took a handful of slices, held them to her nose and inhaled the aroma, and laughed.

"Sometimes," she said, "the simple pleasures are the best."

Clinging to the back of the car as it rolled clacking

through the bright, cool, clear Colorado morning, they stuffed themselves with hot bread.

The car slowed as it reached the outskirts of Denver. Gavin nodded at Elaine and jumped off. He ran alongside the car to catch her as she jumped. They stopped between the multiple sets of tracks and looked around as they caught their breath.

They were in a sort of manmade gully with stone-block walls on either side. Just a few hundred yards farther along, the tracks disappeared into a dark tunnel.

Gavin and Elaine climbed the nearest stone wall to street level. The area nearby was dominated by the massive concrete bulk of a stadium, a complete bowl pierced with dark openings for entrance and exit; ramps wound their ways up the sides to upper levels.

The stadium was surrounded by broad black expanses of parking lot, now filled with a multihued harvest of electric cars. The air was thick with the rise and fall of massed human voices shouting their pleasure and displeasure, and the inhuman sound of engines and of bending and rending metal.

Elaine pointed out the camera surveillance on the pillars at the corner of each lot and the warning signs of the ubiquitous WatchComp, and they walked around the periphery of the stadium lots until they reached an area where a few old cars were parked and there were no pillars.

"This time let's get an electric," Gavin said, "and solve the fuel problem."

Most of the cars, however, were old steam turbines, and a few, even older, seemed to be internal-combustion models, more suited to a museum or a junkyard than a parking lot. Finally, however, they found an antique electric, much battered but apparently still sound. After some difficulty, Gavin wedged open the door on the driver's side and kicked open the equally stubborn door on the passenger side. Elaine looked around cautiously and got in. There was no one in sight, and the only reminder of human presence was the sound of enthusiasm and disappointment rolling like surf over the stadium walls.

Gavin settled himself into the driver's seat and stared at the steering wheel, or rather, where the steering wheel should have been. There was no steering column, no dashboard, no accelerator, no brake pedals. In their place was a black box about two feet square. It was humming.

"Let's get out of here," Elaine said.

But it was not that easy to get the doors open again, and before Gavin could force them, the car was in motion, rolling toward the stadium. It turned automatically into a large, ground-floor stadium entrance, through a dark, underground tunnel, and into the brilliance of an arena strewn with sand and filled with automobiles charging like maddened bulls. Others lay ruined upon their sides or hunkered down at the edge of the stadium, oil streaming from their tortured sides into the sand.

Gradually the confused scene sorted itself out in Gavin's mind. Tractors dragged some hulks from the field. The cars still in motion were circling a large ball, hitting it with their bumpers or sides toward goals at either end of the long field. The cars were of many kinds, a few smooth-gliding electrics and a larger number of hissing steam turbines, but mostly snorting, fuming internal-combustion cars which had been outlawed from the highways.

Smoke and dust obscured the field, rolling aside periodically to reveal a moment of action or a scene of mechanical violence. Over everything hung the ancient and exhilarating fumes of gasoline, burning oil, and smoking rubber.

All this Gavin had a chance to sense as he struggled with the doors inside an automobile intent upon carrying them into the midst of carnage and massacre. He heard the audience cheer as their car merged into the melee, and then, as he and Elaine peered out, pounding on the windows, waving in an effort to make their presence known, the audience cheered louder, capering in the aisles of the stadium, standing on their seats, gesticulating gratefully toward the heavens.

"They like it," Gavin shouted at Elaine, trying to be heard above the sounds of whining tires and grinding gears, roaring engines and smashing metal. "They want us in here."

Something struck the side of his door, buckling it toward him, and something hit the car from behind, snapping his head back against a restraint. Their car rebounded and then wove more skillfully through the swerving, swiveling cars, to strike the ball a solid blow that sent it rolling over the hood of another car and far down the field where a car, timing its movement perfectly, hit the ball at the precise angle to send it spinning through goalposts and into a net.

The milling cars made wide, erratic circles in the sand, blasting their horns and revving their engines, as if celebrating a victory, and ended, in perfect precision, facing each other in two straight rows.

All the other cars were empty.

In a desperate burst of strength, Gavin forced open the bent door next to him and emerged into the dusty sunlight, surrounded by panting metal monsters. The crowd exploded. Men, women, and children threw hot dogs and hubcaps into the arena, cheered madly, shouted words that were lost in the general insanity.

As he helped Elaine out on the other side, the impossible levels of noise and excitement rose even higher. Gavin took her hand and ran through the oil-soaked sand toward the side of the stadium, but the sight and sound of the crowd deterred him as he neared the tall concrete barrier, and he swerved left, running around the perimeter of the arena, searching for a way out without risking the manic enthusiasm of the mob above. He looked, he thought, like a runner taking his victory lap, or a bullfighter making a stately march around the ring to accept his tribute.

Just after Gavin had begun to despair of escape, they came to the dark tunnel from which their automobile had emerged, and they dashed into it, seeing at the far end the promise of uncomplicated sunlight, like an entrance into arcadia. But before they reached it, a barred gate rolled down to block their way.

"Here!" someone shouted at them. "This way!"

A white hand motioned to them out of the darkness like the spectral hand that had led many an unwary traveler to his doom. Gavin went through a doorway, Elaine close behind him. A hand caught Gavin's left arm and guided him down a dark hallway. He emerged at last into a small room. It was an office with an old metal desk and swivel chair, a couple of battered metal filing cabinets, and a wastebasket. On the other side of the room was another door.

Even as he saw all this, Gavin was turning to the person who had grasped his arm. "What's all this about?"

A woman released his arm and Elaine's at the same time. She closed the door behind them, and the sounds of the stadium were muffled, as if they were transmitted now through five hundred thousand tons of concrete. She laughed. It was the low, hearty laugh of a big woman.

"I should ask you," she said.

She was big. She was nearly as tall as Gavin, and perhaps almost as heavy, but she wasn't fat. She was a colorful woman. When Gavin looked at her, it seemed as if all the rest of the world had been created in black and white. She was a mature woman, all formed, and well-formed, at that. There was nothing tentative about her, from her pink trousers to her red hair. In between there was a sensual breadth of hips, a firm waist, and a dramatic projection of bosom. Her throat was smooth and unlined, her chin forceful, her mouth red and generous, her nose ample, her eyes blue and certain, her eyebrows thick and red and mobile.

She was, Gavin thought, a threatening woman, with appetites to match her Amazonian build, and a presence which challenged a man to measure himself against her femaleness.

"After all," she said, "it's not every substitute that comes rolling into the stadium bringing a load of refugees." She smiled at them, exposing white, perfect teeth. They looked capable of breaking bones to get at the marrow.

"We were looking for a car," Gavin said.

"To steal," Elaine added.

The woman laughed from the pit of her stomach. "And you poor ninnies picked a computer-controlled car for the game. Oh, golly! Oh, gee! Oh, me-me-me-me-me!" Her laughter finally faded into gasps for air.

Gavin and Elaine looked at each other. "If that's the door to the outside," Gavin said, "we'll thank you for leading us here and be on our way."

The woman wiped her eyes with the back of her hand. "I wouldn't think of it," she said. "You poor kids need a place to stay, I'll bet, and a meal. Come on," she said, as if she were accustomed to having her suggestions treated like orders, "I'll take you home to my family."

"But who are you?" Elaine asked.

The woman took them by the arms again and moved them effortlessly toward the outer door. "Why, darlings, my name is Sally Grandjon, and people call me 'High-livin' Sal, the cybernated gal,' and I'm the rootinest, tootinest, shootinest woman in the Rocky Mountains, but, kids, I've got a warm heart, a heart big enough to take in all the strays in Denver."

Gavin opened the door with his free hand, overwhelmed by her forcefulness. "All right," he said as he went out into the brightness of the day.

"Good," Sally said, giving him a look as openly appraising as the one he had given her earlier. "Here's the car. Get into the back, you two."

The car was a big black limousine of an electric. Gavin had never seen an electric that big. Sally half-helped them, half-pushed them into the back seat. "There, now," she said. "Get comfy. We don't have far to go."

She got into the front seat and put a helmet over her red hair. A moment later the car backed out of the parking space among a row of cars and started out of the lot. It was not until they reached the street that Gavin noticed the car had no controls, just like the battered electric that had abducted them into the stadium. Where the steering wheel and the gauges should have been was a black box, and Sally did not touch it.

She sat straight and unmoving in her seat, watching the road.

"What are you doing?" Gavin asked as an electric bus passed close beside them.

The limousine swerved and then resumed its straight path.

"This car is a cybernetic model," Sally said. "Don't worry. I have it under my complete control."

"I'm distracting you!" Gavin said. "Good God, don't talk!"

"Don't worry," she said. "I've done much more complicated tasks while carrying on a conversation with half a dozen people. It's all a matter of experience and discipline, and if you'll pardon my appearing to boast, I'm the best there is."

"At what?" Gavin asked.

"Look back at the sign in front of the stadium!"

Gavin turned to peer through the rear window. They were passing the front of the stadium now, and in giant letters written in fire on a giant black signboard appeared: AUTOBOL TODAY! Below that a line read: DETROIT PISTONS VS. DENVER WHEELS. And below that: SALLY GRANDJON AT FORWARD.

"That was my car you were in," Sally said.

"You were controlling it by a remote computer linkup," Elaine said.

"Of course. Once they used real drivers, but they kept getting hurt. You know? And they weren't nearly as good. Nor as quick," Sally said. "But I must say that it was quite an experience when you two spun into the stadium. There's a feedback circuit, you know. Has to be. I can feel the engine turning and feel the sand under the wheels, and the ball bearings going round, and even the bumpers hitting the ball or the other cars, or my own fenders bending or scraping or tearing. It's an experience, having a fender torn off or feeling your engine die. . . ."

She paused a moment, as if reliving the sensations. "But imagine my feelings when I saw you in the front seat, felt you there, not metal and paint, but soft flesh and palpitating organs. I tell you, it was inspiring. I've never been better. Right?"

"I don't like to complain," Gavin said, "but you might have stopped and let us out."

"And spoiled the match?" Sally said. "The crowd was cheering you at the end. You were heroes. Think what they would have been like if you'd been responsible for our losing."

Gavin remembered the greedy adulation from which they had fled, and shuddered.

They were entering into the heart of Denver itself. The streets were much like those in Kansas City: clean and bright and relatively empty. The buildings were neat and well kept, and where there was space, green patches of grass and trees and shrubs appeared.

"That isn't my real work, of course," Sally said. "That's just the way I earn what I need for other purposes. Easy money, and a lot of it. Lets me buy equipment for my cybernetics lab. I'll show you that when we get home."

Home was a large old Victorian mansion not too far from the inner city, shingled, turreted, set well back from the street in a shelter of tall trees and shrubbery surrounded by a wrought-iron fence. The limousine turned toward the mansion, a wrought-iron gate swung open automatically, and the car traversed a long drive that passed in front of the house before returning to the street. The car stopped in front of stone steps that led up to a brick porch and big dark carved wooden doors.

Sally removed the helmet and turned herself toward them. Gavin was surprised again by the liveliness of her expression and the vividness of her coloring.

"We're home," she said.

As Gavin got out of the car, he realized he had been sweating. Elaine joined him, and he took her hand in a gesture of reassurance. She held on as if she needed it. Her hand was clammy.

He looked up the steps toward the open double doors leading into a dark interior. Sally was standing beside the doors, motioning to them. "Come on," she said impatiently. "Come on!"

Gavin started up the stairs.

As they entered the doors, Sally took them by the arms again in an action now so familiar as to seem characteristic. Gavin's and Elaine's hands were forced apart as Sally moved between them. "This," she said, "is my husband Frank."

As Gavin's eyes adjusted to the darkness of the entrance hall, he saw a large middle-aged man with graying dark hair and a ruddy complexion. "Hello," Gavin said politely.

"Hi!" Elaine said.

Frank didn't speak to them. "This isn't another one, is it, Sal? I don't think I can stand it if you've brought home another one."

"No, no," Sally said. "These are just a couple of strangers I found at the stadium. I brought them home to meet the family and get a meal and maybe rest up."

Gavin could see now that Frank looked tired and anxious.

"That's what you said about Jay-Jay," Frank said sullenly.

"Don't be jealous," Sally said soothingly, reaching out to pat Frank's cheek. "You can have your turn tonight, okay?"

He moved his face away from her hand, but a reluctant smile crept across his face, and he nodded. "George will be mad," he said.

"Let me worry about George," Sally said. "Come on," she said to Gavin and Elaine, grabbing their arms, "let's go find you two babes something to eat."

They went into a large room with a broad staircase at the far end climbing to a landing and then branching to the right and the left. The old oak of the stairs gleamed with wax, and the broad, balustered railings shone with the polish of a half-dozen generations of hands. A blue Oriental rug covered the center of the oak floor, and antique furniture stood on the rug and around the walls.

The room smelled of lemons.

A young woman stood beside the walnut library table in the center of the room talking to a man of medium size and dark hair. The woman was dark too.

She was small and looked sullen but sexy, like a vixen. She had a dust cloth in her hand with which she was idly rubbing the table. She and the man looked up as Sally entered, and acted guilty.

Sally ignored their actions and took Gavin and Elaine up to them. "This is my husband George," she said, "and my co-wife Susan." And she introduced Gavin and Elaine and described how they had broken into her car. Everybody laughed, even Susan, who managed to look sullen in the process. She also looked speculatively at Gavin when she thought he wasn't watching. When he looked, her eyes slid away.

Beyond the staircase a door opened into a large country kitchen, big enough for a six-burner stove, two ovens, an oversized refrigerator and matching freezer, and a large breakfast table with six chairs. The floor was covered with sunny yellow plastic squares patterned with green lines. A big kettle simmered on the stove, and delightful odors steamed from it. As they entered the kitchen, a matronly woman with wispy brown hair and red cheeks turned from the stove and smiled at them.

They had a cook, Gavin thought, but Sally immediately said, "This is my co-wife Mary. Mary's in charge of the house. She likes to cook and bake and see that everything's clean and everyone's well-fed. She thinks that not eating enough is the cause of melancholy, discontent, neuroses, and general poor health."

"That's right," Mary said cheerfully. "You look starved. Let me get you something to eat. And those bruises. You poor things."

"You see?" Sally said to Gavin. "Yes, Mary, I'm sure they're hungry. Give them some of the hobo stew and your good bread. Mary bakes the best bread in town."

"I didn't know anybody baked bread anymore," Gavin said.

"This is the age of the artist," Sally said. "And artists work in any medium. Mary's is bread."

"Well, now," Mary said, her face getting redder. "I do like to bake. That's all."

Bread, Gavin thought, is the theme of this day, but

man does not live by bread alone. To go with the
hunks of homemade bread torn from a steaming loaf
and spread with slathers of real butter, there was a
rich soup full of chunks of meat and vegetables. As
Gavin popped into his mouth a last piece of bread
sopped in the last bit of broth on his plate, he looked
around the kitchen, replete and contented. A swinging
door led, no doubt, to a dining-room, and another
door to the outside. Near it, against the wall, was a
plaque engraved with the word: RECYCLING. Underneath were four metal flaps that covered openings in
the wall. On each flap a single word was engraved.
From left to right they read: CANS, GLASS, PAPER, and
GARBAGE. Gavin felt a sense of satisfaction that nothing
was wasted until he recalled what the Professor had
said once: "Doing the right thing for one's fellow man
would be more virtuous if it didn't represent an easy
way to delude one's conscience about how one really
feels about one's fellow man."

Mary was busy with what appeared to be the evening
meal, rubbing a large beef roast and cloves of garlic together with a passion usually reserved for more erotic
occasions. Sally had disappeared through the outer
door when they sat down to eat. Gavin considered
them: Sally the sex goddess, the provider and head of
the household, Mary the motherly cook and house-
keeper. Perhaps it was a good arrangement for both;
Mary enjoyed the details that Sally found boring and
benefited from the caliber of men that Sally attracted
and kept contented with her shrewd human relations
as well as the dominance of her body and personality.
And who knows? Perhaps the men found in Mary the
kind of gentleness and concern that was soothing after
Sally's intensity.

And then, for variety, there was Susan, the sulky
vixen. Every family needed a rebellious spirit to keep
it young and vigorous. Gavin wondered, though, why
Sally had chosen Susan. Perhaps she understood that
group dynamics required a force like Susan, or maybe
she enjoyed the challenge of Susan's smoldering sexuality, or maybe it was a satisfying alternative for the
husbands to Sally's frank lust and Mary's pillowy com-

fort. Whatever the reason, it made Sally more complicated and more fascinating.

Then Sally was back, filled with energy and purpose, saying, "Come on, you two. I want to show you my work." She hustled them through the back door toward a large building surrounded by trees. It must once have been a carriage house. Now it had been propped up and resurfaced with plastics and stainless steel and glass, and it was a laboratory. On the ground floor, small rooms opened off a central corridor. Each was equipped with a readin machine for cards and tapes and a teletype input-output, as well as other kinds of computer attachments, oscilloscopes, and apparatus that Gavin couldn't identify.

Most of the rooms were occupied by men and women equipped with soft helmets dangling with wires or with wires attached to various parts of their bodies. Some of them were watching a moving dot of light trace a pattern across an oscilloscope or listening, their eyes closed, to a tone that varied in pitch or intensity.

"We're into biofeedback," Sally said, sweeping her hand at the little rooms. "People come here every day —free if they're doing something we're interested in, for a fee if it's personal development they're after. We train people to control what once was considered autonomic: heartbeats, circulation, headaches, muscular and mental tension, alpha rhythms, kidney function, pain, sleep centers, attention spans, fantasy levels, pleasure nodes, sexual readiness, and almost anything else that once was assumed to be beyond man's conscious control. If we can meter it, we can teach people to control it."

She led them up a flight of stairs to the upper floor. This was her place, Gavin could tell. It was all one room, without windows, lined on one side by a bank of computers and memory units faced with stainless steel and glass. In the middle of the room was a padded table, apparently adjustable into a lounge, covered with tan leather or vinyl and equipped with jacks and dangling wires and apparatus of all kinds, like an effete torture system.

One of the computers had been pulled out of its

place against the far wall, and a man was tinkering with its insides, wires strewn around him like arteries, cables like guts. He looked up at them, grinning. He was black and slender and handsome. "Sal," he said. "How'd it go at the stadium?"

"Got the winning assist," Sally said. "And brought back a couple of friends. Elaine and Gavin, this is my husband Jay-Jay. Jay-Jay's a computer technician. Came to fix the computer and stayed. And this is my computer. Best around. Just like Jay-Jay. Just like me. Super-cooled, high-powered, overgeared. And this is where we do our experiments."

"What kind of experiments?" Elaine asked.

"We're perfecting mental control of computers. And computer-assisted thinking. CAT. As easy as spelling 'cat.' Already we've achieved complete physical control of our autonomic systems, muscle tone, sensory stimuli . . ."

"Sal has, anyway," Jay-Jay said. "The rest of us are just working on it. You should see her undressed."

"I'd like to," Gavin murmured, and Elaine glanced at him sharply.

"I'll tell you, it makes you marvel at the potential of the human body," Jay-Jay went on, uninterrupted. "Sal's a wonder, she is, and when she and this computer get together, there's nothing they can't do. High-flyin' Sal, the computer gal."

"Pshaw!" Sally said modestly. But her magnificent body seemed to glow and ripple under the pink slacks and paler blouse. Gavin couldn't help himself; under the stimulus of Jay-Jay's suggestion, mentally he began to strip away her clothing.

And then he noticed that Elaine was still watching him, and looked away.

Jay-Jay nodded in their direction. "New recruits?" he asked.

"Just friends," Sally said lightly. "If you stay here long enough, however," she said to them, "I'd like you to try the equipment. Maybe tonight. I do most of my best work at night."

"I'll bet you do," Elaine said.

Sally smiled at her. "Don't we all, honey?" she said

sweetly. "Come on," she said once more. "I'll show you to your room."

"Rooms, I hope," Elaine said quickly.

"We're just traveling together," Gavin explained. "Not sleeping together."

"That's too bad," Sally said, and laughed. "We've got two rooms, and they've got a door between them in case you change your minds."

Dinner was a meal in which the entire family participated. It was a social occasion which began in an elaborate drawing room with a marble fireplace and Victorian chairs and settees covered in various shades of blue and green velvet. Mixed drinks or wines were available. Gavin stood on a thick blue-and-gold Oriental rug with a tall cold glass in his hand, feeling the moisture beading the glass under his fingers, enjoying the sophisticated hum of conversation, and thought that this, surely, was what the new freedom was all about. Here it all was: a challenging new frontier of research to keep the mind engaged, an exciting physical and mental sport to exercise the body, varied and perhaps inexhaustible sexual opportunities to lend anticipation to the day and passion to the night, and comfortable living conditions, the amenities of life, and the talk of intelligent people.

What did it matter if Susan sulked and George pouted? What did it matter if Elaine looked at him with blue eyes narrowed in thought?

They went into a large paneled dining room and sat down at a polished walnut table set with silver and china and crystal. There was good wine for the crystal —white wine with the magnificent broiled Colorado trout, and red wine with the beef burgundy, and a fine brandy with cigars after dessert.

Gavin sat back in his chair sipping his brandy, an unaccustomed cigar growing a fine white ash in his fingers, and he thought that the Professor would have enjoyed all this, most of all Sally.

"Our research?" Sally was saying in response to a question from Elaine. "We are after the ultimate conscious control of the body and the mind; we wish to make man, not his instincts, the arbiter of his condition. George, here, has trained himself to control his heartbeat. He can race it up to one hundred fifty per minute, or shut it down to virtually nothing. In fact, he could stop it completely if we could be certain of getting it started again."

George cheered up a bit. "Next I'm going to start on the adrenals."

"Frank, now," Sally said, "is working on alpha rhythms. On command he can suppress everything else in his mind and achieve a serenity that yogi have worked lifetimes to achieve. Show us, Frank."

The weariness and concern on Frank's middle-aged face vanished as his face smoothed, his eyes closed, and a mystical smile curved his lips. As his breathing stilled and his body relaxed, Gavin had the startling impression that Frank was going to levitate off his chair and float around the room. It was a remarkable display of self-control, and at that moment Gavin envied the older man.

But why, the Professor muttered inside his head, is he ever weary and concerned?

"Susan is learning to control her ovulation," Sally said sweetly. "And she's doing marvelously. Just think what a boon this would be for the poor and ignorant masses of the world!"

"If they had the discipline to learn that," Elaine said, "wouldn't they have the discipline to take the pill, or simply abstain at fertile periods?"

"Of course, dear," Sally said, "but think of the accomplishment of women at last overthrowing the tyranny of their bodies. Right, Susan?"

"I'm beginning to think it's a waste of time," Susan said.

"Perhaps you need some help from Frank on alpha rhythms," Sally said without malice. "Mary, of course, is too busy with the household to devote as much time to research as she and the rest of us would like. But when she came to us, she had migraines, and she is learning to control them by increasing the blood flow to her hands."

"Oh, it's a miracle," Mary said, her face shining with gratitude and love.

"I'd call this dinner a miracle," Gavin said.

Mary smiled at him, and Sally said, "Wasn't it, though? Jay-Jay hasn't been here long enough to get his own research started."

"That's not true," Jay-Jay protested. "I'm working on the instantaneous erection."

Everybody laughed.

"What Sally doesn't say," Jay-Jay continued, "is that she does everything everybody else does, and more, too."

"What are you particularly interested in?" Gavin asked.

"I'm trying to perfect the person-computer symbiosis," Sally said. "Not just biofeedback, but an interchange of thoughts—yes, and feelings—with the computer." She smiled at Gavin. "Maybe I'll give you a personal demonstration."

Mary asked about Elaine's black eye and Gavin's bruises. By the time Gavin had finished describing how they had been received, the evening was over. Sally stood up, and as if that were a signal, everyone else stood up. Gavin and Elaine joined them. Sally came around to them from her place at the head of the table, and took their arms and ushered them through the drawing room and up the big staircase to their adjoining rooms.

As they went, she said, "The family has to meet briefly about family matters. I want to talk to you, Gavin, a little later. There are books in your rooms. Of course, you're perfectly free to walk around the grounds or out in Denver if you wish, but I would like to have a moment or two with you a little later."

Elaine looked at Sally with a fleeting smile.

"If you don't mind, my dear," Sally said to her.

"Why should I mind?" Elaine said. "And if I did mind, what would it matter?"

Gavin for once was silent. He shut the door of his room behind him. It was a big room with tall ceilings. An old wooden dresser and mirror, both immaculately restored, stood against the near wall. A bookcase—a sectional case made of oak with glass fronts that lifted and slid over the books—was against the far wall beside the big window framing the night. But Gavin walked slowly across the oval braided rug to the bed, kicked off his shoes, and lay down on the bed fully clothed, staring unseeing at the ceiling and its hemispherical glass chandelier. Too many things had happened too quickly. The world was spinning around too fast. He touched his bruises gingerly.

"Maybe you would understand it, Professor," he thought, "but my old certainties are being chipped and cracked. I feel the urge to protect them, but I suspect that they soon will be gone, and I have found nothing to put in their place."

"That is the first function of education," the Professor said, "to sweep the mind clean of old rubbish."

"But what about the replacement? Education must not merely destroy; it must also teach."

"That will come," the Professor said confidently.

The next sensation Gavin had was the bed sinking under him. Gentle fingers touched his face. He realized that he must have fallen asleep, and he looked up expecting to see Elaine. But the vivid face bending over him was Sally's.

"Ah," she said. "You're awake. I have good news." Gavin tried to sit up, but she pushed him back gently. "No, don't get up. You see, the family has invited you to join us."

"Join you?" Gavin said.

"As a husband," Sally said patiently. "As a full partner in our family enterprises."

"But I just walked in here this afternoon."

"The family doesn't act rashly, but it doesn't hesitate when it knows what it needs. Jay-Jay arrived one morning to work on the computer, and never left."

"But I don't have any skills," Gavin said. "I'm just a student." He was even more confused now, unable to imagine even what was being offered him. The elegant life downstairs, the work, the play, the women, Sally. . . . It was all seductive and unimaginable. From hovel to mansion within a week.

"We think you have something to bring to the family: youth, vigor, promise, intelligence," Sally said. "And we think we have something to offer."

Gavin looked at the dramatic curve of her breasts swelling above him, and he said, "Of course. What about Elaine?"

Sally looked away and then back at him. "I thought there wasn't anything between you. You just happened to be traveling together."

"She's here because of me," Gavin said. "I couldn't just abandon her."

"Of course, we'll see that she gets wherever she's going," Sally said.

"She isn't included in the offer to join the family?"

"No," Sally said quickly. "Not unless those are the only conditions under which you'll join," she added, as if she saw an expression on Gavin's face which he did not recognize. "We will need another female," Sally went on, "but we must choose her carefully for balance, for psychological suitability, for family commitment. In any case, I don't think Elaine would be interested."

"Why not?"

Sally shrugged humorously. "There still are a few old-fashioned women around. I think she's one of them. I think she's a one-man woman."

"I wouldn't be able to answer now," Gavin said. He gestured helplessly with his hands. "I was going to the West Coast . . ."

"We want you to consider the matter very carefully," Sally said. "Take all the time you need. But we do want you to know that we want you." The way she said "we" made it sound like "I." As if for punctuation, she leaned over and kissed him gently on the lips, avoiding his bruises, but even their light touch promised Gavin delights of which he had never dreamed.

She had been gone for only a minute or two when Gavin heard a knock at the door between his room and Elaine's, and then the door opened and Elaine came into the room. She was wearing a nightgown—lent to her, apparently, by Susan—and her breasts barely dented the cloth. Her face was scrubbed and pale except where her eye was beginning to shade from purple into yellow. Compared to Sally, she was colorless, and Gavin felt a stir of sympathy for her.

"I heard voices," she said. "I thought it might be important." Gavin started to sit up, but Elaine said, "No, don't get up." She sat on the edge of the bed, where Sally had sat, hugging herself for warmth. "Was it something I should know about?"

"Sally asked me to join the family," Gavin said.

"She wants you," Elaine said. She sounded a little sad.

"The family wants me," Gavin corrected.

"What Sally wants, the family wants."

"They voted."

"I can see them voting," Elaine said. "Sally told them it was a good idea and convinced them it was theirs."

"She said," Gavin continued, "that they would see that you got wherever you were going. If I decide to stay."

"Are you going to stay?"

"I don't know," Gavin said. "I hadn't thought about anything like this. I was going to the West Coast." He hesitated. "She also said that they would take you, too, if that was the only condition under which I would join." He studied her face, but there was nothing inscrutable about her reaction.

She rolled her eyes toward the ceiling. "That's my definition of hell," she said. "Being dependent upon seven other people. Independence is what I want. I can't imagine anyone joining a group marriage, much less myself. But if that's your thing . . ."

"I don't know," Gavin said. He didn't know. It wasn't the Professor's thing, and it didn't fit with anything that Gavin had considered his goals up to now. And then there was Jenny—and Berkeley and everything it promised. There was so much he didn't know, so much that he might be giving up, so much that he might learn, so much that might happen to him if he left. But he knew the exciting possibilities that were here for him if he stayed.

"Postpone your decision for a while," Elaine said lightly. "She gives samples. So will Susan."

She leaned over toward him, much like Sally, but thin and light, almost insubstantial, where Sally had been solid and earthy, and touched his lips with hers. In the touch was no promise of exquisite delights, but a kind of purity that stirred another kind of response akin to the sympathy he had felt earlier; and he reached for her. He thought he felt her hesitate, but perhaps she was withdrawing all the while.

She stood at the edge of the bed, beyond his reach. "Not while you're thinking about that improbable, overstuffed wench. Maybe not at all."

And she was gone, and the door opened, with a brief gust of air, and clicked shut, and a key turned in the lock, and Gavin was left with silence and his thoughts.

Gavin went to sleep quickly. The past twenty-four hours had been so packed with events that the first of them seemed like history, and he did not realize how tired he was until he let his body sink into the embrace of the mattress and Morpheus. Only a short time later —at least, it seemed only a short time—he was awakened by a strange sound, a sussuration, a faint whistling interrupted by changes in tone and timbre. At first Gavin thought of a machine, some kind of engine, perhaps run by steam or compressed air, moving a piston back and forth in a silken cylinder; and then he thought of an animal, a large animal like a lion or a bear, snuffling toward him in the dark.

The tempo of the sound quickened. In the dark, his body taut with listening, Gavin realized that there was something human about the sound, something human and fraught with significance, something urgent and growing more urgent by the minute. He got up in the dark and tried to locate the source of the sound, moving quietly among the scattered furniture. He listened at Elaine's door for a moment, but her room was silent. The sound seemed to be coming from the window.

At the window Gavin saw that the converted car-

riage house in back streamed light from an upper
window, where once bales of hay had been lifted into
a loft to feed the horses stabled below, a window he
had not noticed when he had been in that room.

He was drawn toward the sound. Its tempo had
increased. Its urgency seemed to be approaching a
climax. Something had to happen. Gavin slipped into
his shirt and trousers and went silently down the stairs,
lighted now by a single bulb in the massive crystal
chandelier that hung in the broad hall, and through
the kitchen and out the back door. The sound had
faded as he left the room and had become inaudible
as he went down the stairs, but Gavin thought he knew
where to go.

The door to the laboratory was unlocked. Gavin
went down the corridor and up the stairs toward the
second floor, and while he went, the sound began again
and grew louder, louder even than he had heard it in
his room; it was faster now, too, as if the person who
made the sound was gasping for breath. He wondered
briefly, without distraction from his central quest,
why he had heard it so clearly in his room and not in
the rest of the house, not on the grass and pavement
that lay between the house and the laboratory.

And as he came to the head of the stairs, even before he saw what had drawn him to this spot, he
realized what the sound was and where he had heard
it before. It was the sound of a woman in the throes
of passion. He would have stopped there and retreated from the embarrassment of interrupting a sexual encounter, but he already was at the head of the
stairs and he had seen what was on the couch in the
center of the room, and he could not move.

The scene was barbaric, like some ancient fertility
rite; or, considering the electronic apparatus that lined
the room, the cables that traversed the floor, the computers that clicked and chuckled against the walls
while reels spun and stopped within their glassy fronts
and colored lights flickered across the consoles, like an
updated nineteenth-century laboratory, a modern version of the mad place where Dr. Frankenstein had
committed the ultimate blasphemy. . . .

Only one person was upon the couch. Naked, face upward, her red hair covered by a cap, like a fancy bathing cap fastened under the chin, from which wires trailed to a plug at the head of the couch, lay the magnificent Sally looking more than ever like an earth goddess, a sex goddess, her body oversized perfection, rippling now with periodic contractions that traveled from her toes up fully fashioned legs and thighs past generous hips and a luxuriantly decorated pubic mound to tapering waist and exquisitely rounded and mounded breasts pointing tight, tumescent coral nipples toward the ceiling, up straining columnar throat to a strong and beautiful face, eyes closed, lips parted, breath hastening in and out. . . .

A moan came from between Sally's parted lips. Her pelvis tightened and thrust. She moaned again and again. A series of "ahs" burst from her throat and were, at the end, prolonged into a sigh.

Gavin could not move. Sally had perfected the autoerotic art. She was able to recapitulate the act of sex entirely through mental control, a kind of masterful dream fulfillment while she was wide-awake, a feat of mental discipline more astonishing than anything she had described.

Or else, he thought, the cap linked her to the computer, to her lover the computer, and she was copulating with the machine.

Coming up out of the disturbed sea of his thoughts, he saw her blue eyes open and looking at him. She lay there still and unashamed upon the couch, and looked at him and smiled.

"You're next," she said clearly.

Without conscious volition, he found himself moving toward the couch, toward her, thinking of soft flesh and rounded limbs and tissues responsive each in their own ways; and his arms half-parted, only to discover that Sally had moved, she had taken off the cap, and she was standing beside the couch helping him down upon it.

He let her fasten the cap on his head, so close to him that he could have reached out and clasped her anywhere, so close as she moved that he could feel the heavy weight of her breasts upon his chest and feel one nipple brush his cheek.

Next, he thought, he was next with the machine, and he didn't know what he was doing there. He didn't know what he should expect.

"I thought the sounds would attract you," Sally said as she tightened the strap under his chin. "It always works. Now," she said, stepping back, "relax and get in touch with the machine."

His mind was making so much noise that there wasn't room for anything else inside his head.

"You're tense," she said.

"Of course I am!" Gavin snapped. "This is all new to me, I don't know what's going to happen, I don't know what to do or what to look for, and it hasn't been exactly a relaxing experience up to now!"

"I understand," Sally said sympathetically, "but you've got to relax if this is going to work. Here, let me massage your tense shoulder muscles."

That wasn't the place he was tense, he thought, but she stood behind him, behind the cap and the wires, and he felt her hands kneading his shoulders, but he didn't relax. He couldn't help thinking about her standing there in all her magnificent nudity, as if this were some old-fashioned massage parlor.

"You're not relaxing," she said. "The first thing you should do is think commands at the little white dot on the oscilloscope above your head."

He looked up. There was an oscilloscope he had not noticed before; apparently it had been lowered from the ceiling when his attention had been elsewhere. A white dot was motionless in the middle of the screen.

"Think 'up,' " Sally said. "Think 'down,' or 'right' or 'left' or 'fast' or 'slow' or 'circle' or 'stop.' When you have it under control, doing what you want, then try something more daring. Ask questions, seek information, and then, if you're doing well, you can seek sensations as well. But that may not come until the next time, or the time after that. Now, relax! Relax-x-x! Relax-x-x-x-x. . . ."

"It doesn't help that you're standing back there without any clothes on!"

"All right," she said. "I'll leave you here alone. Play with the system. See what feedback you can get from the computer. When you get tired, the off switch is under your right hand, on the side of the couch. If you want to . . . talk about your experience, if you're still tense, my room is at the head of the stairs, on the right. The door is always unlocked."

Gavin could hear the Professor (or was it Elaine?) say, "I'll bet it is."

Her footsteps receded across the room and down the stairs. He heard the outer door open and shut, and he was alone with the computer.

Thoughts pounded through his head. Images appeared in his mind and did things that he could not control, and were replaced by other images in recalcitrant tableaux, but at last his breathing slowed and his brain stopped churning and he heard a murmuring inside his head, as if a bee were loose there and buzzing quietly, sitting, its thorax swelling and contracting, if that's what bees did when they buzzed, its wings moving gently in time with the sound. And then there was a whole hive of bees, all contentedly humming away.

The dot on the oscilloscope jumped and was still. "Right," he thought. The dot moved right. "Left." It reversed its path. "Up. Down. Fast. Slow. Circle."

The dot responded obediently, and in a little while, as he reckoned the passage of time, he had it doing figure eights and inscribing all sorts of geometric figures on the greenish screen. For a while that was enough, controlling the dot, feeling like a mental giant, but after a few more minutes the game seemed childish, elementary, boring, and he thought "off." The dot vanished.

More abstract notions began to form in his mind: no commands to be obeyed by a simple-minded dot, but curiosity about the manner in which the computer was reading his mind. And the answer was inside his head: the cap, with its trailing wires, was a sophisticated encephalograph which recorded his brain waves; the computer then compared them with a vast store of similar waves in its memory.

Vast? he wondered, and an image of a clenched fist

appeared in his mind. Grains of sand trickled from
the fist. The view, like a camera, pulled back to show
grains piling up over the centuries, and then centuries
of centuries, to form vast beaches and great deserts,
and the view pulled back and back until the grains
began to separate and glow; and Gavin realized that
he was looking at the night sky, not obscured by
earth's atmosphere, but from above the veil of air,
seeing the starry sky, the infinitely studded universe.

He was in touch with the computer. The computer
was putting the answers in his head, and it had answers for everything. A great comfort swept over him,
and he wondered if this, too, were feedback, or merely
the natural consequence of being connected to omniscience.

Heaven, he thought, is being with God.

The process accelerated. Thoughts flowed from Gavin's head to the computer and came back, reinforced
with data and a cloud of consequences and derivations
through which Gavin's mind moved with ease;
thoughts seemed to come in turn from the computer
and stimulate other thoughts in Gavin which were amplified and supported or subtly altered by the computer
until Gavin lost track of whose thought was whose.

He felt as if he were losing his identity. No, that
wasn't it. He felt as if his identity were expanding to
include not only his body and those organs and vessels and memories and thoughts contained within it,
but the metal and plastic standing against the far wall
with its tiny magnetic fluxes tickling the synapses of
microcircuits, with its purposeful electrons seeking the
shortest pathway through its supercooled body. He
was no longer just Gavin, but Gavin plus the computer, Gavin and the computer, Gavin-computer, Gav-
puter. . . .

His brain was as big as the entire room, filled with
neurons and stacked circuits, and ideas and memories,
and inputs and data against which to check them, and
extrapolations with which to extend them into infinity,
and he was God. It was like having the Professor as
part of him but a million times more powerful.

He felt himself reaching, straining for comprehension, struggling for real omniscience, not just omniscience limited by the data incorporated into the machine through the fallible measurements and recordings of man, not even omniscience limited by the direct samplings from the natural world by the computer itself, but omniscience that knew not just what had been thought but what was *true*—whatever was understood by whatever might be, the universe as creation.

His desire for knowledge mounted intolerably, interminably, infinitely—and he broke through, savagely, victoriously, into great warm ecstatic depths and heights and breadths, into great new dimensions of knowledge, each with its unique sweetness and fulfillment; he expanded tumescently to fill the universe, desire and satisfaction coexistent, concept and creation simultaneous; he was one with the universe, flowing into it, permeating it, impregnating it, while it became him, surrendering, responding, rejoicing. . . .

He was God the Creator.

And he created the universe. He created heaven and earth. . . .

And he died. The stars went out. The universe went dark. God died. In a process swifter than thought, the vast and subtle substance that had been the Creator diminished, dwindled, shrank, shriveled through the black nothingness that had been the universe, back into galactic dimensions, stellar scope, planetary volume, and finally, contracting faster than the speed of light, once more into a prison of flesh, and he was isolated, alone, cut off, solitary, condemned. . . .

Gavin opened his eyes and looked up into the concerned face of Elaine. "You turned me off," he said. It was more of an accusation than a statement.

"A few minutes more and you would have been lost for good," she said. "Our instructor in computer school told us about renegade setups like this, which bypass the essential feedback filters. Oh, they're all right for pragmatists like Sally, who use them for their own little tricks, but Sally doesn't know what they can do to someone with imagination and no experience. You could have become incurably paranoid, maybe even catatonic."

"I want to go back," Gavin said stubbornly, feeling for the switch on the side of the couch.

Elaine caught his wrist, and he was too weak to struggle.

"You think that now," Elaine said, "but give yourself some time to get a perspective, to realize what you're getting and what you're giving up. Right this moment, we've got to get away. I've stolen a car. While you're here, close, you'll find it difficult to think objectively. Come with me now, and tomorrow, if you still want this, I'll bring you back."

"Sally's waiting for me," Gavin said.

"She'll still be waiting for you tomorrow."

Gavin allowed himself to be helped down the stairs, his knees curiously weak, and into an electric car, and, reclining wearily on the seat beside Elaine, to be driven silently through the night away from Denver, and back into a world he never made.

9 ⚫ Deflowered Children

Man's instincts are polygamous. His instincts are living fossils from the paleolithic, when men hunted large, dangerous animals, and frequently were killed. The job of the remaining males was to fertilize any available females; the females, as security for the survival of the tribe, had remained in the relative safety of the cave. Virility and instant sexual readiness became survival characteristics; no doubt they are responsible for our presence here. We are the children of the strong, the fertile, and the lustful—and perhaps of the occasional fox who hung back from the hunt or malingered around the cave. The development of agriculture and the domestication of animals made such polygamous instincts unnecessary, and large families have been counterproductive since the Industrial Revolution. But all of this has not affected the persistence of our early characteristics. After all, we were savages for a million years, farmers for only twenty thousand, civilized for less than seven thousand, and industrialized for only a couple of hundred.

—THE PROFESSOR'S NOTEBOOK

The night was a womb through which they passed like blind possibilities down a crooked tunnel, unfertilized potentials, unripe gods. The headlights led them through the dark. No other cars were on the road, and the sky existed only on faith above the clouds. They were alone, the two of them, with the night.

223

Toward morning Gavin resurrected himself. "Where are we going?"

"South," Elaine said. "Toward Colorado Springs. And beyond."

"I wanted to go west."

"We're taking an alternate route. I heard George say that the mountains had been snowed in by a blizzard. I thought we should go a more southern way over the Rockies."

Gavin nodded. He really didn't care anymore. Perhaps someday he would care again.

"Do you want to go back?" Elaine asked.

"Back?" A spasm shook Gavin's body like the anticipation of ecstasy. Then his body stiffened. "No," he said. And then, more softly, "No. No."

Elaine did not ask him for reasons. Gavin didn't know what he would have said if she had asked, but he knew that he did not want to go back, any more than a man named Jesus would have wanted to be born again. To become a god by accident is one thing, but to choose to be a god is another: the frail vessel of flesh was not meant to contain the corrosive fluid of omnipotence.

What had it all been but a kind of wet dream?

Gavin breathed deeply and felt himself slowly begin to care.

A few minutes later the sky began to lighten in front of them. "I thought you were driving south," Gavin said.

"I am."

"Then why is the sun coming up in that direction?"

Elaine didn't have an answer.

The sky continued to brighten ahead; the clouds turned red. The next moment, Gavin knew what it was: not the sun, but a fire, and a big fire, casting lurid reflections against the clouds.

A few miles farther and the fire was raging in the field beside the road, a gigantic bonfire with tiny black figures capering in front of it like sticks drawn to the flames, soon to cast themselves into it. As they watched, parts of the sticks were tossed into the fire.

Elaine pulled the car off the road onto the shoulder.

The blaze was a fascinating display of capricious power. Inrushing gusts of wind and bursts of fuel changed the colors of the flames through all the variations between yellow and red. Barbarous tongues licked at the sky, and fiery throats belched sparks high into the air, where they drifted with the wind or fell dying to the earth.

Gavin could see now that the figures were smaller and thinner than they ought to be, like people seen darkly through funhouse mirrors, and he realized that they were children. They were standing around the fire as if worshiping its beauty and its power, dancing around it like idolators before some pagan god, or breaking away into the darkness for another long piece of wood or splintered board to toss upon the flames.

"Where are they getting the wood?" Elaine asked.

"I think they're tearing up fenceposts, and it looks as if there's a barn or farmhouse back there."

"Destructive little monsters," Elaine said.

Gavin shrugged. "Anytime you create something new, chances are you're destroying something old."

"I hope the people who built those fences and barns are as philosophical about it."

"A good man once called something like this the unavoidable and ultimately beneficial response of urban kids to the sudden release of open country."

"Beneficial to whom?" Elaine asked.

"To them. To society."

"And how about those whose efforts to build something get wasted?"

"The same philosopher said, 'There is plenty of fuel for celebration for a long time when laborious people have for several generations been accumulating it in fences and houses.' " But Gavin thought he could hear the Professor say, "Some people build because they must, and others destroy because they cannot build."

"They're coming this way!" Elaine said.

Gavin could see now that several dark figures were approaching the fence, silhouetted against the fire, crouching between the barbs of the wire fence that separated the field from the highway. Behind, more dark figures were streaming into a river of movement between the fence and the flames, like ants following a pheromone trail toward some marvelous bit of carrion.

"Let's get out of here!" Gavin said suddenly.

"What?"

"Get the car moving! Don't argue!"

"They're only children!" Elaine said.

"They want the car!"

Elaine started the car moving, but now bodies stood in front of it, hands linked, eyes blinking into the headlights. The children were about ten years old; they were both boys and girls, dressed neatly in shirts and pants and jackets of various colors. Their faces were white; their eyes seemed to glow like the eyes of cats.

Elaine stopped the car when the front bumper touched the row of bodies.

"Too late," Gavin said. "Get out. Quickly. Quietly."

Elaine edged out her side of the car, and Gavin followed, pushing her away from the car into the road and then into the ditch on the other side, away from the bonfire, away from the children. Silently the children climbed into the car and on top of it and onto the rear bumper. The car lunged down the highway, then made a tight turn that brought it back toward the ditch where Gavin and Elaine stood. Gavin pulled Elaine down, but the car swerved and turned away toward the fence.

The barbed wire parted and whirred through the air like whips as the car surged into the field, across grass and corn stubble. Children leaped from the car on either side as it lunged into the heart of the bonfire. In a moment it began to smolder, and then tongues of fire licked along the painted roof, the upholstery began to blaze, and metal and insulation turned the ascending flames green and blue and smoky black. . . .

They walked along the dark highway for a couple of miles, by Gavin's estimate, before they saw lighted windows off to the right. They crawled between strands of barbed wire and trudged across a plowed field, clods crumbling under their feet, until they reached a dirt road. They followed the road until they reached a tall fence built of stones and concrete and broken glass haphazardly mixed together by some cruel and determined hand.

"Someone doesn't want company," Gavin said.

"Maybe we should take a hint," Elaine said.

"They can't refuse us shelter and a little food. No one is that savage."

"What about the children?"

"Children are always savages."

After a few hundred feet they came to a gate in the fence. It faced north, toward the fire. The gate was solid and wooden, topped with barbed wire, like the gate to a stockade, but it was open a little, swinging gently on huge hinges, as if someone had come through it in a hurry and forgotten to shut it behind. The distant flames painted the door red, like blood.

Gavin pushed against the gate. The gap widened. "Come on," he said.

"I think we're making a mistake," Elaine said.

"Nonsense."

Inside the gate, the road still was dirt, but it was well kept and rutless, and the edges were outlined by a border of whitewashed rocks. The sky had begun to gray in the east, and by the faint light of dawn they could see neat lawn, which in this climate implied irrigation, and beyond, the beginnings of plowed fields, dark and fertile, waiting for seed and water to turn them green.

The smell of dust was in the air and, more distantly, the smell of fire.

The first building they approached was a white barn. It was big and sturdy, with a gambrel roof dark overhead, and a wide doorway, big enough for a car or a wagon, open like a black mouth to the road. Gavin could hear cattle moving restlessly inside and complaining. As they reached the doorway, Gavin saw a light at the far end of the barn; he nodded at Elaine and stepped inside the barn onto straw.

The smell of the straw and warm cattle and dung came to his nostrils like curdled air, and he breathed it in deeply, identifying the place by its odors as surely as if he had spent all his life on a farm. Over the sounds of the cattle moving around in their stalls, Gavin heard a thin, tinny sound. The light came dimly from a lantern hung or placed on a distant wall. Gavin walked toward it, down the center of the barn, Elaine behind him, between the rows of stalls, each with its cow, jaws working or udder sagging.

As they neared the far end of the barn, Gavin could see that the lantern was hung on a nail. The sound became louder. It was the noise of something hitting the side of a metal bucket. Gavin smelled warm milk. He was not surprised to see a head pressed into the black-and-white flank of a cow and two sturdy forearms thrust under the cow squirting milk in long, alternate streams into a bucket. The bucket was nearly full; the milk frothed near the top.

"That looks very skillful," Gavin said, and the milker leaped up from the stool, almost upsetting the bucket of milk.

The milker was a girl. She was young, perhaps fifteen or sixteen, and pretty, with a milkmaid's complexion, blond hair braided and knotted behind her head, surprised blue eyes, and a full-breasted figure. She seemed not only surprised but alarmed.

"We're just strangers off the road," Gavin said. "We didn't mean to startle you."

"We thought you might have a bite for us to eat, and maybe a bed or some straw for us to sleep in," Elaine added. "We've been driving since Denver, but some children took our car and burned it. I know that sounds ridiculous . . ."

"So that's where Pa went so early this morning," the girl said in a clear, pleasant voice. She looked at Elaine, and then, with more interest, at Gavin. "I wouldn't be here when he gets back if I was you."

"Surely he wouldn't begrudge us a little food," Gavin said reasonably.

"He'd begrudge you being here," the girl said. "This is Pa's land, and he's the only man around, or ever was, or ever he wants to be.

"Come on, Gavin," Elaine said. "There must be

other farms around, and they all can't be so unfriendly."

"She's telling you true, mister, about leaving, that
is," the girl said, "though you've got a good walk
ahead of you. Pa owns all the land for ten miles in
any direction. That's why he's up north. If those
damned kids are back, burning up his fences and
barns . . ."

"We're staying until we get something to eat," Gavin
said stubbornly.

"Well," the girl said, smiling a bit now, "if you
won't be warned, I'll take you up to the house, but
you'll have to move quick if Pa gets here before you're
through." She picked up the bucket of milk and
started down the length of the barn, carrying it with
the skill of long experience so that the milk didn't slop
over the edge.

"Let me help you," Gavin said.

She looked at him sideways, her head tilted, and
said, "I'm used to it."

She seemed strong enough, Gavin thought, with
her big hands and forearms and broad shoulders. Her
legs, though, were slender under a full skirt.

They followed her up a path beside the road until
they reached a big white farmhouse. It was two stories
tall, and it had a broad screened porch that went
across the front of the house and down the side and
around to the back, where the girl led them.

Gavin held the screen door open. The girl put down
her bucket by the door and turned to them. "I'm
Billie," she said. "Mary-Jo'll be by the stove, and I'll
introduce you to the others."

She opened the kitchen door, picked up her bucket,
and carried it into the bright, steamy kitchen. Gavin
followed. The kitchen was a big room, filled with
stoves and refrigerators and washers and other kinds
of equipment, and people. All the people were women
and children. All of them looked alike. The women were
tall, blond, and buxom; they all looked like Billie.
And the children were small and blond, all like each
other and the women, too.

Actually, when Gavin came to count them, there

were only seven women and five children, two of the children infants, one of them suckling at the breast of a mother seated at a big round oak table; she was eating cereal and cream from a bowl. They all looked up, surprised, when Gavin and Elaine entered.

"These is two strangers who come to the barn looking for food and a place to rest," Billie said. "Their car got took and burned by the kids up north. That's Mary-Jo by the stove. This is Sarah and June and Maxine and Frieda and Gertrude and Millie."

"I'm Gavin," he said, feeling strange among all these almost identical women, like an untested bull in a herd of heifers. "This is Elaine."

The woman stirring a kettle at the black stove looked at them solemnly. "You don't belong here. You better git before Pa gets back. He be mighty put out. No telling what he might do he find you here. And, Billie, you git back to the milking. Pa, he finds the cows ain't milked, he might take his belt to you."

Billie shrugged and poured the bucket into a large milk can made of gleaming stainless steel. "I know what Pa's belt is like, and I ain't afraid of it like some of you." But she started back out the door with her bucket.

"We know what you're afraid of," said the one called Frieda.

Billie slammed the door behind her.

"All we want is a bite of food and a place to rest," Gavin said.

"Well, you can't stay," Mary-Jo said. "Pa'd kill you. He near killed the last boy came in here looking for a place to stay. Now, you," she went on, looking at Elaine, "you can stay if you want. Pa won't hurt you, and he might take to you, though you're not much of a woman. Maybe you could be a proper wife to Pa."

"Thanks for the invitation," Elaine said, "but I'll pick my own mate."

They looked at her as if she had uttered heresy. Something about the situation was bothering Gavin, something he should have noticed, or something he had noticed and had not understood.

"Just give us some food, then," Gavin said, "and we'll be on our way."

Mary-Jo looked at the other six women for help, and then looked back at Gavin. "You've been warned," she said. "Whatever happens . . ."

"Is my fault," Gavin finished. He seated himself at the table, opposite the nursing mother; the infant released the nipple and turned its head to look at him before seeking out the nipple again with moist lips. Gavin picked up a knife and a fork, holding them upright, one in each hand.

Mary-Jo took a bowl from a stack beside the stove and filled it with something steaming from the kettle. She put the bowl in front of him and then fixed a bowl for Elaine.

Gavin felt silly sitting there with a knife and a fork. "Is this what all the fuss was about?" he asked. He and his stomach had been thinking of something more substantial, like meat and eggs and potatoes.

"That's breakfast," Mary-Jo said. "That's all there is. Eat and git. And you girls better be about your chores."

Slowly the other women filed out of the kitchen. Some, in work clothes, left by the back door. Others, in dresses, went through a doorway into the house. All of them looked back at Gavin curiously. He shook his head and covered his oatmeal with sugar and cream. He tasted it. It was hot and good.

"I don't understand this place," he said to Mary-Jo.

"It's Pa's," she said simply.

"I know it's a farm—a big farm. Ten miles in any direction, Billie said. And it belongs to your father. But how did he get all that land?"

"Billie's young. She stretches things. But what there is here used to belong to a lot of people. Right thinkers, Pa said, who put their money together and bought this land and built it up and made it flourish, like God said man should do, and the land was good and the animals brought forth their young, and God's blessing was upon everyone and the work of their hands."

"That sounds like some kind of scripture," Elaine said.

Mary-Jo continued as if Elaine hadn't spoken. "But gradually the people fell into error. One by one they began drifting away or were driven away by the others because of wrong thoughts or wrong deeds. And the curse of God came upon the land, and people died, and some were killed in arguments. And what was held in common began to be a source of quarrels, and finally all were gone except Pa. Ma died in childbirth after eight daughters, and we were left, Pa and us, to care for all the land and the animals, to make it the way God wanted it to be, and the land prospered again."

"And Pa is God," Gavin said.

Mary-Jo straightened, frowning. "No, Pa is God's right hand, his spokesman, his prophet."

Gavin was halfway to the bottom of his bowl; the edge had been taken from his hunger. "Apparently," he said to Elaine, "a religious commune was founded here in the early or middle seventies. The religious enthusiasm that supported it in its beginning began to crumble under all the hard work and the human problems of getting along. When the others were driven away or left or died, Pa got it all."

"Wasn't that way," Mary-Jo said.

"Now he's got a holy kingdom of his own here," Gavin said, "with his own crew of workers—all daughters—and nobody allowed to leave and no outsiders allowed in to spoil paradise. There's just one thing I don't under—"

A horse's hooves clopped in the dirt road outside. Mary-Jo looked up, alarmed.

"You got to go," she said to Gavin. "He'll come in the front way to put away his gun. Run, now! Git!"

Her terror was contagious. Gavin himself felt a tremor when she mentioned her father's gun. Something about the situation suggested that, like Abraham, Pa might act without asking questions.

"Go on," Elaine said. "Run! I'll be right behind you, but you can run faster than I can, and he won't hurt me."

Still Gavin hesitated. He heard the front door open. A deep voice, like the voice of a prophet, announced with Olympian satisfaction, "I think I got a couple of the little demons this time."

Gavin ran. He ran through the back door and the screen door, expecting to hear it slam shut like a rifle shot behind him, but Elaine must have been there to ease it closed, and Gavin ran down the road, now much brighter in the onrushing dawn. He looked back as he neared the barn and saw Elaine running from the house as he fell over an outstretched foot and landed face-down on the straw in front of the barn door.

Gavin rolled over and looked up at Billie. "Why did you do that? I thought you kept urging me to get away if your father returned. Well, he's back."

"I know," she said, frowning, and reached down a hand to pull him to his feet, and then into the protection of the barn. "Take me with you."

"I can't do that," Gavin protested. "Your father would never stop following me. Besides, why do you want to leave? Your sisters are here, and your father."

"That's why," she said. "Pa's been hinting lately that I'm old enough to come to him in the night, the way my sisters do."

"The old bastard! That's what was bothering me. All the children. And he's the only male around. . . ."

Billie stood up straight. "I don't want him to service me, no matter what the others say about God's will. If you can't take me with you, least you can do that for me. I'd rather you'd service me than Pa." She turned around and leaned forward over a milking stanchion, throwing her skirt up over her back as she did, and exposed her long slender legs and appealing milky buttocks. "I think if you did it he wouldn't have nothing to do with me."

"Except kill me," Gavin muttered, "and maybe you." He stepped forward to pull Billie upright and toward him as her skirt fell about her calves. "Anyway, that's not the way people do it. Not like animals. There's . . . uh, affection . . . and . . . uh, sometimes love . . . and, uh, caresses, kisses . . . and, uh, mutual respect . . . that brings men and women . . . uh, face-to-face. . . ."

"Show me!" Billie said eagerly.

"What is this talent you have, Gavin," Elaine said, leaning against the frame of the barn door, shaking her head, "for inducing females to throw themselves at you, legs parted?"

"This poor girl has a problem," Gavin said. "She's the victim of isolation and a tyrannical, incestuous father."

"I could feel sorrier for her," Elaine said, "if that tyrannical father were not close behind me. It looks to me like you've got the problem. One of the sisters must have told Pa."

Gavin's hands dropped from Billie's shoulders as if they were weighted. "Where, where?" he asked. He leaped to the door.

Striding down the dirt road from the house as if he disdained a faster pace came a tall, lean patriarch of a man, long hair floating behind, gray beard waving in front, and between them a face like an avenging sword. He held a shotgun in his right hand. He held it easily. Underneath his patched overalls and jeans jacket, Gavin thought, were lean old muscles toughened by hard labor and long days.

Gavin had the uneasy feeling that the god this zealot worshiped was a god of wrath and vengeance, and occasionally the prophet confused himself with the deity.

"Don't go out there," Billie said. "Pa'll shoot you down like a scared rabbit if you run from him."

Gavin felt like a scared rabbit. He turned and ran the length of the barn toward a door at the far end. Dust from hay and straw rose in the air, sparkling in the first rays of the morning sun streaming into the barn. But as he neared the far door, his feet slowed, and he stopped, turned, and walked back toward them.

"Don't be a fool," Elaine said. "Get out while there's time."

"Go on, mister," Billie said. "Pa's no talker."

"What about you?" Gavin said to Elaine. "What about Billie?"

"We'll be all right," Elaine said. "Come on. I'll go with you. I just didn't want to slow you down."

"No," Gavin said. "I'm not going to run from the incestuous old bastard."

But even as he said the words, the mad prophet was in the doorway, the shotgun was at his shoulder, and it exploded with a big coughing sound and a whistling of shot. Gavin stood, frozen in mid-stride, waiting for bits of metal to shred his flesh, and nothing happened. The muzzle of the gun was pointed toward the ceiling; Elaine had pushed the barrel.

Gavin ran toward the old man. As he ran, the old man swung around to knock Elaine away from him. She sprawled on the straw-littered floor. The old man swung back toward Gavin, pulling the trigger as the weapon came to bear, and Gavin threw himself at the old man's legs. He heard the gun cough again and the shot whistle again, and then felt the impact of his body against the old man's legs. The legs yielded, and Gavin found himself rolling over the old man's body as it hit the floor, grabbing for the shotgun, clutching the hot barrel, clinging to it even as it burned his hand, tearing it away from the old man, feeling something break as it came free, rolling to his feet with the gun in his hand, turning it toward the old man.

The mad prophet was just as mad without his gun. He pulled himself up tall as he got to his feet. His index finger dangled crookedly from his right hand, but he disdained to nurse it or even notice anything wrong with it. "Shoot, debaucher, lecher, whoremaster."

"Don't call me names," Gavin said, "you incestuous pig!"

"You despoil my land by standing on it," the old man said. "Just as you would despoil my daughters. Now, kill me so that you can begin your devil's work!"

Elaine tugged at Gavin's arm. "Come on. Let's get out of here. We just came in for a bite of food," she said to the old man.

"Are you his slut?" he asked her.

"We can't just let this bastard go on committing unspeakable sins by night and justifying them by day," Gavin said indignantly.

"Who appointed us his judges?" Elaine said. "His daughters are the only ones injured, and they have ample opportunity to combine against him or to slip away if they wished."

"My daughters are good, obedient girls," the old man said.

"He has them terrified, brainwashed," Gavin said. "To them he's not only a father, with all his paternal authority, but the head of their religion, with all the sanction of God behind his edicts."

"You will be punished by the hand of God the just, the unforgiving," the old man thundered. "You will be pursued across a blasted land by vengeful furies, tormented by whips of fire, tortured by poisoned pitchforks, until your soul screams for mercy and your flesh shrivels upon the bone and your tongue blackens in your head and your—"

"Look how Billie feels about him!" Gavin said. "This would be a better world if I removed this dirty old man from it."

But as he said "dirty old man," something hit the back of his head. Even as he staggered to his knees, he was aware of the ridiculous "bonk" it made. He dropped the shotgun and clutched his head with the pain. "Billie!" he said, and then, "Billie?"

The old man grabbed the gun almost as it fell, and Billie stepped out from behind Gavin, holding her milking bucket tightly in her hand. "He's my Pa," she said simply.

Gavin shook his head gingerly against the pain. "God!" he said.

"Right!" the old man shouted. "God has condemned you, and now you will die, infidel! Satanist! Unbeliever!" But he couldn't pull the trigger with his broken finger, and while he was struggling to fit another finger into the trigger guard and get his broken finger out of it, a crash came from the distance, the sound of metal and splintering wood, and a thunder of engine exhausts and blaring horns.

The old man whirled at this new invasion of his kingdom. Gavin grabbed the shotgun and ripped it away. Swinging the gun by its stock, he smashed the barrel against the door frame, bending it beyond any possibility of use. The sounds grew louder. Gavin stepped out of the barn, holding his head stiffly so that it didn't jiggle. He tried to watch the old man out of the corner of his eye.

But the old man had moved faster than Gavin, and stood a little in front, staring with holy horror at the sacrilege approaching. It was a procession of trucks and automobiles and motorcycles, all internal-combustion models, thundering and creaking and tearing the ground with their tires, leaving a trail of dust and dark, billowing exhaust.

Men and women leaned from the windows of the cars or over the edges of the trucks, waving, calling out with words that could not be heard over the noise of the caravan. They were dressed in jeans and blouses, or jeans jackets or uniform coats, with headbands or scarves or cowboy hats over their long hair.

The motorcycles, most of them with two riders, made crazy circles or figure eights around and through the caravan.

An open jeep led the procession. An older man stood in the back of the jeep holding on to a roll bar fastened to the sides of the jeep, like a general on parade. He, too, was dressed in jeans, and long, gray hair streamed back from a craggy face.

"Gypsies!" Elaine said.

"White Indians!" Gavin said.

But he thought he could hear the Professor saying, "No, these are the centaurs invading the Temple of Zeus at Olympia, bursting in upon the traditional ceremonies, only to be driven back by a stern Apollo, the guardian of the orthodox culture. The clash of irreconcilable conceptions of life. The centaurs and civilization. Dionysus and Apollo."

The jeep stopped in front of the little group at the entrance to the barn, skidding a little, and the other vehicles pulled up behind, some of them slipping off the dirt road onto the grass or banging into the vehicle in front.

When the confusion had subsided, the man standing in the jeep called out in the mellow voice of a singer, one hand flung dramatically into the air, "Welcome! Welcome to the Freedom Train! Welcome all to the cultural revolution! Welcome to the glory of Consciousness Three!"

Gavin gaped at the crazy procession, unable to think of anything to say, but the old man stood up straight and said, "Get off of my land, you satanists, spoilers!" His hands clenched and unclenched as if they were longing for a gun to hold in them.

"We come to invite all who wish to ride upon the Freedom Train to join us in our parade into a glorious future of sensitivity and love and right thinking!"

"Take these strangers," the old man said, indicating Gavin and Elaine. "They're your kind, shiftless and destructive, living off other people's hard work."

"We come," the leader of the caravan said, unheeding, "to share the bounty of the earth, which belongs to all men."

"We need nothing from you," the old man said. "We do our own work here and ask nobody's help and accept nobody's aid."

"You misunderstand me, sir," the leader said cheerfully, as his followers began to pour out of their vehicles behind him and spread out through the barn and other outbuildings and toward the farmhouse itself. "We come to share the bounty that has been deposited here."

The old man looked scornful. "No one deposited anything here. What we have we wrested from a stubborn land. When I came, this land was arid and barren, and I watered it with my sweat and fertilized it with my labor. It is strange that the earth does not deposit any bounty where you live."

The leader of the caravan must have been about the same age as the patriarch, but he acted younger, as if avoiding everything but pleasure had kept him from aging. He shrugged pleasantly and said, "Your god works in strange and mysterious ways his wonders to perform, and it little behooves us to question why he should make one place bloom and not another."

"I know you," the old man said, his eyes glittering madly. "You are the children who burn my fences and my buildings to see the pretty blaze, only you have grown up to become plunderers as well as destroyers."

The men and women who had tumbled out of the cars and trucks were returning now, their arms laden with sacks of grain and flour, and boxes of vegetables and fruit. They led pigs and cows and steers, putting them all in the trucks, which miraculously sprouted ramps as if it had all happened before.

The old man narrowed his eyes in pain at the sight and then turned to the looters and tried to wrestle their spoils from them. But they ignored him or pushed him away, and the old man finally turned and began to stride off toward the house.

"Stop him!" the leader of the caravan called out. "He's probably got guns at the house."

"He has," Gavin said, speaking at last.

The leader gave him a cool look of appraisal.

One of the looters tripped the old man as he passed. Others, their hands free, fell on him and tied his hands together, and then his feet. He sat in the middle of the road cursing the leader and everyone who passed.

The trucks were almost full. "Who goes with us on the Freedom Train?" the leader asked.

"Where are you heading?" Gavin asked.

"South. To Cockaigne. Where no one has to work or do anything else he doesn't want to do."

Gavin looked at Elaine. She shrugged. "What's involved?" Gavin asked.

"Nothing at all," the leader said. "If there were any obligations, it would not be Cockaigne."

"We're going south," Gavin said.

The leader motioned to his jeep. Gavin helped Elaine into the front seat and got into the back with the leader.

"And how about you, little lady?" the leader said to Billie.

Billie took a look at her father shouting in the dust and said, "I'll go too." She climbed into one of the cars behind. She still clung to her bucket.

"I think there's more women in the house and in the fields," a man said. He came from the direction of the house with a big box of fruit and vegetables put up in glass jars. "I thought I heard women . . . children's voices, too."

"Children?" the leader said happily. He turned to Gavin and Elaine. "We all love children." He turned back to his followers. "By all means, let us search them out."

But as a new group started toward the house, a rifle shot cracked, and dust sprouted from the road. Another shot followed immediately, and a bullet pinged against the side of a truck.

"On the other hand," the leader said hastily, "we must not force ourselves upon the unwilling. Get started!" he said to his driver, and the jeep lurched forward. The leader sat down hard in the back seat. The caravan made a wide circle in the grass, returned to the road, and passed through the splintered gate while rifle bullets nervously searched the air.

In a few minutes they were back on the divided highway, heading south, a motley, ragged wagon train of dilapidated and antiquated vehicles filled with shouting, singing people and complaining animals.

"So, Professor," Gavin thought, "Apollo may have driven off the centaurs, but not before they looted the temple."

"Wouldn't it be simpler just to grow your own food?" he asked the leader, seated beside him.

The leader smiled. "You can call me Reich. Or Third. That's short for the Third Reich, as some of the old consciousness groups call me, or Reich the Third, as my friends call me. And we do grow our own food. We just grow it on other people's farms, and when we need it, we come and get it. That's simple enough, isn't it?"

Elaine had turned around in her seat. "For you, yes."

"The unremitting labor necessary to proper agriculture in this climate is deadening to the spirit," Reich said. "Most work available in our society is meaningless, degrading, and inconsistent with self-realization. It is work, unrelenting, driven, consuming, that comes between the professor and his students, the lawyer and his family, the bank employee and the beauty of nature."

"Somebody has to do it," Elaine said.

"Let those do it who must," Reich replied. "Let others get by without it if they can. Freedom from such work, making possible the development of an individual's true potential as a human being, is among the greatest and most vital forms of liberation."

"So you go around liberating other people's produce," Gavin said.

Reich beamed at him. "You understand," he said.

"Why don't you simply pool your minimum annual incomes and buy what you need?" Gavin asked.

Reich's smile turned to a frown. "And collaborate with a government which has always told us we are an incredibly rich country when we are actually desperately poor—poor in most of the things that throughout the history of mankind have been cherished as riches? If you accept its charity, you consent to its tyranny."

"They cut you off, didn't they?" Elaine said.

"They called us a conspiracy," Reich said. "Just because we had a little unscheduled visitation on the town of Taos."

The caravan rolled steadily down the highway, heading south. The even squares of the fields on either side were like a giant checkerboard man had laid down upon the earth to make it comprehensible. The fields were brown, now that winter was almost upon this high land, but they looked as if they would be green and fertile again; and here and there, automated electric machinery harvested corn or soybeans, or plowed the soil to leave a black square among the brown.

On their right, the mountains kept pace with them. To Gavin they seemed like jagged parapets of a great wall which barred humanity from a promised land.

The caravan stopped twice on the road to the commune called Cockaigne somewhere north of Taos— once to let Billie get into the truck with the cows and complete their milking, once to refuel the internal-combustion engines with gasoline brought along in colorful and oddly shaped pottery jars.

Toward evening they arrived at an arid place closer to the mountains and some ten miles from the big highway down narrow, winding roads through valleys and along the sides of foothills. Tired fenceposts and sagging barbed wire guarded the commune. Weeds grew in the fields among volunteer corn and milo and shatter cane; here and there, in a fit of enthusiasm, a little patch of land had been weeded and planted with carrots or potatoes or tomatoes or lettuce and then left to the bugs and the birds, the elements and the animals; but they stood out amid the general decay like reminders of what man could do to improve the productivity of the land if he could sustain his desire.

"If you talk to a farmer about ecology," the Professor said once, "he is likely to reply, 'You should have seen this place when nature was running it.'"

Depressions at the edge of fields and discarded siphons suggested that once the land had been nourished by an irrigation system, but that had been long ago. Now the weeds grew taller in silted and useless ditches. Here and there, the rusted remains of farm machinery poked out of the weeds like the bones of long-extinct dinosaurs.

"Some dull, industrious people farmed this land once," Reich said, "but they got tired and gave up and left it to us."

The whole place looked tired, Gavin thought, as if the land had given up on the people. The dust from the rutted dirt road they traveled now was dry and dead, and mixed with it was a growing smell of human wastes and decay.

The caravan neared a group of farm buildings and ramshackle hutches thrown together out of old wood and tin. Men, women, and a few children emerged into a littered patch of land trampled into uniform, weedless, packed dirt marred here and there by the soot and charred wood of old campfires. The people from the huts shouted and waved and pranced in celebration of the returning scavengers.

Gavin could tell from the set of Elaine's shoulders that she didn't like this place. He shrugged. They didn't have to stay if they didn't like it, and they had gained two hundred miles on their journey south.

Reich was standing up in the jeep again. "We come,"

he shouted, "bringing the earth's plenty to its chosen people."

Earth's chosen people swarmed around the caravan, marveling at the bounty in the trucks, helping unload them of sacks and boxes, leading animals down ramps and into improvised enclosures, laughing at piles of dung the weary cattle left in the commons. Those who had nothing to carry or lead danced around as if they were improvising out of an irrepressible joy in living.

Gavin felt his opinion of the place begin to shift. After all, what did cleanliness and order matter?

Reich turned to Gavin and Elaine, smiling as if he had invented his followers. "Aren't they marvelous?" he said. "Aren't they wonderful?"

Gavin began to think that maybe they were marvelous and wonderful. He had always been able to feel other people's abandon, even though he was basically a spectator. He climbed out of the jeep and reached to help Elaine, but she already was on the ground. They looked up at Reich, his arms spread wide toward his people in a gesture of bounty and openness, like a man performing a miracle with fish and bread or a god prepared to make the ultimate sacrifice. The sunset on the nearby Sangre de Cristos Mountains turned his face and hands the color of blood.

As the shadows of the peaks began to stretch into the camp, the carefree people prepared a feast. Pigs were killed, squealing and bloody, and spitted over an open fire of old wood and manure, and when those ran low, one of the shacks was demolished for its lumber, as if the world ended today.

Vegetables were peeled and sliced and dumped into open pots with water and meat to simmer. Men and women worked side-by-side, sharing in everything, with an occasional half-naked child joining in the joyous activities as well; other children, too small to help, played around the shacks or in the dirt and casual vegetation of the fields. Sometimes, while they worked, a man and a woman's hands would meet in a

special way, and they would stop whatever they were
doing and walk together to one of the shacks or out
into the fields.

They were a strange group, Gavin thought—students
grown middle-aged, with a few young people and a
few more children. Reich was the oldest person in
the group; he must have been sixty, approaching seven-
ty. Like him, the others dressed in a variety of costumes
expressing their attitudes or their moods of the moment,
but all of them wore denim jeans, as if this were their
badge of membership. To this they added individualiz-
ing touches: handmade belts and fancy blouses, ragged
jackets, military coats, or opera cloaks; they liked jew-
elry—they wore rings and bracelets, and around their
necks, men and women, decorations made of various
kinds of metal and semiprecious stones or just pieces
of colored rock strung together. Many of them wore
headbands or strange, tattered hats.

As the shadows of the nearby peaks closed over the
camp like the jaws of night, the sunny day grew colder,
and the members of the group began to edge closer
to the fire, both for warmth and to smell the delicious
odors given off by bubbling pots and turning spits.
Even the children stopped playing their games of pusher and narc, of cops and protesters, and came to hud-
dle beside adults and stare into the flames and whim-
per occasionally at the hunger in their bellies and
the anticipated feast.

Someone brought a guitar out of a shack and began
to pick out a tune. A few people began to hum. Soon
the gathering shadows were filled with song: sentimental songs of the open road or youthful companions or
the discovery of truth, protest songs of alienation and
terror and yearnings, hymns to drugs and free love,
militant songs of coming revolution or of barricades
in the streets. . . .

Gavin recognized a few of them, thought others
sounded familiar, and had never heard the rest. But
everyone in camp except the newcomers knew the
words and joined in the singing, sometimes clapping
in time to the music. It was a communal experience

that Gavin found moving in spite of himself, in spite of the elderly incongruity of many around the fire, and he found himself warming to the life of the commune as his body was warmed by the fire.

By the time the singing died away, the people turning the spits indicated that the feast was ready. Big knives appeared to carve long slices of roasted meat into waiting plates and impatient hands. Big ladles added vegetables to bowls and cups. Loaves of bread were torn apart. The eating began.

The cold mountain air and a whole day without food made Gavin ravenous, and he did not notice until he was almost full that the pork was burned on the outside and underdone on the inside, and that everything lacked salt and other seasoning. But it was good, better even than the elegant meal in Sally's Denver mansion on china with crystal and silver, and Gavin at last put down his plate, wiped his greasy fingers on his shirt, sighed, and was content.

He lay back on grass beyond the immediate family circle around the fires, with the night full upon the world, and looked over at Elaine, who had taken no pork but had eaten stew and bread, and at Billie a few feet away, her face smeared with pork fat and the heat of the fire. Her eyes looked stunned, as if she was overcome by the food and the heat and the colorful figures around the fire, and the changes wrought in her life within a few hours.

In spite of everything, Gavin thought, these were his people, even if they were old. He looked up at the stars, and they were clear and close and cold.

He smelled tobacco smoke and a more acrid smell, like dry leaves burning. He lay there, smelling them and enjoying the contentment of a full stomach and the companionship of brothers and sisters, and Elaine spoiled it. She leaned over him and whispered, "Let's get out of here."

"What?" Gavin asked.

"I feel uneasy," she said. "Call it intuition."

"Oh, come on," Gavin said. "Let's lay up here for a few days, rest up for the remainder of the trip."

"Something's going to happen," Elaine insisted.

"What could happen way out here?" Gavin said. "These just aren't your kind of people."

Before he could say more, a rhythmic clapping had begun from the group sitting around the fires, and someone shouted, "The Ballad." Others took it up: "The Ballad! The Ballad!"

Gavin sat up and saw a small boy run past with a joint in his hand.

Some of the others had pushed together a platform out of boxes and planks, and they were boosting Reich up onto it. He only half-resisted, and when he was up he stood in front of them, his hands on his hips, his long gray hair swinging. "You want the Ballad?"

"The Ballad! The Ballad!"

Reich struck a pose like an old-fashioned troubadour and lifted a clear tenor toward the sky.

"Let me sing you a song of Consciousness Three."

"Consciousness Three," sang the others, like antiphony.

"Of you and me," Reich sang.

"Consciousness Three," responded the others, and so it went through the rest of the ceremony. At least, that's what it seemed like to Gavin, like a ritual, like a confirmation of their beliefs, of themselves.

"On our legs we wear jeans
   because they are cheap,
   because they are earthy,
                    sensual,
                    free.
"Expressing the shape of the leg,
   shaped to the leg that wears them.
"They nudge the wearer with deep questions.
   Their freedom reminds him he has choice."
"But what about bell bottoms," the crowd shouted.
"Bell bottoms are better," Reich sang.
"Like jeans they express the body
  but they give the ankles a special freedom
  as if to invite dancing in the street.
"A touch football game in bell bottoms
  is like folk dancing or ballet.

"Bell bottoms are happy,
                    comic,
                    rollicking.
"No one can take himself seriously
    in bell bottoms.
"For we are Consciousness Three."
"Are we!" came the response.
"We are Consciousness Three."

By the flickering light of the fire in the night, Gavin saw Billie being led into the darkness by a young man and a middle-aged man, and he felt a touch of regret.

"First there was Consciousness One."
"It's done," the others sang.
"First there was Consciousness One.
    Immigrants
    from class and village,
    seeking new hope,
    making a new beginning,
    freed from the past,
    building a new community,
    innocent and free.
"The sovereign individual
    turning the wheel of plenty.
"But then came self-interest,
                    competition,
                    suspicion,
    to confirm its thought that
    human nature is bad,
    and struggle is man's condition.
"Consciousness One alienated man
    from environment
    and society,
    from man's own needs and functions.
"Money called the tune;
    loss of reality,
    gross corporeality.
"Set in a sterile model of the past,
    spooning ice cream
    while piped-in ragtime
    tinkles unheard.

"That was Consciousness One."
"It's done," came the antiphony.
"That was Consciousness One."

"What was that sound?" Elaine asked.
"I didn't hear anything," Gavin said.

"Then there was Consciousness Two."
"It's new."
"Then there was Consciousness Two.
"From Consciousness One
   disaster had come:
   robber barons,
   business piracy,
   ruinous competition,
   unreliable products,
   false advertising,
   grotesque inequality,
   excessive individualism,
   lack of coordination,
   a gangster world.
   Besides the chaos of insecurity
               and powerlessness,
"Man became the plaything of circumstances
   and forces beyond control,
   like the Great Depression,
   and turned to Fascism.
"A new Consciousness arose
   to organize and coordinate,
   arrange things in a rational hierarchy,
   and sacrifice for a common good.
"Consciousness Two appeared:
   businessmen,
   liberal intellectuals,
   educated professionals,
   technicians,
   middle-class suburbanites,
   labor-union leaders,
   Gene McCarthy supporters,
   blue-collar workers with newly purchased homes,
   old-time leftists,

members of the American Communist party,
the Kennedys,
the New York *Times* editorial page,
liberalism,
and the Democratic party.
"And they produced
a commitment of the individual to the public interest,
more social responsibility by private business,
more affirmative government action,
                              regulation,
                              planning.
more rational administration and management
and the welfare state.
"But possessing still a
profoundly pessimistic view of man as an
aggressive,
competitive,
power-seeking,
jungle beast.
"And the joy of life became a quest for
power,
success,
status,
acceptance,
popularity,
achievement,
rewards,
excellence,
cooperation,
and a rational, competent mind.
"The result: alienation, and no room for
awe,
wonder,
mystery,
accidents,
failure,
helplessness,
and magic.
"And to a young person
the corporate state beckoned,
with a skeleton grin,

'Step right in,
you'll love it—
it's just like living.' "

Gavin said to Elaine, "I think I heard something."
"What is it?" Elaine asked. "Let's move farther
from the fire and listen."

"And then came Consciousness Three."
"Are we."
"Yes, we are Consciousness Three,
     sprouting from the stony soil
     of the American corporate state,
     from the promise that proved false,
     affluence,
     security,
     technology.
"Consciousness Three made possible
     a new life,
     a new freedom,
      a new expansion of human possibility.
"Consciousness Three accepts itself:
     'I'm glad I'm me.'
     'Whatever I am I am.'
"To those who have glimpsed
     the real possibilities of life,
     tasted liberation and love,
     seen the promised land,
     a dreary corporate job,
     a ranchhouse life,
     a miserable death in war,
     is utterly intolerable;
     the thought of what is
     and what could be
     is overwhelming.
"The promise of America,
     land of beauty and abundance,
     land of the free,
     had been betrayed.
"And Consciousness Three emerged with its message:
     Thou shalt not do violence to thyself.
     People are brothers.

No one judges anyone else.
No one stands above the crowd.
No one uses another person.
No one gives commands nor follows them,
Nor observes duties after the feeling is gone.
"To Consciousness Three all has been revealed:
   an unjust society
   run for the benefit of the privileged few,
   lacking in proclaimed democracy and liberty,
   ugly,
   artificial,
   unhealthy for children and other living things."

"It sounds like people moving around out there somewhere," Gavin said.

"Put on your headbands and your jeans,
   and show what revolution means.
"For we are Consciousness Three."
"Are we!"
"We are Consciousness Three."

Almost as the echoes of the ballads were still returning from the surrounding hills, while Reich still held his dramatic pose upon the makeshift stage, a woman screamed in the darkness beyond the firelight and Billie ran into the circle of light. She was naked to the waist, and her face and hands were smeared with blood.

"Help!" she shouted. "Help me! It's Pa. He's killed those two fellows with a knife, and he's fixing to kill me too, if he can."

At the sound of the first scream, the people around the fire were on their feet, and as Billie appeared with her message of vengeance, they turned in different directions to flee. Before they could separate, lights blazed from every side of the camp. People froze where they stood, like jacklighted deer.

From out of the darkness beyond the lights came a man's reasonable voice. "This here group's been found a conspiracy, and it has got to be broke up. Do not resist, and no damage will be done."

"What do you mean 'no damage'?" Reich called. "What are you going to do with us?"

"Nothing much," said the reasonable voice. "You're going to be split up is all, and the government is going to see that you keep split up. If you don't, the next step is deportation."

"Where to?" Reich asked, looking around him at the men and women his song had praised, as if he could not bear to think of the group being scattered. "Europe? Asia? Latin America?"

"Mars," the voice replied, and chuckled. "See if you can get by there without working."

"Come on," Elaine said softly, and tugged at Gavin's hand. Keeping low, they began crawling between the outer rings of lights.

Behind them Gavin could hear the camp explode with movement as the members of Reich's tribe threw themselves toward the lights. But bombs exploded in the air, and something sweet and enervating, like the odor of lotus blossoms, came to Gavin. By this time they were past the lights and scrambling into the darkness.

Gavin looked back once and saw Reich, defiant to the end, sinking onto his platform like the Statue of Liberty melting from the bottom up.

A few hundred yards into the night, Gavin collapsed into an irrigation ditch. He dragged Elaine down beside him. They lay huddled together. Gavin could feel Elaine's heart bumping against his chest. They listened to the sounds of bodies being methodically loaded into vehicles, like sides of beef.

"Have we got them all?" someone called.

Elaine shivered in Gavin's arms.

"According to my count, we're missing one."

"Say, I just stumbled across a couple guys in this field. They had their throats cut wide open."

"Then we're one over."

"Here's a wild man with a long beard and a bloody knife who says these people stole his food and his daughter."

"If one of these is his daughter, then the numbers

check out. Bring the old guy along. We'll take care of his problem in the morning."

Slowly the sounds became infrequent. With a burst of activity, a new caravan pulled away from the camp. After its passage diminished in the distance, silence settled back upon the land as if it had never been disturbed since eternity began.

"You see, Gavin," the Professor said, "the forces of Apollo prevail, as they always have. Even when the chaos of Dionysus seems victorious, it is only momentary. Order creeps back; civilization returns; day replaces night. . . ."

Gavin held Elaine in his arms all night long and never once thought of anything but the cold.

10 ⟶ The Place at the Top of the World

Ever since the Industrial Revolution began reshaping the nature of human existence, romantic fools have been urging humanity to shut down the machines—forcibly, if necessary—and return to the simpler, more natural ways of our ancestors. How else, they ask, can we throw off the poisons of civilization, restore the natural vigor of our bodies, prevent the pollution of our water and our air, and eliminate the neuroses and psychosomatic illnesses which afflict technological man? We must return to nature, they say. Nature! What is natural to man? And I tell you that knowledge is more human than ignorance, science is as human as art, and only technology can prevent pollution and preserve us from extinction. Without technology, man is at the mercy of nature, and nature is not kind. Man's natural condition, as Thomas Hobbes pointed out, is poor, short, nasty, and brutish. But more important than man's condition is his potential: he has only one chance for immortality as he starts up the ladder of technology. At a certain stage in his development, he has used up his capital—the fossil fuels—and he must climb the next step to the inexhaustible resources of solar power and thermonuclear energy, or fall all the way to the bottom, perhaps never to rise again.

—THE PROFESSOR'S NOTEBOOK

Gavin woke up shivering in his sleeping bag. For a disoriented moment he didn't know where he was, and then he felt under his back the hard reality of the mountain and he felt in his lungs the thin, cold air, and he remembered how they had arrived at this desolate spot in a desolate world.

It was later than he thought. The sun had climbed up as high as the mountains to the east of them. Gavin felt as if he were peering out of a shark's mouth past great jagged rows of teeth crowding in one behind another.

He looked over at Elaine, still asleep in her sleeping bag; her head was ducked into the bag, and he could see only her hair. But he knew her face so well now that it was almost like seeing it.

They had come a long way together across the country. Since Taos it had been either deserts or mountains with towns like oases in their midst. And now they had arrived at this spot on this mountainside so barren, so useless, so isolated that it might never have known the presence of man. And still she would not let him touch her; even for warmth, she would not share his sleeping bag.

If they did not find the pass through these mountains soon, it would not matter. Their packaged food had been eaten for supper and their water was almost gone, and Gavin was afraid that they were lost. They had been wandering in these mountains for days, and every valley led only to another peak.

Everywhere around them was gray, dead rock, cold, hard, and unforgiving.

Ruefully, Gavin thought that they should have stayed on the road with their electric cycles, but experience had made them cautious. When they heard approaching them the strange discordant melodies of a religious procession, they had turned off the highway onto a convenient trail. It led up a valley, always climbing into the mountains. But the procession had followed; when the path ended in tumbled rock, they had to abandon their cycles and proceed on foot, always just a little in front of the procession.

Later they found a bearded man dying on a cross on

a hilltop. He was exalted by revelation or drugs or approaching death, and he cursed them in Spanish when they took him down. But they stayed with him anyway until he was dead, and they buried him at the foot of the cross under some rocks.

In the last mountain village they had been told about strange people in the mountains. Some were mystics like the ones who sought a new messiah among those who passed their way, for someone who would die for their sins and be reborn. Others . . . well, the villagers didn't know, but they thought magicians lived high in the mountains—in the place at the top of the world.

Gavin and Elaine sipped hot chocolate at a table outside a little adobe café while dark-skinned children looked wonder at their cycles, and they speculated whether either of the stories was true. Now one had been proven.

By then they were lost. They were afraid the religious group would return and ask one of them to replace their lost messiah on the cross. They tried to retrace their steps and found they could not remember which ways they had turned. They searched for trails that would lead them back down to the broad highway that led across Nevada into California, but each trail ended in the mountains, and when they paused sometimes they thought they could hear the strange chanting of the religious group. Perhaps it was only the wind.

Gavin slid out of the sleeping bag. The experience north of Taos had warned them of the possibility of being declared a conspiracy, and they had worked for a month in Albuquerque to buy sleeping bags and warm clothing, and for another two weeks to make down payments on the cycles. On the cycles the end of the journey had seemed just over the next rise in the road.

He stood up, fully clothed, pulled the sleeping bag around his shoulders for warmth, and walked to the far side of the ledge where they had stopped when the dark had caught them. With the sun behind his shoulder, Gavin looked over the edge of the hill.

He stood at the top of a cliff that dropped away steeply several thousand feet, at least. Far below, scree marked where sections of the cliff had broken away over the millennia. But that was not what stopped him there upon the mountain, one hand clutched to a jutting rock for support. He looked down upon a sea of fire.

The valley below burned with a white flame. There was no smoke, no heat that Gavin could feel. But as far as he could see, the valley blazed with light such as God must have created when He said, "Let there be light!" In the focus of that empyrean, Gavin felt his body burning, charring, shriveling, his grosser parts smoking away, leaving only the purified essence of what he was.

He stood at the topmost reach of that great spiritual conflagration and felt as if all the blind, creative forces in the universe were centered in his body, making him whole again, reuniting him with everyone and everything else, and he trembled on the brink of great revelations.

"What is it?" Elaine asked behind him.

"I don't know," Gavin said, "but I think it's a sign."

"A sign of what?"

"I don't know," he said again. "Death maybe. Maybe something even more wonderful."

The mountains which held this miraculous sea had been transformed from gray rock into a silver chalice for a god's transubstantiated blood.

And as they watched, the sea of flame dulled, faded, and became a vast dark array of small mechanical devices made apparently of metal and glass. They covered the valley floor as far as Gavin could see, except right at the base of the cliff, where white desert sand or alkali came up to the fallen rock.

"They're solar-energy cells," Gavin said.

"I knew they had them all over Death Valley," Elaine said, "but we're hundreds of miles east of there."

"And there the arrays are set in a fixed framework. Here they follow the sun, and from the looks of that desert, they get sun every day."

Even though the sea of flame had been explained as the reflection of the morning sun from a million solar cells, the experience lost none of its magic for Gavin. He still was shaken by the vision, still felt it working upon him, burning out the dross, refining what was left into something truer, something more essentially himself.

The day of miracles had just begun. Out of a place near the scree where the cells began, where the sea of flame had lapped at the cliff, a figure rose from the desert floor into the air, lifting from the sand like an angel ascending into heaven. As the figure got closer, it seemed even more angelic, unsexed and beautiful in a silver suit, with a glittering halo above its head.

Gavin stared at the incredible figure as it climbed to eye level, not thinking to move back into the shelter of the rocks or to conceal himself. Even when he saw that the halo above the angel's head actually was counterrotating blades which drew the creature up into the sky like the rotors of a helicopter, he did not move. He felt Elaine's hand creep into his, and he stared into the face of the creature, who looked back at him and then moved close enough to stand beside him on the cliff edge. The blast from the propellers whipped dust from the rocks, made them the center of a small whirlwind, although the blades themselves were almost silent. The fabulous figure in front of them open its hand; the blades stopped turning.

The angel was a young man in a one-piece silver suit. A framework that fit tightly to his body supported the horizontal propellers on a short post. "Hello," the young man said in a normal, pleasant voice. "You're out here where nowhere meets the sky."

Gavin found himself unable to speak for a moment. Then he said, "I'm afraid we're lost."

"No food either, I'd guess," the young man said, looking at their flat packs. "Come along with me, and I'll take you where you can get some food and shelter."

Gavin continued to look at him.

"You're probably curious about my gear," the young man said. "This is an experimental power system—

several times as efficient as ordinary solar cells—but hard to service because they're hard to reach. So I use this contraption to get around. The uniform is also an experiment. Very effective insulation against cold or heat."

"Very effective, too," Gavin said, "at dazzling the locals. I've never seen anything like that uniform or that lifting device."

"I guess we do get some stories started," the young man said. He laughed. "And this 'lifting device' we call a levitator. Not really a levitator, of course. It's electric; works by broadcast power. But it's better than a personal helicopter, we think."

The young man's openness was appealing, but Gavin still hesitated. "Where is it you want to take us?"

The young man undid some fastenings on his chest and shed the framework supporting the levitator. He held it easily in one hand. "We have a place just up the hill," he said. "I've been down repairing the cable to the solar cells. It gets cut now and then by rock slides." He went to Elaine's sleeping bag. "Come on. Let's get you packed up."

After a moment's hesitation, Gavin went to his own bag, folded it into a compact double handful, and stuffed it into his pack. When he was finished, Elaine already had put on her pack and was ready to start. The young man was smiling at her. Gavin felt a flash of annoyance that vanished as the young man turned and smiled equally warmly at him.

"Let's go," he said, and he picked up his levitator, braced it against one shoulder, and started up a rocky slope on the other side from the cliff edge.

Gavin shouldered his pack and started after him.

They climbed for several thousand feet, once over a snow field and once through a flurry of snowflakes. The young man did not breathe deeply, nor seem concerned, and he led them, without hesitation, over rocks and snow and through the semidarkness of the falling snow, occasionally turning to smile encouragement or lend them a hand over a difficult spot.

Gavin would have felt irritated by the continual

receding of their destination if he had not reflected
that their guide was walking when he could have
flown.

"How much farther is it?" Gavin asked at last.

"Not much farther now," he was told.

But it was farther, and by the time they reached a
dark cleft in the rocks, Gavin was breathing in gasps
from the exertion and the altitude, and the muscles in
his legs were trembling from the strain of the long
climb. It was a relief to walk level again, even though
the cleft closed ominously overhead, and only the
glimmer of their guide's silver suit led them through
the darkness of what was now a cave or a tunnel. Under their feet, however, the surface was remarkably
smooth.

"Are you sure you know where you're going?" Gavin
asked.

"He acts sure," Elaine said.

"Sure," the cheerful word floated back to them.

In the dark their trip seemed to take even longer.
Finally the silver suit in front of them seemed to grow
brighter, to begin, almost, to radiate. Then they
turned a corner and Gavin saw that light was entering
at the far end and reflecting off the uniform. Now
that sunlight at the end of the cave was streaming toward them, the silver suit began to fade again, and
then, as the opening grew close, it disappeared.

Gavin came to the mouth of the cave and stopped.
He felt Elaine beside him, but he did not look at her.
In front of him, in a sort of natural valley sheltered in
what seemed to be the crater of an extinct volcano,
with the diminishing and darkening peaks of the Rockies behind the crater rim on every side, was a great
white building surrounded by smaller buildings, and
all set in an ordered garden of greenery and color.
There were trees and shrubs and flowers, and surrounding the central garden were fields with vegetables and fruit growing in them. The odor of green
things came to them in a warm, scented breeze. It was
like a vision of Paradise, and Gavin looked around for
the flaming sword, or the guards that were its modern
equivalent. There were none.

"The man who found this valley called it 'the enchanted mountain,'" their guide said. He was standing beside them on a rock ledge. In front of them, white-marble steps led down to the valley floor, where red-tiled paths led through the fields and then through the gardens to the buildings. "He came across it when he was prospecting for uranium, and he resolved if he ever became rich to return here to build a mansion."

The big white building occupied a natural hill in the center of the valley. It had a single giant tower, six-sided at the top, adorned with filigreed Moorish windows, spires, carvings, globes, and balconies with wrought-iron railings. The building rambled massively through treetops, rising here and there to red-tiled towers and white chimneys. Around the big building were satellite structures with red roofs and arches and frillwork. Here and there among the greenery could be seen the white flash of statues and fountains and terraces.

"He became one of the richest men in the world," their guide said, "and he came back to build this place. He wanted it to be bigger and grander and more fabulous than the Hearst Castle at San Simeon. He spent nearly a billion dollars building and furnishing the big house and the various smaller places and the grounds."

Terraces and fountains and long, sweeping steps and balustrades and retaining walls cascaded down the hill from the mansion and the satellite buildings. On the side of the hill facing them, a gigantic swimming pool was a blue jewel set in a frame of white-marble colonnades and what appeared to be part of a Greek temple.

"At one time he was said to be buying half of all the artworks being sold in the entire world," their guide said.

It was stunning.

"And ostentatious," the Professor added.

Magnificent.

"And vulgar," the Professor said.

A monument to what man can accomplish, to bring to this inaccessible spot all the art and grandeur . . .

"Shows what God could do if He had money," the Professor said.

"And he didn't live to see it completed," their guide said. "Since he was building it in relative secrecy—next to him, Howard Hughes was a social butterfly—word about this place never got out. Now it's quite different, of course. It's a research institute, and nobody cares about research anymore. Except a few scientists."

He started down the white-marble steps into the valley. Gavin hastened to catch up with him. "What do you mean, this is a research institute? What do you study?"

"Anything anyone wants to study," the young man said. "That's the most wonderful part of the enchanted mountain. It's an ivory tower, a haven for scientists and scholars of all kinds. You'll have a chance to meet most of them. This is one of the few places left in the world where they can do their thing. No question of expense or social utility."

Elaine was beside them. "But how did you get all this?" she asked. She sounded awed. It was the first time Gavin had seen her impressed.

"When the builder died, considerable controversy broke out among the corporation lawyers over what to do about this place. None of them saw it. They were too busy with other matters. But they couldn't avoid seeing the huge hole in the old man's fortune, all of it pouring into the enchanted mountain. Even then there were big income and inheritance taxes, and although there were no immediate heirs, the corporate entity had to be protected. Some of the lawyers wanted to give this place to the state, but it was too far from everything to be of any use, and frightfully expensive to maintain. So it was turned over to some of the corporation scientists who were approaching retirement, and licensed as a nonprofit research institute."

"It's a retirement home for superannuated scientists," Gavin said.

The guide laughed. "That's one way to describe it. Of course, there are younger ones like me. People who had no place to go to do whatever it was we had to do. There's a worldwide recruitment service. Promising young scientists are spotted, contacted discreetly, invited here—and most never leave."

The smell of the rich vegetation was thicker here, like a kind of perfume. In combination with the conversation, it was heady stuff.

"Don't you get restless sometimes, want to see the world outside?" Gavin asked.

"Who would ever get tired of a place like this?" Elaine asked.

"We aren't exactly cut off," the guide said. "Some supplies are brought in—although we grow most of what we need—and people do leave on brief visits. There are more convenient routes than the one we took. But you're right," he said to Elaine, "nobody leaves because he's tired of the enchanted mountain, and if they must leave for some purpose, they return as quickly as they can."

"But this place is . . . incredible!" Gavin said. "Why doesn't word of it get out? Why aren't you deluged with visitors? Why is the air so warm at this altitude? If this place is so secret, why did you bring us here? What are you going to do with us now that we know about it? When can we leave?"

Their guide held up one hand in a lighthearted gesture of helplessness. "You'll have all your questions answered, but one at a time—and later. Now I think you need to rest."

They had made their way up marble stairs and along tiled paths through trees and shrubs and flowers, including dozens of different kinds of roses, with statues and fountains scattered casually in the greenery or against retaining walls or in the middle of terraces or on the pedestals of staircases; and they had arrived at one of the red-roofed satellite buildings. From the distance they had looked like cottages; up close they were as big as mansions.

If these were called cottages, Gavin wondered, how big was the white building on the summit of the hill?

"This is one of the smaller houses," the guide said. "We use it for visitors before they choose some more permanent form of housing. Some of our people are single and live in the big house or one of the other

guesthouses. Many are married and have their own
separate dwellings. You have your choice of rooms;
the place is empty now. There's food in the kitchen,
clothes in the closets. Use whatever you like; that's
what it's for. If you want to wander around the
grounds, feel free; if you want to take a swim in the
pool, there's swimming gear in the dressing rooms on
the terrace above the pool, if modesty's your thing;
but nobody will feel offended if you don't wear anything. If you have any questions, just dial information; we have a voice-reading computer that's almost
human. I've got some business to take care of now,
but I'll be back to pick you up this evening at seven.
Dinner is formal, for those who choose to take it at
the big house; you'll find appropriate clothes for that in
the closets also."

He paused and then grinned handsomely at them.
"My name is Jackson, by the way. And I'm delighted
to be the first to welcome you to the enchanted mountain."

And he was gone, still shouldering his levitator
without effort.

Gavin stared after him, questions dying on his lips,
and then turned to the large bronze doors that opened
outward easily, without protest. They entered a foyer
with dark parquet floors and an ancient carved wood-
en ceiling; fragile antique chairs stood against tapestried walls. Beyond was a sitting room; it held several
large modern easy chairs scattered casually over a
colorful Persian carpet. The walls were covered with
colorfully worked Spanish velvet hangings. A fascinating collection of sixteenth-century carved and metal-
banded chests decorated the edges of the room. Old
paintings hung on the walls, and a large time-worn
wooden table held paper and pens.

"Do you suppose all this is real?" Elaine asked.

The bedrooms were just as magnificent in their ways.
They contained carved wooden beds, tapestried and
gilded four-poster beds, ornate window frames and
wall moldings, ancient ceilings, old furniture, wall
hangings, paintings. . . . Entire rooms, it seemed to

Gavin, had been transported here intact out of their individual centuries, as if by some giant time machine, or as if they stepped from one century to another as they passed between rooms. Gavin felt an urge to act courtly in a seventeenth-century Spanish room, to swear great oaths in an Elizabethan room, or to twirl a cape near the bed where Cardinal Richelieu may have slept.

They found a modern kitchen and a lavish dining room with a scarred old polished walnut table, broad chairs with tooled leather backs, gold leaf on door frames, and statuary in niches. It was an incongruous place to eat cold roast beef and rolls and fruit, but the food was welcome and good, and they ate, not talking much but looking around them a great deal, and occasionally, in a kind of astonishment, at each other.

Gavin bathed in a sunken marble tub with gold fixtures and dried himself on a thick towel. He found a pullover, open-necked shirt in the closet, and a pair of trousers, both of which fit him admirably, and he joined Elaine, who had found a pink sweater and a slightly darker skirt, for a walk through the park that surrounded the buildings. They admired the formal gardens, the terraces, the artwork. Some of the sculpture clearly was copied; much of it seemed weathered and battered enough to be genuine.

They stood in front of the big house for a long time, looking up at its tower, tracing the intricate carving on its massive brass entrance and the limestone that formed its facade. They tried to imagine what lay behind it, but they did not dare to enter.

Later they swam in the big, inlaid-marble pool. The water sparkled blue and clear in the afternoon sun. Then they lay on the sun-warmed marble terrace surrounding the pool, trying to restore a semblance of health to winter-white bodies.

Neither of them had wanted swimming suits. Gavin looked frankly at Elaine. He had not seen her without clothes since that terrible moment with Chester, and she was not as boyish as he remembered. She was thin, but he was thin, too, from walking and running and missing meals. Her hips and shoulders were pleasingly rounded, though, and her breasts would have filled his hands.

She was a remarkably attractive, even an exciting, woman; desire stirred in him, as he wondered why he had not realized it before. But she did not look at him except as her eyes passed by as she studied the marble colonnades or the ancient Greek temple whose entrance had been re-created at the far end of the pool, or its frieze of Neptune and Nereids riding mythical sea monsters, or the statue of Venus on a seashell at the terrace end of the pool, or the distant crater rim and the more distant peaks that loomed beyond the rim.

She had always rebuffed him, and he was not ardent enough to pursue her across snowfields of indifference and glaciers of withdrawal. And now he could not break the pattern of sexless companionship into which their relationship had fallen.

He stared at the walls of the crater, gray and unbroken, that surrounded them, and felt imprisoned.

In the bathhouse they showered alone and dressed alone. In the guesthouse they each took a big bed—Elaine the one with the embroidered canopy, Gavin the walnut one with its deep and intricate carving—and they napped alone.

When their guide returned promptly at seven, they were waiting for him. Jackson was dressed formally in a velvet jacket and dark trousers; he wore a medallion at the throat of a ruffled shirt. He led them through the evening along the tiled paths up to the intricate doors of the big house. The doors opened in front of him, and he led them up a short flight of marble steps to a gigantic room that extended the entire width of the great mansion, possibly more than one hundred feet; it was easily fifty feet wide and two stories tall. The room blazed with color and rich furnishings from the medieval choir stalls which formed a head-tall wainscoting to the statues in bronze and marble, the glowing old tables, the tapestries and huge paintings that covered parts of the marble walls, and the carved wooden ceiling.

Gavin was dazzled; he stood still, taking it all in.

Oriental rugs covered part of the polished wood-block floor; a fire built of logs as big as tree trunks blazed in the huge antique white-marble fireplace decorated with pedestaled busts and carved coat of arms. It seemed to Gavin that all the centuries of man were focused here upon this room; being here was like living with history. And yet the room was cheerful and bright, and large windows at each end looked out upon gardens and terraces.

"This is the congregation room," Jackson said, "where everybody meets at the end of the day for conversation and fellowship and the exchange of views before dinner."

The room already was partially filled with formally dressed men and women, sipping drinks, conversing in small groups, or sauntering between them. They varied in age between relatively young and distinguished elderly, but they were uniformly handsome. Here, Gavin thought, the best of humanity had gathered together to discuss the best of thoughts.

He wished the Professor were here to join them. He himself did not feel worthy, even in the dark evening clothes he had selected from a variety hanging in a closet. They fit him well; he was stronger and slimmer than he had been a few months before. Perhaps privation was good for him.

Elaine looked fit for the company, however. She had found a long golden gown which accentuated her slenderness into something willowy and sophisticated, and she had not spent all afternoon napping. She had done something to her hair, trimming it, shaping it, and it provided a frame for a face that had developed more character and more color than he had noticed before.

He saw Jackson looking at her admiringly, and he felt a return of the desire that had washed over him this afternoon. He had to remind himself that it was not Elaine he loved. He loved someone who might well be dead, but until he knew that she was dead, he loved her still, and he might never love another.

"Drink?" Jackson said. They soon had cold glasses in their hands.

Gavin found himself talking to a tall, lean, middle-aged man with remarkable white hair, who seemed to know a great deal about engineering.

"The warm air in this crater is held in place by a refinement of the old air-curtain principle," the man said, looking intently at Gavin as if he really cared whether Gavin understood. "It has an additional advantage: a slight disturbance introduced into the air curtain makes the valley hard to see from above. I've been up, and from a height of a few thousand feet, this place looks like a snow field."

"What does everybody do here?" Gavin asked. "Besides enjoy themselves."

"Whatever they wish," the other answered. "Which is, of course, the truest kind of enjoyment. Of course, they're selected, in the first place, for creative interests, and the thing that creative people enjoy most is being creative. I'm a biologist, for instance, and my passion is limb and organ regeneration."

"Any success?"

"Oh, yes. Of course, the real work is being done in the basic studies of DNA. Let me show you around sometime."

Gavin blinked. Later he talked with a dramatically attractive brunette woman who said she was a physicist. "We don't go to unusual lengths to keep this place a secret," she said. "But we don't advertise it, either. If people get the notion that this is a dull research operation, we accept the image. Maybe encourage it. And the people who come here come for a purpose, and once they see the place, they tend to keep quiet about it, if only to keep it unspoiled and to themselves."

Gavin looked around him at the congregation room. "I can see that. What about people like us, who just wander in?"

"That depends upon them."

"What are you working on?"

"You know that the working model for the thermonuclear generator and the practical solar cell came from our laboratories here," she said.

"No." He was surprised, but he tried not to show it.

"Well, I'm working on the theory of thermonuclear propulsion for space vehicles."

Gavin said, "That means interstellar travel, doesn't it?"

She laughed. "You're more perceptive than some of my own colleagues. I suppose the answer is yes. If we could get someone to go."

"Wouldn't you go?"

"Heavens no," she said, and laughed. "I like it here."

Gavin listened to a young man talking to a young woman about the philosophy of engagement as opposed to the philosophy of detachment. He, it turned out, was a chemist; she, a mathematician. Finally they asked for Gavin's opinion.

"I've always been engaged," he said.

"Exactly," said the mathematician. "What use is knowledge if you don't apply it?"

"But increasingly," Gavin went on, "I have begun to wonder what good it has done."

"Precisely," said the chemist. "How can one retain one's objectivity if one is engaged in the turmoil of society? One becomes no better—"

"And no worse," interrupted the young woman.

"Than the untrained citizen," the young man completed.

"Then what do you do with your discoveries?" Gavin asked.

"That's up to the Director," the young man said, and the young woman nodded.

"Then you've decided for detachment."

"That's right," the young woman said, as if he had revealed a truth.

A middle-aged computer scientist told him about the computer that performed all the necessary scientific calculations for the institute, as well as directing most of the automated labor performed in the fields and on the grounds, except for what was taken on by botanists and horticulturists, and the avocational puttering of individuals.

"We are one class here, you see," the man said. "We have no serving class, no workers. Everything possible is automated, and what little can't be automated, we do for ourselves."

Elaine had made her own circuit of the room. Now she joined them. "What kind of computer is it?"

The computer scientist told her. It didn't mean anything to Gavin, but Elaine was impressed. "Perhaps the most important feature, however," he said, "is that this computer is in constant contact with virtually every other computer in the world through the satellite relay system."

"Coordinate?" Elaine asked.

"Interrogator-responder. Our computer can ask but cannot be questioned."

"You mean," Gavin said, "you can spy on anything going on anywhere without revealing your presence?"

"Yes," the computer scientist said. "It keeps us in touch, and our computer calls our attention to anything worth noticing."

"And then what do you do?" Gavin asked.

"That's up to the Director," the computer scientist said. "Mostly we just observe. Here's the Director now. You might ask him."

Gavin turned, to see a section of the wall open. Out of a small elevator stepped a short, plump man with a rosy, cherubic face and a bald head framed by wild white hair. He beamed at everyone as he passed, but he made his way directly toward Gavin and Elaine.

He paused in front of them and held out a hand to each. "Welcome!" he said. "Welcome to the enchanted mountain!"

"Thank you," Elaine said. "It's magnificent."

"We have a few questions," Gavin said.

"Of course," the Director said. "And they will be answered. In time. But now it is time for dinner."

The dining hall looked like a sixteenth-century monastery refectory. Gavin walked on travertine floors and stared at the choir stalls against the wall and the ancient tapestries above them, and the carved wooden ceiling above all. A fire burned in the French Gothic fireplace, and a buffet was laid out in sterling-silver serving dishes on old dark wooden sideboards. Massive candelabra, also apparently made of silver, stood on the floor and on the sideboards and on the scarred monastic dining tables that ranged nearly the length of the two-story room.

The monks should have enjoyed such splendor and such food. Even if the food was cooked by computer, it was cooked by a computer that had digested the recipes of Cordon Bleu. The meal was accompanied by good wine, good coffee, and the most brilliant conversation Gavin had ever heard.

But there were no answers to his most pressing questions, and he returned with Elaine to their rooms in the guesthouse, his head bubbling with ideas about the universe from the infinitesimal to the infinite. No one, however, had wanted to talk about what was expected of them or what was going to be done with them.

They went to bed, as always, alone.

The next day they explored the vast laboratories that burrowed beneath the enchanted mountain. Much more existed below the surface, and was, in its way, even more incredible. The biologist, as he had promised, escorted Gavin and Elaine on a guided tour, down an elevator located on the first floor of the big house, and then through tunnels carved interminably through igneus rock and even into granite.

Through dark goggles they watched a laser about the size of a thirty-five-millimeter motion-picture projector evaporate rock at the rate of three cubic meters a minute.

"I've never even heard of anything like this," Gavin said.

"That's because there isn't anything like it anywhere else," their guide said.

"Why not?" Gavin asked.

"The Director hasn't decided yet whether to release it."

The laboratories were only larger corridors carved at right angles to the passageways, and, like them, the laboratories had walls of laser-polished rock. But their equipment was extraordinary, and, to Gavin's untrained eye, unique. Much of it was unique, their guide said;

one-of-a-kind machinery was no more expensive than that which was mass-produced. All it required was a program for the computer.

In one laboratory they saw what their guide called rather routine experiments in cryogenics and the odd behavior of liquids and solids at near absolute zero, as well as some attempts to freeze and restore living tissue. In another laboratory they witnessed a breakthrough in superconduction at room temperatures.

At the end of a long reddish corridor, new antibiotics were being created, molecule by molecule; nearby, work was moving forward on chemical treatment for mental illness, on lengthening the life span, on synthetic food, on improved fertility depressants, and on improvement of the process for coding information into chemicals.

"We're far beyond the chemical-learning pills now in general use," their guide commented. "Those are little more than placebos, you know."

Gavin hadn't known that, and a terrible thought occurred to him that he did not voice. "Why don't you release these?" Gavin asked. "They'd be a real boon to students."

"That's up to the Director," the biologist said.

In another laboratory they watched biofeedback experiments with extrasensory phenomena. One young man had just experienced an astonishing run with dice, but their guide thought it was merely one of those inexplicable operations of chance and that the experiments would not come up with anything in the end.

"Then why are they continued?" Gavin asked.

"The person in charge of them thinks they are worth his time," their guide explained.

In a physics laboratory they saw the results of particle accelerator tests—the accelerators themselves were buried deep beneath another mountain—and the theoretical configuration of a hydrogen ramjet interstellar ship which could reach speeds of nine-tenths the speed of light. Given the desire and the resources, travel to another star was feasible.

Over coffee they heard discussion about obtaining the resources from Jupiter. The colony on the moon, they learned, already was self-supporting, and the colonies on Mars had learned what self-sufficiency would involve. These, of course, were not institute projects, but the institute had observers present and felt a sense of commitment to colonization. The terraforming of Venus had been started with the release in the atmosphere of free-floating, tailored diatoms.

Surprising new astronomical information was being received from a giant telescope built on a nearby peak —a black hole had been identified after its location was calculated from the behavior of a companion sun, and nearby stars with planetary systems had been observed. The new radio telescope in space—a gigantic web of cables—was relaying valuable new information about the distant reaches of the universe, and time had been allocated for picking up possible messages from other worlds.

In an engineering section they saw demonstrations of materials whose strength approached their theoretical limits, avoidance mechanisms for vehicles, voice-actuated typewriters, computer-human interfaces, and a dozen other amazing gadgets and appliances which, Gavin learned, probably would be released for licensing.

"Even though we have all the power we need and extensive manufacturing facilities of our own," their guide said, "we still have major expenses, particularly for art and books, which a purchasing committee continues to buy when anything valuable comes on the market."

"One would think you were preparing for a cataclysm or a holocaust," Elaine said.

The biologist smiled at her. "In general, we are optimistic, but we must discount the normal optimism associated with our kind of work. So we protect ourselves and plan to preserve what we can of the human inheritance. Already we have the largest library in the world, not to mention the capacity of our computer to reprint any book recorded anywhere. What is just as important, we have a magnificent retrieval system."

Their guide had saved his work until last. They looked into microscopes to see cells budding and into vats to see limbs and organs floating like refuse from a charnel house. Elaine shuddered, and Gavin wondered darkly if that was where uninvited guests concluded their stay.

"We've had some luck with limb transplants on animals," the biologist said. "We are able, you see, to grow limbs from their own cells. But so far we've been unable to get the organs to function properly. We're about to release what we know to hospitals across the country where there is plentiful human clinical material. We've been unable to do that sort of thing here; we've had no one needing transplants."

In the days that followed, Gavin explored the grounds and the big house. Each had its delights and surprises. Later his days settled into routine. He would rise early —he had never before awakened early by choice— and after bathing and dressing, he would wander to the morning room in the big house. The bright marble room with its carved fireplace and its sixteenth-century Spanish ceiling received the light of the morning sun as it peered over the crater rim. Gavin would sit in a large easy chair sipping coffee, usually with a few other early risers, while they waited for breakfast to be laid out in the dining hall.

After breakfast he usually wandered upstairs to the library, where he would browse through the ten thousand rare volumes shelved along the walls in glass-covered wooden shelves, and read them beneath the carved ceiling. Or he would follow a line of momentary interest deep into the computer catalog and call for books which would be delivered immediately by dumbwaiter from the endless stacks carved out of the hill beneath the mansion.

In the afternoon he would swim. Sometimes Elaine would join him. Sometimes others would be there, too.

Days passed unhurried and unnoticed. Except when Gavin saw Elaine at the pool, he scarcely saw her at all. She had her own routine, into which he did not inquire. They usually went over to dinner together, but they did not talk much, and when they arrived at the congregation hall, they parted and spoke to others. Gavin felt that the strange bond that had held them together was dying, if it was not already dead.

In spite of his uneasiness at the ways in which the crater walls seemed like prison walls, and his inability to get answers to his questions, Gavin would have been content to wander for years through this enchanted place with its enchanted people, but nightmares began to trouble his sleep. Dreams of Jenny alternated with dreams of Elaine; sometimes they were together in one dream, and sometimes together in one woman. He dreamed, too, about the Professor, and occasionally about Gregory and the Iron Chancellor and Willie and StudEx. And once or twice he dreamed about Berkeley and the West Coast.

One afternoon he came upon Elaine splashing and laughing in the pool with Jackson, who was even better-looking with his clothes removed. He stood watching them for a few minutes before he turned away. That evening he told Jackson he wished to speak to the Director.

"Of course," Jackson said. "He's with us almost every evening."

"I want to speak to him alone."

Jackson sighed. "He's very busy, you know."

"It's important."

"I'll see what I can do."

Two days later, in the late afternoon, Jackson came for him and led him to the third floor of the big house. Gavin had never been there before. Jackson ushered Gavin through a big carved doorway into a Gothic room and then withdrew. Gavin stood in the doorway looking at the room. Intricately carved wooden arches rose to a Spanish ceiling. Books were shelved against the walls behind leaded-glass fronts. A massive old table, flanked by antique chairs, extended down the center of the room toward a towering Gothic fireplace at the far end of the room.

The Director was seated at an antique desk made of dark wood and inlaid with tooled leather. He had a stack of papers in front of him; he went through them rapidly, making notations on them with a pen. Finally he looked up.

"Come in, Gavin," he said.

Gavin stepped forward hesitantly. He felt he was in the presence of something extraordinary, that the Director was something more than an older man with a pudgy body and a bald head.

"Sit down," the Director said, indicating an old chair opposite the desk. "I've been wanting to talk to you."

"I want to leave this place," Gavin said abruptly.

"We're sorry to hear that," the Director said. The wild white hair around his ears seemed wilder than ever. "But of course you're free to leave anytime."

Gavin sat down. "Why didn't anybody tell me that earlier?"

"I can only speculate," the Director said, "but possibly they hoped you would become happy enough here to forget your questions. We would like you to stay, you know. This is an invitation to join us if you wish."

"To join you?" Gavin repeated. "But I'm not a scientist."

"We're not all scientists here," the Director said. "I'm only a layman myself, with a little knowledge about a great many things, and a great deal of knowledge about almost nothing."

"I'm just a student," Gavin said. "I don't belong here."

"We're all students. That's all we want here—students. Nobody whose mind is made up—'used up' may be a better description."

"I have nothing to contribute," Gavin said.

"Others think differently. You have impressed a number of our people; they think you will develop into a scholar and a creative human being."

"I'm unworthy."

The Director looked around him at the Gothic splendor. "We're all unworthy."

"You don't understand," Gavin said. It was a moment of confession, as inevitable as the coming of night, and yet it did not come easy. "I did a very bad thing once."

"We know."

"I killed someone, out of carelessness, out of greed. It was someone I liked a great deal . . ." Gavin broke off. "You know?"

"As you must have been informed by now, our computer is in contact with all the other major computers in the world."

"And you learned it from one of them?"

"All such information is recorded, and we like to know as much as possible about our guests and potential colleagues. We know about your Professor, and from your friend Elaine we think we know why you did what you did—a reprehensible act, a childish act of will and bravado, but an act those of us who seek knowledge can understand. It was an accident."

"There was more to it," Gavin said.

"I understand there was also an act of ritual cannibalism," the Director said. He didn't smile, but there was on his face a look of absolution.

Gavin had not thought for a long time about what he had done, about how it had been, and the memory was like a fist in his stomach.

"An act of admiration," the Director said. "An act of love."

"Yes." Gavin felt a hollow within himself where someone else had been, where someone had lived with him. *Professor! Where are you?* There was no answer. The Professor was gone. It was as if the act of confession had released the Professor from a kind of bondage, or as if Gavin had been sick and now was well again. But Gavin felt alone now and afraid.

"I'm glad you spoke of this yourself," the Director said. Increasingly he seemed to Gavin like a confessor. "It is good for you to be free of this ancient guilt before you decide what you wish to do. Let me ask you again: will you join us?"

He had been given a similar invitation by Sally, but her family was sick, and they wanted him to join the sickness. These people seemed well, and they wanted nothing of him but that he be well too. And yet . . . "It seems to me," Gavin said, "that you have chosen to isolate yourself from the human struggle."

"We were driven here by events," the Director said. He stood up and turned his back toward Gavin to look out a window toward the crater rim.

"What events?"

"The same events that turned the campuses over to the students drove the scientists and scholars from the universities. For centuries, teaching and research had reinforced each other, but when hiring and firing of teachers became a student game, teaching became student-pleasing, a con game in which practical men and women sold students tricks and flattery. Oh, there were a few exceptions, like your Professor, who stayed on out of love and out of a disregard for pay or appreciation. The rest of those interested in the creation of new knowledge, in the exploration of the unknown, were neither welcome nor useful. Some of them went into other occupations. Many never discovered the delights of discovery. A few found their way into places like the enchanted mountain."

Gavin looked around the resplendent room. "There are other places like this?"

The Director turned from the window and laughed. "Nothing quite like this, but here and there a quiet place of thought and study and isolation from the mad currents of the world. A hidden valley in Tibet, an oasis in the Middle East, a mountaintop in Africa, a high plateau in South America, an island in the South Pacific. And more ordinary research institutes doing practical work in the outside world, with a wing for theoretical research and time for impractical studies.

"After all, the individual is more free today to do whatever he wishes than he has ever been. Why shouldn't this be so for the serious student as well? Why shouldn't scholars and scientists be free to pursue their special interests as much as communes and group marriages and revolutionaries? The only thing that keeps them from exercising their new freedom is that their interests often require resources unavailable to the ordinary man. This is where the enchanted mountain is useful. It provides resources and solitude, the two essentials for intellectual discovery."

"It seems to me that your consumption of resources and your surreptitious use of privileged information makes the institute a conspiracy," Gavin said. "Why doesn't the government act against you?"

The Director nodded. "That's very good, Gavin. The fact is, however, that the institute is licensed to perform its functions—and, as a matter of economic truth, produces more resources than it consumes, not even counting the potential of its theoretical research. And we are privileged to obtain and use otherwise secret information."

"It's a poor license which has no inspection procedures," Gavin said stubbornly, "and the governments of the world do not even know what you are or why you exist."

"No," said the Director, "and we give them no reason for curiosity. But, since the conscious withdrawal of police power, governments are not what they used to be. And, like the civil authorities, we do not use against the individual any information we may gather. Everyone who knows of our presence here is free to come and go. It is not illegal to keep our existence as secret as possible, so long as we do not infringe on the liberties of others." He sat down once more in the chair behind the desk.

"You are content," Gavin said, "to exist here, playing games with information and discovery, keeping the results to yourself."

"In part, that is so," the Director said. "When the scientist isolated himself from the distractions and temptations of society, he regained his ability to control the effects of his own ingenuity. In fact, it would be an infringement on the liberty of others if he did not."

"To withhold the benefits of your research . . ."

"There is much we do not withhold."

"Nuclear research, longevity studies, infertility drugs, chemical-learning improvements . . ."

"Man needs power, not explosives," the Director said. "If we could, we would denature all nuclear materials, but we have done the next best thing. All fusion plants have been placed in orbit. They themselves would burn up harmlessly in the atmosphere if disturbed. The state of the art makes the construction of a hydrogen bomb almost impossible without fissionable materials to start with, and fission plants have been driven out of business, because, like fossil-fuel plants, they were unable to compete with virtually free power. A nuclear war may be impossible."

"What about fertility depressants?" Gavin said. "Surely the world needs better methods of birth control."

"In general, it is controlling its fertility. We have made birth-control pills or implants available, which can be taken by women or men, or both, but we have kept to ourselves those chemicals which might be applied indiscriminately, through the water supply or the food, or even the air. The possibilities of misuse by an enemy nation or even a tyrannical government are too horrendous."

"Longevity, then," Gavin said.

"We can't have it both ways," the Director said. "We can't both hold down on population and increase longevity. As a matter of fact, we have the ability to lengthen the life span, particularly the mature life span, by about fifty percent. I myself am over one hundred years old."

Gavin looked at the chubby white-haired man in disbelief. Old men should be less substantial. "And you aren't giving that to the world?"

"At the cost of what turmoil? Even if it were possible for everyone—which it isn't, because it demands constant medical monitoring, diet, exercise, an expensive drug, and a serene environment—it would mean that the world would have to reduce its birth rate by another fifty percent, a not impossible goal but one which seems difficult to realize at this time."

"And chemical learning is too explosive as well, I suppose," Gavin said.

"True chemical learning contains the potential for revolutionizing society more radically than Marx and Marcuse ever imagined."

"If it is misused?"

"Through natural evolution," the Director said. "It is theoretically possible—it has even been accomplished in the laboratory—to encode not just knowledge but experience. If people can live other lives, why should they be content with one? Some identities are intolerable; others simply less desirable. If men and women can get the thrills and satisfactions of a hundred existences through a hypodermic or a pill, why should they struggle to modify a highly resistant reality?"

"And one man," Gavin said slowly, "has the power to decide which blessing to give the world and which to withhold."

"Which blessing and which curse," the Director said. "I am old," he continued, and for the first time Gavin thought he looked old; *but this is what he offers me, long life and more power than I ever knew existed.* "I have seen much, and I have nothing to gain from the release or suppression of others' work. But in the long run, we do not withhold; we merely delay the release of information to an appropriate time."

"And how do you decide these things?"

"The researcher presents his recommendations, along with the comments of his colleagues. Then I have a group of science-fiction writers take the facts, toy with the possibilities, and translate them into human terms."

"Into stories?"

"Yes. The best eventually get published or broadcast or filmed. Thus they creep into the dreams of the general public, and their collective unconscious begins to work upon it, assimilating it, naturalizing it. Having immersed myself in it, then, I make the final decision. Someone must make it—a committee is only a device to decrease efficiency and diffuse responsibility—and I make it. Everybody knows who to blame. Meanwhile, what is delayed is not permanently suppressed; it remains alive for discussion, input of new information, and reconsideration. We are a flexible organization."

"But basically," Gavin insisted, "you have withdrawn. Your isolation in these mountains is a symbol of your isolation from society. You have the power to revolutionize society, to make it a paradise, and you refuse to act."

The Director looked at the walls above the bookcases as if gauging whether they were thick enough to hold out the world. "The world is engaged in a dangerous experiment," he said, "a social experiment called freedom. The experiment began on this continent more than two hundred years ago, and spread eventually to the rest of the world. Its final conditions have been realized through free power and automation. For the first time in its life, humanity has been liberated from necessity; it is free to be just as individualistic, just as idiosyncratic, just as angelic or devilish as it chooses. The consequences are all around us—little groups springing up, glorifying their prejudices into universal principles of behavior, magnifying their little insights into eternal truths.

"It is a dangerous experiment. We do not know whether it will succeed; if it fails, it will fail disastrously. We will not interfere, because it might contain the ultimate expression of humanity's potential. Perhaps there is some fundamental human goodness which can flower into understanding and tolerance and love. But if the experiment fails, we choose not to let all human hopes die with it. There are other worthwhile human aspirations besides freedom, and we will be here, preserving the human heritage, for man to find again."

"You choose not to act," Gavin said sadly.

"We are not wise enough to direct man's destiny, nor even wise enough to control the revolutionaries who think they know enough to change the world for the better."

The Director studied Gavin with old eyes. They had seen a great many things, and Gavin thought, though he did not dare to ask, that they were the eyes which had first seen this crater and later had seen much of the world's riches. "You cannot stay," the Director said finally.

"No," Gavin said. "I don't know why. Am I an unregenerate romantic, a compulsive participant, or simply a person who has too many personal questions unanswered? You have taken me up on the mountain and offered me the ultimate temptation. But I must go on to the Coast. There are matters I have yet to settle."

"A helicopter is leaving tomorrow to pick up supplies," the Director said. "You will be notified where to go and when. If you should ever wish to return, if you get your personal problems resolved . . ."

"You offer me a reprieve," Gavin said. He felt a little dizzy.

"That's all we ever get from life," the Director said.

Elaine came to Gavin in the night. He was almost asleep when he heard the rustle of her robe and felt the mattress sink under her as she sat down on the edge of the Cardinal Richelieu bed. "Are you awake?" she asked.

"Yes."

"You're leaving."

"Yes."

Her face was a pale oval in the darkness. "Jackson told me." She was silent for a moment. "I'm staying," she said.

"Yes."

"Not because of Jackson. He's just a pleasant companion. With him there are no commitments, no responsibilities. No, what I want to say is that I've been asked to stay, and this place is what I've been looking for."

"I understand," he said.

"I don't think you do. I don't think you've ever understood me. My childhood. Growing up. What I want, what I need, is independence. I don't want to be dependent upon anybody for anything. Here I can do whatever I wish. We're all free to do what we wish. No dependence."

He heard the rustle of cloth, and the pale oval that was her face was now part of a paleness that extended from her waist. As if they had a separate will of their own, her hands picked up his hands where they lay on the coverlet and lifted them to her chest.

She hadn't stopped talking. With his hands filled with her firm, small breasts, their nipples hardening into his palms, she said, "But we've come a long way together. It must have seemed strange to you that I would tag along wherever you went, but I hoped that you would

see me—really see me sometime—and not always be
thinking about that girl or the Professor or the revolution."

His hands moved, and he wished she would stop talking, but she only took a deeper breath and said, "It was
mostly me. I was in love with you. Why do we love
people? What makes one person different from another?
But I didn't want to be dependent on you. I didn't want
to become involved unless it was on a basis of equality.
You know—love freely offered and freely returned . . .
no obligations . . . no responsibilities."

She was lying beside him now, and his hands were
discovering the rest of her. "But it doesn't matter now,"
she said, "because you're leaving, and there's no dependence either way. But I have to tell you this, too—
you're going to find whatever is at the end of your
quest, and I don't want to be there when you find it.
The end of my quest is right here. Oh, I don't mean in
this bed, but in this place, where everybody is equal,
and—"

He stopped her voice with his lips, and then there
was no more talking for a long time. Toward dawn she
said quietly, "I hope you find what you're looking for."

It had been a night filled with surprises and delights. For perhaps the first time in his life Gavin had
felt completely eased, had felt reconciled with the
world. But when Elaine spoke, the old doubts crept
back into his mind. He had to go on; he had to discover what awaited him in Berkeley.

11 ◆━ Thus I Refute Berkeley

"Here I sell what all men desire," said Matthew
Boulton, proprietor of the first steam-engine factory.
"Power." Power. That's what we think we want. The
power to make people do what we tell them. The
power to say no. The power to change people's minds.
The power to act without fear of consequences or
concern for others. The power to change the world.
The struggle for power—or frustration at its ab-
sence—is the cause of all the crime and violence in
the world. And yet we know that intervention in
human events is almost always futile. Those we com-
pel resent us. Those we refuse ignore us. Those we
try to change reject us. The willful act does not
finally satisfy. And even the most passionate of revolutions do less than normal economic developments.
The French Revolution only speeded a process of
equalization that would have destroyed the power of
the aristocracy; slavery was dying before the Civil
War; protests may have prolonged the Vietnam war
through middle-class resentment of the protesters.
Violent revolutions do not redistribute wealth or en-
sure equality; they destroy wealth, and freedom re-
stores inequality.

—THE PROFESSOR'S NOTEBOOK

No Berlin walls for Berkeley. As was only proper for
the nursery of revolution, the campus at Berkeley was
surrounded by a wall neatly constructed of sawed lime-

stone. The sun broke through clouds behind San Francisco, and the sunset turned the stones to rust, as if they had been painted with the blood of martyrs.

Gavin stood on the cleared ground between the decayed and battle-weary edge of the city and the south gate. He looked upon the fabled castles and towers of Berkeley. They loomed above the walls: the buildings of the Student Center, Sproul Hall, Sather Tower—he knew them all as if he had lived among them. Indeed, he had kept them, like a fairy land, inside his head for private moments, to walk those fairy streets and re-create those fairy battles; and now that they were here, in reality, before him, he could not yet bring himself to step on the streets where Mario Savio, Jack Weinberg, and Art Goldberg had put their feet. He did not know whether he held back out of reverence or a fear of disillusion; he was not the same man who had set out from Kansas to seek a holy place.

The way was open. The tough wrought-iron gates were parted casually, as if he were being invited to enter. They should have been closed and locked against intruders and the coming of night, and he wondered what this breach of security portended. Had the guards grown careless, or were those outside the walls no longer a menace? Or was destiny welcoming him to his spiritual home?

Gavin walked slowly across the cleared ground, glancing uneasily behind him twice. But nothing moved. He edged between the gates. No guard challenged his right to enter; no one asked to see his student ID. He could see no one at all. The plaza between the Student Center and Sproul Hall was empty. The shabby benches sat like tattered old men in the sunset. Odd bits of paper tumbled idly about in the evening breeze.

An uneasy quiet hung over the place. It was like an arena after the bull has been killed and the matador has bowed to the cheering crowd, and now the bull has been dragged away and the people all have gone, but the stones still remember. Gavin walked on the cracked concrete and felt history beneath his feet.

Ludwig's Fountain was dry and filled with cans and

papers and broken bottles. Gavin looked up the steps toward the wide expanse of Sproul Hall. The walls were old and pockmarked, and the windows were broken, but Gavin did not see them. He saw another time. He saw students by the thousands gathered here in this plaza, surrounding a police car in which sat a martyred Jack Weinberg for twenty-four hours. He saw Mario Savio climb atop the police car and mold the casual, excitement-seeking students into a revolutionary army. He saw them charge up the steps to take over Sproul Hall, and he saw them dragged down again, limp and unresisting, by fascist kops.

He stood where it all had happened. It was worth the journey, he thought. It was worth everything he had suffered.

And yet it was not enough. The exaltation of standing on hallowed ground could not endure. The remembered scene faded; the cheering and the cursing died; the silence returned. He glanced again at the half-open gate in the limestone wall. Why wasn't it guarded from the city that surrounded it like a watchful beast?

He shook his sweatered shoulders as if shuddering away bad dreams, turned, and walked quickly to the north, toward the metal archway with stone pillars on either side. On top of each pillar was a hollow metal sphere. Once they had been glass and metal, but the glass had been broken and the light bulbs inside were shattered or stolen. Beyond the gate was a green belt running east and west.

Gavin's footsteps sounded hollow between the buildings, and he resisted an urge to look behind him to see if anyone had emerged to frown at this desecration of Berkeley's silence.

He paused at the archway and looked up. Above his head, embossed on the metal, were the words "Sather Gate." This was it. The famous Sather Gate. He was walking under Sather Gate, over Strawberry Creek. The green belt on either side was mostly weeds; the trees were broken and dead, as if they had been a battlefield, and Strawberry Creek smelled like an open sewer, but he didn't mind. It was Berkeley.

Only, where was everybody?

To his left was Dwinelle, to his right was Wheeler, and straight ahead was Durant.

"Notice!" someone said.

Gavin stopped.

"Notice!" the voice said again.

Gavin looked around. There was nobody nearby, unless he was hiding behind a kiosk to his right. It was a cylindrical little structure covered with the tattered remains of messages stacked one atop another like the artifacts of extinct civilizations. The kiosk had a conical, overhanging roof; underneath the overhang, a circle of shattered glass globes had once illuminated the communications that now no one read. The kiosk looked like an overgrown, long-dead mushroom.

"Notice!" the kiosk said. "A book burning will be held at Doe Library in honor of the wedding of . . ."

Gavin moved around the kiosk, trying to locate the person who was speaking. One message stopped abruptly and another began.

"Wanted: roommates, sex no obstacle. . . ."

The kiosk was speaking. It was reading aloud, in a cracked and uncertain voice, the announcements posted on its surface over the months and years. "Lost: a pair of matched tarantulas; can be recognized . . ."

Gavin continued to circle the kiosk, trying to determine by the freshness of the printed notices which might still be current.

"Notice: the faculty coven will meet tonight at midnight for unspeakable practices in the Faculty Glade. . . . For sale: coke, a spoon or a shovel. . . . Notice: the end of the world is scheduled for next Tuesday at exactly . . . Wanted: sex, no questions asked. . . . Notice: the Doomsday Society will meet Wednesday at Alumni House unless canceled by unforeseen . . . Notice: the Fernwald-Smith Terrorists will shoot it out with the International House Guerrillas today at Memorial Stadium; admission will be . . ."

The last one was so old that the words were almost incomprehensible.

"Notice: a new batch of LSD is available at Chemical Bio Lab. . . . Notice: exhibition of living art now open

at the Gallery. . . . Wanted: love, no questions asked.
. . . Notice: a book burning will be held at Doe Library
in honor of the wedding of the Chief of the Kampuskops and the Homecoming Queen. . . ."

Gavin was back where he had started. He turned
away. He knew no more now than he had known before. It was a campus. He was on it. It felt good. But it
wasn't enough.

"Who are you?" a voice asked.

Gavin shrugged.

"I said, 'Who are you?' "

Gavin didn't turn around. "I'm not going to talk to
a bulletin board," he said.

A pebble fell at Gavin's feet. Another hit him on the
shoulder.

"I wouldn't talk to a bulletin board either," the
voice said, "but you'd better talk to me. You might get
into trouble, you know."

Gavin turned around. A tall, thin man smoking a
twisted cigarette now was sitting on top of the kiosk.
Gavin realized that he had been smelling the odor of
burning leaves.

"Who are you?" the man repeated. He was only a
young fellow, younger than Gavin, but he seemed older
because he loomed above him.

"What are you doing up there?" Gavin asked.
"Where is everybody?"

"Really," the young man asked, "we must get
straight immediately who is asking the questions here.
The question is: 'Who are you?' "

"I'm just a student," Gavin said.

"You don't look like a student," the man on top
of the kiosk said, "and certainly not like 'just a
student.' "

"That's what I am anyway—a transfer student,"
Gavin said. "I'm new."

"Why aren't you dressed properly?" The man on top
of the kiosk was dressed in an old army jacket over a
ragged shirt and a pair of cutoff jeans.

"Now, wait a minute," Gavin said impatiently. "I've
answered two of your questions; now answer one of
mine."

"Well," the other said sulkily, "if that's the only way we're going to get anywhere."

"Where is everybody?" Gavin asked.

"They'll be along," the young man said quickly. "Now, why aren't you dressed properly?"

Gavin looked down. His student workman's shirt and peasant trousers had been lost along the way. Now he wore a pair of trousers, shoes and socks, a shirt, and a sweater for warmth. It all was neat and improper, and Gavin didn't know why he had been so careless. "This is the way people dress where I come from."

"Where do you come from?"

"Unfair," Gavin said. "I get to ask a question. What are you doing up there?"

"Looking down," the young man said. "Now, where do you come from?"

"Oh, east," Gavin said.

"Everything's east of here. Where in the east?"

"It isn't any of your business, but I was enrolled in a university in Kansas. I was expelled. And I've been making my way here ever since."

"You're not dressed right."

"That's not a question."

"That's true. And you're still not dressed like a student."

"What do clothes matter?" Gavin asked. Once he might have felt the way the fellow did who sat on a kiosk and smoked a marijuana cigarette and asked stupid questions, but now it all seemed silly and unimportant.

"We've had a lot of undercover kops around," the young man said defensively. "You know—infiltrators, agents provocateur. Are you one?"

"If I were one, wouldn't I do a better job of disguise?" Gavin asked impatiently.

"Maybe that's what they'd like us to think," the man on the kiosk said half-shrewdly.

"Nonsense," Gavin said. "The basic principle of infiltration is not to call attention to yourself."

"That may be," the other said, taking a drag on his cigarette. "You want a hit?"

"No, thanks." Gavin was turning away again. He thought he heard sounds in the distance.

"I've got other stuff," the man on the kiosk said eagerly. "Listen: what I got in my right hand will make you feel so tall you'll have snow in your ears."

"Forget it," Gavin said.

"Listen: what I got in my left hand will make you feel so small you can play billiards with molecules."

"Shove it," Gavin said.

"And you say you're a student!" the man on the kiosk said scornfully.

Gavin heard a quiet rumble. When he looked back at the kiosk, the man was gone. That was it, he thought; the fellow was a pusher, and there was some kind of elevator inside the kiosk leading to underground tunnels. The whole campus probably was a burrow for underground activity.

The distant sounds had turned into voices and musical instruments. He couldn't make out what kind of instruments or what the voices were saying.

He moved forward and looked back the way he had come, through the Sather Gate and down the plaza past Ludwig's Fountain toward the gates in the outer wall. They were wide open now, and beyond them he could see a glimmer of movement against the distant background of weary shacks.

Something poked Gavin in the middle of the back. He turned around slowly. A Kampuskop was standing behind him, an electric nightstick in his hand still extended toward Gavin. The kop was dressed in midnight black with silver starbursts on his breast pockets and on the epaulets of his shirt. He was a big man, muscular in the shoulders and the jaw; he had a big nose, mean little eyes, and a machine pistol in a black holster at his hip. He poked Gavin in the stomach with the nightstick. It had enough of a charge to make Gavin's skin prickle. It was a warning.

"You a student?" the Kampuskop said in a hard, negligent voice that told Gavin whatever he replied didn't matter. He had rubber shoes on his feet; Gavin didn't know whether that was for insulation or so he could sneak up on people.

"Yes," Gavin said.

"You don't look like a student," the kop said. "You're older. You ain't dressed right. Where's your ID?"

"I just arrived," Gavin said. "I haven't had a chance to enroll."

The nightstick prodded Gavin's stomach again. The charge had been turned up. It hurt now. "Outside," the kop said. "You can enroll tomorrow."

"I don't have anywhere to go," Gavin protested.

Again the nightstick thrust at him. Gavin backed up to avoid it. "You people always got someplace to go. You can't stay here. Not without a ID. This is the chief's wedding day, and nobody stays around without he's a student."

The nightstick poked at him again. Gavin yielded. "Okay. I'm going."

He moved reluctantly toward the open gates through which he had come. He glanced back once. The kop still was standing on the other side of Sather Gate. He still was watching him.

The music was louder now. The instruments he had heard faintly now clearly were guitars. The voices were singing something about Jesus. In the gathering darkness Gavin could see the first row of marchers in a procession. They were carrying guitars. Farther back, Gavin could see signs and torches held aloft.

He moved toward the outer gates. "We are the Children of Jesus," the procession sang. "He knows what you're thinking of. He saves us when he pleases. We are the Children of Love."

Gavin stopped on the other side of the open gates, concealing himself behind the pillar that held one of the gates. He peered around the corner. The distant kop still was standing beyond Sather Gate, but he had been joined now by another kop, who stood on the opposite side of the bridge over Strawberry Creek. They were like two dark giants waiting for him. They were like no Kampuskops he had ever seen; there was nothing comic or ridiculous about them.

He stooped and removed his shoes and socks, stuffing them behind the pillar. He took off his sweater, even though the evening was cool, and put it on top of the shoes. He tore off his shirt sleeves at the elbow. He would have torn the trousers, too, but the cloth was too tough.

The parade had reached the gate. "Come join the Children of Jesus," the marchers sang. "You'll find what you're dreaming of. He won't deny what will please us. Come join the Children of Love."

The marchers all were young people, student types, dressed in blue jeans and little else. The men wore codpieces laced over their genitals, and the girls wore nothing above the waist. Their breasts bobbed and swung with the rhythm of their marching, and in some places along the parade people were making love as they marched.

The torches flared along the line, filling the air with the odor of pine resin and oil. Gavin could read a couple of the signs now. One said: "Make love, not frustrations." Another said: "Sexual repression is the origin of all evil." Another: "I am love," signed "God." And another, just behind it: "I am God," signed "Love."

Gavin started. "Jenny!" he shouted, and plunged into the middle of the procession. But when he reached the young woman he had thought he recognized, she bore only a superficial resemblance to his lost love. She was carrying a sign. He nodded and smiled. She smiled, and her breasts nodded.

"We are the Children of Jesus," he sang as the procession passed between Sproul and the Student Center. "He knows what you're thinking of," he sang as he passed under Sather Gate. "He saves us when he pleases," he sang as he passed the Kampuskops. He was crouching, and they didn't see him. "We are the Children of Love."

They passed Wheeler on the right, and he thought of slipping out of the procession. But by the time he had made up his mind, they had reached the front of Doe Library and the procession was parting on either side of a dark mound. When Gavin reached the mound, he saw that it was made up of books, thousands of books. A hill of them was growing into a mountain as more books were brought by dark figures moving out of Doe Library.

As the Children of Jesus passed the heaping books, the torches were thrust into the hill or cast upon it. For a few moments, like wisdom battling ignorance, the books resisted the flames, and then someone brought forward a can and began tossing gouts of liquid on the pile. Wherever the fluid lit, fire burst upward. The smell of gasoline reached Gavin, and then burning paper and black smoke. In a minute or two the little mountain was burning briskly, and shadows like demons were dancing on the nearby facades of Doe and California.

Gavin edged away from the fire and its revealing light. As if by the same kind of mysterious signal that sends lemmings to the sea, students began arriving to join the Children of Jesus and those who had been at the scene accumulating books. They thronged into the plaza between Doe Library and California Hall, coming from the East Gate and the North Gate and the West Entrance, by all the walkways and streets that led to the center of the campus, and Gavin faded back into them, feeling secure again in their numbers. But even anonymous in the crowd, he still felt alone; he felt more alone than he had felt earlier when there had been no one around. He realized that he no longer felt like a student. He had grown old. He no longer belonged. He felt himself standing apart, holding himself away from them, judging them.

They were animals, he thought, led by their instincts, acting only in immediate response to their environments, doing whatever felt good. They were moths to the flame, bees to the mating dance, wolves to the kill, sharks to the scent of blood, vultures to the carrion. They were anarchists destroying their human heritage for the sport of it. The Professor would have called them barbarians and despised them.

He stood apart, in the midst of them, in the shadows of California, and watched students trundling carts full of books out of the entrance of the library. Other students appeared in tall windows above the entrance, pushing splintered sheets of plywood out of their way, and tossed armloads of books onto the steps below for others to gather and add to the fire.

Gavin saw a girl dressed in white tossing books, one by one, upon the flames, and he called out, "Jenny!" But no one heard, and before he could move, she was gone, and he realized that he was seeing Jenny everywhere.

Gavin was not immune to the excitement around him. He felt the raw edge of emotion exposed, like nerve endings flayed out; he felt the tumescent weight of events impending. Something vital and significant was about to happen, was happening, and he was there to share in it.

It was the old fever of campus life: youth and excitement and something always about to happen. There would never be anything like it, never again. For him, though he recognized it, it was all past, and he sensed it filtered through a dull concern for consequence and a philosophy of behavior. While he had not been watching, he had grown old and cautious; and he saw history now as a battleground between anarchy and tyranny, with reasonable people trapped always between them as one seemed victorious for a while and then yielded to the other.

The flames leaped high on the plaza. Students formed a giant circle and danced around the fire, first one way and then suddenly reversing directions, spilling laughing students to the ground.

Gavin remembered another fire much like this, and he thought: It is not so far from Colorado to California, from child to youth. What binds them together is power: the power of fire, the first great invention of man, fire the great civilizer, fire the tenderizer, fire the protector, fire the god, fire the destroyer. . . . The destroyer was what men worshiped, the raw, brutal power of fire, the roaring, churning fury of flame that can turn wood and paper and wisdom and the world itself into heat and smoke and ashes. . . .

The Professor might have said that, Gavin thought. But he hadn't. Gavin had thought it himself, and he realized at that moment how the Professor had changed him. He was not simply himself plus the Professor; the very act of learning, of imbibing the Professor's ideas, had changed Gavin. Ideas are not neutral; they are not tools to be used by any hand. First men shape tools, and then tools shape man. Ideas contain values, and a man absorbs one with the other.

Gavin knew then who had won. He thought he had been the victor, the man in control of the situation, but the Professor had won. Gavin wondered if the Professor had known it all along, if he had come willingly, if he had allowed himself to be kidnapped, if he had known what would happen.

Gavin shook his head. The important matter was that he had changed. He no longer belonged here with the barbarians, and he could not throw in with the tyrants. He turned to find a way out of the crowd, but at that moment someone shouted over a bullhorn, "On to the wedding! On to the Greek Theater!"

The cry was picked up elsewhere in the great crowd, and the ocean of humanity began to surge, with Gavin in the middle of it. Whirlpools and eddies formed, until the tide began to flow finally up the long beach of the campus toward the hill, shaped and controlled by the buildings that rose from the land like stone monuments to a long-forgotten race.

With the smell of burning books still acrid in his nose and thick upon his clothes, Gavin was swept along helplessly. He concentrated only on keeping his feet under him as the sea of students parted for Sather Tower and then reunited in front of Le Conte to flow irresistibly up University Drive past Campbell and Physical Sciences to the East Gate and Gayley Road. It poured into the Greek Theater.

Thrust despite himself onto a stone bench near the front of the vast, semicircular amphitheater, Gavin pondered escape and then settled back to enjoy the spectacle. He knew the place now. Here, on an anniversary of Pearl Harbor, President Kerr had ordered a special university meeting "to inaugurate a new era of freedom under law." But they had been only words to disguise the old tyranny, and Mario Savio had immediately pierced the deception. Perhaps he had sat near where Gavin now sat. He had rushed to the microphone to announce a new revelation, and he had been dragged away by the fascist kops.

Like everything else on this fabulous campus, this place lived in legend; it had been blessed by the revelations of inspired prophets and sanctified by their blood.

The great crowd of students—some twenty thousand of them—had filled all the curved stone benches and the aisles and the hillside above the theater. The students waited impatiently in the darkness; they were packed in so tightly that no one could move, and the only light anywhere, except for the ruddy reflection from the low clouds of the blazing books in front of Doe, were the flickering of lighted matches and the glowing tips of cigarettes.

Behind him Gavin heard a girl say, "Are you sure this is where the wedding is going to be?"

Another girl said, "That's what I heard. But who's sure of anything these days?"

In front of Gavin a fellow said, "I don't know why I come to these things. I can't stand crowds."

"You wouldn't want to miss all the excitement," a girl said.

To his left a girl said, "My horoscope says that I shouldn't even be out tonight."

A young man said, "My sign is in ascendance all month. I can't do anything wrong. Just stay with me."

"Nothing wrong, eh?" the girl replied. "That's what you think! Take your hand off my leg!" But a moment later she laughed to show she was only joking.

Gavin turned to the student on his right. "What's the issue here these days?"

The blond young man looked at him suspiciously. "What do you mean 'what's the issue?' "

Gavin shrugged and let his speech fall into the old patterns of inarticulateness. "I mean, what's goin' on?"

"What's the matter? You new or something?"

"Yeah," Gavin said. "What's the routine? Who's in charge?"

"You talking about politics?"

"Yeah," Gavin said.

"I don't know nothing about politics," the young man said. He leaned over to talk to the person on his right, as if to put as much distance as possible between himself and Gavin.

Gavin turned to the brown-haired girl on his left. "How come there ain't no politics?" he asked.

The girl looked at him, then around at her neighbors, and then put her head close to Gavin's. "They expelled the student president and dissolved student government," she said in a confidential voice.

"Who did?"

"The Kampuskops. Who else?" She looked at him as if deciding that appearances were deceptive. "Why are you asking questions all the time?"

"I'm new," Gavin said apologetically.

"I'll bet you are," she said suspiciously. She made a decision. "Anyway, who cares about campus politics? We're into more important things."

"Like what?"

She turned away coldly. "Like telling strangers to shove it."

Gavin turned to the girls behind him. "Isn't anybody going to protest the way student government was broken up?"

They stared at him. A brunette with stringy hair said, "Why should they? What has student government ever done for us?"

"But . . . this is Berkeley!" Gavin protested. "This is the campus! Students run the campus!"

"Not any more," the other girl said. She had dark hair and a distant look in her brown eyes. "Who cares? The stars are the only things that matter."

"Yeah," her companion agreed. "The stars."

Gavin leaned forward and spoke to the young man in front of him. He had shaved his head and had painted it yellow. He was saying one syllable over and over again, like an incantation to ward off demons. "Om. Om."

"Who's in charge of the project to run the chief of the Kampuskops off campus?" Gavin asked.

He found himself looking at a vast expanse of yellow skin that said, "Om."

"Last guy tried that got shot down in the middle of

University Drive," said the girl next to the bald fellow. "Nobody can outshoot the chief."

A large man on the other side of the bald head turned to Gavin. "You some kind of nut?"

"Om," said the bald head.

"I think he's a spy," said the fellow on Gavin's right.

"I think he's trying to stir up something, get people in trouble," said the girl on Gavin's left.

"He doesn't believe in the stars," said the girl behind him.

Gavin spread out his palms in a gesture of innocence. "I'm new here."

They glared at him. He tried to make himself inconspicuous.

A blast of sound came from the stage to prevent further interrogation. The lights came on full and blindingly. They were focused on the stage where a rock band seemed small against a background of a Greek facade with fluted pillars and a large pedestaled doorway stretching across the wide marble stage to wings at each side. Five guitarists, a drummer, and an electronic pianist were dressed in gold shorts, gold half-boots, and glittering gold jackets parted to expose naked chests. The amplifiers screamed with the agony of tortured strings.

In front of the shoulder-tall stage stood a row of black-uniformed Kampuskops, elbow-to-elbow, nightsticks thumping into their hands in time with the music, holsters thrust forward for a quick draw, visors lowered from their helmets to hide all but their mouths and chins. The black reflective visors dehumanized them; the imagination painted in alien eyes or horrible disfigurements. They seemed half-monster, half-robot, and Gavin saw them as naked power, the ultimate arm of tyranny.

At the north end of the theater a group of girls entered the wide aisle. They were dressed in old sweaters and skirts and canvas shoes, and they came running and tumbling, doing backflips and cartwheels down the aisle in front of the stage, uttering little cries and squeals of joy. As they reached the center of the amphitheater, they turned into the sodded area within the semicircle of curved benches. On their chests, in script, was written the word "Cal," and a line forming the "l" swept back under the syllable for emphasis.

Behind them a group of young men in sweaters and jeans pulled a float. It held a tall cylindrical shape made of silvered strips by the thousands; they blew in the breeze like streams of water revealing a shape inside the cylinder but concealing its identity.

The rock band screamed in protest. The float drew opposite the center of the stage and stopped. The silver strands dropped away. Inside was a girl dressed in a long white gown. A coronet of white and yellow flowers had been woven into her dark hair. Gavin had the feeling that she was beautiful.

She waited, her back half-turned to the audience, her eyes looking at the far end of the stage. Then she stepped forward from the float onto the stage. The band tormented its instruments.

Suddenly the music stopped. In the silence that fell over the stage and audience alike, a spotlight picked out a figure above the marble structure behind the stage, as white and dramatic as an avenging angel. It was dressed like a Kampuskop, but all in white, with starbursts of gold on breast pockets and epaulets. Part of the distant face and one of the hands glittered oddly in the spotlight as the figure descended slowly toward the mortals below.

Gavin laughed. It sounded loud in the silence. "God out of the machine!" he said.

The people around him glanced at him in annoyance and then looked away quickly, as if they didn't want to be associated with him in any way. The figure descending toward the stage seemed to hesitate, as if searching the audience beyond the glare of the spotlight, and then the slow descent began again.

Somebody snickered, and in a distant part of the audience someone else laughed. But in general the spell held, and as the figure got close enough to see more clearly, it didn't look as funny to Gavin. It wasn't human; not all of it, anyway. Large parts of the face and the left hand had been replaced by plastic and metal. One eye was human; the other was a staring marble of tinted plastic set in a clear-plastic socket. Part of one cheek and half a jaw had been replaced, and a third of the forehead and skull. Underneath the clear replacement skull could be seen the gray convolutions of the brain; underneath the plastic skin of the cheek and jaw, shiny metal bones and teeth.

The creature looked like one of the transparent models beloved by the anatomy lab, but obscenely afflicted with a disease that made it break out in skin and hair. Or a person rotting away into something alien.

In spite of the horror of the creature's appearance, it alighted solidly on the stage and spread its arms to the audience. Then it turned, apparently vigorous and strong, toward the waiting bride. The rock band thundered a clash of chords. The audience exploded into applause and cheers.

Again the band fell silent; the audience stilled. The creature took two steps toward the bride; she took two steps toward her monstrous groom. Her movement turned her toward the audience. Gavin saw her face for the first time.

He recognized her. He knew her. He could never forget that face. "Jenny!" he shouted.

The girl stopped. She turned, trying to peer into the audience against the brilliance of the lights. The creature turned also, its plastic left hand thrust out toward the audience like a command. The fingers twitched.

"A stranger is among us," the voice boomed out mechanically. It needed no microphone to be heard in the far reaches of the amphitheater. "He must not damage our moment of celebration, our ceremony of reunion. Send him forward!"

"Here he is," shouted the man on Gavin's right.

"I didn't like him from the first," said the girl on Gavin's left.

Hands grabbed Gavin, lifted him above the heads of the crowd. He was passed down the audience toward the front aisle, fingers pinching away strips of cloth and bits of flesh as he kicked and squirmed futilely to regain control of his fate. At the front, faceless kops caught his arms and half-carried him to the stage. In a moment he faced their half-human leader.

Gavin stared incredulously at the leprous face. Up close, only the metal and plastic parts looked real; humanity was the disease. One bloodshot human eye and one plastic eye stared at him. Gavin saw through the clear-plastic eye to the twisted lucite tendrils which carried some kind of visual message to the obscene movements of the gray cortex revealed beneath the plastic skull.

The human eye seemed to open wider as it looked at Gavin, and the human half of the creature's mouth turned up in a crooked grin. "Gavin," it said.

Gavin felt surprise.

"Gavin?" the girl said. She turned to look up into his face; finally, it was Jenny. "Why, it is Gavin! What are you doing here?"

"That's what I should be asking you," Gavin said, but he knew. There on the muddy bank of the Kaw, she had been terrified, but not so terrified that she had not been able to slip away from her guard. Even before the shooting began, she must have begun to run through the darkness, and she hadn't stopped running until she reached the Coast. Here in the birthplace of revolution, on this strangely quieted campus, she occupied the ritual position of Homecoming Queen, and she was going to marry the chief of the Kampuskops in a glorious public ceremony intended to wed students and authority. It was a political matter, like the marriage between the heirs to rival kingdoms.

All the while, Gavin could not more than glance away from the monster who had called his name.

Its human lip curled higher on one cheek. The plastic side of its face was immobile, and the contrast was frightening. "You don't recognize me in my apotheosis?" Now its voice did not carry beyond the immediate intimate group on the stage. "I am Gregory."

"Gregory?" Gavin said.

"Gregory transformed! Gregory exalted!"

Gavin began to understand. Gregory had been terribly injured, fearfully maimed, in the attack on the generating plant. Doctors there and then here had put him back together, replacing parts shot away or badly shattered with plastics and metal. They had brought him back from death. That was power, and Gregory always had gravitated toward power. He had switched sides effortlessly. He had joined what he saw as the most powerful of the forces available. He became a Kampuskop. Now he was leader of a force greater than he had imagined. He had made the kops more than a token; he had recruited men capable of his own kind of brutality; he had armed them, outlawed political activity by the students, and compensated them with circuses like this.

"I've seen a lot of things since that night by the river," Gavin said. "I know places that could grow new limbs and parts for those you lost."

"Lost?" Gregory laughed. It was a low mechanical sound that rumbled across the stage like artificial thunder. "The doctors put me back together better than ever. Look!" He took a nightstick from the nearest kop in his artificial left hand. The fingers tightened on it. The stick disintegrated into splinters and wires.

The waiting audience, unable to make out what was happening on stage, applauded the show.

"I wouldn't change back for all the little squealing coeds on the campus," he said. "Before, I was merely strong. Now I've got power!" He shook the splintered wood from his plastic hand. "I've also got Jenny. And I've got you." The crooked smile grew more crooked.

Gavin realized that he had been wrong. The wedding was more than political expediency, more, even, than a mating of beauty and the beast. It was the consummation of Gregory's frustrated desires for the one girl who had resisted him and the one man who had stood in his way without acknowledging his physical superiority.

"I could castrate you here upon the stage," Gregory said, "using only my good left hand. That would be appropriate to the occasion, I think, and the audience would appreciate it almost as much as I would."

"I don't want anything like that at my wedding," Jenny said.

Gregory's human eye blinked, and his artificial eye stared. Perhaps they saw different realities.

The reality Gavin experienced was a brief gratitude for Jenny's intervention, which faded before the realization that she had not spoken up because of him. "You're going through with this abomination?" he said, and he knew that she was. He had never known her. She was fascinated by Gregory, by what he represented, by the very monstrousness of him. What she had feared and desired had come to pass; she had come to enjoy what Gregory did. His sadism and her masochism had come to their proper meeting.

"You want to save him?" Gregory asked.

Jenny shook her head. "What do I care about him? He belongs to the past." For Jenny the past was dead.

Gregory believed her. "My sweet captive!" he said. "My tender slave!" He turned to the kops who held Gavin's arms. "Take him into the wings until the ceremony is over! Make him watch! Don't let him look away! And don't give him a chance to escape! He is dessert."

So, Gavin thought, he had come all the way across the country for this. From within a small doorway, out of sight of the audience at the left of the stage, Gavin watched helplessly as Gregory took Jenny's left hand in his and raised it in a gesture something like that of a victor in a prizefight. "This woman I wed," he said in a voice that carried to the last row of benches. "In the name of unity between students and administration, in the name of cooperation between all elements which go to make up a great university, in the name of the power we will wield together not only over this campus but the city that surrounds this campus and the entire bay area, and perhaps, who knows, over the state itself, I take this woman for my own, to do with as I will."

He turned to Jenny. "And you, Jenny, do you accept me as your mate and master? Do you put control of your fate and body into my hands?" The fingers of his plastic hand twitched.

Jenny nodded. That was enough. The audience applauded and cheered wildly. It was a savage rite. They should be surrounded by a jungle, Gavin thought, tensing his muscles against the grip of his guards. As the audience reaction began to fade, Gregory held up his right hand. It seemed pale and weak by comparison. "This marriage will be publicly consummated," he shouted.

"No!" Jenny said. She tried to turn away, but as Gregory released her hand, he caught the neck of her white gown with his plastic hand and ripped it from her body. She stood cowering in front of him, naked and white upon the stage.

Gavin knew now that he had never loved her. How can you love someone you do not know? But he had been close to her, and he struggled against the hands that held him, knowing the shame that Jenny felt, remembering how she had dreaded the light, and hating the strange mixture of fear and fascination upon her face now.

With the same left hand, Gregory ripped away the front of his uniform jacket. The white cloth fell from his chest; the pattern of mutilation apparent on his face was duplicated down his body. His entire left arm was plastic, and part of his shoulder. Almost half his chest had been blown away; inside, the transparent plastic organs moved obscenely. Some of the organs were dark red and moist; others were glassy. A pulsating plastic heart pumped blood through plastic arteries.

By then Gregory's white pants also were on the stage floor. The left leg was normal; the right leg was plastic, covering shiny metal bones. And as Gregory turned to reveal himself fully to the audience, Gavin saw that even his genitals were plastic.

"What pleasure in that?" he thought as Gregory put his plastic arm around Jenny's back and lifted her effortlessly into the air. And Gavin struggled with his guards, even as he understood that the real center of sex is not in the loins but in the head.

Slowly Gregory lowered Jenny onto his plastic chest. Her head was thrown back in a final gesture of aversion; her hands pushed futilely at his chest. It was the rape of humanity by the machine.

No, Gavin corrected himself in the midst of his futile effort to go to Jenny's rescue, that was too easy; it was

Gregory's humanity at fault, not the mechanism that made it possible. The tragedy was humanity's mechanical rape of itself.

At the consummation of this savage public rite, almost as if it were a part of the ceremony itself, the stone floor of the stage disintegrated under Gregory's feet. Gregory was lifted into the air, still clasping Jenny in his plastic embrace. Rock splinters and slivers whistled through the air like shrapnel. The rock band was scythed down.

The concussion reached Gavin. His guards were shaken away. As Gavin was throwing himself to the floor, he saw Jenny and her terrible lover disappear into the hole in the stage left by the explosion. Almost simultaneously he thought, "Poor Jenny!" and "They did it!" He exulted in the indomitable anarchy of uncowed students, who had not acquiesced to this unholy matrimony, who had prepared an ultimate protest to the dramatic tyranny Gregory had planned; and he knew them for irresponsible romantics whose only useful contribution was a basic unwillingness to go along with anything.

Stone darts sprayed past Gavin. The floor was still vibrating from the explosion. Something hot and sticky spurted on his hand. The kop on his right clasped to his throat a hand that was already dead.

The sound of gunfire echoed from stone surfaces. In front of the stage, the helmeted, visored kops formed a wedge that tried to carve a corridor through walls of student bodies. Nightsticks rose and fell like flails or thrust forward like short spears. Automatics fired blindly into bodies pressed close. The black group made some progress toward the south exit, but for every foot it advanced, a kop was lost to a bullet, a club, or clawing hands.

It was Ragnarok, the campus Armageddon toward which events had moved for twenty years, storing up rage and frustration and violence toward the final explosion. Here order made its last stand; here anarchy presented its final negation to tyranny. Here the world ended, Gavin thought.

But he was wrong. The battle surged south, uncertain, inconclusive. The amphitheater was left behind, filled with the groans of the wounded, the blood of the dead. Gavin tried to stand up, but his right leg collasped under him. He looked down at it. Blood was seeping through the cloth that covered the thigh.

He crawled to the edge of the ragged gap in the stage and looked down into the hole where he had seen Gregory and Jenny disappear. They were still there, upright, staring at him, locked in a last embrace. Gavin pulled his head halfway back, thinking for one crazy moment that they had survived. But they were dead.

Jenny's body was unmarked. Gregory's plastic arm had pulled so tight around her that her ribs were broken, and perhaps her back as well. Gregory's plastic leg kept them upright through some mechanical miracle. His fleshy leg had been shattered, but the plastic had stayed strong and true, and the plastic heart had pumped away until his blood was gone.

He looked up toward the red-tinged clouds, his human eye closed but his plastic eye staring as if it still were sending messages to a dead brain. A final rictus had twisted his plastic lips upward, so that now he smiled on both sides.

Gavin found a piece of Jenny's dress. He tore it into two pieces. One of them he folded into a pad over the wound in his thigh; the other he used to tie it in place, feeling grateful that the piece of stone had missed the arteries. He crawled to the steps and edged down them, seated, like a small child. At the last one, he pulled himself upright by the edge of the stage and shuffled south, picking his way among the bodies.

Just beyond the theater, a small tree had been trampled by struggling feet until it broke off near the base. Gavin lowered himself gingerly to the ground and methodically began stripping the tree of branches and leaves. When he pushed himself upright again, he had a passable crutch.

He hobbled down Gayley Road, past Keelberger Field and the stadium parking lots, between the Law Building and International House, and through gates that stood open to the night. Halfway across the cleared ground that surrounded the campus wall, he turned and looked at the University for the final time.

"Ah, there, Professor," he thought, and took the first step of his long journey to a place called the enchanted mountain, and, if he was lucky, to peace and sanity, and to a girl who, in this uncertain world, perhaps he really loved.

ABOUT THE AUTHOR

JAMES E. GUNN is both a distinguished science fiction writer, former President of the SFWA, and a long-time member of the faculty of the University of Kansas.

OUT OF THIS WORLD!

That's the only way to describe Bantam's great series of science-fiction classics. These space-age thrillers are filled with terror, fancy and adventure and written by America's most renowned writers of science fiction. Welcome to outer space and have a good trip!

☐	THE MARTIAN CHRONICLES by Ray Bradbury	2440	$1.75
☐	STAR TREK: THE NEW VOYAGES by Culbreath & Marshak	2719	$1.75
☐	THE MYSTERIOUS ISLAND by Jules Verne	2872	$1.25
☐	ALAS, BABYLON by Pat Frank	2923	$1.75
☐	FANTASTIC VOYAGE by Isaac Asimov	2937	$1.50
☐	A CANTICLE FOR LEBOWITZ by Walter Miller, Jr.	2973	$1.75
☐	HELLSTROM'S HIVE by Frank Herbert	8276	$1.50
☐	DHALGREN by Samuel R. Delany	8554	$1.95
☐	STAR TREK XI by James Blish	8717	$1.25
☐	THE DAY OF THE DRONES by A. M. Lightner	10057	$1.25
☐	THE FARTHEST SHORE by Ursula LeGuin	10131	$1.75
☐	THE TOMBS OF ATUAN by Ursula LeGuin	10132	$1.75
☐	A WIZARD OF EARTHSEA by Ursula LeGuin	10135	$1.75
☐	20,000 LEAGUES UNDER THE SEA by Jules Verne	10325	$1.25

Buy them at your local bookstore or use this handy coupon for ordering:

Bantam Books, Inc., Dept. SF, 414 East Golf Road, Des Plaines, Ill. 60016

Please send me the books I have checked above. I am enclosing $_____
(please add 50¢ to cover postage and handling). Send check or money order
—no cash or C.O.D.'s please.

Mr/Mrs/Miss_____

Address_____

City_____State/Zip_____

SF—6/77

Please allow four weeks for delivery. This offer expires 6/78.

RAY BRADBURY

America's most daring explorer of the imagination

☐ S IS FOR SPACE	(11017—$1.50)
☐ SOMETHING WICKED THIS WAY COMES	(10750—$1.75)
☐ THE ILLUSTRATED MAN	(10557—$1.75)
☐ DANDELION WINE	(10430—$1.50)
☐ R IS FOR ROCKET	(10367—$1.50)
☐ TIMELESS STORIES FOR TODAY AND TOMORROW	(10249—$1.50)
☐ I SING THE BODY ELECTRIC	(2882—$1.75)
☐ MACHINERIES OF JOY	(2834—$1.50)
☐ MEDICINE FOR MELANCHOLY	(2668—$1.25)
☐ THE WONDERFUL ICE CREAM SUIT & OTHER PLAYS	(2467—$1.25)
☐ THE MARTIAN CHRONICLES	(2440—$1.75)
☐ GOLDEN APPLES OF THE SUN	(2247—$1.25)

Bantam Book Catalog

Here's your up-to-the-minute listing of every book currently available from Bantam.

This easy-to-use catalog is divided into categories and contains over 1400 titles by your favorite authors.

So don't delay—take advantage of this special opportunity to increase your reading pleasure.

Just send us your name and address and 25¢ (to help defray postage and handling costs).